P9-ECP-498

4/22

In The Shadow Of Lewis And Clark

Marilyn Kilpatrick

Copyright © 2017 by Marilyn Kilpatrick

All rights reserved under International Copyright Conventions.
Published in the United State by

ISBN-13 9781542661546
ISBN-10 1542661544
Library of Congress Control Number: 2017900989
CreateSpace Independent Publishing Platform
North Charleston, South Carolina

All rights reserved. This book or any part thereof may not be reproduced in any form whatsoever, whether by graphic, visual, electronic, filming, microfilming, tape recording or any means, except in the case of brief passages embodied in critical reviews and articles without the prior written permission of the author.
For permission write to:
Marilyn Kilpatrick
P.O. Box 1216
Fort Jones, CA 96032

OTHER BOOKS BY MARILYN KILPATRICK

The World Is My Oyster, Travels With A Cheapskate

How To Drive Your Daughter Crazy

Dedication

To Joshua Kilpatrick and John Hans Junior.

They encouraged me to keep writing the original draft by saying "I can hardly wait to see what happens next."

List of Characters

COAKLEY

Wesley Coakley – born in 1768 in Boston where he became a shipbuilder. As a bridegroom to Jane he became a carpenter for Putnam and Cutler in 1787 in Marietta, Ohio. He later opened his own furniture factory and established a farm.

Jane Coakley – born in 1771, married in 1787 to Wesley Coakley. Their first child, William James was born in 1788, fourth child, Ephraim born in 1792, tenth child, Lydia born in 1810.

PAUGHS

Joshua Paugh – son of revolutionary soldier, Nicholas Paugh who planted a wine vineyard near Athens, Ohio.

Julia Coakley Paugh – born in 1816 to Ephriam Coakley and Evette Laureau Coakley, reared by Wesley and Jane Coakley, married in 1834 to Joshua Paugh. Mother of Emily and Jenny.

Emily Paugh – born in 1835 to Julia Coakley Paugh and Joshua Paugh, married in 1853 to Matthew Kilkenny.

Jenny Paugh - Emily's younger sister, born in 1845.

KILKENNY

Ian Kilkenny - from Scotland, arrived in America at age 20, June 25, 1825, migrated to Athens that year, met and married Lydia Coakley in 1827. Died in 1844 in mine accident.

Lydia Coakley Kilkenny – born in 1810 to Wesley and Jane Coakley, married in 1827 to Ian Kilkenny. Mother of Matthew, Mark, Luke and John.

Mark Kilkenny – born in 1828, eldest Kilkenny brother, went to work in mine at age 12, left job of mucker at age 18 to marry Becky and move to Pittsburgh. Worked in foundry with Becky's father as his foreman.

Luke Kilkenny - born in 1830, second eldest brother, subject to lung disease, worked as a mucker in the coal mine.

John Kilkenny – born in 1832, third eldest brother, worked as a mucker in the mine.

Matthew Kilkenny – born in 1834, youngest brother, worked in mine. He was six months older than Emily Paugh, whom he married in 1853.

LAUREAU

Emil Laureau – father of Evette.

Jeanette Laureau – mother of Evette.

Evette Laureau - married to Ephraim Coakley, mother of Julia Coakley.

VARIOUS

Rufus Putnam – fought in revolution, founded Marietta, Ohio in 1788, founded Ohio University in 1804 in Athens, Ohio.

Manasseh Cutler – fought in revolution, co-founded Ohio University in 1804.

Caleb Fitzgerald – arrived in America with Ian Kilkenny, married Ian's widow, Lydia.

ON THE TRAIL

Jerome Jeffers – slave born in Lexington, Kentucky, given freedom by his owner in 1853.

Beth Simmons – married to Jerome.

Michael O'Brien – soldier from Fort Louisville who retired and traveled west to seek gold, married Deborah Dawkins on the trail.

Deborah Dawkins O'Brien – school teacher on way to Beaver Valley, California to teach school.

Elijah and Hester Jackson – four children, Marie is youngest, Rebecca second youngest.

Katherine Reed – Deborah's friend headed for a prearranged marriage to a farmer in Beaver Valley.

Doctor Brian and Jesse Jamison – traveling with two adolescent sons, Josiah and Robert.

Sam and Katie McCafferty – wagon master and wife, owner of boarding house in Oregon City.

Brown Eagle - scout and guide on trail.

Rhys Watson - resident of boarding house.

Juanita Garcia - employee of boarding house.

Westward Expansion

*T*he United States of America was a dream of oppressed people throughout the world in the tumultuous years of the Renaissance. In the seventeenth and eighteenth centuries the country was populated by immigrants looking for a better life. That dream still exists today. The first Europeans landed on the eastern shores looking for religious freedom, fortune, and/or land. Some migrated westward to find gold, ranchland, freedom from slavery, or any of a myriad of other reasons. All of the people who wandered into the unknown were as brave as the astronauts of today. They were the forbearers of generations of adventuresome people.

After Great Britain lost the American War of Independence, started in 1775 and ended in 1783, they ceded their rights to The Northwest Territory to the United States of America. Congress enacted the Land Ordinance, establishing conditions for distribution of the land they now claimed as their own. Revolutionary soldiers formed the second Ohio Company of Associates and received the right to facilitate that land distribution. They saw to it that men who fought in the War of Independence received the free allotments promised by Congress as their payment for military service.

In 1787, Rufus Putnam and Manasseh Cutler were sent by the Ohio Company to establish a shipping port on the Ohio River. The chosen site, Marietta was the first non-Native settlement in the Northwest Territory.

The Natives, called "Indians" by Columbus because he thought he had landed in the West Indies, considered themselves the sole owners of the land and fought to retain possession. There was a series of frontier wars between Natives and settlers. A United States military was formed to protect the immigrants. After many battles, Native American hostilities in the Northwest Territory were squelched in 1795.

Rufus Putnam and Manasseh Cutler were then free to pursue their plan of establishing Ohio University, the first college in the territory. They did so northwest of Marietta in the township of Athens, Ohio in 1805. Athens grew with the influx of university staff and students and mushroomed after the discovery of rich veins of coal ore. Many of the settlers were coal miners from Europe.

At about the same time President Thomas Jefferson assigned his personal secretary, Meriwether Lewis the task of forming a company to explore the possibility of a Northwest Passage to the Pacific Ocean. The explorers were to use river systems, which extended from the Atlantic Ocean to the Mississippi River and then across to the western edge of the continent.

Meriwether Lewis and William Clark formed the Corps of Discovery and started an extensive exploration in 1804. They arrived at the Pacific Ocean in Oregon in 1805 and returned to Washington the following year with volumes of information on the fauna, flora, geology, and indigenous peoples. They inspired pioneers to follow in their shadow.

Chapter 1

*I*n February 1787, Wesley Coakley, nineteen years old, and a new bridegroom hired on with Rufus Putnam as a boat builder. He had nearly five years' experience at the Boston Shipyard and a reputation as a reliable, hardworking carpenter. He and his sixteen-year old bride, Jane, eager for adventure, left their comfortable family life in Massachusetts and headed for the frontier. They traveled by stage coach with other Ohio Company recruits southward along the eastern seaboard. New roads were being built every day and old animal trails that had become Native American trading routes became commercial roads from city to city. Village roads became highways wide enough for two vehicles to pass each other in relative safety as they approached cities like Boston and Philadelphia.

"My! Look at that grand palace," Jane said as they pulled to the front door of a two-story inn at Philadelphia. "They could house fifty people all at one time in such a large establishment."

The inn's kitchen fed the Putnam group a full meal of meat, potatoes and other vegetables, as well as peach cobbler for dessert. Wesley and Jane felt pampered and were happy with the private bedroom with a large four-poster bed they were given for a night's rest.

"It seems a shame to fall asleep in here instead of lying awake enjoying the luxury of such a beautiful room," Jane whispered to Wesley when they snuggled under the plush comforter.

"Don't expect all our rooms to be this extravagant. I suspect we'll be living in a log cabin once we get to Marietta. It may take a year or two before we can afford a four-poster with down comforters," Wesley said.

Early the next morning the parade of coaches turned west leaving Philadelphia. Soldiers accompanied the pioneers between Philadelphia and Fort Pitt to discourage possible attacks by Natives. At first the Pennsylvania countryside consisted of established farms. After living in Boston proper all her life, this looked like the wilderness to Jane. She could see no problem in learning to live in such a place. The travelers spent the night at a smaller inn where plain nourishing hot stew was served and married people assigned austere private bedrooms.

The third day out of Philadelphia, the environment changed. Domestic animals were replaced with deer and the occasional raccoon or possum. The sounds of wolves were heard at dawn and dusk. There were no more tilled fields, no pastures of beef cattle and no pleasant farmhouses. The route became progressively more primitive. The roads were thick with the mud of early spring and wheels of loaded wagons and coaches were easily mired. Darkness had settled before the soldiers stopped at a way-station. After dinner of beans and bread, Wesley and Jane lay on straw strewn on the floor along with twelve other people. The room where they ate was their sleeping quarters for the night.

"So, is this the type of housing you want me to live in when we arrive in Marietta?" Jane whispered to Wesley.

"I doubt we will be so fortunate for the first couple of years. Don't get used to this luxury. Remember, you said you would support me in this adventure," Wesley whispered in response.

"Oh, ho, so this is what you meant by adventure!" Jane said slapping a cockroach that ran across her arm.

"By adventure, I meant running the rapids in the Ohio River and sleeping under the stars for a couple of months until I had time to pitch a lean-to in the corner of Fort Harmar. The ride to the fort is the holiday part of the experience. Go to sleep, the sun will be up before you know it," Wesley said pulling something wiggly out from under his cover.

There were a few settlers scattered across central and western Pennsylvania but the soldiers found no one who could accommodate the group of travelers with food and shelter. On the sixth night, Jane longed for the luxury and security of the way-station as she and Wesley made their bed under a wagon on the cold ground. They lost the draw for places inside the coaches.

They arrived at Fort Pitt at the confluence of the Monongahela, Allegheny and Ohio Rivers nine days after leaving Philadelphia.

"I'm as tired as if I've had no sleep for three nights," Wesley confessed. "I hope the boat waiting for us on the Ohio River has comfortable sleeping quarters."

There was no boat docked outside Fort Pitt on the fast flowing waterway. The Ohio Company recruited fort employees for the journey down river and the Boston boat builders started their first job.

They cut timber from the surrounding forests under the watchful eyes of soldiers standing guard. No Natives bothered them and work went smoothly. When two sturdy boats were finished, fifty men, five with wives, completed the trip from Fort Pitt to Fort Harmar.

This fort was named after Brigadier General Josiah Harmar, a veteran of the Revolutionary War and the first commander of the United States Army following a peace agreement with the British. Harmar was assigned the daunting task of guarding immigrants in the vast frontier. Putnam and Cutler's employees were to be the garrison's closest neighbors.

The workmen pitched company owned tents side-by-side and four people slept in each tent. At least they did have cots made of canvas to get their tired bodies off the ground at night. The five wives were expected to help company cooks prepare meals.

Surveyors laid out the town of Marietta on the banks of the Ohio River. The port was at the mouth of the Muskingum River, which drained from the north-eastern hills. Workers cleared away brush; Wesley Coakley and other carpenters felled and planed trees and constructed a boat dock and a storage facility for Ohio Company supplies. The materiel was removed from boats tied to trees at the river's edge and put in storage. Over the next two months, carpenters built a general store, blacksmith shop, corral, and a saloon much to the distress of a couple of wives, and the delight of most of the men. Bachelors built a dormitory near the saloon where they planned on living until they decided whether to settle in the frontier town or return to the eastern seashore.

Some of Putnam and Cutler's men wanted isolation, in spite of threatened dangers from wild animals and Natives, and they bought land away from Marietta. Wesley and Jane Coakley were among those people and obtained a quarter section of land five miles out of town. It was dangerous getting to and from work on the animal path that lead to Marietta, but that didn't deter the newly married duo.

The young couple thrived on accomplishment as they cleared a plot, dug a well and latrine pit, and planted seeds in the roughly tilled soil of their own land. They slept in a discarded army tent that leaked during the frequent summer rains. By late autumn, Wesley and his co-workers built a one-room cabin, which seemed enormous and luxurious to Wesley and Jane after spending the summer in the tent.

"I'll repay you for your services with help building your home when you choose a site," Wesley said as he shook hands with the carpenters on their last day of cabin work.

"I'll cut some dried grass to use as a mattress so we can sleep indoors tonight," Wesley told his wife as she unpacked cooking utensils and hung them on pegs wedged between logs on the wall next to the stone fireplace.

"Don't bring back a wagon of dried autumn leaves. They may smell nice but the noise will keep us awake," Jane called after her retreating husband.

By mid-October Jane had time to can wild fruits she found in the woods. Wesley killed and dressed two deer to hang in the smoke house built several feet from the cabin.

"Why don't you unpack your violin and play me a tune?" Jane asked one evening as she took out her knitting needles and yarn.

"I'd like that. I haven't played any music since we left Boston," Wesley said and headed for the packing crates in the corner of the room.

He tuned up the violin and strummed a few chords. Then he played a Beethoven rhapsody memorized from his days in a Boston church orchestra.

"Oh, that was beautiful. I hope we always have time for music in our home," Jane replied when he finished.

From then on Wesley played at least one song each evening as Jane knit warm socks and gloves to sell to the single men working for Rufus Putnam.

Wesley was sanding boards for a proper bed and suggested Jane read him a story while he worked.

"I have a book of Shakespeare plays I brought from home. Is that all right?" she asked.

"I love Shakespeare, which plays do you have?" He asked.

"I have King Lear, Hamlet, and Merchant of Venice. Which one do you want?"

"Start with Hamlet," he suggested.

The cold, rainy winter evenings passed pleasantly as the young couple shared their love of music and literature. One entertained while the other worked.

Jane was making good money from her sales of socks and gloves. They used the money to buy nails, varnish, and sandpaper and their supply of furniture grew. The young carpenter built a table, two chairs, a chest of drawers, and a kitchen cupboard over the first winter in the cabin.

They were delighted in December to discover Jane was pregnant. She counted her blessings that she didn't have to till or hoe the garden while tolerating morning sickness. She would be well past the sickness part before spring came. She worried about giving birth in this desolate place but her strong faith consoled her. In the early months of 1788, Jane made baby clothes and bedding from material brought from Boston as well as her socks and gloves for workers. She had added warm, wooly hats to her inventory after speaking to the general store manager.

"You know, most of the men now have the gloves and enough socks to make it through the winter. The requests I get the most, and can't supply, are for hats and scarves," he told Jane. "If you can make me a dozen of each, I could sell them before the warm weather comes on."

Wesley built a crib and carved a design of evergreens and the words "Baby Coakley" in the headboard. He didn't know at the time that the crib would be used by generations of Coakley babies. Wesley made Jane a rocking chair as a Christmas gift and she spent every evening there-after using it instead of the straight back chairs at the kitchen table.

Jane enlarged the garden patch. She and Wesley had nearly an acre of land tilled and planted by the end of May. The garden was Jane's domain, pride and joy. June and July was consumed in adding a room to the cabin, with the heavy lifting done by Wesley and his co-workers. Wesley worked on their cabin and a second out building from the time he returned from Putnam's job until dark each evening.

Together they studied the book on birthing sent from Boston by Jane's mother. Jane had sheets, towels, a blanket, baby clothes, diapers, whiskey, and anything else suggested by the book neatly organized in a drawer of their clothes chest. A soldier's wife with two children that lived at Fort Harmar promised to assist in the birth.

In early-August Jane felt a prolonged pain in her lower abdomen. Her first reaction was panic. Wesley was in town putting the finishing touches on Manasseh Cutler's home. She was alone. No one lived within three miles of their cabin. She sat on the ground and calmed herself. She had time; the first baby wouldn't just fall out. She might not give birth for twenty-four hours. She picked up the basket of fresh tomatoes and headed for the house.

Jane cleaned house, made dinner, changed the sheets on the bed and tied a strong strip of cloth to the bedpost by her pillow. Then she took a bath, donned a clean nightshirt, fixed herself some tea and went to bed. She was interrupted every few minutes with another pain but wasn't alarmed; Wesley would be home by six p.m. He'd have time to eat his dinner and get the lady from the fort before the pain became unbearable.

Wesley was late getting home. He arrived at almost eight o'clock with a surprise for his wife.

"Sweetheart, come look what I bought," he called cheerily as he approached the cabin.

Jane didn't appear and he took the Guernsey dairy cow and calf right up to the front door. The bovines arrived on a barge of animals destined for Fort Harmar and he purchased the mother-daughter pair from the company commander. He burst through the door with a beaming smile on his face.

The smile turned to shock when he saw Jane. She was on the bed writhing in pain. She had hold of the cloth tied to the post pulling on it with all her might. She had a round peg between her clenched teeth and uttered a long deep moan.

"It's time!" Wesley rushed to the bed and looked at her with anguish.

"I'm sorry, I didn't think it would be this soon. I would have hurried home instead of...," he pointed at the door but let the explanation die in his throat. "What should I do?"

When the pain subsided, Jane told him it was too late for him to fetch the woman from the fort. The pains were two minutes or less apart. He would have to deliver the baby.

A startled look crossed his face, "I can't. I don't know how. I'll hurt you. Can't you wait? It'll only take me two hours to get to the fort and back."

"No, don't leave me," another pain wracked her body and she returned the peg to her mouth and gurgled. She was sweating profusely, her twisted nightgown stuck to her body; she drew her knees up as far as she could and rolled away from Wesley.

"Water, we need to boil water," Wesley said trying to remember what he had read.

Wesley found the kettle on the fireplace hook boiled dry. He rekindled the dying fire and filled the kettle from the well.

"Where's the book? I need to read the book," he said as he tore open drawers.

The book lay on top of the bedding and towels. Everything in the drawer looked so clean and neat, it helped calm Wesley.

"I'm going to wash up, I'll be right back," he assured his wife as he ran to the well. He stripped off his work clothes and washed all over with cold water and soap.

He took the time to tie the Guernsey cow to a tree so she wouldn't wander off.

When he returned to the house stark naked, Jane was between pains and burst out laughing.

"Not now, if you don't mind, I'm not in a romantic mood at the moment," she choked out. Her clinging wet hair partially obscured her face but the smile made her beautiful.

Her remark momentarily broke the tension. They both laughed as he quickly put on clean clothes and arranged towels and baby clothes on the kitchen table.

"Do you want a drink of whiskey?" he asked.

"No, that would just make me sick. I can do this," she said bearing down harder than she ever thought possible.

An hour later, Wesley was washing his son in warm water and marveling at the miracle of birth. He wrapped the baby in a warm towel and laid him in his mother's waiting arms.

Jane rolled to one side and kissed the child on the forehead. "Welcome to our world William James Coakley," she cooed softly. She was exhausted and exhilarated at the same time. She had never been happier or more tired.

"You are the most beautiful woman in the world, Jane Coakley. Thank you for being the mother of my child," Wesley's eyes were filled with tears.

Chapter 2

For the next seven years, the soldiers at Fort Harmar battled hostile Natives. President Washington sent reinforcements to the Ohio valley bringing about the end of the Indian Wars in 1795. The Treaty of Greenville was signed by the Western Confederacy on August 2.

Homesteading after the cessation of hostilities resulted in a population large enough to demand organized government. Ohio was separated from the remainder of the Northwest Territory, and March 1, 1803, it became the first state of the territory to be admitted into the Union.

"Well, my sweet, what would you think of being married to the first governor of Ohio?" Wesley asked Jane.

Jane mulled over the question before answering, "I think it would be a tremendous change to our way of life. How could we possibly continue the progress we've made to the farm? What about all those orders you have for furniture in your carpentry business? Would I have to give up my garment business? I'd hate to put the lovely ladies working for me out of a job. Why, Ellen Ellis is a widowed mother after her husband was killed the Battle of Fallen Timbers. What would she do to support herself and her children? What about your own children? Who will help me rear them?"

"I think you are getting way ahead of me. There will be a campaign. I'm not the only man in the territory, er I mean state, who has political ambitions. You and I could solve problems as they came up-if they came up. What I wanted from you was an enthusiastic 'Great idea Wesley!'"

Wesley Coakley, a popular man along the Ohio Valley went into politics and ran for governor against Edward Tiffin. By 1800 Wesley had an established farm and a profitable carpentry shop. His wife, Jane owned Coakley

Creations brand of clothes which were sold at the Marietta General Store and in villages popping up throughout southeastern Ohio.

Wesley wanted to see better roads between townships, and also pushed for more schools to be brought to the district. He spent days, and then weeks away from the farm while campaigning for the governorship. He made impassioned speeches to weary pioneers, budding entrepreneurs, and coal miners. Never-the-less, he was defeated by Edward Tiffin. However he made influential friends by stepping forward with his recommendations for governing the new state. The new state's population exploded for a variety of reasons.

Almost thirty years after the signing of the Declaration of Independence, Frenchmen who had fought beside colonists arrived in Ohio to collect their military pay-free land-as promised by Congress. Many of these arrivals were family men that had been waiting for the Native problems to be settled.

Goods and livestock arrived in Marietta on barges and were sold to settlers or kept at the fort for the dwindling army. Most of the soldiers had moved to Fort Washington (present day Cincinnati) over the previous years when General Harmar decided that was a more advantageous point from which to stage battles. It was located at the confluence of the Licking River and the Ohio River.

Rufus Putnam and Manasseh Cutler, original surveyors of Marietta went up the Hocking River and located a place in the hills filled with Virginia and pitch pines, sassafras, and black, scarlet, white and chestnut oaks. There they built their university. The young area was growing fast and the Coakley family along with it.

Wesley and Jane prospered and reared their family, which eventually consisted of six children. Four boys and two girls were born between 1788 and 1810.

Wesley and his hired hand, a retired soldier, built split rail fences and filled the pastures with sheep, dairy cows and pigs. Each of the first ten summers after Wesley and Jane moved to the Ohio Valley, Wesley added rooms to his house. By 1803 it was considered a mansion with four bedrooms, a sewing room, a parlor and a large eat-in kitchen. The original little log cabin was now Wesley and Jane's bedroom and the room he had added the summer they were expecting William James was Jane's sewing room.

Survival in the wilderness meant family effort. The boys worked as hard as their parents but were glad when a school was finally built in town and they were given a few hours of respite from the physical labor. They had been taught reading, writing, and rudimentary arithmetic by their parents but none of them was considered a scholar. Of course, each had chores to attend to when they arrived home from school, but after autumn harvest the farm work became minimal giving them time for study, music lessons, and play.

As the years went by, Jane had all she could handle tending her younger children, two daughters named Ruth and Lydia, born several years after the boys. She was also doing all the household chores, and sewing clothes for her family. Jane hired two women to sew the clothes she designed for sale. She was a rare female entrepreneur living on land that had so recently been wilderness.. Jane was thirty-eight years old when her final baby, Lydia was born.

The Coakleys had become one of the wealthier and most respected families in Ohio.

Chapter 3

As adults Wesley and Jane's son, William, Elias, and Aaron Coakley were content to live on or near their parents' farm and continue family enterprises. Elias and Aaron built homes on property adjacent to their parents' land. Elias ran the furniture factory after his father decided to spend his declining years working with politicians. William spent his whole life farming the same land. He married a stout Irish lass and refilled the family home with a new generation of Coakleys. Each of his children started life sleeping in the crib crafted for him by his father.

Ephraim left Marietta when he was eighteen and went up the Hocking River to Athens, a town not only famous for Ohio University, but also for its coal mines. Coal was becoming a popular way to fuel the many steam boats plying the Great Lakes. Mining companies built villages for their employees and paid them with script which could only be used in the company store. Still there was a draw to the independence offered by the companies. Young men were drawn to the idea of having their own home away from their parents.

Athens Coal Mine brought in Irish, Scottish, and Cornish miners. It seemed adventuresome to work with immigrants. Ephraim joined the workers, made friends easily, and became a leader among the men. He was a favorite with his employer because of his good work ethic. He started at the mine as a mucker and three years later became a blaster responsible for setting and firing the blast that produced the debris for the muckers.

Blasters drilled holes manually. Ephraim held a steel chisel in one hand while swinging a four-pound sledge with the other. This was called "single jacking." He was good at his job but the effort was time consuming. His supervisor learned Cornish techniques and the process was speeded up by "double jacking." Ephraim held the chisel and two partners rhythmically swung eight-pound sledges. After each hammer blow, Ephraim rotated the steel a fraction of a turn to reposition the cutting edge of the chisel. The average face, or working end of a drift, a horizontal tunnel off a vertical shaft, required at least seven holes.

After drilling the holes to a precise depth, Ephraim loaded them with black powder, a mixture of saltpeter (potassium nitrate), sulfur, and charcoal. The black powder was packed in paper cartridges and gently tamped in place with a wooden stick. This was the most dangerous part of the operation as the black powder was unstable and a spark would ignite it. With the fuse extending outward from the powder, Ephraim packed each hole with mud. The timing of each of his charges was of great importance. A logical sequence was employed. The center holes, closely grouped were angled to meet within the rock. They were exploded first to blast out a center. The remaining outer charges could then direct their energy inward, breaking the rock in keeping with the desired configuration of the drift. Timing was achieved when Ephraim lit each fuse in sequence, or he cut each fuse to an appropriate length and lit them all simultaneously.

With all in readiness, Ephraim lit the fuses, shouted the traditional "Fire in the hole!" and quickly retreated to safety. If all went as planned, the drift would be advanced about two feet and tons of mud, rock, dirt, and coal awaited the shovels of the muckers.

Ephraim and his fellow workers left the deep shaft of the mine on a pulley elevator ascending into the bright light of day. They were covered from hat to boots with fine powdered coal dust. The fossil fuel filled their nostrils and throats and the men frequently blew their noses, coughed and spoke of ancestors in the "old" country dying of black lung disease. They talked of giving up the dirty work as soon as they learned a new trade, or got enough money to move on, or paid off their mortgage, or... Few ever escaped the mines.

Ephraim's off-work hours were spent at a miner's boarding house owned by Athens Coal Company where he entertained others with his folk music adeptly played on the violin. His father, Wesley had given his sons music lessons and they were assigned a thirty-minute time slot to use their father's old violin for practice each day. The Coakley house was filled with music, amateur to be sure, but music no less for two hours each evening. The effort and patience paid off; the boys grew into musicians that could entertain themselves and others. When they reached that stage, the parents sent to Boston or New York for a finely made violin that the son could call his own.

Ephraim played the fiddle with a group at the church hall where Saturday night dances were held. It didn't take long for the handsome young man to become a sought after bachelor. A hard-working Christian with the added talent of being a musician was a good catch for any woman. He was outgoing and popular. It was not unusual for him to show up at Sunday morning services with a fetching young woman on either arm. Then he wouldn't be seen with either of the women again for weeks on end. He took his time choosing a lady to court.

He eventually found such a woman and fell in love with a fragile, delicate beauty with a French accent. Evette Laureau was a devout Catholic, shy, dark haired, with big brown eyes. After almost a year of keeping company, Ephraim and Evette married and settled into family life in a rented cabin owned by the mine. Ephraim converted to Catholicism and proved to be just as much in demand as a musician with members of that denomination. He played his violin at weddings, funerals and church parties, and became a well-loved and respected man in the community.

Julia, daughter to Evette and Ephraim arrived a year after the marriage. She was their first and last child. Julia was only two years old when her mother got word the black powder had blown prematurely and killed Ephraim instantly. The Coakleys, Laureau family, and the towns of Marietta and Athens mourned the loss of this beloved man.

Evette tried valiantly to support Julia and herself. She did laundry for miners from dawn to dusk; her fingers grew gnarled and callused. She still didn't make enough to keep up with the cost of rent, food, medicine, and clothing. Evette's parents weren't any better off than she was and could offer nothing but moral support. By the time Julia was four years old, it became painfully clear that Evette had to take drastic measures. She requested Ephraim's parents take over Julia's care.

Wesley and Jane Coakley took the child into their home and hearts. Jane was in her late forties by this time and didn't have the strength to chase after a precocious child. It became the duty and pleasure of ten-year-old Lydia Coakley to see to the little girl. Lydia filled the roles of caregiver, big sister, and aunt all at the same time. A bond formed between the two that would never be broken.

The frail, grieving Evette returned to her parent's home in Athens and continued her job as a laundress until her death from consumption three years later. Her parents, Emil and Jeanette Laureau, were unable to overcome their exposure to the dread disease, later called tuberculosis, and followed Evette to the grave within a year.

Julia was an orphan with no connection to her French ancestors. Julia's inheritance consisted of nothing more than her father's violin and her mother's rosary. Grandfather Wesley Coakley took on the task of teaching one more family member to play music. She started her lessons at the age of six and the next couple of years she slowly advanced beyond caterwauling squeaks from the instrument.

Chapter 4

By 1827, Lydia Coakley, the youngest of Wesley and Jane's children had grown to womanhood and married a Scottish miner named Ian Kilkenny. He was employed by the Athens Coal Company and took his bride away from the Coakley farm complex near Marietta and to the town of Athens where Lydia's brother, Ephraim had lived and died..

Lydia and Ian lived in the hilly village and eleven-year-old Julia lived with them. The lack of Coakley kin was felt, as there were no Kilkennys in Athens to replace the large family the girls were used to having around. The mining community including Ian's friend, Caleb Fitzgerald became their new family. Caleb had come to America from Ireland on the same ship as Ian and never married. He spent Sunday afternoons at the Kilkenny house at least once a month. He and young Julia entertained the family with their music. Caleb was a singer and Julia played her violin.

Julia attended the public school in Marietta for five years before Lydia's marriage. In Athens, she was home schooled by Lydia and could read the classics, write poetry and short stories, and solve mathematical problems as well as anyone who had a formal education.

Julia helped care for the children that followed Lydia and Ian's marriage. They had two sons, Mark and Luke at the time Julia first met Joshua Paugh. She was immediately smitten with the good-natured Franco-American who worked in the mines with Ian. Lydia convinced Julia being infatuated was a natural part of adolescence and assured her she would outgrow the phenomena.

A third son, John arrived to Lydia and Ian the following year, and Julia had her hands full caring for boys and doing her own school work. She had little time for daydreams about romance.

Joshua Paugh, like Caleb Fitzgerald, became a frequent visitor at the Kilkenny home. He taught the family a French game called croquet and they spent Sundays in the summer knocking colorful wooden balls around the front yard. It was evident to Ian that Joshua was biding his time waiting for Julia to mature enough to be courted. When she turned seventeen, Joshua began bringing flowers to her when he visited the Kilkennys. Occasionally, he would take her to the Athens' Hotel for a meal in their dining room, or invite her to join him in a stroll along the Hocking River. Then he asked Julia if he could walk her to church on Sunday mornings. By the end of the summer, they were considered a courting couple. Julia's sheltered life had precluded her meeting other boys her own age. If she suffered from this loss of social companionship, she never showed it. She adored Joshua and the feeling was reciprocated.

At eighteen Julia Coakley married Joshua Paugh, son of a French soldier who fought for the United States during the American Revolution. Nicholas Paugh, Joshua's father served in New England's battle with the British. Nicholas had received a quarter section of land outside Athens in the late 1790s from the Land Ordnance Act as payment for his services. Nicholas planted grapevines and coaxed them into producing a dry, red table wine. The hard work paid off and the vineyards shipped wine throughout Ohio. The widowed Nicholas and his two eldest sons loved tending the grapes but his third son, Joshua was drawn to the more lucrative work of mining.

At the age of fourteen Joshua went to work in Athens Coal Mine like so many of his neighbors and friends. He had been there ever since.

Joshua purchased his own home site in Athens and he and his brothers built a two room cabin for the newlyweds. Julia loved her life as woman of the house, but missed the boys she had cared for on a daily basis and used any excuse to traipse to her Aunt Lydia's home to visit. Lydia announced her fourth pregnancy soon after Julia's wedding.

A few months later Julia was thrilled when she found she was with child herself. She had seen Lydia sail through pregnancies without any distress and was taken by surprise when her own pregnancy brought about a near death experience. Julia was ill most of the nine months she carried her child. Some days found her too weak to get out of bed. Joshua fetched her aunt to look after her on those days. Lydia arrived with three little boys trailing behind. The boys ranged in age from two to six and were of little help so played in the yard as Lydia nursed the ailing woman.

After a long, hard three days of labor, Julia and Joshua celebrated the arrival of Emily Evette. Emily, named after her grandfather, Emil Laureau and her mother Evette Laureau Coakley, wife of Ephraim, was a healthy, vociferous child from her first squall. The birthing process had taken its toll on Julia and she required several months to recover. Emily was a robust baby and showed no signs of suffering from her mother's lack of health.

Emily grew up playing with the Kilkenny boys as though they were brothers. She started school the same year as Lydia's fourth son, Matthew, and gradually learned to play with girl classmates. She had a natural nurturing tendency and occasionally talked friends into dressing cats or puppies in baby clothes and carrying them about like children. Emily was equally at home playing house with girl friends from school, or playing sports with Matthew and his older brother, John Kilkenny.

Emily's mother, Julia was not keen on having more children for fear of losing her own life. She avoided pregnancy for ten years. Then one sunny autumn day, Jeanette, known as Jenny was born and was named after Julia's maternal grandmother. Julia was back on her feet within two weeks and delighted with her precious new daughter.

Emily thought of Jenny as a special gift and raced home from school to care for her. She considered the baby an assignment and wrote reports on the child's behavior, accomplishments, and any fussiness. She entertained the baby while Julia did household chores, not out of duty, but out of love.

Matthew's brother, Luke was particularly fond of taking Emily and Matthew on outings. It was Luke who taught the two to swim in the Hocking River and to swing from ropes hung in trees over the river. By the end of the summer after Jenny's birth, both Matthew and Emily had developed a natural affinity toward the water.

John Kilkenny was twelve when the baby girl was born. That was the year that he and Matthew joined their brothers, Mark and Luke at work in the coal mine, and playing with the Paugh girls gave them time to act like children for a few hours a week.

Little Jenny was carried around so much that it's a wonder she ever learned to walk. But walk she did, and grew along with the other youngsters in the love of an extended family.

Chapter 5

"Ow!" Emily's knuckles were blistered and every downward stroke brought new pain. She changed tactics and rubbed the wool blanket against the corrugated washboard using the heels of her palms. She didn't mind doing laundry, she liked the clean fragrance of the soap as she chipped it from the bar into the boiling water. The large washtub sat on the stone fireplace her father, Joshua built in the yard. Emily liked being outdoors in most any kind of weather, but this morning was mild and sunny making it especially pleasant.

Blankets were different than washing clothes; they were heavy and awkward. Normally, blankets were only washed once a year, and she had her mother's help. Now, Ma was so weak she couldn't stand let alone maneuver heavy wet blankets.

The breeze blew Emily's auburn curls into her face and she pushed them out of the way. She inhaled deeply noticing the damp earthy odor from last night's rain.

September's a good time of year. Ma and Jenny should be outside enjoying the sunshine. It won't be long before the maples turn red and gold then lose their leaves. Trees with colorful leaves are so pretty against the dark green pines, Emily thought. She looked around her at the Appalachian foothills. The sun was rising over the hilltop bringing vibrancy to the scene.

Julia and Jenny were huddled in winter clothes under blankets piled on for extra warmth. They had a gastro-intestinal illness, chills and fever, as well as vomiting and diarrhea. Their care was up to Emily; her father was working his twelve-hour shift in the coal mine. Emily was fifteen and old enough to handle the responsibility, but would rather be in the library or at school.

"I should be at school," Emily sighed. She enjoyed nursing people and watching their progress from misery to good health, but schoolwork was very important at this stage of her life.

Athens High School was built the year before and had twenty students. Emily was an excellent student and helped less intellectually endowed pupils with their reading and ciphering. Emily hummed a tune from the school play and watched the silhouette of a man on the crest of the hill as she rubbed more soap on an oily stain.

She recognized Matthew Kilkenny's swagger and smiled. She'd known Matthew all her life but lately when he was near she experienced a strange stir deep inside. She'd invoke his help getting the blankets on the line. She knew beyond a doubt that he'd stop to say, "hey" on his way to work.

Matthew approached the picket fence with a tin can under his arm. He carried his dinner in the closed container to keep coal dust off his food.

"Hey, Matthew, give me a hand twisting these blankets," Emily greeted him.

"Hey, yourself, Em," his blue eyes twinkled with delight at seeing her.

"Got yourself soaked to the skin, girl. Where's your ma? Why ain't she helping you?" he asked then answered his own questions. "Bet you're being punished and have to do the washing alone."

"Am not. Ma and Jenny are sick in bed. Jenny's got a fever and puking her insides out. Ma's just as sick."

Matthew stammered, "Oh, I'm sorry to hear that. I didn't really think you was being punished. I was just teasing."

He put his can down and took the corners of the blanket handed him. "Put the corners together then bring the bottom corners up to meet the top ones," Emily instructed.

"Okay, now start twisting the blanket corner over corner," she said.

She held her end of the blanket taunt so the center wouldn't sink to the dirt. The first blanket went well and water drained onto the ground. They carried it to the wire strung between two maple trees and draped it over. With the second blanket, instead of twisting the blanket, Matthew twisted his body around and under the blanket while holding the corners high over his head.

Emily laughed at his creativity. He made it look like a graceful dance. Of course, this maneuver strained the water from the dripping blanket over him. With the third blanket, the teenagers circled and twisted in opposite directions caught up in a fit of mirth. When they met at the middle of the blanket, they were standing two feet apart. Their eyes met and the laughter stopped. Neither said anything. They didn't move, it was like seeing each other for the first time. Emily felt her heart flutter and shyly looked at the ground.

Matthew cleared his throat and said, "Let's get this here soaking thing on the line. I'm going to be late for work."

The blankets hung, Emily ran to the house and got a towel for Matthew to blot his clothes. Neither person could think of anything to say. They glanced at each other then quickly away.

"I'll see you tomorrow. Maybe my ma can fix some soup or something for your family," Matthew said as he retrieved his dinner pail and swung his long legs over the gate.

Emily emptied the laundry tub and put her tools away. She tiptoed into the house to see if Ma or Jenny needed assistance. Both patients slept soundly, so Emily sat by the window and opened her book. She was in the tenth grade and a voracious reader. She hoped to attend Ohio University, the college in the valley down from her home. There was so much she wanted to learn.

She had discovered the wonders the university library held one day while delivering a message from her teacher to the librarian. Books for adults and older students were found on any number of subjects. The ones that interested her the most involved medical science.

When Emily visited the library, she stopped by the portraits of Manasseh Cutler and Rufus Putnam and read the history of their struggle to start the university. In the year following the founding of Marietta, the first European settlement in the wilderness known as the Ohio River Valley, Putnam procured a charter for a seminary. However, he had to wait until after General Anthony Wayne's winning campaign against the Native American's Tribal Confederacy before he could survey and select two townships for the university's land. The Indian Wars ended in 1795, when the Natives under Shawnee leader, Blue Jacket were defeated by The Legion of the United States led by General Wayne.

Once buildings were actually under construction, Rufus Putnam hired twenty men to travel from the country's eastern seaboard and become instructors. School began at the University in 1805, two years after Ohio became a state, and slowly attracted pupils of prospering families.

Now, forty-six years later, Emily took books home to read even though she wasn't a college student. The librarian had two daughters near Emily's age and had a definite opinion about proper reading material for young ladies. He discouraged her reading scientific books saying they were fit only for boys' eyes.

"I'm serious about learning the workings of the human body," Emily convinced him. "I want to be a doctor in a few years. I need to learn how we're put together."

The librarian eventually let her checkout books on anatomy after he caught her reading them in the aisles of the public building. He knew they would both be in trouble if word got out that he allowed a young lady to see pictures of the human physique.

She had such a book at home now and perused the digestive system trying to diagnose her mother's and sister's distress. There were so many causes for digestive tract ailments she got totally confused. She soon found her mind wandering. She took up a turkey quill and drew hearts then printed Matthew's name in the center.

I wonder if Matthew ever thinks of me, she mused.

In fact, Matthew had trudged to work with Emily on his mind. *What a fine woman she's grown to be. She's strong, smart, and hard working. She's going to be a fine wife for someone. Well, except for being high spirited. That'll test a husband's mettle*, he chuckled to himself.

As a small child, Matthew looked forward to visits from Emily and her mother, Julia. Emily was six months younger than him and they played under the kitchen table while their mothers enjoyed a cup of coffee and an update on Coakley gossip.

When Matthew's father, Ian Kilkenny died of a concussion caused by an explosion at the coal mine, it was Joshua and Julia Coakley Paugh that consoled the distraught Kilkennys. Julia sadly helped her Aunt Lydia with funeral arrangements. It was the first funeral the children attended and four-year-old Matthew trembled in fear when he saw the men lower his father into the ground. His mother hugged him to her breast and sobbed uncontrollably during much of the ceremony. Ten-year-old Mark Kilkenny stood erect in his Sunday school suit with his hand on his mother's shoulder. His eyes were wide with fear as the pine box was nailed shut and he knew he was now the man of the family. Eight-year-old Luke and six-year-old John stood on the other side of their seated mother and cried openly for the loss of their beloved father, Ian Kilkenny.

Ian had regaled his sons with stories he'd learned about Benjamin Franklin, Thomas Jefferson and Paul Revere. His youngest son, Matthew's favorite stories were the ones his father told about Meriwether Lewis, William Clark, Sacagawea and her husband, Charbonneau's journey of 1804 and 1805. Matthew inherited his father's dream of crossing the continent, seeing Natives, bison, antelope, beaver, and mountains so high they had snow all year round.

Joshua Paugh, made good money as a blaster at the coal mine and he supplanted Lydia Kilkenny's meager wages as a baker for two years until Mark and Luke were old enough to take over family responsibility. The boys quit school at the ages of twelve and ten and went to work as muckers. Muckers cleaned the mine debris out of the way after a blast. As the boys loaded the coal cars with rock, coal and dirt, other miners shored up the walls and ceiling with timbers.

Mark worked his twelve-hour shifts in the mine without complaint until he was eighteen. At that time he married a young lady from Pennsylvania he'd chanced to meet at a Grange dance. Becky was attending Ohio University and decided after a year that further education was not her forté, she wanted to return to her family's home in Pittsburgh. Mark was in love by that time and proposed marriage. Becky was smitten with the tall, handsome blonde and promptly accepted.

After the tearful departure of Mark and his bride, the Kilkennys had a family conference.

"I can't support a family of four with baking and mending," Lydia said. "Luke's off work so much with his breathing problems, he doesn't bring in enough for us to get by, and we can't continue accepting Joshua's charity every time we need an extra coin or two."

It was decided that John and Matthew would have to go to work. Employment was scarce in town and the mines paid best so the youngsters talked to Joshua Paugh about working for him.

As a twelve-year-old, Matthew was prime age to learn the underminer's position. Joshua told Matthew that was the job his father held for many years in Scotland and it was his first job in the United States. Joshua told the Kilkenny boys about Ian's arrival in America just as he'd heard it many times over lunch in the dark drifts of the mine.

It was June 25, 1825 when Ian stood on American soil for the first time. Ian was oblivious to the cacophony around him. Nervous cattle were bawling. Men were yelling instructions. Machinery and chains were clanking and clattering. Horses were screaming with agitation. Somewhere in the distance, a player piano was heard accompanied by bawdy singing and laughter.

Cattle were being offloaded and herded into pens. Ian earned his passage by tending those animals in the hold of the ship for the previous three months. He reeked of malodorous living conditions and felt his first action should be to find a bathhouse.

"Come on mate, I'll shout you a brew," Caleb whacked Ian on the back. "We deserve a thirst quencher for surviving the crossing."

"I'm looking for a bath house first, mate," Ian exclaimed. "Don't want those beautiful American women to get the wrong idea about Scottish blokes."

Both men were twenty years old and had bonded while distributing hay and shoveling manure on the ship. They shared their dreams. Ian wanted to spend the rest of his life under blue skies, not underground. He'd spent the past decade working in coal mines in Scotland.

Just in case he couldn't immediately start trekking across the wilderness in pursuit of the snowy mountains of the west, he'd brought a wooden chest packed with tools. A four pound and a ten pound sledge hammer, several steel wedges, three picks, a drill with a tamping bar at the opposite end, and a scraper were carefully stored. He'd managed to find room for two changes of clothes, a small painting of his parents and two precious books on life in the United States.

The books were tattered from repeated readings. Ian almost memorized the story of the rag tag menagerie that had taken on the British Empire and won independence for the colonies approximately forty years earlier.

The second book told of the adventures of explorers, Meriwether Lewis and William Clark, the intrepid surveyors and recorders of geography, biology, zoology, and human life west of the Mississippi River. Ian wanted to follow in their footsteps before overcrowding ruined the west. It had only been twenty years since the explorers returned to Washington and told President Thomas Jefferson of their findings. There was surely still room for him to spread his wings without infringing upon another person's right to privacy.

In Scotland, Ian worked as an underminer at the end of drifts where he struck the coal seam several mighty blows with a pick until he had a shallow hole. Then he sat on the ground with his legs spread wide and carved the hole deeper and wider. With his upper arms on his thighs, he struck the coal seam forty or fifty blows per minute until he had a small room four feet high and twenty feet wide. It was body-torturing work accomplished best by men grown into the job from adolescence.

Ian walked across the bustling Philadelphia wharf and saw a boarding house advertising baths for twenty-five cents. He headed there. On the way he passed a bulletin board outside a pub where a flapping piece of paper caught his eye.

"Wanted! Experienced Underminers!
Athens Coal Mine, Athens, Ohio.
Good wages plus a substantial starting bonus."

"Oh well, in the scheme of things, what's a few more long hot days underground," Ian muttered as he looked for someone to direct him to Ohio.

He went on to the bathhouse and soaked in a tub of hot soapy water while ruminating on his future. He could work his way to Ohio on a freight train. Wagons were headed west with supplies from Philadelphia to Pittsburgh every week. He would catch a paddle-wheeler from Pittsburgh to Marietta. If he worked on the boat, he'd have enough money to buy a mule, maybe even a horse, to haul his tools the short distance to Athens. If not, he'd build a boat and pole his way up the Hocking River. He'd work in the mine for a year and earn a sizeable poke. With that money, he'd buy an ox cart and team and drive to Oregon. There was a valley called the Willamette that was begging for farmers; it was filled with the clean, fresh fragrance of pine trees from the surrounding mountains. He'd get himself some acreage, a cabin, a good plow horse and a sturdy wife and live happily ever after. Ian lit a cigar and luxuriated in his dream.

Chapter 6

"Hey, Em, want me to carry your books," Matthew said as he saw his friend leaving school.

"I'm going to the library, I need a book about bones," she responded handing her stack of textbooks to him.

The two walked in comfortable silence from the high school to Ohio University library.

"I planned a picnic for Sunday," she said breaking the silence. "Do you want to go down by the cave?"

Matthew readily agreed. He knew Emily was speaking of their secret place, a swimming hole in the Hocking River unknown to anyone else.

During the hot October Sunday they removed their outer layer of clothes and swam in the pond just as they had been doing since they were six years old. They dried off lying on a flat rock.

The sun warmed and soothed them as they talked lazily of their future.

Emily told Matthew, "I want to be a doctor although I know it will take lots of study. Dr. Six said he'd hire me as an assistant as soon as I finish high school. I'll learn quickly with him as my teacher."

Matthew divulged his desire to travel across the continent. "I want to live Pa's dream in the Willamette Valley of Oregon. I want to have a farm and live in the clean air. I need to get out of mine work. I know it's a good job for someone living in Athens, but I want something healthier, cleaner. Mines killed Uncle Ephraim Coakley and Pa, and now Luke's sick all the time. Ma's afeared Luke has consumption. John's beginning to have breathing problems and won't get no better as long as he works in the mine. If I can get a farm going, they can all move to Oregon and work beside me."

When Matthew finished his speech, he closed his eyes and let the sun lull him into drowsiness.

Without preamble Emily whispered, "Matthew, I love you."

Matthew sat bolt upright, "You do? You mean love like a wife for her husband? Or does you mean like friends?"

Emily blushed and stammered, "I want to be your wife."

Matthew danced in place like a man who had stepped on hot coals. "Emily, I want to marry you more than anything in the whole world. I didn't think you felt that way about me. I was afeared we'd have to be friends all our lives."

"Could we be married and still be friends?" Emily asked laughing.

Matthew grabbed her hand and pulled her to her feet. "Ouch, not so rough! What're you doing?"

Matthew danced around and around with Emily in his arms. "Do you suppose it's too late to get married today?"

She laughed, "Oh Matthew, can we really marry? We're only sixteen and…"

"You forget, I'm seventeen. I bet we could get married in Kintuck. Let's go find out," he jumped down off the rock and held out his arms to catch her.

Emily gathered up their outer wear and jumped into his waiting arms. Her heart beat wildly as he held her tightly.

"Well, if we are getting married, does you think it'd be all right for me to kiss you," he whispered into her hair.

Both of them were blushing deeply now. Emily dropped the clothes to the dirt and threw her arms around his neck. Their lips met in a soft gentle touch. Then he kissed her cheeks and forehead and then back to her mouth. His insides were steaming hot and he never wanted the feeling to go away.

Finally, they pulled apart, "Are we going to run away or should we tell our folks?"

"Oh no, I don't want to elope. That's sneaky. I want the whole town to know we're getting married. I want to wear a white dress, and have everyone come to our wedding, dance, sing, eat, and rejoice in our happiness."

"You been reading love stories from the library, I bet you," Matthew said laughing.

"Come on, let's go tell Ma," Emily pulled Matthew toward the path. "She needs something to plan; this wedding will be just the thing to make her feel better. She's been sickly for a month. Never really got over that stomach distress she and Jenny had."

"Wait a minute. Don't you think we'd best keep it to ourselves for a little while? We've a lot of talking and planning to do. If we get married right away, you'll have to drop school. Do you want that?" Matthew queried.

"No, I still want to finish high school, go to medical school at the university, work for Dr. Six and..." Emily saw what Matthew meant.

"Let's wait for a week afore telling anyone. That'll give us time to figure out what we want to do," Matthew kissed her gently again. "I love you, Emily Paugh, and I'll be the best durn husband in the whole country, I promise."

Julia Paugh and Lydia Kilkenny made plans for their children's upcoming wedding.

"It seems like only yesterday that Emily and Matt said they were engaged," Lydia said checking off names on the list of guests.

"I know, where does the time go? That was two years ago! Emily is graduating from school in one week and getting married in two weeks," Julia replied. "Our babies are grown up."

"This will be nothing like the little wedding and reception we had for Mark and Becky. Becky didn't know many people in Athens. It was just a family affair," Lydia said.

"I remember, there were only about twenty folks. Emily and Matthew know everyone in town and we have our relatives from Marietta coming. This'll be a big affair. I hope it doesn't rain. Don't know where we'd put all these people," Julia said pointing to the list.

Emily had been working as Dr. Six's hired assistant for the past two years. She helped with medical emergencies, birthing, broken bones, and routine health care. Her assignments ranged from washing and boiling surgical instruments, to preparing women for childbirth, to assisting in mine related injuries. Her favorite part of the job was watching people heal and the lowest times were when the doctor had been unable to save a patient in spite of his best efforts. Then, the two of them sat with the grieving family and prayed for the departed soul.

Matthew had been promoted to assistant blaster and worked with Joshua, his future father-in-law. The betrothed saved every penny they could toward their life together. They had a substantial nest egg. It proved to be a good idea to wait the two years until Emily graduated, but it had been hard. Now the day was fast approaching when they would be man and wife.

"The ceremony will be held at the chapel on the university campus," Emily told her classmates. "Reverend Perreaux is looking forward to joining us in holy wedlock. He baptized Matthew and his brothers and instructed both families in the Baptist faith."

"Joining you in 'holy wedlock.' Oh, that sounds so romantic!" one girl said dreamily.

"It's a good thing you're both Baptist. My Ma is Methodist and Pa is Catholic. They argue religion all the time," a sixteen-year old said twisting her braids.

"I'd love to talk about the wedding more but I have to get home and help get ready for it. All of you had better be there," Emily said waving as she left the schoolyard.

Julia and her daughter, Emily worked together on a white Irish linen dress with crocheted highlights. Julia crocheted faster and better than Emily so the trim was her job. She made wide panels to decorate the skirt and delicate strips to sew around the neck and sleeves. She made a veil to match the trim of the dress.

"Emily would be a beautiful bride even if she wore a grain-sack, but this dress will make her appear angelic," Jenny said seeing the work her mother was doing.

Emily used the sewing machine at Lydia's house to put the linen panels together. The Singer pedal machine whirred away several hours each day as the bride's dress as well as the attendants' dresses took shape. Lydia used the opportunity to teach Emily some sewing tricks. She'd never had a daughter and knew no other girls she loved more than Emily and Jenny Paugh. She was happy to have the one on one time alone with her future daughter-in-law.

Eight-year-old Jenny joined in preparations by tying bows on bouquets of dried flowers to decorate the pews lining the center aisle of the chapel. She also made flowered centerpieces for the tables at the reception. Jenny looked forward to her grownup part as maid-of-honor and hummed the wedding march as she worked.

Lydia organized food for the celebration. She'd make the cake herself. It had to be special and the task could be trusted to no one else. She scheduled others to fry chickens, bake hams, and fix side dishes. It would be the biggest feast the town had seen in years.

Two blasters that worked with Matthew and Joshua said they'd play fiddles for the ceremony and reception. Ian Kilkenny's friend, Caleb Fitzgerald wanted to sing at the service. He and Ian had come to America working for their passage by taking care of Dutch Friesian cows being sent to American dairy farmers. The Kilkennys were his adopted family. He'd continued attending church with Lydia and her sons after Ian's death. Frequently, rainy Sunday afternoons were spent with Lydia playing her violin and Caleb singing.

The university librarian said, "I'll have students carry tables and chairs to the shaded area beside the chapel for the reception. I'll see to it that the area is clean and the grass cut. Just let me know anything you need and we'll have it for you."

Joshua Paugh watched the excitement mount as his daughter's wedding approached. He worried about his sweet child going off to start her own life. Joshua knew Emily was educated, responsible, and capable of being a good wife and mother. He also knew they would leave for the wilderness shortly after marriage. Matthew made no secret of his desire to see the whole continent. Like his father before him, he was drawn to the majestic mountains teeming with animals, flowing with rivers of giant fish, and crowned with snow year around. The daily news brought stories of gold finds in California and Oregon. Joshua thought that would be an extra lure for young Matthew.

Several coal miners had gotten gold fever and left for the west. Like most fathers, he was reluctant to turn over the safety and care of his beloved daughter to another man. Even if that man was already loved like a son.

The week before the wedding guests started arriving. Matthew's brother, Mark and his wife, Becky brought their three toddlers from Pittsburgh and stayed with Lydia.

"We stopped off in Marietta and looked at Matthew's barge. It's huge, have you seen it?" Mark asked his mother.

"No, but it's been Matthew and John's main topic of conversation for the past several months. Is it finished?" Lydia responded.

"All except the loading would be my guess," Mark said.

Lydia felt her stomach muscles tighten but said nothing, just nodded. She too worried about her youngest son and his bride traveling across an untamed land.

Lydia entertained her grandchildren with stories about their father and his brothers as children. The youngsters soon bored with that and wanted outdoor activity. In desperation, Lydia requested Jenny take over the children's entertainment so the adults could work.

That was a new experience for Jenny, at ten years younger than Emily everyone looked after her. Now she held a position of responsibility. She rose to the occasion and spent the days exploring the woods with Mark and Becky's children. She did such a good job she was assigned the chore of entertaining everyone under the age of ten that arrived for the wedding.

Mark brought commercially made suits for his brothers to wear for the big occasion. "These were made by the best tailor in Pittsburgh," He proudly announced. "Becky's pa has all his suits made by this man. I guessed at measurements, so hope I'm close."

Lydia and Becky altered the suits as needed. Luke was so thin; his suit required major work. John and Matthew required sleeves enlarged to cover their massive biceps and forearms developed from years of swinging a sledgehammer and lifting mineral laden shovels.

Julia's and Lydia's family, the Coakleys arrived from Marietta. Jane and Wesley had passed away, but their sons and daughter attended along with their own families. The Coakleys stayed in the newly constructed hotel in downtown Athens. Reunions were planned and people happily traveled from one household to another. Visiting, gossiping, and eating were in full swing.

The wedding rehearsal was mass confusion. John was Matthew's best man, and his other two brothers were ushers. Jenny was Emily's maid-of-honor. Becky was an attendant and a cousin from the Paugh family filled the last position.

Emily and Matthew smiled at each other during the rehearsal and hardly seemed aware of the noise around them. After the practice, all wedding party members were to meet at the Athens' Hotel for dinner as guests of the Coakleys. Everyone was there except the bride and groom.

Emily and Matthew went to the rock where they became engaged. They swam in their underwear and sat dripping dry where they had first professed their love. They shared quiet conversation and affectionate touches. It was an evening of reflection and a chance to step back from the rush and tension of the past few weeks.

The next morning, women were up before dawn. They were busy with last minute wedding apparel preparations and packaging food to avoid contamination by insects or heat. Houses were overheated with the constant boiling of bath water. Kids were scrubbed and threatened with permanent physical handicaps, if they dared get dirty before the wedding was over.

Vehicles made continual circuits between the Paugh and Kilkenny houses and the chapel. Food arrived and nets were secured to keep flies at bay, the church was decorated, musicians tuned their instruments, flowers and ribbons donned every tree in the vicinity.

An hour before the ceremony was due to start a deadly calm fell over the church and grounds. Reverend Elijah Perreaux walked outside to look for an impending storm. The skies were clear, the wind calm, and the holiday-decorated grounds contained no people. He returned to the rectory and donned his clothes for the ceremony.

By the time he'd finished, the area resounded with carriages of people dressed in their Sunday best arriving at the front door. Ushers escorted giggling school girls in crisp, ironed dresses and hair bows to their seats. They helped the elderly find pews close enough to hear the minister. Family members shared privileged places down front. The bride's and groom's mothers sat across from each other in the first row, both smiling and dignified. The flower bedecked pews filled with guests. The musicians in suits reserved for weddings and funerals and shirts with starched collars took their place in the back of the church and played Appalachia's favorite hymns. Caleb sat beside them erect and alert, watching for the first signs the bride had arrived.

At Caleb's signal, the music changed, notifying the guests the ceremony was about to start. People turned in their seats to watch the bridesmaids walk down the aisle on the arms of the smiling ushers. The ladies' hair was piled high on their heads and decorated with fresh flowers. Their pastel gowns were admired by the ladies in the congregation. Jenny Paugh entered with her small, gloved hand tucked under John Kilkenny's muscled forearm. She tried hard to look serious and adult, this was the most important day in her whole eight years of life.

Caleb stood next to the musicians and sang Ave Maria in a strong, clear tenor voice. Emily appeared, radiant with her white gown back lit by the open church door. The graceful crocheted veil hung from her auburn curls to the outside edges of her shoulders and down her back to her waist. The lace on her dress cascaded from her tiny waist to the floor. She was lovely. Matthew could hardly believe this vision would soon be his wife.

Emily took her father's arm, gripped the bouquet of flowers in her other hand and locked her wide green eyes on Matthew. Had a more handsome man ever existed? Did she really deserve to be married to this wonderful, kind, gentle, hard working person? She knew there were much prettier girls attending the university and easily within his reach. Should she politely say "no" when the minister asked her if she would be Matthew's wife? Should she free him to marry a better woman?

Matthew smiled as he reached for her hand. The two of them stood facing Reverend Perreaux and the music stopped. The minister intoned a blessing upon them and talked to the guests. Neither Matthew nor Emily heard what he said, they were suspended in space holding each other's hand tightly.

Suddenly, Matthew realized the minister looked directly at him and had said something. "I do!" Matthew responded much to the audience's delight.

The minister looked indulgently at Matthew and said, "I asked you to repeat these words after me. 'I, Matthew Joseph Kilkenny, do take thee, Emily Evette Paugh, to be my lawful wife'."

Emily felt Jenny tugging at her sleeve. "Give me the flowers. You're supposed to hold both of Matthew's hands like you did at rehearsal," she whispered.

"Oh, I do!" Emily responded to Jenny. Giggles were heard from the row of school friends sitting behind Emily's parents.

Matthew and Emily blushed as Reverend Perreaux took the flowers from Emily and handed them to Jenny. He took Emily's hands and put them on Matthew's extended ones and patted her left hand where a ring would soon be attached.

"Now, shall we proceed with this holy sacrament?" he asked.

The rest of the ceremony went according to tradition and was over in a matter of moments. Emily and Matthew sat in chairs provided while the good minister gave a short sermon on the sanctity and challenges of marriage. He said a prayer asking the Lord to give them strength to live according to God's plan. Caleb sang a stirring rendition of an Irish love song, women blotted their eyes on embroidered handkerchiefs and the bride and groom exited the church and went into the rectory to sign legal documents.

"Well, that went well," Reverend Perreaux said as he signed his name as officiate of the ceremony.

"I know you'll always cherish each other but there'll be times when you disagree. When that happens, think about this day and the feelings you had when you were saying your vows. Keep those feelings alive in your hearts always and you'll be able to weather any storms ahead," he looked from one to the other then motioned to the two witnesses that it was time to leave. Emily and Matthew were left alone in the room.

They sat still not sure what to do next.

Emily blurted out, "Matthew, I know I'm not really good enough for you. I've just thought of my own selfish feelings. I've wanted you so badly for so long, it never dawned on me until today that I didn't deserve you. If you want to tear up that certificate before it goes to the courthouse to be legalized, I'll understand."

Matthew inhaled noisily; he was astounded, he was speechless. This was the most unexpected thing he'd ever heard. How could such thoughts have entered Emily's mind? When he regained his breath, he stood and pulled Emily off her chair. He kissed her passionately and held her so tight it hurt. He didn't attempt to say anything, he continued kissing her until they were both sweating and breathless.

Somewhere in Emily's subconscious, she heard knocking on a door. She pulled her lips back from Matthew's and opened her eyes. Matthew loosened his grip on her and they both took several deep breaths.

"Emily Evette Kilkenny, if you ever say anything that silly again, I'll take you to the looney bin for testing," Matthew said, taking out his new handkerchief to wipe their faces.

Mark opened the door, "Hey! Are you two going to join the rest of us? Or are you already on your honeymoon?"

Matthew and Emily heard laughter behind Mark. They straightened their clothes, he reached for her hand and they walked through the church to the waiting throng.

They were cheered and hugged for the next ten minutes. Women dabbed at tears, blew their noses, and kissed the young couple offering a brave smile of encouragement.

"Are we being sent off to war?" Matthew whispered to Emily. "Why all the tears?"

Men shook Matthew's hand exuberantly, slapped his back, and winked before giving Emily a gentle hug.

"What's the secret? Do men know something women don't?" Emily whispered to Matthew.

People migrated to the tables of food. Plates were layered with a multitude of tempting delights and people found seats at tables. They ate, talked, laughed, and reminisced about their own wedding days or experiences from early marriage. Teenagers flirted and gossiped. Children ran around the tables and ducked under them free from the confines of staying clean until after the wedding. They ran in and out of the trees decked out in full summer foliage as well as bows and flowers.

Marital advice was passed along to Emily and Matthew. By the time the phrase had been passed from person to person along the tables it reached the newlywed's ears as unintelligible garble. They looked for the originator, who was easy to spot from the expectant stare he or she gave them. They nodded and raised a glass acknowledging receipt of sage advice.

Music played joyfully after the musicians took time for a quick lunch. Children danced with chicken drumsticks or slices of watermelon in their hands. An hour later, adults joined the children with jigs and reels or weaved around the lawn in romantic slow dances. Every person from the high school attended and girls danced with other girls until the boys finally submitted to the flirting of classmates. People married for more than half their lives held each other tenderly and whispered about remembered moments as they waltzed. The party didn't end until night descended and people couldn't see.

Emily and Matthew went to a decorated surrey and rode off into the night amid cheers.

Chapter 7

"Don't forget to write," Julia called to Emily as she shaded her eyes from the rising sun.

"Take care of yourself. Be safe," Joshua said untying the last restraint holding the boat to the pier.

"Send me something the Natives made," Jenny said blowing kisses to her big sister.

Lydia had tears streaming down her cheeks as she smiled and waved at the departing duo. John and Luke stood on either side of their mother calling farewells and giving last minute traveling tips to their younger brother.

The Coakleys of Marietta filled the balance of room on the pier. Each had come to bring gifts and well wishes to their young kin.

"Remember," Uncle William called, "We were one of the first families in Marietta. We're pioneering stock. You follow our example, set up a new settlement in the west. Call it Coakleyville!"

"Keep your Christian principles, pray often, and spread the word along the trails," Aunt Ruth called out waving a soggy handkerchief.

Mr. and Mrs. Matthew Kilkenny left the wharf at Marietta, Ohio resembling Noah and his wife. The Kilkenny brothers had built a barge that was crammed with animals and equipment leaving little living space for the humans.

Four sturdy calves were at the front of the barge in a ten-foot square pen. The bull had been weaned from his mother the previous week and was still a bit flighty wanting to kick up his heels at anything that moved near him. A roof was built over their pen making a second story where farm implements were secured.

Behind the calves were a young mare and a stallion in a similar size pen. There was a lifetime of work in their future. Matthew planned to trade the barge for a covered wagon when they reached St. Louis. The horses would pull the wagon across the plains then spend the rest of their workable days pulling farm equipment.

Shaded crates of fowl were tied to the roof over the horses. There were six hens, one rooster, three ducks, a drake, three geese and a gander. Emily reasoned that she could sell excess eggs. If they settled along the route over the winter, she could set the hens and use older fowl for meat as younger ones began producing eggs.

Behind the pens was a closed-in storage room for barrels of beans, corn, wheat, molasses, and oats. Dried meats hung from the ceiling. At the rear of the barge was a small cabin for human occupation. On top of the storage container and cabin was hay to be fed to the stock while traveling on the rivers, straw for the pens' floors, and a small skiff with oars.

Matthew stroked the ears of Ole Blue while day-dreaming of a farm carefully laid out with fields of crops and pastures for his stock. The hunting dog enjoyed this rare show of affection and growled at his mate, Betsy, when she tried to place her head under the man's hand. The dogs snarled and snapped at each other. The distracted man didn't notice their behavior and rose to see if Emily needed help.

Emily was busy making the cabin into a living area. The drinking water barrel was covered with a square of calico representing a tablecloth. A box of ammunition sat beside the "table" against a burlap bag of potatoes. She spread a sheepskin over the two and thought it made an acceptable "chair" for her man.

The chest holding her trousseau, bed linens, bolts of material, sewing box and skeins of yarn was a perfect chair for her. It would be too high and miserably uncomfortable to sit on but that didn't deter her fantasy housekeeping.

A straw mattress and two woolen blankets lay on top the twin boxes holding Emily's medical equipment and Matthew's mining tools. Matthew hoped his tools would never be needed. Emily hoped she'd save many lives with hers. The boxes lay on a barrel of brandy and a wooden box of Uncle Harold

Paugh's bottled wine. Those were two items the Kilkenny's didn't expect to use while on the barge.

In the meantime the boxes would make a narrow but serviceable bed. She had plucked a water lily from the flower-bedecked cove while waiting to leave Marietta. She impulsively laid the flower on the pillow of the bed and felt her neck and face flush with embarrassment as Matthew cleared his throat. She realized he was standing right behind her.

She didn't turn to see him but busied herself smoothing the wrinkle free blankets. His arms encircled her waist and he squeezed gently.

"Is the flower for me per chance, Mrs. Kilkenny? Or was you expecting someone else?" Matthew teased.

"Why, Mr. Kilkenny! What a surprise seeing you here, of all places," Emily replied as she turned toward him.

"As a matter of fact, I thought this would make a nice room for Jerome," she smirked as she referred to the black middle-aged man poling the barge along the shore.

The current flowed southwest in the Ohio River and only required one person to pull the long pole used to steer the heavy barge. Once they headed north on the Mississippi River, it would take both men to pole while Emily worked the rudder. The rudder was currently locked in place, holding the boat in a straight path.

"Well, in that case you and me will just have to sleep in the fish-net hammock in the bow of the boat. You know it might be hard to avoid one person rolling on top the other, if we sleep in the hammock," Matthew kissed Emily's neck and she responded by throwing her arms around him and kissing him passionately.

"Oh, Matt, can you believe it? We're really on our way. Every day for weeks and weeks, we'll see something new," she whispered as her lips were right beside his ear.

Matthew pulled her back and held her at arm's length, "Aren't you a bit afeared of that? I mean, everything new and different. We're going to have to deal with strangers and strange things all the way across. Even when we get to Willamette Valley, it'll take a year or so to get established and make friends," Matthew's forehead furrowed with concern.

"A stranger's just a friend we haven't met yet," Emily's fingertips smoothed Matthew's brow.

"No, I'm not afraid. I hate the thought of not seeing our families, but I'm looking forward to establishing life in the frontier. Hopefully we'll be so successful, the families will join us," Emily responded before changing the subject and spreading her arms out straight. "How do you like our new home?"

Matthew looked around the tiny room. The floor was crammed waist high wedding gifts. The walls were filled with cooking utensils hung from nails, spare parts for the barge were suspended from pegs, two rifles were mounted over the door, and a lantern hung from the ceiling between fishing poles. Every bit of space was utilized. Matthew appraised the room then picked up the water lily and smelled it.

He said very seriously, "I think we'll be very happy here."

Jerome stayed out of sight as the newlyweds bid farewell to their families in Marietta. He had no one on shore to see him off. Then he took his station at the front starboard side of the barge.

He had a hammock suspended from the roof extending in front of the cattle pen. The hammock held a pillow and neatly folded wool blanket. His meager belongings were in the carpetbag in the storage container. As soon as the boat was in motion, he watched the traffic, he watched the shoreline, but mostly he intently watched the water in front of the boat. This was his first job since receiving his freedom. He wanted to do it well. A submerged log could ruin everything.

His master in Kentucky had promised Jerome his freedom years ago. Arnold Jeffers owned half a dozen slaves and each had been promised papers making them free citizens along with a new suit of clothes and train fare to Ohio.

Mr. Jeffers inherited three slaves from his father. Jerome was the son of two of those slaves. No one knew which male had sired him and it seemed unimportant. His mother was fond of both men and each treated the boy as his own.

Arnold Jeffers spent most of his waking hours in his laboratory and worried little about the morality or customs of his slaves. He was engrossed in books and test tubes and strange smelling chemicals. None of the slaves were allowed to enter the laboratory. Indeed, they feared the place and showed no desire to learn its hidden secrets.

The adult males were expected to keep the house, gardens, tools, and buggy in good repair. They were also to care for the few animals. Jerome's mother did the cooking, laundry, and house cleaning. As Jerome reached an age of ability, he helped whichever adult needed assistance.

His mother had two additional children, which weakened her physically. She never regained her full strength after the stressful breach-birth of her youngest child. Jerome did more and more of the household chores as her health deteriorated. He was fourteen when his mother died. His younger sisters were twelve and eight.

Mr. Jeffers decided the youngest girl, Harriet, needed a mother. He had no intention of selling the child, which was the custom of Kentuckians overstocked with slaves in the 1850s. The child was given emancipation papers, as was one of the adult males. The two were sent to Cincinnati where Mr. Jeffers's lawyer met them.

The lawyer got the Negro man a job, housing, and a live-in maid. The maid was expected to be a surrogate mother. Within a year, nature took its course and the man and woman married and adopted the child. Arnold Jeffers paid all legal expenses as he felt a sense of responsibility toward his slaves even after their emancipation.

With one adult, a fourteen-year old boy, and a twelve-year old girl in his house, Mr. Jeffers set about educating them as a hobby. He instilled a sense of fear into the slaves concerning their lessons. It was illegal for slaves to know how to read or write. He convinced them they must never let anyone know he was teaching them white man's secrets.

By the time Jerome was twenty, he had an education equivalent to a fourth grader. He also knew how to do household repairs, took care of Mr. Jeffers two horses and two dogs, and did the gardening. The second father figure passed away that year and Jerome assumed his responsibilities of maintaining the buildings, fencing, buggy, and household tools.

Jerome and his eighteen-year old sister, Eliza, were now the only slaves in the house. Housework, laundry, cooking and nursing were completed by his sister. Jerome did everything else. This setup continued fifteen years.

Jerome and Eliza had minimal social life with other slaves. They occasionally attended Saturday night socials at an abandoned hall where some dancing took place if the mouth-organ specialist or other musicians attended. Sometimes men played cards. On rare occasions someone brought alcohol to be shared with others. Mostly the people talked. They told stories about their life experiences, religions, superstitions, living conditions, and the loss of their family members to disease or sale. The stories were enough to let Jerome and Eliza know they were well off living with Mr. Jeffers.

Arnold Jeffers, Eliza, and Jerome shared a mutual respect, the slaves were never mistreated. They were fed regularly, and given ample time for rest. The differences between them and free people were that they weren't allowed to leave Mr. Jeffers's home without permission, they weren't paid, they weren't to have visitors at the house, they didn't attend school, and they were expected to respond to Mr. Jeffers' needs.

At the time Jerome received his emancipation papers and a train ticket to Ohio, Mr. Jeffers was confined to bed and had a young man in medical training caring for him around the clock. Jerome read the paper saying Eliza would be given her freedom upon Mr. Jeffers' death. She didn't want to leave Lexington and a friend of Arnold Jeffers promised her a job as his hired maid. It never entered the mind of any member of this household that Jerome and Eliza should inherit anything from Mr. Jeffers. Upon his death, Mr. Jeffers' property was sold and the proceeds went to Ohio University, his alma mater, as his will directed.

Jerome gave Eliza a perfunctory hug and left home the day after Mr. Jeffers was buried. His first stop in Ohio was Cincinnati. After a week of search, he located his father figure. The fifty-five-year-old man was suffering from senility and couldn't recall Jerome, his mother, Mr. Jeffers, or life as a slave in Kentucky. His wife was polite but distant. She recalled her husband mentioning another family the first year or so after they married. They had moved forward with a life of their own centered around their church, their daughter and her family.

Jerome obtained his youngest sister's address and visited the twenty-nine year old woman. Harriet was now married to a minister and had three children. Her only topics of conversation were the bible and her children. Jerome knew nothing of either and their communication ground to a halt. They sipped tea and smiled but found nothing to say. Jerome excused himself, gave his sister an awkward hug and bid her farewell.

He returned to the shoddy hotel room and thought about his options. Cincinnati was a busy, crowded city. The Negro section was nothing more than a shantytown. The sound of street brawls, drunken singing, women screaming at their men and each other came through the broken window and thin walls. He spent a restless night tossing on the foul smelling bed.

Jerome was sure he didn't want to stay in the big city. The next morning, he poured water into the wash stand bowl and cleaned himself from head to toe as he had been doing every day since childhood. He used the home-made soap brought from Mr. Jeffers' that contained a floral scented chemical. He was attired in his new suit of clothes including a vest, tie and hat and making his way down the street by seven a.m.

Jerome carried a small carpetbag with two changes of underwear and socks and one worn but clean set of outer wear. He also had the sealed envelope containing his release papers. Five dollars' worth of coins lay loose among the clothes. Mr. Jeffers' caretaker had given him the money as he left the house. At the bottom of the bag was a pocket watch Mr. Jeffers gave him at their final farewell. The watch was placed inside socks for safe keeping. He also had six bars of Mr. Jeffers' soap, a shaving mug and razor.

Few people noticed Jerome as long as he strolled through the Negro section of town. A prostitute approached him with a bright smile and tired desolate eyes. She offered her wares and Jerome declined. Her smile dropped into a sneer as she mumbled something and walked away.

Jerome decided to follow the Ohio River and see where it took him. There was a busy road along the waterfront. Jerome walked all day, stopping only once to buy some food and water at a fish shanty. The owner seemed curious about Jerome's appearance. Jerome explained he was new in the area and his master had bought him the clothes. The fisherman asked no more questions and went on with his net mending.

An hour later, an uniformed man on horseback approached Jerome.

"Hold up there, boy. I want a word with you," said the policeman.

Jerome stopped at the command, fear mounting in his throat, he looked at the road afraid to lift his eyes.

"Mighty fancy duds you're wearing. Where'd you steal them?" the officer inquired.

"I didn't steal them! Master Jeffers bought them for me," Jerome choked out.

"*Master* Jeffers, eh. Where's *Master* Jeffers now? He letting you strut all about the countryside showing off your new clothes?" the constable leaned down and pulled the necktie out of the vest.

"No, sir, Mr. Jeffers not doing nothing. He's dead," muttered Jerome. His heart was pounding so loud he was sure the lawman heard it.

"Dead! You don't say. Did you help him get dead, nigger?" the officer said while dismounting his horse.

"No, sir! I didn't do nothing to Mr. Jeffers. He just got old 'n sick 'n plum up 'n died," Jerome stammered, sweat now pouring down his face.

"You don't say! What about your mistress, nigger? Did she up 'n die too?" the policeman was patting Jerome's clothes, checking each empty pocket.

"There weren't no Missus Jeffers," Jerome could feel the sweat trickle down his back. He didn't know why the policeman stopped him but he did know he was about to be arrested for some mysterious crime.

"Now, look here, nigger. This is the way I sees things. You feel free to stop me, if I say something wrong," the policeman's face was close enough to Jerome's that he could smell remnants of the officer's lunch.

"You are a run-away slave, from Kentucky, say, maybe somewhere else," the lawman verbalized.

"No, such thing! I ain't no run-away!" Jerome spoke loudly and clearly now that he knew what the policeman was thinking.

"And you killed your master and stole his money...," the constable continued ignoring Jerome's interruption.

"No, sir, I didn't kill Mr. Jeffers nor nobody else!" Jerome was agitated and wringing his hands.

"Then you made your way across the river by hiding on the ferry. Went into Cincinnati and bought some fancy duds with your master's money. Let us just see what else you stole from this here Mr. Jeffers," the policeman dumped the contents of the carpetbag onto the edge of the dusty road.

A cloud puffed up as the clean clothes landed in a heap. The sock with the watch was now on top of the pile.

Jerome saw the white hand reach toward the socks and he panicked, "No sir, no such thing. I ain't no run-away. And I didn't hurt nobody nor steal nothing."

Jerome kicked at the clothes exposing the envelope. He grabbed it and handed it to the policeman.

The officer eyed Jerome's agitated state as he fiddled with the sealed envelope.

"Fancy clothes, smelling purdy as a flower, and now a wax-sealed envelope. Right proper nigger, ain't you, boy?"

"To whom it may concern," was written on the front of the envelope.

Jerome fidgeted from foot to foot and wrung his hands again. "Read it, sir. You'll see."

The policeman slid a small knife under the flap, "You sure you want me to break the seal. The proof of your misdeeds might be inside."

Jerome started; the thought that the envelope might contain incriminating evidence hadn't entered his mind.

"Yes sir, you just read that letter from Master Jeffers. You'll see I's all on the up 'n up."

The wax seal snapped as the knife hit it. The flap was open. The lawman slipped the official looking paper from the envelope and unfolded it. He read silently, glancing up at Jerome from time to time.

Suddenly, the policeman shouted, "How much is three times six?"

Jerome was taken aback and stared at the man blankly.

"I said, how much is three times six, nigger?" the officer was in Jerome's face again.

Jerome took a step backwards, "Niggers don't know how to read and write and cipher numbers. It's against the law."

The lawman grabbed Jerome's arm and swung him around. He pushed him face down in the dirt and wrapped a leather thong around the black man's wrists. Jerome was breathing heavily and the dust from the road filled his throat and nostrils. He coughed violently.

The policeman stood up, walked to the scattered clothes, and stuffed them back into the carpetbag. His hand fell on the hardened sock and he dumped its contents onto the ground. The watch rolled to a stop two inches from Jerome's nose.

The officer picked it up and dusted it off with his hand. "My, my, what does we have here? Motive for a murder, perhaps?"

The gold watch flipped open and the engraving was read aloud, "To Arnold Jeffers in recognition of his contributions to the science of chemistry. Ohio University, Athens, Ohio."

"Very interesting," said the voice hovering over the prostrate man.

Jerome was yanked to his feet and marched down the road. The sweat and dust made him feel gritty. The leather thong on his wrists was humiliating as passersby stared. The prodding by the policeman's riding crop made him angry.

They passed the fish shack and the owner tipped his hat to the policeman. The officer touched his riding crop to his cap brim in a return salute. Jerome knew the fisherman had sent the police after him but he didn't know why.

The township of Riverton had a small jail and it was crowded because of the zealous police force. Jerome was shoved through the front door. The weary desk clerk looked up, "What did he do?"

"Possibly murder. He claims to be the nigger in this release form but he's not," the arresting officer tossed the important document on the desk.

"What's your name, boy?" the desk sergeant inquired.

"Jerome, sir. My master said to use his surname - Jerome Jeffers. I never had no last name until I got my release papers," Jerome politely responded.

Jerome noticed the clerk had more stripes on his sleeve than the arresting officer and wanted him on his side.

"I never done no murder. I don't never fight nobody. I never been in trouble afore. Why is I arrested?" Jerome asked.

"Where you from, boy?" the sergeant asked.

"Lexington, I lived with Mr. Jeffers all my born days. Never lived nowhere else but Lexington until I was freed. Mr. Jeffers, he said he's sending me to Ohio with a new suit to start a new life," Jerome talked fast hoping to explain everything before he was asked a trick question.

The desk clerk turned to the arresting officer, "What makes you think this isn't the man described in the paper?"

"He didn't know how much three times six was. Said he couldn't read or write cause it's illegal," the policeman responded.

The sergeant read the emancipation paper aloud, "'and in conclusion, let me say that Jerome is an educated Negro. He can read, write, and cipher numbers to a hundred. I taught him to do his sums, subtraction, multiplication, and short division. He can sign his name, write legibly and spell words to a fourth grade level.'"

The room became very quiet. Finally, Jerome asked, "Is it against the law for niggers to read and write in Ohio?"

"Nope," the desk clerk replied.

"Eighteen. Three times six is eighteen," Jerome muttered.

The arresting officer sighed audibly, "Why didn't you say so before? And what about the watch? How come you hiding it in your socks?"

"I wasn't hiding it. Mr. Jeffers gave it to me the day he died. I wanted to keep it someplace safe," Jerome explained.

"Well, I reckon we ought to hold this feller until we check on the cause of Mr. Jeffers' death," the arresting officer defended his actions.

"Do you know how long that'd take? We'd have to feed this here boy for two weeks while someone went to Lexington to check on an old man's death. Take off that leather strap and set him free," the sergeant instructed.

The arresting officer tried to save face by adding his own statement as he untied the thong, "We don't want to see you around these parts tomorrow, you hear? Get out of town tonight." He roughly shoved Jerome toward the door.

"Wait, just a minute," the clerk called. "You better take these papers just in case you get into more trouble," he held the release papers and envelope out to Jerome.

Chapter 8

*J*erome walked several miles that day and was physically and emotionally drained. He would have liked to go to hotel, take a bath and sleep a few hours. Instead he retraced his steps out of town heading east.

He walked until the lights of town were out of view then made his way to the river's edge. When he found an under water rock ledge protruding from the shore, Jerome stripped off his clothes, hung them over a tree limb, waded into the cold water up to his armpits, ducked his head underwater and released a pent up yell of anger and frustration. The water absorbed the scream and string of foul words that followed.

When Jerome was out of breath, he raised his head and scrubbed his scalp furiously. He walked into shallow water and reached to the ground gathering two handfuls of sand. He scoured the offending brown skin until it hurt. He was sure white men were never stopped and dragged off to jail for failing to answer a simple question like, "How much is three times six?"

When the anger subsided, Jerome climbed from the water and put on dusty worn clothes from his bag. He thought of throwing the new suit into the river but decided against it. He might be able to sell the clothes for a train ticket far, far away from Ohio.

The following day Jerome was ten miles from Riverton. He had resisted the urge to beat the crap out of the fisherman and walked straight past the darkened shanty at about two a.m.

At six a.m., he heard a wagon approaching and chose to hide until it passed. From behind the boulder, he saw the wagon was being pulled by a mule. The driver was an elderly black man.

Jerome decided to chance meeting this stranger. He walked around the boulder and startled the dozing driver. The old man was sure it was a hold up and threw his arms straight up.

"Take what you want. I won't need nothing much longer," he said.

"I was hoping for a ride. I can pay you," Jerome responded.

"I'm heading for Portsmouth. Where abouts you needing a ride?" the gentleman said lowering his arms.

"Portsmouth do me just fine. Long as Portsmouth's not in Cincinnati or Kentucky. I was hoping it wasn't in Ohio, neither, but that's probably asking for too much," the weary traveler proclaimed.

"Throw your bag in the back 'n we'll be off. Glad to have some company. Portsmouth's two days ride for ole Lazrus 'n me," the Negro laughed.

"Whose this here Lazrus feller?" Jerome asked.

"Lazrus is my mule. Named him after the feller in the bible cause he almost died when he was born, but I prayed 'n he lived. I should of named him Molasses, slow as he pokes along," the man impressed Jerome as being right congenial.

The ride with a friendly person was just what he needed. "My name's Jerome. Jerome Jeffers. What you want me to call you?"

"Well, I expect we'll be friends afore we get to Portsmouth. My friends calls me Pappy Jack. Been called lots of names I'd rather not repeat. Pappy Jack will do," Pappy gave Jerome a knowing smile that said he realized Jerome Jeffers was not his real name.

The two men rode in companionable silence most of the way to Portsmouth.

Jerome was learning the hard way that the less said about his past, the better off he'd be. Pappy Jack dozed from time to time but the slack reins didn't change the mule's gait.

Jerome crawled into the back of the wagon and slept for several hours the first day of the journey. They stopped for the night in a clearing near the flowing river. Pappy caught some fish and they were fried with grits for dinner.

Once they neared Portsmouth, Pappy told Jerome he was going to live with his sister. She was a widow and younger than Pappy. She had written to suggest they spend their last years together.

Pappy offered to sell the mule and wagon to Jerome for four dollars. Jerome had no idea where he was going and was carefully weighing his options. Which would he need more, four dollars or a mule and wagon. He hesitated so long, Pappy said, "OK, make it two dollars. I can't go no lower."

"Sold!" said Jerome, rather surprised to hear the word come from his mouth.

Jerome took the empty wagon and mule further east along the Ohio River after dropping Pappy off at an unpainted shanty on the edge of Portsmouth. He smiled at the gleeful, round lady that clasped Pappy to her breast with such force it took his breath away. Pappy coughed and laughed and lifted the lady off the ground in his return embrace. Jerome knew Pappy had found a welcoming place to spend his final days.

Jerome figured he would know his stopping place when he saw it. He still had no idea where he wanted to settle. He did love watching the activity along the waterfront and seeing the boats plying the water.

His meals were costing two bits a day so he knew it wouldn't be long before he ran out of money. He'd better watch for a job opportunity the next day or two.

It was Sunday afternoon as he approached Waynesville. He heard singing. The voices were sweet and clear and he recognized the sound as church music.

The mule automatically turned toward the music. No amount of persuasion by Jerome seemed to deter the mule from walking right up to the church picnic.

Black women were setting bowls of tempting food on a long white tablecloth. Children played tag around the edge of the woods. Men sat on the grass or on concocted stools enjoying sounds emanating from the choir of teenagers.

Jerome descended from the wagon with the intention of leading Lazarus back to the main road. Some children ran up to him and asked if he would take them for a ride in his wagon.

"No, you go back over there by them other folks. I'm going up the road," his answer was short and curt.

A boy of four or five didn't join the other children running back to their game of tag. He kept walking beside Jerome.

"Please, mister, please, can I ride," he pleaded.

"No. Git! Go play with them others," Jerome motioned with his hand.

"Just one little ride, please," the boy entreated.

Jerome stopped walking for the purpose of speaking to the boy sternly. As soon as the wheels of the wagon stopped turning, there were half a dozen children climbing aboard. It was assumed Jerome had come to an agreement with their young counterpart.

He led the wagon back and forth along the path from the highway. The children's excited whoops drew the attention of two young fathers. They approached Jerome with outstretched hands, "Welcome, brother, glad you could join us."

"You're going to work up a thirst walking back and forth. Better come get a glass a lemonade," a muscular man in overalls said.

Suddenly Jerome was very thirsty. He thought of the cool refreshing lemonade his sister made for Mr. Jeffers and himself.

"Well, maybe just one glass. I's just passing by and my durn fool mule turned down here to listen to the singing," Jerome explained.

"The little whelps wanted a ride in the wagon," Jerome felt he should explain why children were climbing on and off his wagon and feeding Lazarus handfuls of grass.

"Mighty kind of you to accommodate the little folks," the man said picking up two chipped cups next to the pitcher of lemonade. "Most folks would of shooed 'em away."

He held both cups in the palm of one hand as he extended them toward Jerome.

"I work as a farm hand here abouts," the man continued conversationally. "Always plenty more help needed in the summertime. You want a job?"

Jerome thought about plowing, sewing, harvesting the fields from dawn to dusk. "Well, I's hoping to get some work on a riverboat. Want to see some country. Ain't never been nowhere but Lexington 'n Cincinnati."

The words were out of his mouth before he could stop them. His stomach contracted in fear as he watched for the man's reaction. The man now knew he had been in Kentucky. The only Negroes in Kentucky were slaves.

"Went to Cincinnati once. Hated it. That's the first 'n last I want to see a big city," the man intoned showing no sign of knowing Lexington was in a slave state.

"Guess, I'm just a country bumpkin," he continued. "I wouldn't even go to Waynesville excepting my woman likes to take our children to church."

"Come along. I'll introduce you. They's good folks. Might know about a job on the river, if you got your heart set on that," he said after draining his cup.

Jerome secured his mule to a tree then followed the farmer to a couple of men playing checkers.

They chatted amiably and invited Jerome to take part in the repast. They knew of no river jobs available and mentioned he might have to go to Cincinnati or Marietta to get such a job.

The men were served dinner first, then the children, and the women chose from the remains. The men joked about who made the best fried chicken and about saving room for pie. After dinner they stretched out on the grass and listened to more hymn singing while the women cleared the grounds of dinner debris.

One man sat next to Jerome and started a conversation. He said he was new to Waynesville and from what he could see, it would be a good place to settle.

"I kind of think I'll see the world afore settling. I's hoping to get a job working on the river. Want to see where it goes," Jerome explained.

"I been working in coal mines in Athens. Been there nigh on to ten years. Got tired of breaking my back in the dark. Got so I dreaded waking up in the morning. Decided it was time to get an outside job," the stranger said.

The two men talked awhile and the stranger rose to leave.

"You know, a feller from the mine was fixing to travel up river to St. Louie. He and his brothers was building a barge to take some animals.

Matthew, name was, Matthew Kilkenny. Square shooter all the way. Young feller, eighteen, nineteen or so and getting hitched up to a Athens' girl and going west," the stranger said almost as an afterthought.

"If you find him in Athens, tell him Gabriel Goshen sent you. Bet you he'd find a job for you."

"Sounds good! How would a person get to Athens from here?" Jerome asked with excitement. Traveling with two people and some animals sounded considerably more enticing than shoveling coal on a steamboat.

Chapter 9

Jerome arrived in Marietta, Ohio a week later. He and Lazarus meandered along the waterfront until they came to a likely camping spot. Jerome wanted to stay out of sight of the uniformed men on horseback. The small contingency of soldiers from Fort Harmar and policemen looked much alike to Jerome.

He needed to find someone who could direct him to Athens. He wanted to find Master Kilkenny as soon as possible. Jerome watched the faces of people traveling along the road. He was trying to find one that looked friendly. Darkness overcame his search.

Jerome ate the last of his church picnic donations, some stale biscuits, and lay down on the floor of the wagon. He used the carpetbag as a pillow and listened to the waterfront sounds. He could hear cows lowing and the chug, chug, chug of paddle wheelers making their way into the docks. He heard wagons as they entered or left town.

Soon it was quiet. He looked at the moonlit river. It was like a siren calling him. He wanted to ride that silvery beam to a place where he could read a sign in a window or write a letter to Eliza without fear of reprisal. Somehow that shiny path on the water led to the new life Mr. Jeffers wanted for him.

Out of his reverie came the sound of a man's voice, "John, help me get this critter back in his pen. Some fool left the gate unlatched."

"Matt, I swear, that horse knows how to unlatch the gate himself," came a reply.

Jerome listened intently as the two men yelled at the horse and each other.

"Contrary animal, don't he know there's oats waiting for him in the pen, Matt?"

There it was again, "Matt", could that be short for Matthew? He had to take a chance. He was going to wander over to the place where the voices were coming from and ask. Jerome pulled on his boots and jumped off the wagon.

He made his way toward the commotion. He heard laughter, "Doggone, that was close, he almost went right through the gate."

Jerome approached the open field just as the horse was about to run into the woods. They were face to face and the startled horse spun around and ran straight through the open gate into his pen.

John got to the gate before the horse realized his predicament. He swung the gate closed and latched it securely.

Jerome came into the opening, surprising the two men.

"Whoa, you gave me a start!" Matthew smiled at Jerome and the latter responded nervously, "You happen to be Matthew Kilkenny, per chance?"

"Could be. Who wants to know?" the smile hadn't left Matthew's face.

"I's Jerome Jeffers. I's looking for work on the river and Gabriel Goshen said Matthew Kilkenny might help me."

"Well now, Jerome Jeffers," Matthew grabbed and pumped Jerome's hand. "Come over by the fire and set a spell. We'll talk. We got a cup of beans left from dinner. You hungry?"

Jerome sopped up the gravy from the beans with fresh bread.

"Your missus make this? It's lip smacking good," Jerome commented.

"John made it. My missus is still in Athens waiting for me to finish off our barge," Matthew said pointing a thumb at his brother.

John started to say something but succumbed to a paroxysm of coughing.

Matthew poked at the fire violently, "John if you don't come west with Em and me, you're going to cough yourself to death."

When John finally got his breath, he said there was no way he was going to a dangerous place like Oregon. He'd leave that to youngsters.

The two brothers joshed about bravery and respecting elders. Matthew knew John wouldn't leave his mining job or Athens out of a sense of duty to his mother.

Matthew, John and Jerome spent the evening getting acquainted. They agreed to meet the next day to discuss a potential job.

Jerome slept better that night than any since he left his Kentucky home.

The next morning, he was waiting beside the dead campfire when Matthew and John awoke.

Not sure whether or not it would be acceptable for him to offer to prepare breakfast, he paced back and forth between the penned animals and the campfire. Finally, he blurted out, "I ain't got no food to offer you, but I'd be pleasured to cook something if you got fixings."

"You can cook? Great! Would you start coffee while we feed animals?" Matthew asked.

Glad for something to do, Jerome fell to his knees and stacked twigs and kindling into a conical shape. He struck a match to the twigs and was relieved a blaze started with the first try. He felt making good coffee was part of the job interview. When the fire was going, Jerome filled a pot with water and a handful of freshly-ground coffee beans. He broke an eggshell and put the contents into a bowl, then he threw the shells into the bottom of the coffeepot.

He sliced left over bread, set out a can of sugar, three mugs and a spoon.

Matthew and John returned to the campfire and squatted after pouring coffee into mugs. The three ate bread and drank coffee before business was discussed.

"What kind of experience you got with poling a barge?" Matthew asked.

"None, never done it," Jerome admitted. Then he quickly added, "I can fix most anything that breaks. I can build boxes, pens, furniture, stalls 'n fences. I can plant 'n care for a garden. I can cook 'n wash clothes 'n clean house - errrr a barge. I'll work all day without a break 'n be up and raring to go the next morning."

He stopped for a breath searching Matthew's face. He could see the corners of Mr. Kilkenny's mouth twitching but didn't know Matthew was trying to suppress a smile.

"You didn't say nothing about animals," Matthew narrowed his eyes and put his eyebrows together.

"Well, I ain't specifically worked with animals except two horses and two dogs. But I can read 'n write and spell some and sign my name 'n cipher numbers. Not many niggers do that," Jerome brought himself upright and proudly put his shoulders back.

"Maybe you could teach me some of that stuff. I ain't got a whole lot of schooling myself. Now, my missus is smart as a whip. Graduated high school just afore we married. She can do doctoring too. Been helping the Athens doctor for quite a spell," Matthew bragged.

There was a lapse of a full minute when nothing was said. Jerome swore silently when he felt the sweat roll down his face.

He knew Matthew wasn't going to hire him. "I know nothing about the river. Why would you need a useless nigger tagging along?"

"The first thing we got to get straight here is language. I don't never want to hear you say 'nigger' again. Got that?" Matthew shook his forefinger at Jerome.

"I won't! Oh, I won't never say that word again! What you want me to say?" Jerome beamed as he realized he had the job.

"If you're talking about a Negro and it's real important you tell me his skin color, say 'Negro.' Otherwise just say 'man, woman, boy or girl' according to what you mean," Matthew explained.

Jerome was confused but willing to follow any rules his new master set down.

"Does you want me to call you Master or Mr. Kilkenny?" Jerome inquired.

"Lordy, no, my wife would skin us both. Call me Matt or Matthew same as everybody else," Matthew laughed.

"Yes sir! I can do that. I got to call your wife Missus Kilkenny if that's not offending. Master Jeffers said it's always proper to call a lady 'miss' or 'missus'," Jerome looked serious.

"Deal," Matthew shook hands with Jerome. "Say, hadn't we ought to discuss wages? How much money you want for poling this here barge from Marietta to St. Louie?"

It was Jerome's turn to look serious. "This here 'St. Louie.' Is it in Cincinnati or Kentucky? I reckon I don't know just exactly where it's at."

"Well, it is a long way away from Cincinnati, Kentucky, or even Ohio. It'll take about a month of poling on the river to get there. We want to get there by July so we can sell the barge and be on our way to the Willamette Valley by first of August. We want to spend the first winter in a military fort along the Oregon Trail." Matthew explained.

It sounded like a foreign language to Jerome. He knew none of these names. His education never extended to geography. He heard the part about St. Louie not being in the places he wanted to leave and that was all that was important to him.

"You can give me food to eat, a place to sleep, and maybe a change of clothes when we get to St. Louie, if that ain't too much. I just want to get to someplace I can read 'n write without being thrown in jail," Jerome was very serious now.

Matthew flinched as he appreciated Jerome's concerns, "You got proper emancipation papers don't you?"

"Course, I does! What's 'mancipashun papers' mean?" Jerome asked.

"Papers proving you are a free Negro, not a slave," Matthew explained.

"Oh, yes sir! I does have those. Mr. Jeffers called them freedom papers. Mr. Jeffers signed them and so did his lawyer friend from Cincinnati. They are safe in my carpetbag," Jerome was relieved to learn he had the papers Matthew wanted.

"Where's that carpet bag? I don't see one around here," John spoke for the first time during the job interview.

"It's over yonder with Lazrus and the wagon," Jerome motioned.

"Lazrus! Who's he?" Matthew asked.

"He's my mule. Good ole boy. I reckon I'll sell him afore we starts out for St. Louie," Jerome answered Matthew's question as well as the one that had been floating in the background of his thoughts.

Various questions were asked and answered on both sides and a verbal contract was agreed to within the hour. Matthew promised to give Jerome twenty dollars when they reached St. Louis. Jerome had no idea if that was a lot of money for a month's work or a little. All he cared about was that he would be gaining his immediate goals.

He brought the mule and wagon to the campsite, showed Matthew and John his emancipation papers and started his first job helping with the construction of a private room on the barge.

Chapter 10

John went home Sunday afternoon. He felt confident Jerome and Matthew could put the finishing touches on the barge. John told the Kilkennys and Paughs the barge should be ready to depart in a week's time. He also told them about Matthew hiring a man to help with the labor.

Four days later, Emily, Jenny, and their parents arrived at the campsite. They were in a wagon filled with wedding presents and foodstuff for the journey.

Emily's father, Joshua took Jerome to a lawyer in Marietta where they had copies of Jerome's release papers made and filed at the courthouse. He gave a second copy to Emily for safekeeping and returned the original to Jerome. Joshua was concerned about Jerome's safety, as the entire trip would be made on river ways separating slave states and free states. Suspected run-away slaves were treated harshly, sometimes killed.

Matthew planned on spending a day in Paducah, Kentucky. The settlement which was surveyed and laid out by one of his heroes-William Rogers Clark. Matthew thought he might be laying out the plans for a town in the wilderness and wanted the learning experience of seeing Paducah. Joshua suggested Jerome wait for Emily and Matthew across the river in Illinois.

Emily's mother, Julia could see no sense in taking a Negro on the excursion. It was an added unnecessary element of danger. Emily said she would stand by her husband's decision. She was sure he had a good reason for hiring Jerome. That evening, when she knew no one was within hearing range, she asked Matthew to explain his reasoning.

"Jerome wants to go somewhere he can read and write without fear of being thrown in jail," Matthew answered simply.

Emily thought of the precious hours she spent at Ohio University library. She thought of the secretive ways she and the librarian had developed for her to read books on anatomy. She needed no further convincing.

"Jerome will be the perfect employee for our trip," she said kissing Matthew tenderly.

June 1, 1853 was set as the departure date. A farewell party was planned for the day before departure. Jerome thought of notifying his sister, Eliza, still living in Lexington. Jerome knew she wouldn't come to Marietta, so he just wrote her a note telling of his plans to work his way up river to St. Louie, where ever that was.

John arrived in Marietta with his mother, Lydia and brother, Luke on the twenty-ninth of May. Matthew was surprised but happy to see his father's old friend, Caleb, in the wagon.

Matthew could tell his mother had been crying. He was sure it was because she doubted she would ever see her youngest son again. Matthew felt bad about leaving his family but discerned fulfilling his father's dream, indeed his own dream, was important to them all.

Ian Kilkenny had come to America to see the whole continent and only got from Philadelphia to Athens, Ohio. Matthew would complete the trip across the continent. Then, he would establish a farm and send for his mother and brothers. She could sit on the porch and rock while admiring the giant frosted mountains. His brothers could help with the farm work that would support the family. They could enjoy the good, clean, fresh air and sunshine instead of breathing deadly coal dust underground the rest of their lives.

The farewell contingency was staying with Coakley relatives. The family had grown considerably. They owned four large farms as well as a garment factory and a furniture store.

The party was to be held at Uncle William Coakley's farm. His son, William Junior and his pleasant wife ran the original farm now with the knowledge they would eventually inherit it. Wesley and Jane's daughter, Ruth Coakley, who had never married lived there and was responsible for her widowed brother's care. The brother-sister couple had a cabin a short distance from the large family home occupied by William Junior and his family.

The Coakleys had visited Julia and Lydia and their families over the years and knew the young adventurers well.

The party was a gay event. Family musicians played their instruments, singing, dancing, and feasting was the itinerary for the evening.

Jerome felt strange, being an outsider, and tended to spend much of the time outside wandering about the outbuildings. In the tack room of the barn, he found a shelf filled with books. He flipped through the pages of a few of the books on veterinary care, animal husbandry, methods of training horses, and so forth. He sounded out the words under the pictures over and over until they made some sense to him. He was so engrossed in the information, he forgot to return to the house. It was only when it was too dark to see the words that he remembered where he was.

Jerome wondered if Matthew was still in the house. He walked through the kitchen door and found Emily and other women doing the washing up.

"Jerome! We thought you had gone back to the barge. Come sit down, I'll fix you a plate," Emily said and headed for the pantry.

Jerome flinched at the thought of a white woman serving him, "No, thanks, ma'am. I ain't hungry."

Emily hesitated only a moment, "Oh, well then, I'll just fix a plate for you to take back to camp and eat whenever you're ready."

"Where you been, Jerome? We missed you," Matthew asked walking into the kitchen.

"I was out in the barn looking 'round. Nice place. I can learn a lot about animals just by seeing where they live," Jerome answered.

"Especially, reading the picture books in the tack room," a ten-year-old girl added giggling.

Jerome flushed and wanted to escape. He took hold of the door handle ready to bolt in case anyone showed alarm at a Negro reading books.

"Now, why didn't we think of that," Emily's great aunt Ruth remarked. "Matthew, you and Jerome go to the tack room and see if there's any animal books you want to take west with you."

"Could we? That's mighty generous, Aunt Ruth. Come on Jerome, show me the books you think is best," Matthew took Jerome's elbow and the two men walked back to the barn.

They spent fifteen minutes in the tack room then emerged with a book on veterinary medicine and one on range cattle.

"Okay if we take these two? Powerful lot of learning in them," Matthew showed the books to Aunt Ruth.

"Sure thing, take more if you like. Knowledge needs to be passed on to younger people. Uncle William and I aren't about to try to heal or raise any new animals. Young William is already smart as a man could get. Those books are just gathering dust," Ruth responded, handing a heaping plate of food to Jerome.

"You better eat up Jerome. You'll need lots of energy to pole that heavy barge," her smile relaxed Jerome somewhat. He was uncomfortable being treated as an equal, a feeling he would never overcome.

Chapter 11

*M*atthew, Emily and Jerome made their way along the river. The early morning fog was lifting. It would be a muggy, warm day.

Their spirits were high with the excitement of the new venture. The trio cheerfully called out to people they saw along the banks.

Sometimes a farmer's children would run barefoot along the shoreline plying the floating visitors with questions about their animals. "Are you Noah from the bible?" "Where you going?" "Can we ride along?" The hunting hounds usually drowned out any responses with their barking.

Occasionally, a solitary fisherman shouted out a word of encouragement. "Settle in Kansas, that's where the best farming is." "Are you going to the gold fields? Hope you find a wagon full." "Good luck in injun country." "Don't let the bears eat you."

They passed a few commercial fishermen with their nets stretched across the river catching fish for the Marietta market. They saw a shanty from time to time with people peering out from doors or windows and waved cheerily.

Matthew noticed Jerome steered the barge toward the center of the river when approaching a wharf or fisherman's shanty. For the most part Jerome seemed engrossed in doing his job. When he took a break, he picked up the book on veterinary care and attempted to read it.

This was Emily's clue to make herself available nearby. When Jerome stumbled over a medical term, Emily was glad of the opportunity to explain it. Sometimes Jerome was so embarrassed by the explanation that he quickly closed the book and returned to the long pole. Emily tried to make the birthing sequence of a colt sound like something she experienced every day. She fooled no one.

The first night on the barge was idyllic. Matthew and Emily lay in their bed listening to crickets and frogs and the soft slap of water against the sides of the barge. Jerome lay in his hammock looking at millions of stars. He had checked and double-checked the ropes securing the barge to trees on the shore. All was well with the world. The trio drifted off into a restful sleep.

At first light of morning, Jerome awoke. He emptied his bladder and went into the section of the storage container set aside for his privacy. The space was barely six-foot square. He had made a box into a table where he could set a basin of water and take his morning bath without worry of intrusion. The smell of the soap as he lathered his hair reminded him of Mr. Jeffers. He wondered anew if his education would be beneficial or detrimental. He longed for the knowledge held in books and hoped he would soon be able to understand all the words. He sure didn't like having a woman, a white woman, teach him secrets only men should know.

Jerome heard movement among the animals and quickly dried himself and dressed for the day.

"Morning, Jerome. My, don't you smell purdy. I might have to buy some of your soap for Em. She'd like smelling like flowers," Matthew greeted Jerome as he hauled in water to wash out the horse and cattle pens.

"Mr. Jeffers made the soap. I don't know if it's for sale in stores," Jerome imparted the idea that he wasn't about to part with his personal bars of rose and glycerin soap.

Jerome removed the shovel from its bracket on top of the horse stable. He shoveled manure overboard and stepped out of the way for Matthew to throw the buckets of river water onto the slightly sloping floor. The water flowed over the sides of the barge. Jerome put clean straw on the floors as Matthew filled the drinking troughs with fresh river water. In an hour, all animals had clean cages, food, and fresh water.

Matthew stripped off his clothes and dove into the river. He called to Jerome to jump in. Jerome said he would rather wash up with Mr. Jeffers soap. He neglected to tell Matthew he didn't know how to swim. Plus, he wasn't about to get naked when there was a woman nearby.

Emily could be heard humming as she prepared coffee and biscuits for their breakfast.

It was almost eight a.m. by the time breakfast was cleared away and they were underway once more.

The first people they saw were fishermen who told them they were near the town of Gallipolis, Ohio. Matthew looked at his charts and announced he was pleased with the progress of the first day. He added that from now on they would have to get an earlier start in the morning. Jerome and Emily nodded agreement and started thinking of ways to speed up the morning preparation.

Emily spent most of the day at the stern guiding the boat with the rudder. Matthew poled on the river side and Jerome on the shore side for the first hour. They alternated sides hourly to avoid sore muscles since neither was used to this exercise. The current was with them and the ride went without incident.

At two o'clock in the afternoon they tied up to shore for a lunch break. They checked the animals and found them dozing in the mid-day heat. The dogs had been howling and restless for the past couple of hours.

Matthew decided to take them for a short run on shore. He took his gun, as he knew there were bears and mountain lions in the woods. The area was hilly and the dogs whooped and howled in excitement as they easily transversed the terrain.

Ole Blue stopped every few feet to sniff at foreign aromas. Betsy made great circles howling in delight; she appeared to feel she was winning some undetermined race. After she made such a circuit, she raced back to Matthew for his approval.

He patted her head and assured her she was a good dog. Then she tore off again, always making sure her path was close to Ole Blue. He recognized the game and chased after her until something caught his attention. Then he stopped in his tracks and investigated.

One such stop stirred up a covey of quail. In a flurry of feathers and clucking, half a dozen quail reluctantly took flight. Ole Blue barked wildly to tell Matthew it was time to shoot. Matthew was busy negotiating loose boulders and in no position to shoot. Ole Blue seemed to give Matthew a look of disgust before sniffing out more quarry.

Ole Blue pounced on a clump of grass and more quail took flight. Matthew was ready this time and pulled the trigger. The single blast from his shotgun felled three birds. Betsy appeared out of nowhere and gently picked up a dead quail and took it to her master. She arrived before Ole Blue who was carrying a second bird. The two dogs quarreled over who deserved their master's praise. Matthew laughed and patted and scratched both dogs before giving the command "find."

Both dogs turned tail and crisscrossed each other's trails several times while keeping their noses to the ground. Ole Blue found the third bird and yelped in triumph. Betsy ignored him and kept searching. Ole Blue returned to Matthew with the quail and received his just reward. Matthew tied the three birds together and started back toward the river.

He whistled for Betsy and yelled the command, "come." Betsy ignored him. Matthew stopped every few feet and whistled. No Betsy appeared. Both dogs were normally obedient and Matthew didn't get concerned until he was back at the shoreline. He whistled several times - no response.

Matthew handed the birds to Jerome and asked him to pluck them. Matthew and Ole Blue started back through the woods in search of Betsy. They had gone only a short distance when Matthew spotted her high stepping toward him with a quail in her mouth. The bird looked like it had put up a valiant effort to escape the determined dog. It had lost most of its feathers and suffered bite wounds on the head and neck. There were no signs of shotgun pellets.

Matthew laughed at the competitive nature of his female hunting dog. He scratched her neck and praised her while wondering what the animal training book would have told him to do to the disobedient animal.

Matthew handed the bedraggled bird to Jerome and shrugged his shoulders. Jerome puzzled over the condition of the fourth bird and held it by a leg well out in front of his shirt.

Chapter 12

$\mathcal{E}$mily fried bacon to go with left over breakfast biscuits and made a fruit salad out of apples and pears Aunt Ruth had given them. Aunt Ruth had handed her a picnic basket filled with fresh fruit and nuts just as they were ready to disengage the barge from the wharf in Marietta.

Other relatives surprised them with homemade breads and desserts for the trip. It had been a challenge to find space to store the goodies on the overcrowded boat. Matthew suggested putting them in the hidden compartment under the floor of their bedroom. It was a cool dry box attached to the bottom of the boat that contained birth certificates, a copy of Jerome's emancipation papers, and cash. The limited space was filled once two pies were added. The gifts added greatly to the plain, quick meals Emily had planned for their trip down river.

Matthew's brother, John made a waterproof box from sheet metal and wood and attached it to the rear of the boat by cables. The box was submerged under water. It could be raised with a pulley. That was the perfect location for meats and dairy products and the box was loaded to capacity at departure.

The second day of travel came to an end at sunset. Jerome secured the boat to shoreline trees. He was careful in selecting trees in a cove where the boat could set out in the water far enough to discourage land animals from boarding it. He didn't want to be parked under overhanging branches and have a snake drop into his hammock for a surprise visit.

Emily roasted the quail with fresh potatoes. Leftovers would make a quick tasty breakfast. An early morning procedure was worked out and agreed upon among the three. If all went according to plan, they would be underway an hour after first light. Whoever awoke first was to rouse the other two.

After dinner Matthew took the two dogs for a swim. Jerome and Emily watched jealously as the animals chased each other or sticks thrown by their master.

Finally Jerome said, "Missus Kilkenny, why don't join them. I'll just sit on the far side of the boat and watch out for snakes 'n such."

Emily didn't need a second to make a decision. She joyously started undoing the laces on her boots. She knew the cool water would be refreshing. When she was stripped down to pantaloons and a camisole, she dived headfirst into the murky river. The water got colder as she swam deeper. When her hand hit the gooshy mud on the bottom, she turned, bringing her fingertips to her toes. Then she straightened out with her arms at her sides. Emily's natural buoyancy brought her body back to the surface.

She bobbed up a few feet from Matthew and quickly splashed water into his face. "Got you first," she quipped before she jackknifed and dove back under water.

She barely obtained an upside down position when she felt Matthew grab her leg. He held onto her ankle and tickled the bottom of her foot roughly.

A pocket of bubbles emerged from Emily's mouth as she fought to stop laughing and free herself. In her exuberance and desperation to get loose, her free foot kicked out. Her heel landed squarely on Matthew's eye.

He let go of her ankle and grabbed his face. Emily surfaced, "Oh, Matt, I'm sorry! Where did my foot hit you?"

Matthew was temporarily breathless from the pain and said nothing. Emily was in front of him in one stroke and reached for his shoulder.

"Oh Matt, not your eye!" she exclaimed.

Emily reached to touch his face and Matthew swatted her arm away.

"Matthew, I'm sorry. I didn't do it on purpose. You know that don't you?" Emily's eyes filled with tears.

"Yeah, I know. I'm as much to blame as you. It was an accident," he mumbled. "But it hurts like hell."

"Let's get back to the boat so I can put some fresh beef on it," she said.

"What? What're you saying? Are you nuts?" Matthew's pain brought out his irritation. "I'm going to need leeches to drain the blood. Not meat to draw a bunch a flies to my face," he turned away from her and swam toward the boat.

Emily quietly followed. When she was on board, she turned and called to the dogs, "Betsy, Blue, come."

The dogs ignored her and continued their own form of horseplay.

Matthew gave out a long, shrill whistle to the dogs, "Damn, that hurt!"

The dogs immediately swam toward the boat. Once aboard, they shook violently, spraying everything in the vicinity.

Matthew ignored the dogs and headed for his cabin totally unconcerned with his nakedness. Jerome glanced up at Matthew's retreating derriere just as Emily walked behind him on her way to the dairy locker. Her wet pantaloon leg brushed Jerome's bare back. He was startled and jumped, instantly falling overboard.

The splash brought the dogs to the scene barking and howling. Jerome flailed his arms propelling himself to the surface long enough to yell, "Helllllllp!"

Emily realizing Jerome couldn't swim dove in and tried to grab him. She got his chin under the crook of her elbow and his body facing away from her.

Jerome was more scared than he'd ever been in his life. He knew he was going to die. Then he felt the warm womanly body against his back and was struck with a new wave of panic. A woman, a white woman, a young white woman with almost no clothes on was clinging to his back! A quick death by drowning was preferable to what was in store for him if he survived.

Jerome's adrenaline was pumping and he easily removed Emily's arm and pushed her under water. Emily surfaced and screamed for Matthew to help. She hoped she could be heard over the animal noises.

Matthew appeared at the doorway.

"Come quick, Jerome's drowning," Emily called.

Matthew dove into the water and surfaced facing Emily.

"Where is he?" Matthew asked swiveling his head.

Emily's answer was drowned out by the two dogs jumping into the water between she and Matthew. They barked furiously at the commotion.

Emily raised her arm and pointed behind Matthew. He turned in time to see a small stream of bubbles coming to the surface. They were barely visible in the diminishing daylight.

"Get away, dogs!" Emily shouted in despair.

The barking dogs swam around Matthew as they thought a new game was underway. They were effectively blocking his view of Jerome's air stream.

Matthew dove under water followed by Emily. They reached Jerome's body simultaneously. Each took an arm and swam back to the surface.

Jerome's body was dead weight and they struggled to get him back to the barge. One thing was in their favor. The dogs had spotted a perceived tres-passer and were busy running along the shore.

Emily held Jerome's body afloat while Matthew climbed aboard. Matthew placed his discarded shirt under Jerome's armpits and braced his own feet against the lip of the barge. He then levered himself backwards dragging Jerome up over the side of the boat.

Jerome would be bruised but it was the only way Matthew could think of to get him aboard quickly.

Emily pulled herself up the short ladder attached to the rear of the boat. She and Matthew were exhausted from their efforts. Matthew's eye was swollen shut. He lay with his back against a crate with the black man's head on his knees.

Jerome's thighs were extended over the edge of the boat. Emily crawled on all fours to his side. "We have to get his head lower than the rest of his body."

The two managed to move the heavy man so his torso was across Matthew's legs and his head was on the floor. Then Emily turned his head to one side and stuck her fingers down his throat.

Matthew was too exhausted to make sense of her procedure, "I guess your fancy medicine book says your supposed to choke a man after he drowns."

"I'm trying to get him to vomit out the river water," Emily barely whispered.

She had no more said so than Jerome spewed a large quantity of water onto the boat deck. Most of the discharge landed on Emily.

Jerome moaned and Emily smiled weakly. Inside she felt like jumping up and down and cheering loudly, "Yes! I saved a man's life!"

Matthew helped her get Jerome onto the deck and lying on his side so more water could drain from his nose and mouth. Jerome started coughing, choking and spewing water. Matthew smiled at Emily. She thought her heart would burst with love for the naked man with the purple, swollen face.

"Woman, you better get some clothes on afore Jerome comes to. He'd have a heart attack if he saw how beautiful you look right now," Matthew said with pride.

Chapter 13

The third morning, Matthew opened one eye and decided it was a perfect day to sleep in late. He closed the unswollen eye and hoped to go back to sleep. His head throbbed and he knew there was little chance he could lie still until his pain went away.

Jerome tried to roll out of his hammock and discovered he had sore muscles in places there weren't any muscles two days earlier. He lay on his back and gingerly touched his abdomen. It felt like he was holding a lit match to his chest. He tried to focus. What had happened? They had a nice day coming up river. Emily and Matthew went for a swim after dinner. Then what? The barge didn't look wrecked. He didn't remember a crash. Had they been attacked by a mob of madmen? He couldn't remember a fight. Had the Riverton police recaptured and beaten him?

"No!" A light came on in his head. "Missus Kilkenny had attacked him!" He remembered her touching him and he fell in the water. He remembered grappling with her.

"Ooooh," he moaned. "She must be one strong woman. But I'm stronger." He sure didn't want to get out of bed and face her. Heaven only knows what he did to her.

I sure hope I didn't kill her, he thought.

"Good morning, Jerome! I'm pleased to see you alive. How do you feel?" Emily greeted him cheerily.

Jerome opened one eye a tiny bit so he could surmise the damage he had probably inflicted on this petite woman. There were no cuts or bruises. There were no bandaged limbs. He opened both eyes wide. Okay, so maybe *she* didn't attack him. Maybe it had been an alligator. He'd never seen an alligator but had heard stories from other slaves. Some had been mighty happy to live to tell the tales of their experiences with alligators in the Louisiana bayous.

"Morning, ma'am. Reckon I'm glad to see you, too," Jerome tried to get out of the hammock. He didn't succeed.

"Matthew will help you get up and do your morning things. Just let me bathe and bandage your chest. It still looks mighty raw," Emily said.

"Yes sir, ma'am. I mean, no, ma'am. I can wash myself," Jerome stammered.

"Look, Jerome. We need to get something straight. I'm a trained medical person. Like a doctor. I've seen hundreds of men's bodies. Well, dozens anyhow. You're hurt and I can make you feel better. Don't think of me as a woman, think of me as a doctor," Emily proudly made her speech setting a bowl of water, disinfectant and a cloth on the floor.

"You sure does look like a woman to me. You look like a white woman. I don't care to get lynched. I'll just wash myself or no one will," Jerome retaliated.

Emily had little contact with Negroes. She didn't know much about the mistreatment of slaves in the south. The only time she had been to Kentucky was with Dr. Six. They had gone to a poor farmer's home across the Ohio River from Marietta. The farmer's wife had given birth to twins joined at the skull. Dr. Six wanted to see if he could separate the babies. It was a short, sad trip. The mother and the twins were near death when Dr. Six and Emily arrived. They were unable to save anyone. Emily put on a brave face and helped prepare the trio for burial. On the return trip, Emily cried softly as Dr. Six held her gently in his arms.

Emily brought her thoughts back to the present. "Okay, I'll let you do it this time, but if you want help, let me know. You need to wring the cloth out and lay it on your bare chest. There's medicine in the water and it'll sting at first. Then it'll feel better. It's important to get medicine on all the scraped skin so you don't get infection. You hear me? All of the skin," Emily shook her finger at Jerome as though disciplining a child. It never occurred to her that he was twice her age; he was a patient.

Emily placed the basin as close to the hammock as she could then turned to go.

Matthew was staggering toward the farm animals. When Jerome saw Matthew's face, he had an awful sinking feeling. He must have had a fight with Matthew instead of an alligator. Matthew looked terrible.

Emily mixed two glasses of water and laudanum. She gave one to each man along with their breakfast of quail and roast potatoes. The men slept away most of the morning. Emily tended the animals. Despite their complaints, she kept the two bloodhounds tied up. She was in no mood for their aggravation.

By noon, the men stirred about a bit. Neither was in a decent mood so Emily kept her distance as much as possible. The boat was never untied from the shore. A whole day was wasted while the men healed.

Chapter 14

A new dawn, a new day. The subdued trio went about their tasks a bit more slowly than normal but they did manage to get underway by eight a.m. Matthew wanted to make up lost time so there was no midday stop. Emily brought the men sandwiches, pie, and jugs of milk at dinnertime.

They poled past the busy settlement of Portsmouth in the afternoon. There was no reason to stop. Matthew certainly didn't want people inquiring about his black eye. Jerome still didn't know how his chest got scraped raw and thought it best not to ask. He was afraid if they went to town, he might learn the whole story as he heard Matthew explain it to a lawman. Emily had eggs to sell but thought better of suggesting a stop. She would have bacon and scrambled eggs for supper. That would make nice leftovers for the following breakfast.

At sunset, the weary trio found a quiet cove and tied up. Matthew looked at the water longingly. Emily knew he wanted a cool swim but said nothing. Finally, Matthew announced he was taking the dogs ashore. He invited Jerome to accompany him; he said nothing to Emily. The skiff was removed from the roof of the cabin. Jerome moaned at the strain on his abdomen as he helped lift the boat down. He hoped Matthew hadn't heard.

The men and dogs were gone for a long time. Emily could hear the dogs barking from time to time but heard no sounds of distress. She took care of the fowl, made biscuits, beat eggs and sliced the bacon. There was no sense in cooking the food until the men returned.

At nine o'clock, Emily heard the skiff approaching. A funny sound was emanating from it and she listened more closely. There it was again. Laughing! She heard men actually laughing. She went to the shore side of the barge and listened intently. Yes, yes it was laughing. She had never heard Jerome laugh out loud but now he guffawed heartily. Emily returned to the stove Luke Kilkenny had made for their journey. Her heart felt light as a feather as she popped the bacon into the skillet.

Shortly, Matthew came up behind her and embraced her, "Well, all's forgiven. We've decided to keep you. It was touch and go for a while but we took a vote on it. Betsy broke the deadlock. We wouldn't let Ole Blue vote cause he don't understand women," Matthew nuzzled her ear.

"Oh, I see. You and Jerome understand women, do you?" Emily put her hands on her hips.

The three of them laughed together. The tension was broken. Matthew tried to tell Emily that Jerome mistook her for an alligator but told such a disjointed tale between bursts of laughter, she never really understood the story. She chuckled politely and went on with her cooking.

The next morning the men were feeling much better and the preparatory routine went well. It took an hour and a half from the time the first person awoke to embarkment.

Matthew's face was more green than black this morning. It also had tinges of blue, yellow and purple showing. The swelling had receded to the point he could open his bloodshot eye halfway.

Jerome's chest was streaked with rows of tiny scabs and in places the normally brown skin was black or dark red. He refused Emily's offer of a mild dose of laudanum saying he didn't need it and didn't want to be groggy.

They were underway by seven a.m. Cause for celebration. Emily poured each man and herself a glass of apple cider as a treat for a job well done.

The hazy sun rose on their backs and turned the ripples of water into a path of sparkling silver.

The current was getting faster and they made good time. Spirits were high and the men joked back and forth as they poled.

Emily worked the rudder and couldn't quite hear the jokes over the cackling fowl, lowing cows and barking dogs. She was elated to see her men happy again. She allowed herself a congratulatory compliment that one of those men would be dead, if it wasn't for her medical expertise.

Matthew spotted two small fishing boats on the river ahead. They were traveling parallel, one on the south side of the river about twenty yards from shore and one on the north side about forty yards from shore.

Matthew motioned to pull the boat to the north and Emily turned the rudder. As they got closer to the fishermen, Matthew could see men at the rear of the boats pulling in heavy ropes. He knew the two boats were dragging a net between them. Matthew told Emily and Jerome to proceed as slowly as possible. He wanted to give the fishermen as much space as possible and didn't know where the net extended under the brown water.

A man wearing a slouch hat emerged from the small cabin on the boat closest to the animal laden barge. Jerome recognized him immediately. It was the person who reported him as a run-away slave. The two men stared at each other as the barge worked its way past the fishing boat. The animosity was thick in the air. Matthew called out a greeting to the fishing boat. The man working the net returned a salutary wave. The second man's eyes never left Jerome's face.

An hour passed before Jerome could breathe easily again. Matthew noticed the change in demeanor but said nothing; he waited to see if Jerome wanted to explain the situation.

At their lunch break they discussed whether to attempt getting past Cincinnati before camping for the night. Emily was afraid it might mean traveling after dark. At their current rate of speed, they would reach the major river port about sunset. Matthew said he really wanted to take the animals ashore and let them graze for a day. Jerome fidgeted through the conversation. He showed no interest when Matthew said the town was formerly known as Fort Washington and was settled by General Harmar, who had moved his point of operation from Fort Harmar at Marietta to the location of present day Cincinnati. The General thought that Fort Washington would be a better spot from which to defend settlers from warring Natives.

It wasn't Indians Jerome was worried about, he could keep quiet no longer, "I doesn't want nothing to do with land between here and the far side a Cincinnati."

Matthew and Emily looked at Jerome, waiting for an explanation. None was forthcoming.

Matthew cleared his throat and said, "Well, I guess that settles it. We'll move on to the far side of town afore we stop for the night."

Emily looked from one man to the other, "You mean you're willing to chance smashing into a rock or submerged log in the dark? Why don't you want to land, Jerome?"

Jerome knew he owed the couple an explanation but hated telling about the humiliating experience with the fisherman and the lawman.

"I first come cross the river on the ferry at Cincinnati. It's a terrible place-noise, dirt, drinking, fighting. The bad news kind of folks spread out long ways round that town," he said.

"Has it something to do with the man on the fishing boat?" Matthew asked.

"Yes sir, he's bad news to me. I just might have to beat the living day lights out of him, if we was to meet up on solid ground." There, Jerome felt he needed say no more. That was all the explanation necessary.

Matthew looked to Emily for the final decision.

"Let's travel the center of the river where the current's strongest from now until sunset. Then we can make the best time. At sunset we pull ashore. We could go to the Kentucky side, if that makes you feel better, Jerome," Emily offered.

The ball was back in Jerome's court. He wasn't used to making decisions and knew this could be an important one.

"Let's just try that and see where we is when the sun gets low," he procrastinated.

Chapter 15

Jerome worked harder that afternoon than any previous day. The water was too deep for poling in the center of the river. Jerome and Matthew manned the other end of the poles, which had been hewn into oars. Matthew was leery of the speed they were traveling. One submerged log could destroy the barge if they collided at their current speed. Jerome rowed like demons were on his tail.

He stood on a box so he could see further ahead. He too wanted to avoid a collision or anything that would cause a slow down. Jerome breathed a sigh of relief when they rounded a bend and saw the Cincinnati harbor. Sunset was still an hour away. They would be well past the despised location before pulling ashore.

Matthew wanted to avoid the traffic of the wharf and motioned to Jerome to pull to the south side of the river. Emily turned the rudder to avoid the dozen or so boats of various sizes and types plying the waterway.

The town was only thirty some years old and was mushrooming with growth. The surrounding land was ideal for farming and was being populated with migrants from Germany, Ireland and Great Britain who were depressed by poverty and starvation in Europe.

Reluctantly, Jerome followed Matthew's orders to travel slowly and carefully south of the traffic lanes. They coasted in the slower current along the Kentucky shore. He could see slaves at work on tobacco fields. He saw youngsters not more than five or six years old working in the fields. An overseer was prodding an ancient looking black man with his riding crop. Jerome couldn't hear the words coming from the overseer's mouth but envisioned abusive language telling the elderly man to work faster.

Fear gripped Jerome as the overseer looked his way. The white man appeared to bore holes into Jerome's skin trying to decide whether he should stop the barge. Jerome knew exactly where his freedom papers were kept. Should he stop rowing and get the papers just in case the man stopped the boat? He saw the overseer put his riding crop into the leg of his boot and pull a rifle from a scabbard. Papers would be of little use if the man shot at him.

"Jerome, Jerome, did you hear me?" Jerome realized Matthew had been calling him.

"Yes, masta," Jerome answered automatically.

"Come over to this side right now," Matthew ignored Jerome's response.

Jerome forced his frozen fingers off the oar after putting it in its bracket. Matthew was suddenly at his side and put his arm around the black man's shoulders.

"You work on that side for a spell. Give your arm muscles a change," Matthew spoke softly and reassuringly.

"Morning, sir! Great day for working outdoors," Emily cheerily called to the man on horseback.

Her bright smile distracted the man's concentration on Jerome, "Yes, ma'am. I reckon it is a bit cooler floating down river. Powerful hot in the fields."

He placed his rifle back in the sheath hanging from the saddle and gave a grandiose swing of his wide brim hat. He bowed to Emily as she called out, "Might be time for lemonade on a shady veranda."

Jerome and Matthew were rowing faster with each stroke. The trio glided past the point of danger without incident. It was ten minutes before anyone spoke.

"Missus Kilkenny, about your suggestion we camp on the Kentucky side tonight," Matthew intoned. "Jerome and I kindly decline the invitation."

An audible sound came from Jerome. Matthew realized the black man was exhaling. Had he actually held his breath for fifteen minutes or so? "Nah, not a chance," Matthew said to himself.

The sun was nearing the horizon and Jerome and Matthew paddled as hard as their tired muscles allowed. Emily steered the boat back into the center of the river. As the sun sank behind the horizon, Emily headed for the Ohio shore. Matthew watched for a clearing in the thick brush. He saw an alcove entrance from the west when he looked back up river. It hadn't been visible until they were past it.

Matthew called to Emily and Jerome pointing to the hidden waterway. Jerome's white teeth gleamed in the diminishing light; he was smiling his agreement. This surely looked like a safe haven.

The three of them worked in the gathering dusk until the barge was maneuvered up the waterway and hidden from river traffic. They secured the boat, fed and watered animals and sat down to a cold repast. They ate in exhausted silence while listening to the domestic animals settling in for the night. Wild critters could be heard calling for family and friends to join in a search for sustenance.

Daylight shone in the doorway as Emily opened her eyes. She moved her foot back to nudge Matthew and realized she was in bed alone. She rolled onto her back and stretched luxuriously. It was rare she had the whole bed to herself. The yard wide bed felt decadent as she tucked her palms under the back of her head and her legs out straight and wide. This was more room than she had in her bed before marriage. She and Jenny shared a bed four-foot wide in the loft of the clapboard house in Athens.

Emily closed her eyes and lay there reflecting on their trip so far. She was proud of the way they had diffused danger and overcome accidents. She had had more adventure in the past week then in the previous year.

Matthew and Jerome explored the area. Matthew couldn't believe his luck. The brambles surrounded a meadow about an acre in size. Perfect for the cattle and horses!

Emily was aware of movement outside and heard the hushed voices of Matthew and Jerome when they returned to the boat to start their day's work. She knew they were trying not to wake her and smiled at the thoughtfulness.

If I keep my eyes closed, I can pretend I'm the Queen of Sheba with my adoring subjects working away outside my sleeping chamber, she thought.

"Hey, woman, how's about giving us a hand out here," Matthew's voice from the doorway broke her short reverie.

"All right, *man.* Give me time to get some clothes on," she responded emphasizing the word 'man.'

"Wear those ole pants of mine that you cut off to fit yourself. And real boots, the boy's shoes you bought. You'll be walking in brambles," Matthew said with excitement.

"Oh, goody," she answered thinking Matthew sounded like a boy who had discovered a wrapped Christmas present with his name on it. She dressed quickly and emerged from the room looking like a boy except for the wide brimmed sunbonnet Lydia had made for her. It circled her face and a blue ribbon tied it in place under her chin. Her auburn tresses were tucked up under the hat to avoid getting them caught in blackberry bushes.

Chapter 16

*M*atthew led the stallion along the edge of the sandy beach. The animal was skittish about being on solid ground and stepped from side to side as though still trying to balance on a rocking boat. Once he got his bearings, he wanted to break loose and run. Matthew expected that and had Jerome holding the rope on one side while he held the bridle and reins tightly keeping the horse's head lowered.

They led the horse down a cleared path to the meadow then tethered it to a horizontal rope stretched between two trees. The grateful horse nodded his head several times before turning and running.

"Whoa boy, slow down," Matthew yelled.

The horse stretched the rope to its limit and was stopped with a jerk. Upset, he reared and pawed the air. Matthew kept talking to the horse as he approached him. He went hand over hand along the rope until he held the horse close so he could no longer rear easily.

The frustrated horse fought the man demanding his freedom then became calmer as Matthew continued to talk softly and hang onto the bridle. When the horse stood still for a couple minutes, Matthew began walking him up and down the horizontal rope to show the horse his limits. Within five minutes, the horse was standing quietly munching away on the fresh grass.

"Ok, now we knows how NOT to introduce a horse to his new surroundings," Matthew said. "Anyone got a better idea? We've still another horse to bring ashore," Matthew looked from Jerome to Emily.

"Maybe walk the female on a short lead until she feels secure out of the pen but still on the boat. Then bring her onto the beach on a short lead and walk up and down the beach before bringing her into the meadow," Emily offered.

"Or hobble her on the beach for awhile afore bringing her to the meadow," Jerome suggested.

"We'll do both," Matthew answered.

The docile female was confused about being led around the narrow edge of the boat. She went where she was led. She wasn't the least concerned with the strange feeling sand beneath her feet once on the beach. Jerome hobbled her and she made no attempt to move. She looked from man to man as though asking what they wanted her to do next.

Two minutes later, Matthew removed the hobbles and led the horse into the meadow. He clenched the bridle tightly in case she tried to rear or take off when she saw the green grass. She didn't. The horse followed her master's lead to the rope where her partner was tethered. She neighed softly, put her head down and started eating the verdant food.

Emily laughed, "Guess there's more than one difference between boys and girls. Girls are better behaved."

"You better not brag too loud, we have some cows to bring over," Jerome said.

Matthew and Emily exchanged a quick meaningful glance. Jerome spoke directly to Emily in a playful manner. He was beginning to relax in her presence.

"Oh, yeah. You take the bull. I'll take the heifers. Just see who ends up with the most bruises," Emily joked shaking a finger at the black man.

"Hey, you two, no contests. We'll work together as a team," Matthew admonished. His delight with the new friendship was evident.

An hour later, all animals were on shore. They were restrained by one method or another although the blackberry bushes and undergrowth looked impenetrable. Emily shuttered at the thought of crawling around in the bushes trying to retrieve a goose or hen. She was glad Matthew had suggested leaving them in their crates on the beach.

"I'm starving," Emily said, "I feel we have done a full day's work. Let's eat breakfast."

Emily made coffee and cooked ham, eggs, and fried stale bread. Matthew carried a blanket, the square of calico, dishes, cups, and eating utensils to a shady spot in the meadow. Jerome carried fruit, a jug of milk, sugar, and pillows to the picnic site. The three ate while admiring their handiwork of getting all the animals safely ashore and secured.

Ole Blue and Betsy had worn themselves out racing up and down between the boat and the meadow. They were now reclining under a tree near the picnickers. Betsy lay with her chin on her front paws watching every move Matthew made. Ole Blue lay on his back in a most ungentlemanly position. His head was turned to one side and his tongue lolled out of his mouth as he snored, totally unconcerned with his manners.

After an hour's rest, the pioneers decided this was a good opportunity to scrub out the pens. They worked on the boat until sunset. They left the larger animals on land overnight. The fowl were returned to the boat to prevent an attack by raccoons, skunks or foxes.

Emily and Matthew went for a swim. No mention was made of their disastrous last frolic in the water. Neither made any attempt to tease the other on this occasion. They swam out to the main river but didn't enter the flowing current.

The alcove water had been warmed by the sun and was a comfortable temperature. They found soap weed and rubbed it between their palms until it was frothy. Matthew scrubbed his limbs with sand but Emily found that too harsh for her liking.

When they returned to the boat, Jerome was setting out plates of cold sliced beef, biscuits, green salad of wild watercress, and bowls of blackberries.

"This roughing it could be habit forming," Matthew said drying his skin with a soiled shirt.

"Don't use that stinky old shirt," Emily admonished. "We have a clean towel in our room."

Emily had put her towel on the edge of the boat so she could dry off out of view from Jerome. She was wrapped from head to toe in the picnic blanket as she made her way to their sleeping quarters. She caught a whiff of roses as she passed Jerome and felt a tiny pang of jealousy. Matthew had discussed

Jerome's possessiveness about the bars of soap made by his master. She knew better than to comment on the delightful fragrance.

The tasty dinner was consumed and utensils cleaned. The three sat comfortably watching the moon rise on the water.

"Yas suh, masta," Matthew said with a twang. "You know that has kind of a nice ring, don't it? Maybe, Jerome, you ought to address me that way all the time."

Jerome jerked his head around to look at Matthew. He was ready to protest when he caught the glint of moonlight on Matthew and Emily's teeth. They were laughing.

Chapter 17

$\mathcal{J}$erome lay awake in his hammock listening to the night sounds long after Matthew and Emily were asleep. He wasn't sure they were far enough away from Cincinnati and its lower class citizens. Jerome felt a barge full of cargo might be very tempting to hooligans looking to make fast money.

Well into the night, he heard wood scraping on wood. The sound didn't fit in with the normal bush noises. He listened more closely to see if a wind had come up on the river. Maybe two trees were brushing against each other.

There was a splash followed by a chain rubbing against wood. Someone was lowering an anchor. The sounds were far enough away that they had to be coming from the main river. Maybe someone was traveling and chose that spot to pull up for the night. Although, few boats attempted the tricky river in the dark.

Jerome reached for his pants and shoes and put them on. He quietly felt his way into the storage area among the barrels. He lifted the lid of a chest, a gift from woodworker, Elias Coakley. Inside was the musket, powder horn, ramming rod, and powder given him by Joshua Paugh.

Jerome had never fired a gun before receiving this gift. Joshua made sure he knew the loading, shooting and cleaning procedures. Now Jerome wished he could light a lantern and prepare his shot. He knew a light would give away their position so he worked with the fading moonlight. Trying to move quietly took extra time and care but he eventually felt the gun was ready for use.

He stealthily made his way to the front of the barge and sat on the floor by the horse pen. He could see the faint glimmer of water until it was hidden in the dark shadows of trees. He watched the water and listened for unusual sounds the rest of the night.

As the first gray light of day appeared, Jerome realized he was stiff from sitting and exhausted from lack of sleep. *I'd be useless if they attacked now,* he thought.

He stood, stretched and twisted until his muscles felt more flexible. He lay on the floor and brought a pail of water up from the river. He relieved himself into the pond and started his morning ritual. When he opened up the soap container, the smell of flowers confronted him. He thought better of using the scented soap and reclosed the lid. The black man cleaned his teeth and washed his upper body with fishy smelling river water. He was awake and alert again though he didn't really feel clean.

He resumed his position on the front of the boat sitting in the shadow of the pen. He sat still for more than fifteen minutes before he sensed movement. He heard a soft sound of rhythmic water movement and identified it as oars going in and out of water. His muscles tensed as he saw a small skiff moving along the shore. He waited until the skiff passed through a spot not shaded by trees, in the early dawn he could make out two men in a rowboat paddling quietly in the still water.

Jerome picked up his gun and aimed it at the skiff. He cocked the hammer and yelled, "Who goes there? What you want?"

Ole Blue and Betsy were startled into action and howled loudly, drowning out any reply made.

Jerome swore softly, "Darn fool thing to do."

Matthew was suddenly at the door in his nightshirt, rifle in hand.

"Quiet down you dogs," he yelled. "Jerome, what's wrong? Where are you?"

A loud report from the rowboat was his answer. A musket ball whizzed by his head and hit something metal behind him. The fowl were alarmed and set up a ruckus. The dogs ran around the barge barking wildly.

"Stop where you is or I'll shoot," Jerome hollered when he saw the small boat heading across the lagoon toward the barge. The sky was getting lighter by the minute and the men were now easy to see.

One man was rowing with his back to the barge. The second man was reloading his musket. Sweat blinded Jerome for an instant and he wiped his eyes with the back of his hand before re-aiming his gun. He could kill the man rowing and the thought nauseated him. He lowered his aim and fired. The ball hit the side of the boat at water level. Boards splintered and water slashed. The standing man yelped and dropped his gun. He fell to the floor with a thud and the boat nearly capsized.

The oarsman picked up the musket and swung around in his seat. Jerome was busy reloading or he would have recognized his nemesis, the fisherman who had reported him as a run-away slave.

Matthew shouted for the man to drop his gun, warning him that a shot was imminent. The fisherman saw Matthew aiming at him and wisely put the musket on the floor of his boat.

They were now twenty yards from the barge. The dogs jumped into the water growling at the boat's occupants. Matthew held his gun aimed squarely at the oarsman. The second man in the skiff was rocking on the floor holding his foot and crying.

Jerome looked up after loading his musket. A flash of anger gripped him as he recognized the oarsman. He was greatly tempted to pull the hammer on his gun and shoot but something stopped him. The fisherman pointed at Jerome and said something. The commotion from the animals and injured man drowned out his words.

The skiff had floated to within ten feet of the barge and the dogs were climbing aboard. They were showing every sign of an attack. The men threw their arms up in self defense.

Jerome could contain his anger no longer. He laid his gun down and jumped onto the skiff. The boat instantly flipped over throwing three men and two dogs into the water.

"Not again," moaned Matthew. He put his gun down and dove in to rescue Jerome.

The water off the side of the barge was only three feet deep. Matthew's fingers jammed into the mud jarring his whole body.

Emily was now dressed and emerged from the room to see the unbelievable sight.

Yelling men, barking dogs, fists and elbows flying every which direction. The rowboat quietly sank to the bottom leaving no signs of its existence except for two floating oars. Ole Blue had the collar of the injured man's shirt in his teeth. He jerked it back and forth as the owner flailed wildly. Betsy circled her mate and his opponent barking encouragement. Jerome had the fisherman in a hammerlock and his other arm around the man's neck. The man was howling and clawing at Jerome's strangling arm. Matthew stood in the mud rubbing his strained arm muscles yelling at his dogs.

Emily returned to her cabin and started laying out medical equipment.

Chapter 18

*M*atthew rubbed horse liniment on his aching arms and shoulders. The fisherman encased his accomplice's neck in a wooden brace under Emily's tutelage. She was preparing the man's foot for surgery. It looked like the musket ball had passed through cleanly. She would clean the entrance and exit wounds thoroughly and bandage them. Jerome was making the man a crutch. It would be sometime before the injured man walked on his own.

Emily forbid any conversation until all injuries were attended to. Jerome and the fisherman glared and snarled at each other occasionally, but both seemed resigned to Emily's authority. Neither questioned the fact that she was the youngest of the lot or that she was merely a girl.

After the foot was bandaged, Matthew made coffee and all but the patient sat on the shore to discuss their differences. The patient was pleasantly inebriated from a glass of whiskey and a dose of laudanum. He curled up by a tree and slept.

The fisherman started the conversation with his accusation that Jerome was a sneaky run-away slave who had outsmarted the police in Riverton. He claimed it was suspected Jerome had killed his master in Kentucky. He didn't fool the fisherman who wanted to return him to the law in Lexington and collect the reward.

Emily, Matthew and Jerome responded simultaneously negating the accusations. Each gave a logical answer, but it came out as gibberish with everyone talking at the same time.

Within ten minutes, the matter was cleared up. Jerome's innocence was proven to the fisherman's satisfaction once he read the emancipation papers.

"What a mess!" Emily lost her temper. "You went to all this trouble and nearly killed us just because you didn't trust the word of another human being. You are despicable. I hope you don't think I'm going to feed you breakfast."

She grabbed the man's cup half filled with coffee, "Get out of here. You are a disgrace to humanity. The very idea of trying to capture or kill someone just because you didn't believe they had the right to go about their own business."

Emily stormed onto the barge. The fisherman thought she was getting a weapon and took off down the path to the meadow as fast as he could move.

Matthew and Jerome heard the crashing and banging of pots and pans coming from the barge and decided it might be a good time to check on the livestock. They walked to the meadow looking in the brush for the offending intruder. He was nowhere to be seen.

Matthew put ropes around the necks of the cattle and led them to the beach. He noticed it was quiet on the barge and breathed a sigh of relief.

Jerome followed with tethered horses. One by one all the animals were taken aboard and penned.

Emily called the men to breakfast in a pleasant voice as though it was a typical morning.

The two men lifted the sleeping patient and brought him aboard. Within the hour, they were underway. When they reached the main river, they found the fisherman pulling in his anchor.

"Hang on," Matthew called, "Your forgetting your partner."

As they neared the fishing boat, they could see the occupant was badly scratched and his clothes torn from making his way through the blackberry bushes. Jerome and Matthew lifted the groggy patient high enough that he could be pulled aboard the fishing boat. Jerome flinched in remembrance of the bruised chest and stomach he had sustained a few days earlier.

Matthew and the fisherman exchanged acknowledging nods in way of a farewell. Jerome avoided looking directly at the man. Emily stayed inside their bedroom ignoring everyone.

The pioneers caught the current and picked up speed.

"Good riddance," muttered Jerome as they rounded a bend out of sight of the fishing boat.

It was after ten a.m. and the humidity was already high.

"Can we keep floating through lunchtime and go right along until sunset?" Matthew asked.

Jerome was glad to get as far from Cincinnati as possible. Emily agreed to the plan, saying she would bring the men biscuits and smoked ham when they got hungry.

The balance of the day was spent without incident. The animals settled back into their confines after a restless morning. The two hounds lounged in the shade most of the day, occasionally rousing themselves to bark at floating debris.

The next week one tranquil day followed after another. The trio worked well together. The morning routine of assigned chores got them underway by seven o'clock, which was satisfactory to all.

They planned a daylong stop near Fort Louisville, Kentucky to take the animals ashore for exercise and to study the falls and rapids around the islands in the river. Jerome tied the barge to a log on an island beach. Emily and Matthew swam their horses to the mainland then rode them several miles along a country road through the rolling blue grass hills. They returned on a road that ran parallel to the river. The water rushed over limestone outcroppings and dropped several feet in some spots. They made stops to study the water. It looked like it was going to be necessary to portage the boat. A daunting chore. They rode into the fort to ask for advice.

Jerome stayed on the island with the cattle and fowl and wrote a newsy letter to his sister. He only told her the good parts of his life, no sense worrying her with details about unpleasantness. He assured her that when he settled in a safe, slave-free town, he would come get her and they could make a new life together. He missed the Negroes he had known all his life, though he now had white friends that treated him just fine.

Chapter 19

ort Louisville was considerably larger than Fort Harmar or Fort Washington. Matthew tied their horses to a rail in front of the sutler's and looked around. He and Emily decided to get their bearings before making inquiries.

Most of the buildings looked alike, about sixty feet long with two or three doors and a row of small windows. They were built of wood and white washed; each had a railing in front for tethering horses.

Few horses were at these railings; most were in a large corral between the livery stable and black smith shop. Half a dozen men were busy shoeing horses. Others were currying, feeding or watering the animals. The horses were being readied for a trip of some distance.

A tall circular stone structure stood away from other buildings. Instead of windows, it had slots. Matthew pointed and said, "Armory."

Emily nodded. She was more interested in the edifice she perceived to be the hospital. Two ambulances were parked beside the stone building. The ambulances were wagons with two-foot wide boards running down either side in bunk bed style. The wagons could transport eight injured men at a time. She involuntarily shuddered.

They passed three small, neat cabins and assumed they were officer's quarters. Children played in front of a cabin that had a flower garden.

"Captain's quarters," Matthew said.

One building had a veranda along the front and a door as every third opening. It looked like a series of living quarters where two windows were allotted each apartment.

"Married quarters," Emily commented as they passed.

At the far end of the fort was a malodorous building with a door on either end.

"Latrine," Matthew said holding his nose.

On the way back toward the sutler's store, they saw one structure with an uncovered veranda that seemed exceptionally busy. Soldiers were coming and going from the three doors carrying papers or engaged in conversations.

"Office. Captain's office," Mathew said and headed for a door.

Inside he saw five men working at desks. One was tapping out signals on a telegraph. Others were writing or filing. The most popular man was the payroll clerk. It was obviously pay day.

Emily saw a civilian speaking to a soldier seated behind a desk in front of the door marked "Captain" and pulled on Matthew's sleeve.

"This way," she said.

They waited until the civilian finished his business then approached the soldier.

"Can I help you?" the man asked looking at Matthew.

"We're looking for advice on how to get a loaded barge through the rapids," Emily replied smiling.

The soldier looked a bit startled that the woman had explained their business. He looked directly at Matthew.

"At so?" he asked.

"Yep. We've got us several animals and a barge full of farming equipment. We're trying to get out west," Matthew replied.

The soldier suppressed a smile, "Now, you want the army to help you navigate?"

"We just thought, you living right next to the falls, 'n all, would know more about them then us. Can someone help?" Matthew spoke curtly as he had taken a dislike to the soldier.

"Maybe. You want me to give you an appointment with the captain so you can tell him your tale of woe?" the soldier asked rudely.

"Oh, that would be most kind of you," Emily answered taking Matthew's hand and squeezing it.

"How about next Thursday? I see he has an opening at ten a.m.," the soldier smirked.

Emily squeezed harder on Matthew's hand.

"Normally, that would be just fine. But as you can imagine, the captain probably wouldn't appreciate us parking our cattle, horses, ducks, chickens, and so forth in his parade ground for a whole week," her voice dripped with sweetness.

The soldier looked at Matthew and said, "Wait here, I'll see if the captain has time to talk to you now."

The chair noisily scraped the wooden floor as the clerk pushed himself away from the desk. He disappeared behind a door and Emily relaxed her grip on Matthew.

"Now, you've gone and broken my good fighting hand. How you expect me to flatten that servant of the public's nose?" Matthew muttered lowly so no one but Emily could hear.

"He's a 'larrikin,' as your dad would have said, but we'll get more information, if we ignore his attitude. Let's just hope the captain is friendlier," Emily whispered.

"He is," replied the soldier waiting behind them to speak to the captain.

Matthew and Emily turned to find a smiling lieutenant.

"He'll probably send you to see me. The Captain's pretty busy right now with some Indian skirmishes up the Wabash. That's my office in the corner," he said pointing to the far side of the room.

"Up the Wabash? Is that near here?" Matthew asked.

"Two day's hard ride where the redskins have some settlers in their sights. We're hoping to squelch the uprising before it spreads," the lieutenant wasn't smiling anymore.

The door opened and the clerk emerged all ready to give Matthew the news the captain was too busy to see them. He saw the lieutenant and ignored the civilians.

"Captain wants you to assign four men to baby-sit these people," he sneered.

The lieutenant asked Matthew and Emily to wait in his office while he spoke to the captain about another matter.

Emily grabbed Matthew's arm and turned her back on the rude soldier. She felt Matthew's taunt muscles and she hoped they would get out of the fort without a fight.

They waited ten minutes in the lieutenant's office. Emily looked at the picture of a lady and two children in stylish attire. She had never seen anyone dressed in so many flounces and lace. The hat was large and lacey with enormous plumes, obviously not meant for shading the eyes from the sun. The boy and girl standing on either side of the lady were attired in dark material decorated with expanses of lace.

"The lieutenant must be from the eastern seaboard," Emily stated matter of factly.

Just then he entered the room. "My wife and children. These new Daguerreotypes are really something aren't they?" he said gently taking the picture from Emily.

Emily and Matthew looked at him blankly.

"I don't see no daggers," Matthew said looking at the image.

"A Frenchman named Daguerre invented a machine to make images using iodine-sensitized silvered plates and mercury vapor. The machines are known in Paris and my wife brought one home with her about six months ago. Her brother is going to start a photography business. She had taken the children from New York to Paris to visit their maternal grandparents," the lieutenant appeared momentarily lost in thought while studying the picture.

"My son, Geoffrey was a year old when I last saw him," Emily could see the pain in the soldier's eyes.

"Well, back to our problem," Matthew interrupted the man's thoughts.

"Yes, right. Tell me what you have and where it's located," the men were back to the business at hand. A plan was laid out. All animals and loose containers would be brought ashore. The boxes would be loaded on an army wagon and the animals herded around the falls. The boat's contents would be secured in place and ropes would be attached and held by soldiers on horses going along Shoreline Road. Someone would have to stay on the barge and navigate with the rudder. Two men would be needed on the poles to push the barge away from rocks. It was a tricky operation but could be done.

101

"One more thing," Emily said, "we have a free Negro with us. He won't want to come ashore in Kentucky. Please assign him a job poling the barge or using the rudder."

The room was silent for a minute.

"Couldn't you folks think of any more troublesome way to get to the gold fields?" the lieutenant asked with a smile. "He does have emancipation papers or proof that he was born a free man, doesn't he?" the officer continued more seriously.

"Yep, he's got emancipation papers," Matthew answered.

"That brings up another thought," Emily said. "We have boxes bolted to the bottom and rear of the boat. Will they be in danger of being torn off going over the rocks?"

"Sure will. And if that happens, the barge will probably sink," the lieutenant sighed heavily. He made no effort to disguise the potential for trouble.

"I'll remove as much stuff from the barge as Jerome and me can lift. Looks like this is going to take a couple days. Is there a corral where's we can leave the livestock?" Matthew asked.

"The corral inside the fort is too busy right now. There's fenced pasture outside where they can mingle with our other stock. We have a couple of men patrol the pasture at night to discourage thieves. Doesn't always work," he lamented.

A sergeant rode back to the barge with Emily and Matthew. He would be in charge of the project.

Sergeant Michael O'Brien was twenty-two years old. He had been a horse soldier for three years and had been in three skirmishes with Native Americans. He hoped he'd never see another battle. He had been at Fort Louisville for a year and had helped a number of other boats get through the falls.

Matthew thought he seemed young and wanted to ask exactly how many boats he had *successfully* helped through the rapids but he held his tongue.

Jerome left the cattle on the island and brought the barge to the wharf when he saw the Kilkennys approaching. Introductions were made and the sergeant went about a mental inventory of the barge.

"Take off anything that's loose like the stuff hanging in the cabin and the farm implements. I'll send two men and a wagon down here at six a.m. They'll help you unload the barge," the sergeant intoned with authority. "Anything left on the barge will have to be secured. I'll send along extra ropes."

Matthew didn't get a good night's sleep. He thought of many problems that might arise. Of course, his restlessness kept Emily awake in their tight sleeping quarters.

Jerome slept soundly on a bedroll on the island with the dozing livestock.

Chapter 20

Matthew got up before dawn and stood on the bow. The roaring water could be heard in the distance. He pondered what it would take to portage the barge. It was forty feet long and twenty feet wide. It wouldn't fit between the trees lining the road in some places. The road was built to handle eight-foot wide wagons. It looked like they were stuck with the sergeant's idea of pulling the boat through the rapids.

It had taken three months to build the barge. His mother's brother, Elias, had taken a month to design it incorporating the extras Matthew and Emily wanted. Now it didn't seem like a good idea at all. He should have taken the animals overland and caught a ferry across the Mississippi to St. Louis, or gone around the tip of South America in a ship or...

Emily interrupted his thoughts, "Let's go for a cool swim and eat breakfast before the soldiers arrive."

"You won't splash me, will you?" he said grinning.

"Never again," she promised.

The water was cold, deep and moving more swiftly than Emily anticipated. She clung to the bottom of the ladder. "Don't jump in. The current's too strong," she called to Matthew perched above her on the boat's edge.

"Does you need help getting out?" he called back.

Emily was afraid to let go with one hand to grab Matthew's outstretched one. The seconds passed while she tried to think of an escape from her dilemma.

"You want me to put a shirt under your armpits like I did Jerome?" he asked.

"Yes, I'm afraid to let go. The waters pulling me under the barge," she answered.

Matthew quickly removed his shirt, lay on the floor and tied it around his bride. He could see panic in her face. He didn't remember her ever being afraid before.

He took a hold of the shirt and lifted. Emily was able to move her hands to the upper rungs of the ladder. Her legs were being pulled by the force of the water and were banging against the lower portion of the ladder.

Matthew told her to put her arms around his neck. He assured her he still held the shirt tightly. She did so and he pulled himself to his knees and elbows. This allowed Emily to get a foot planted on the ladder. Matthew knelt upright, pulling Emily higher.

She was safe! She climbed up the top step then onto the boat.

Matthew was unable to untie the knot made in the shirtsleeves so pulled the shirt up over Emily's head. She was shaking and he held her in his arms.

"Now, now, Mrs. Kilkenny. That was a little test to see if you would ever need me for anything. You're such a brave, strong woman," he kissed her hair.

She clung to him and continued to shake. "We'll just see how long you love me. I'm not taking a bath again until I have a proper wash tub to sit in."

When she was calm, she went to the cabin to get dressed while Matthew fixed coffee. They ate boiled eggs and cold ham in silence. Each was dreading the task in front of them. By the time they finished eating, the first gray light of day was on the eastern horizon.

They carried the hanging items from their cabin walls to the deck. Emily took the money and papers out of the secret compartment under the floor and stuffed them inside a corset she was wearing. She didn't normally wear such confining encumbrances but it seemed a logical place to hide their precious belongings. She was grateful she had brought one complete outfit of city attire for fancy occasions.

Matthew put the tags Sergeant O'Brien gave him on things to be moved ashore.

Jerome boarded the boat and started work immediately feeding the fowl and cleaning their cages. At five-fifty, the barge was untied from the tree on the island and rowed the short distance to the dock.

The soldiers arrived the same time as the barge. Sergeant O'Brien asked three young privates to start off-loading the barge as soon as the hand shaking

---

was done all around. The work went more quickly than expected and the boat was stripped of everything that could be loaded on a wagon by eight-thirty.

Matthew, Jerome and one soldier went to the island for the livestock while the sergeant ordered the other two soldiers to load the wagon. The cages of fowl were put on last. Matthew returned with the livestock. Emily saddled her horse to herd the cattle. Matthew's, Sergeant O'Brien's and Private Hetterschmidt's horses were tied in tandem behind Emily's mare.

Matthew noticed Emily was very agitated and asked what her problem was.

"Oh, Matthew, do we have to do this? I don't want you on the barge going over the rapids. I have a feeling something bad is going to happen. Can we stop here and live at Fort Louisville?" she pleaded.

"We'll be all right. This bad spot will just be a memory in a couple of hours," he held her and felt her shaking.

"Hey, all your bravery didn't get washed off in your morning bath, did it? You just get my cows down the road safe, you hear? Jerome and me will be just fine," he consoled. "You ain't about to get rid of me this early in our married life. You'll be stuck with me for years 'n years."

She knew he was worried himself and tried to put on a brave face for his sake.

Jerome was glad he hadn't eaten. His stomach was tied in knots. The current between the island and the dock was bad enough; it was about to get a lot worse.

Two soldiers secured ropes to the barge. Each soldier had two ropes. The sergeant double-checked the knots. He checked the barge for any loose items. Matthew triple checked everything.

"What about the horse soldiers getting tangled in trees on the side of the road?" Matthew asked.

"They won't. We've chopped down all trees on the river side of the road specifically for this purpose," the sergeant explained.

The procession started off. Emily was in front herding cattle. The two horse soldiers followed a quarter mile behind her adjusting the length of their ropes to keep the lines taut between the barge and their saddles. The wagon brought up the rear. Sergeant O'Brien could keep an eye on the boat and yell orders to his men from his vantage point on the wagon seat. He had the river hazards memorized. He had worked out a series of hand signals to give Matthew telling him how to turn the rudder. The soldiers knew the signals and could communicate even if they couldn't hear over the roar of the water.

Jerome was on the roadside of the barge and watched intently for rocks jutting out from the shore. He felt his third time in the water would surely be his last. One little mishap and he would drown along with his hopes for a good life in a free state.

Private Hetterschmidt, the second man poling was the only person in the group that smiled. The farm boy from Pennsylvania thought every assignment given him in the army was designed for his enjoyment. He loved adventure and looked forward to the challenge of the rapids. He had been down them once before in a boat half this size. The two and a half mile stretch of river was built for an adrenaline rush. The previous boat had hit a submerged rock and shattered just off Goose Island. Private Hetterschmidt wasn't about to let that happen again. He poled rhythmically keeping his eyes moving from the water to Jerome, Matthew, the sergeant and back to the water.

Sergeant O'Brien signaled Matthew to turn the rudder so the boat would move slightly to the north. The soldiers on horseback saw the signal and released a few feet of rope. Private Hetterschmidt saw the signal and brought his pole up out of the water.

Jerome did not see the signal. He did, however, see a submerged rock just ahead of the boat on his side. He braced his pole against the rock and shoved with all his might.

The boat jerked to the right throwing Private Hetterschmidt off balance. He fell over backward losing his grip on his pole. The pole rolled noisily across the deck and hit the pens.

The ropes snapped tight pulling the horse soldiers toward the water. They yelled at their horses to hold steady. The horses stumbled around regaining their balance. Matthew fell against the rudder handle pushing it further then he intended. The boat hit the first set of rapids going sideways. Jerome was at the front. He had no choice but to ride it out hoping the others could correct the boat's direction.

Emily stood up in her stirrups for a better look at the activity behind her. She could see the boat fast approaching. It appeared out of control and her heart was in her throat.

The horse soldiers were quickly beside her then in front among the cattle. They pulled their ropes trying to get the front of the boat to swing back toward shore. Matthew maneuvered the rudder the best he could. He watched the boiling water and forgot about the sergeant.

Private Hetterschmidt regained his footing and pushed against each rock he saw. Jerome moved to his side. Together they pushed their poles trying to regain the boat's correct position.

The boat dropped down a two-foot drop and smacked against the water in a pool.

The sergeant's wagon was in front of the cows now. He yelled orders and swung his arms communicating to one and all. The boat was righted; the men resumed their normal positions and braced for the whitewater ahead.

Before he went back to the south side of the boat, private Hetterschmidt told Jerome to watch the sergeant for signals. Jerome nodded and looked at the irritated man standing on the front of the wagon with two barking dogs beside him.

The next set of rapids went more smoothly. The movement of the boat was too fast, though. The men with poles held them tightly poised just above the foaming water. The ropes kept the boat about twenty feet from the gravelly beach. Matthew strove to maintain the direction and distance from the shore.

Emily fell further behind the rushing men. Her cows were not interested in a foot race. She sat back in her saddle thinking of things they should have done. She should have kept the dogs with her. She knew they were excitable. The sergeant should have brought one more man to drive the wagon. He should have been on a horse.

Emily saw the front of the boat flip up into the air then disappear. She held her breath until she saw they had descended another falls and were riding across a fast moving pool. There was a bend in the river indicating they were approaching Rocky Island. She was getting too far behind. She wouldn't be able to see the barge when it got around the bend. She slapped her reins against a heifer that had stopped to eat a delicacy.

The startled cow ran alarming the others. All four were running ahead of the string of horses. Emily kicked her heels into her mount's ribs. She picked up speed forcing the horses behind her to run along with the other animals. With the horses in pursuit, the cows ran faster.

The cows rounded the bend with Emily close behind. Suddenly there were flapping wings and cackling geese in front of the cows. The frightened cows split up, each running wildly in a different direction.

Emily's horse barely missed the fallen crate and took off after a cow that ran across the meadow.

The geese flapped and flew to escape the stampede. One goose got tangled in the legs of a cow and was trampled. Another hit the face of the last horse causing him to shy and skid to a stop.

The three attached horses were jerked off balance and stumbled. Emily was thrown off her horse and bounced across the rocks and long grass.

A horse rolled over a goose, killing it instantly.

Emily lay still assessing the damage to her body. Her adrenaline was pumping wildly and it was hard to determine her true condition. Lying still, nothing felt broken. Her arm was scrapped and cut, the sleeve of the shirt filling quickly with blood. She sat up feeling stabs of pain in her side and thought it must be bruised or possibly a rib was cracked. She removed her belt and used it as a tourniquet just below her shoulder.

From her seated position she could see that only three horses had gotten back to their feet. She struggled to get to her knees noting the sharp pain midway between her armpit and her waist. Yes, a rib was broken.

Once standing, she could see Private Hetterschmidt's prostrate horse. She made her way to its side and saw the unusual angle of the head. She knew immediately he had broken his neck in the fall and was beyond help.

"Poor thing, at least you died quickly," she said aloud. She was now very much aware of the pain in her arm and side. She knew she had to stop the bleeding of her arm quickly. None of the horses were bearing saddlebags so there was no clean clothes to use. She would have to improvise from her attire.

She was wearing a riding skirt, a garment meant to be ladylike with the center sewn into wide legs for straddling horses. She wore no petticoats. Her corset was the cleanest article she was wearing.

Emily struggled out of her shirt and corset. The money and papers fell to the ground. She struggled across the road to the river and knelt to wash the open wound. With great effort she laid down on a rock and extended her arm into the water. She winced with pain. The cold water made her arm go numb but the pain in her side was excruciating from her weight on the rock.

She rolled over on the rock, lying on her back and wrapped the corset around the open cut and pulled it as tightly as she could. She tied the laces using her teeth and her uninjured arm. She released the belt and felt the rush of blood. Her arm throbbed and she sat rocking on the boulder until she regained her breath.

She staggered back across the road and stuffed the papers and money inside her camisole. Bending to pick up the papers made her vision go black. She knew she was getting weaker and weaker. She had some daunting tasks in her immediate future, and if she didn't move as quickly as possible, she would pass out from loss of blood.

She returned to the horses and cut the dead one from the string. That had taken such a long time she thought the men would arrive soon to find her. No one appeared. She had to mount her horse. She thought there was no way she could stand the pain of pulling herself up but had no choice but to try.

Her camisole, corset, and shirt were soaking red. She screamed in agony while pulling herself onto her horse. She was instantly dizzy and willed herself not to faint. Her nervous horse danced around. The horse had never encountered such noise from her mistress and was unsure of her duty.

Emily nudged the horse into a slow walk. Each step felt like someone was sticking a knife into her side. She vaguely remembered seeing the shattered duck crate on the roadside. It had one dead duck inside.

Emily walked the horses almost half a mile before she saw the barge and wagon. She was barely conscious. The sergeant and a private were setting the crate of chickens on the ground. She didn't see Matthew or Jerome near the wagon.

She was almost even with the wagon when she saw Matthew and Jerome sprawled on the rocky shore. They were lying on their backs with their arms at their sides. She fainted, falling from the horse to the dirt road.

Chapter 21

*E*mily became conscious of her surroundings; she was lying on an army blanket under a tree, her head on a saddle. Matthew was saying her name.

"Emily, Emily, come on honey, wake up," he was speaking softly and wiping her face with a wet cloth.

Her arm had been re-wrapped in clean white bandages from her medical kit. A streak of red was showing through so the wound was still bleeding. She had been bathed and wore Matthew's clean nightshirt.

"I thought you were dead, Matt," she whispered.

He was grateful Emily had regained consciousness and sobbed a short prayer out loud. "Thank you God for sparing my lovely wife. Thank you, thank you."

He turned back toward Emily and said, "The men are working fast as they can to get the wagon unloaded so's you can ride in it. We'll get you back to the hospital just as soon as possible. Sergeant O'Brien says he thinks you got a couple a broken ribs."

"He bandaged them the best way he knowed how, not being a doctor nor nothing. He just used battlefield know how," Matthew explained.

Emily was too weak from pain and loss of blood to care. She was glad to see Matthew alive. She dropped into unconsciousness. When she awoke again, she was in a proper hospital bed and a doctor was at her side.

"Welcome back young lady. I should say, lucky young lady," he smiled at her.

Her rib cage was bandaged tightly and her arm was encased in solid white and held to her rib cage with further gauze. The doctor was still talking but his words were fading in and out. She tried to look around for Matthew. When she turned her head a gray rim formed around her vision. The grayness grew until she could no longer see anything. She was unconscious again.

Private Hetterschmidt and Jerome stayed on the shore with the unloaded goods. They suffered from fatigue, bruises and scrapes, and were happy to do nothing but sit in the shade and drink hot coffee.

"Man, what a ride!" Hetterschmidt said. "Ever done anything like that before?"

"Nope, and I hope I never does anything like it again," Jerome responded. "Didn't know a man could be scared for so long and have his heart keep on working."

"That last drop was a doozy!" said the private. "I felt like I was flying. Too bad it only lasted a couple of seconds."

"Is that all? I thought it took an hour to hit bottom!" Jerome said.

The soldier laughed, "You got us off to a good start, twirling the boat around like you did. I knew right off, it was going to be a good ride."

"I sure didn't want to tear out the bottom of the barge right off. I don't cotton to drowning," Jerome offered as an explanation.

"Oh, well, it all worked out. The barge can be repaired tomorrow and be reloaded the next day. It'll just be a matter of waiting for Mrs. Kilkenny to heal up enough to travel," the cavalryman said.

"Shore does hope she ain't bad hurt. She's a nice lady. Kind of spirited, but nice," Jerome said.

They sat in silence while they finished their coffee.

"Reckon one of us ought to go get the rest of the animals afore they wander too far," Jerome broke the silence.

Neither man relished the thought of moving. They sat there staring at the river awhile longer.

"We have to make a crate to put the birds in before we catch them," Hetterschmidt said.

Jerome reluctantly made his body take an erect position. "I'll make a couple of cages while you round up the cows. I don't know nothing about riding horses."

"You don't swim and you don't ride a horse! Why you heading out west?" Hetterschmidt asked.

"Is St. Louie out west? I'm just going to St. Louie. You right, though. I better learn to swim if I'm going to live on the river," Jerome admitted.

Hetterschmidt chuckled and shook his head. He forced himself up off the ground.

"Sounds like a good deal. I'll see if I can find the cows. What are you going to make cages from?"

"I'm going to weave green branches off of that willow tree around a frame," Jerome answered.

He took out his penknife, a gift from Uncle William Coakley, and started cutting long branches from the weeping willow.

Just as the private swung his saddle onto his horse, he saw the first cow round the bend. The other three followed. Bringing up the herd was a smiling private that had manned the ropes tied to the barge.

"You people want some steak on the hoof?" he asked.

"Mighty glad to see you, ugly as you are. I didn't feel up to a round up," Hetterschmidt joshed with his friend.

"Where's Henderson? Please tell me he's gathering up the birds," Hetterschmidt said.

"Yep, he's got two ducks in a Hessian bag. He's looking in the grass for more critters," Private Conners said.

"Jerome, would those dogs help us find the geese and chickens, or would they kill them?" Conners asked.

"Can't rightly say. I do know Betsy mangled a quail she found a few days ago," Jerome thought the quail incident seemed like something out of the distant past. Actually, they had only been on the river a couple of weeks.

"I don't want nothing to do with turning the dogs loose on Missus Kilkenny's fowl. If she gets mad, I don't want to be nowhere nearby," Jerome said smiling.

Conners and Hetterschmidt nodded as though they were men of the world and understood exactly what the wrath of an angry woman was like. Both were half as old as Jerome and raised in an entirely different environment.

Jerome had known black men that were beaten senseless by women with horsewhips.

Jerome shook his head vigorously bringing himself back to the present. He knew Miss Emily would never deliberately hurt another human being.

"I'm going to make two cages. I hope you gentlemen will fill them with ducks 'n geese 'n chickens for Missus Kilkenny."

The soldiers took that as an order and agreed to try. The cattle were tied to the same rope that kept the horses in place. The late afternoon sun beat down and they took refuge under spreading maple trees.

Jerome went about his task methodically as though making cages was an everyday occurrence.

Chapter 22

*M*atthew watched Emily sleep. He was exhausted but was afraid to take his eyes off his wife. It had taken three hours to unload the barge and pack the goods on the wagon. The two and a half-mile trip over the rapids took approximately ten minutes. Yet, that ten minutes had worn him out more than the three hours of heavy lifting. He wanted to close his eyes and sleep so badly, but what if Emily woke up and needed him?

As if in answer to his thought, Emily stirred again. She saw Matthew through the haze of laudanum and weakness. She tried to find his hand. It was a feeble attempt but Matthew understood her need.

"I'm here, honey. Everybody's fine except you. You're weak from bleeding. Doc says you'll be just fine in a day or two," Matthew lied.

He didn't want to tell her the muscles and tendons of her upper arm were torn so badly she may never use the arm again. The doctor felt he performed a near miracle by saving the arm from amputation. If his needle work didn't mend, Emily might still lose the arm.

Matthew's heart swelled with pain when he thought that this beautiful woman had been entrusted to his care less than a month and already she was terribly damaged. He didn't know what had happened during that ten minutes he was in the rapids. He did know he had let her down.

Matthew sat beside the hospital bed and smiled at his bride. She smiled back then dozed off again. He laid his head on the bed beside her thigh. She smoothed his hair even though her eyes never opened.

They slept thusly for over an hour. Matthew awakened when the doctor returned to Emily's bedside once more. He checked her bandages looking for signs of bleeding and was grateful to find none. He lifted Emily's eyelid and tsked audibly.

"What's wrong?" Matthew asked alarmed.

"I just wish she would regain some color. We can tell how much good blood she's got by the color of her eyelids," the doctor explained.

"We'll do all we can for her. She'll sleep until tomorrow morning. Why don't you get a bath, some sleep and food, and come back in the morning?" he could tell Matthew was emotionally drained.

"Can I sleep here on the floor beside her tonight?" he pleaded.

"I don't think that's necessary. We'll bring another hospital bed in here and you can sleep in it," the doctor turned to leave. "I would suggest you get cleaned up. It's not good for a person with open cuts to be close to someone so dirty."

Matthew looked down at himself in embarrassment. He was a mess. He kissed Emily on the forehead and left the hospital. He rode his horse along the river road trying to imagine what had caused Emily's disaster. He saw nothing but the two broken crates. The dead fowl had been returned to Jerome who cleaned and boiled them.

Three soldiers and Jerome were eating dinner when Matthew arrived. He joined them in a hearty meal of stew and dumplings. It was tasty but the men felt it was wrong to compliment the cook under the circumstances.

The remaining goose and gander were in a willow cage hung from a tree limb. There were two ducks still alive but without a drake they wouldn't supply Emily with the flock she wanted. The two ducks and chickens were also extended from a tree limb to keep foxes from raiding the flimsy cages.

The dead horse had been dragged further from the road and left for scavengers.

Boxes and barrels sat on open ground beside the beached barge. The soldiers were to spend the night protecting the pioneers and their property from possible human scavengers.

Matthew explained Emily's condition over dinner. The doctor hoped she would be ready for release from the hospital in a week to ten days. He wanted to keep her there in case infection set in. The military surgeon had sewn up her arm to the best of his ability, and he was knowledgeable. He'd studied at Boston General Hospital before joining the army. He had worked at West Point healing injured men from Indian campaigns. He'd been a doctor for twenty years and had an enviable record of medical achievement. The army was lucky to have such an accomplished doctor. Emily was fortunate to have him attend her wounds.

Matthew bathed in the river's edge and changed clothes. He looked, smelled and felt considerably better. He announced his intentions of spending the night at the hospital and mounted his horse.

"Just a minute," Jerome said walking toward him. "Take this for Missus Kilkenny to use. The purdy smell might make her feel better." He handed Matthew a bar of his precious floral scented soap in a little tin box.

Chapter 23

*E*mily got more sleep than Matthew. Medical staff came in with lanterns several times to check on Emily's condition. She slept through their visits, Matthew did not. Each time he would ask, "Any change?" The answer was always, "No."

The next day, the doctor reduced the amount of laudanum he was giving her. Matthew spent the day in the room so he could spoon feed her water or beef broth each time she woke. Sometimes she would stay awake for five to ten minutes. Matthew talked to her, telling of his plans when they arrived in the Willamette Valley. He didn't want her expending energy by talking and doubted she was aware of what he was saying. Her eyes had a foggy, glazed look. She moved her hand in the direction of his voice and appeared to relax when he took hold of it. She swallowed the water and broth and had consumed a cup of each by the time night fell.

Matthew put on the nightshirt an orderly gave him and crawled into the hospital-supplied bed. He slept soundly never hearing the parade of medical practitioners in the room during the second night.

Emily awoke with first light. Her mouth tasted terrible. She was thirsty and felt sweaty. It took a few minutes to focus on her surroundings. She wondered why she wasn't in the bed on the barge. She turned her head and saw Matthew sleeping. She surmised she was the first one awake and needed to wake Matthew and Jerome. It was time to start their daily routine.

Emily tried to get up. Her left side wouldn't move. She looked down and saw the bandages. She lay her head back on her pillow to think. Why was she bandaged? She touched her left arm with her right hand. Bandages reached from her collarbone to her wrist. Her ribs were also bandaged and her arm was secured to the rib cage so she couldn't move it. There must have been an accident! The familiar gray rim closed over her vision and she succumbed to sleep once more.

Matthew woke up when the night staff brought the day staff in the room. The men discussed what had occurred during the night. There was basically no change in Emily's condition. There had been some movement. She changed positions in her sleep. One time during the night she rolled onto her right side and brought her knees up. That was considered a positive improvement.

Matthew took care of his personal needs, bathed and changed into clean clothes. An orderly gave him a clean hospital gown for Emily. Matthew carried a basin of warm water to her bedside and washed his wife with Jerome's soap. When he washed her face, she smiled in her sleep. Matthew's heart skipped a beat.

"She knows! She knows it's Jerome's soap," he thought.

The orderly helped Matthew change her gown so the injured parts would not be jostled. Matthew brushed her hair on the top and sides. As he was putting the hairbrush on the bedside stand, he heard a groan and Emily was turning onto her side. Matthew thought she was indicating she wanted the back of her hair brushed. He walked to the other side of the bed and brushed the auburn tresses he loved to touch.

When he finished, she said, "Mouth, clean mouth."

He looked at her and her eyes were still closed

"What? What did you say?" he asked.

"Brush teeth," she whispered.

Matthew beamed, "You bet you! I'll be right back."

He went looking for baking soda and split twigs used for cleaning teeth. He got soda from the kitchen and twigs from a bush behind the hospital.

When he returned to Emily's room, she was propped up in a sitting position with several pillows. She smiled weakly.

"As milady requested," Matthew said bowing from the waist. He sat a tray in her lap that had a bowl with baking soda, several twigs, a glass of water and a small pan. He explained the pan was for her to spit into.

Emily looked at the tray questioningly for a few seconds. She obviously didn't remember asking for them. Matthew's heart sank.

"I'll help you clean your teeth, then you'll be all fresh to start a new day," he said.

As though a light bulb came on, Emily picked up a twig, dampened it and dipped it in soda. She winced as she put the foul tasting powder in her mouth but brushed her teeth with it. She rinsed and spit and repeated the procedure two more times.

"Kiss," she whispered. "I need a kiss."

Matthew was more than happy to oblige. He kissed her mouth, cheeks, forehead, hair, and back to her mouth again. The effort exhausted her and she sank back into the pillows with a pleasant smile on her face.

"Wait, wait. Don't go back to sleep just yet. Drink some broth first," he held a cup of rich beef broth to her lips.

She stayed awake long enough to drink half a cup of the nourishing liquid. She relaxed and reached for Matthew's hand.

"I'm ok. Just a bit tired right now," she said drifting off slowly into a restful sleep.

Matthew tiptoed out of the room. He found an orderly and told him he was going to check on their belongings and make arrangements for boat repairs. He requested the orderly explain this to Emily if she awoke during his absence.

When Matthew arrived at the spot where the beached barge had been, he was met with a wonderful surprise. The soldiers had brought planks of wood from the carpentry shop at the fort and helped Jerome repair the damage. The barge was sitting in the water fully loaded with the exception of the animals. Jerome was making proper wooden cages for the fowl.

Hetterschmidt was relocating the cattle and Emily's horse to more lush surroundings. He had the hounds with him and was playing a game. He had made a duck decoy out of wood and tied feathers (possibly from Emily's drake) around the decoy's neck. Hetterschmidt tossed the decoy as far as he could and the dogs raced out to retrieve it. Whichever dog brought it back was lavished with praise and affection.

Matthew laughed as he watched the process. It felt like his first laugh in a long time.

"Looks like you fellows been busy," he said simply, unable to express his gratitude until the lump in his throat receded.

"How is the missus?" Jerome asked almost afraid to hear the answer.

"Well enough to be a smart aleck," Matthew smiled broadly.

"That's good! The best kind of a woman is a sassy one," Jerome replied.

Matthew grasped the black man and hugged him, slapping him on the back. Jerome was astounded. His arms hung at his sides. He had no idea how to respond to this foreign emotion from another man, a white boy, well man, really. Matthew regained control of his overwrought emotions and was suddenly embarrassed.

He cleared his throat and said, "I don't know how to ever repay you Jerome. You're like a brother to us. I hope you'll go all the way to Oregon with us. We need friends like you."

"Maybe. Is Oregon in Cincinnati? I changed my mind about Kentuck. It's got some mighty fine folks living here. Them young soldiers is nice to me as if I wasn't even a ...," he caught himself before saying the forbidden word. "An old man what's not white," he finished with a grin.

"There is good 'n bad everywhere, Jerome. Probably even Cincinnati has a handful a nice folks," Matthew replied.

Chapter 24

The less laudanum the doctor gave Emily, the more she stayed awake. The more she stayed awake, the more she was fed. Her strength and coloring slowly returned. She stood up the third day and promptly fainted. Fortunately, she had her good arm around Matthew's neck and he was grasping her waist; he lowered her back onto the bed without causing further physical damage. She spent the rest of the day on her back in bed.

The fourth day, the doctor ordered her to stay in bed, but to sit on the side with her legs dangling. She was to have a man in front of her and one behind her in case she passed out. She felt dizzy and nauseated on her first attempt but didn't let on. She insisted on trying again and again during the day. By the end of the day, she could stand the pain and didn't get dizzy. She fell into exhausted sleep with the feeling she had taken a major step forward.

By the end of the week, she was able to make it from her bed to the latrine behind the hospital unassisted. Matthew walked beside her sideways ready to catch her if she showed any sign of a stumble.

The doctor reluctantly released her. He gave Matthew a list of conditions to be met. He was warned of potential amputation, if the conditions were not strictly adhered to. Emily listened to this respected physician and took him seriously. The doctor put her in his surrey, as a wagon ride would cause her pain and possibly damage. He drove her slowly and carefully to the barge. The doctor inspected the living conditions and found the bed unacceptable. He ordered Matthew to return with him and get a hospital bed for her to sleep in.

Emily and the doctor loved the padded rocking chair Jerome had made. Emily agreed to sit patiently in the rocking chair until Matthew returned with the bed. Jerome made her a cup of coffee and she sat quietly until Matthew and the doctor were out of sight.

Jerome went into their cabin to dismantle the contrived bed. The two boxes of tools were carried to the storage area. He was returning to the cabin to move the barrels when he found Emily hand feeding her ducks.

"Now, missus, if you want something done, you holler at me. You just sit in the chair," he reprimanded.

"I'm just visiting old friends. Thank you for making the lovely new cages," she said sadly.

"Matt reckons you can get a drake and gander in Oregon. It'll be okay. Them Oregon ducks is strong 'n handsome. Those girls will love 'em. Just you wait 'n see," he tried to console her.

Emily smiled, "You're right, Jerome. I know I shouldn't get attached to animals meant for food or stock. I'm being silly."

Jerome took hold of her elbow and escorted her to the rocking chair.

"Where's the cattle and my horse?" she asked.

"The new hired hand will bring them with him when he comes," Jerome stated.

"New hired hand! Matthew didn't tell me. Guess it'll be awhile before I can handle the rudder," she said.

She saw Jerome look away and knew he was trying to hide something.

"What? Jerome. What's on your mind? Do you think I'm never going to use this arm again?" she had the voice of authority again.

"Jerome Jeffers! Is that what you think?" she demanded.

"Yes ma'am, I's sorry. Mr. Matthew says you is real bad hurt. The pain might never go away. Maybe you can't lift your arm ever again. I's sorry, maybe you didn't know," he was wringing his hands, embarrassed at having told a secret after seeing the loss of color on his mistress's face.

"Well, he's wrong. The doctor's wrong. I will use the arm again. It'll take awhile to heal. Maybe I can't use the rudder, but I'll be good as new by the time we get to St. Louis," her jaw was set in determination.

"We won't mention this conversation to Mister Matthew. I'll surprise him as soon as I get the use of my arm back," she said.

Jerome was more than happy to agree to keep the conversation a secret. He hoped he'd do better with this secret than the one Matthew told him about Emily being a permanent invalid.

Matthew returned and set up the bed in the cabin after deciding where to put the two barrels that had been the base of their previous bed. They ended up filling the last of the floor space in the storage container, leaving Jerome with no private area to call his own.

Jerome made up the hospital bed with clean sheets from Emily's trousseau.

Matthew said he would sleep on the sheepskin on the floor. He helped Emily change into a nightgown and kissed her as she prepared to sleep. She was still weak and tired easily. The doctor said she would sleep twelve to fourteen hours a day until she regained her lost blood.

She was sleeping at five p.m. when the new hired hand arrived with the livestock.

Michael O'Brien, formerly Sergeant O'Brien, helped get the animals into their pens on board the barge. He put his own gelding, which he had bought from the government, in the pen with Matthew and Emily's horses. The pen was overcrowded but serviceable.

The extra weight from the third horse, the additional man and his gear made the barge set low in the water. Matthew didn't like the situation but couldn't think of an alternative.

Michael tossed his bedroll, saddle and duffel bag on top of the cabin and covered them with the skiff. He planned on sleeping up there. He, Jerome and Matthew were going over plans for the next day. Chores were divided and assigned. Emily was not expected to do anything, of course, so the men shared her load.

The stove would be returned from the shore in the morning. Tonight they would cook enough food to last for two or three days. Matthew had bought pork and beef roasts and a ham from the sutler and those were cooked. He had replenished vegetables, fruits, and dairy products. Soups were made with rich broth as suggested by the doctor. Emily was to be fed a small meal every two hours when awake.

The men were finished eating and having a cup of coffee and cigars when Emily joined them at the campfire. She had wrapped up in a blanket over her nightgown for modesty sake. She wondered, as she looked at the faces around the fire how many of these men had seen her undressed. Someone had bathed and changed her clothes before she was taken to the hospital. She knew Sergeant O'Brien wrapped her broken ribs. Who had helped him? She hoped it was Matthew but her medical background made her realize it was unimportant.

She sat on Matthew's stool while he brought her rocker from the boat. Emily saw that Michael O'Brien had on civilian clothes so opened the conversation with, "Sergeant O'Brien, are you going to accompany us to St. Louis in a military capacity?"

"No, ma'am. I finished my tour of duty yesterday. Matthew, Mr. Kilkenny, and I discussed me tagging along with you. I want to go to the gold fields near Sutter's Fort in California. Want to try my luck," he smiled and shrugged his shoulders indicating he knew it was a long shot.

"Oh, so, you'll be going on with us after we reach St. Louis?" she inquired.

"We'll see. We want to see if we're both ready to leave about the same time. If you have any problem with me going along, now's the time to discuss it," he had detected a tone of disapproval in her voice.

"No. No problem. I'm just trying to catch up on what's happening. I slept through the past week" she heard Matthew approaching behind her and turned to look at him, "No more laudanum unless I'm in extreme pain. I want to stay awake as much as possible."

Matthew nodded and said, "I didn't mention Michael going along because I didn't think you could understand. You seemed confused sometimes."

"My mind's been in a jumble. Sometimes, I thought I heard Jenny calling. Other times I thought the military doctor was Doctor Six wanting me to help him. Then, when I tried to get up, he wouldn't let me," Emily admitted.

"By the way, Jerome. Thank you so much for the lovely soap. That was instrumental in my recovery," she smiled at Jerome.

"Your welcome, Missus Kilkenny. I hope instamental's a good thing," Jerome was glad to see his friend back among them.

Emily laughed, "It is. The smell of the soap washed some of the cobwebs out of my mind. It brought me back to current time."

Jerome mulled over how she used the soap to wash her mind and all were quiet for a minute or two.

Matthew finally asked the question on everyone's mind, "Can you tell us what happened to you? Does you remember?"

Emily hesitated like she still wasn't sure herself, "It all happened so fast. You disappeared then I saw you going around the bend. I was getting too far behind."

She stopped, straining to think what came next. "I smacked a heifer with my reins to get her to move. Then we were all running. Something white jumped in front of us and I went flying through the air. I must have hit rocks when I landed. Doesn't make much sense, does it?"

"We'll piece it together in time," Michael spoke up. "I do want to offer my most sincere apology. I'm sure I'm to fault, partly anyhow. I shouldn't have been on the wagon. I normally ride my own horse. We were short-handed at the fort with so many men gone up the Wabash."

Emily nodded, hoping that someday she would understand what he meant.

Matthew brought her a plate heaped with way too much food. "You got to start eating better so you'll get your strength back," he said sitting the plate on a box next to her rocker.

He had cut the roast pork and potatoes into bite size pieces. She put a bite in her mouth and chewed slowly. The men were all watching her and she felt self-conscious.

"It's delicious. I'll eat as much as I can. What are the plans? When do we leave? Who's working the rudder? Tell me what's happening," she hoped to distract them so she could dump most of her food in the bush beside the box.

The three men started an animated conversation but they still kept their eyes on her. After six bites, she admitted defeat. She could eat no more.

"It's probably the tight bandage on my ribs. The food was excellent. I'm just not up to eating more tonight," she stood ready to retire to her room after a thirty minute visit.

The men were sitting in silence when Matthew returned to the campfire.

"The white thing that jumped out in front of her was a goose. You know that, don't you Matt?" Michael sounded like a man confessing his sins.

"Guessed it," Matthew said. "It was an accident. She shouldn't have been running the cattle. She should have been riding in the wagon and I should have been driving the wagon. She is more important than a boat load of things."

"I shouldn't have shoved off of the rock," Jerome put in. "It's all my fault. I got scared and got us started off in a mess and now Missus Kilkenny is hurt cause of that."

There was silence again.

"Guess, that's why they is called accidents. It wasn't an 'on purpose,'" Matthew said. "We all done something wrong and now we are going to work together to make it right again."

Chapter 25

They were underway at seven o'clock the next morning. Jerome and Michael manned the poles. Matthew was on the rudder. Emily slept until almost nine a.m. When she awoke she found clean clothes laid out on the end of the bed. Matthew had evidently bought her a new dress at the sutler's store. It was a loose flowing dress with no buttons or fasteners. There were pantaloons, but no camisole, petticoats or stockings. The boots looked like something she could shove her feet into and not worry about ties or fasteners. He must have had them made at the fort. She would later learn they were called moccasins.

There was a wash basin with clean water, a towel, wash cloth, and Jerome's soap. A salt dish of baking soda, tin cup of water, and splintered twigs sat beside the wash basin.

She smiled, "What a man. How'd I get so lucky?"

She knew he understood her need to be as independent as possible. It took her an hour to perform her morning ablutions and dress. She was so tired when she finished; she lay back down to rest.

She knew they were underway and wanted to be outside watching the world go by. The sound of the water, men's voices and animals was soothing. She dozed and awoke when she accidentally rolled onto the injured arm. Pain started in the arm but seemed to shoot through her whole body. She stifled a cry.

Emily rolled onto her back, took several deep breaths and lay very still. The pain receded and gradually became bearable. Tears rolled across her temples and into her hair. Maybe she should take just a small dose of laudanum. She turned her head and saw the bottle sitting next to the tin cup of water. It seemed so far away. She could call out and Matthew would be there in a minute - but she didn't.

She heard Matthew laugh. Michael said something and Jerome exclaimed, "Look at that!" All three men laughed. She wanted to join them. She didn't want to spend the afternoon asleep.

She forced herself out of bed and walked to the door. Matthew had his back to the door leaning easily on the rudder.

"What's so funny out here?" she asked.

Matthew turned grinning, "Come here. You can still see her, just barely."

"See the mother bear and her cubs at the river's edge? She's teaching them how to fish. See them?" he asked.

Emily could just make out movement of brown lumps. She had missed the fun part.

"Next time, call me as soon as you see any wild animals. Also, if you see something pretty or interesting in any way. I don't want to miss a thing," she sounded like her old self, giving orders.

"Yes ma'am," Matthew said bowing. "How do you feel? You look purdy good in your new duds."

"Thanks for the clothes. They're great. I just tucked the useless sleeve inside," she replied hoping she sounded more cheerful than she felt.

She took the three steps to the rudder and gave Matthew a one armed hug. He responded with one arm while keeping his other hand on the rudder.

"We're moving right along. Michael reckons we'll make about fifty miles today. I'm hoping to be in Paducah in a couple of days. Sit down in your rocker. I brung it back here so that you could keep me company," he said.

He took a package down from the cabin roof. It was two pork sandwiches wrapped in a tea towel. He handed one to her and ate the other one himself. He pulled the pulley bringing the coldbox to the rim of the boat and got out a jug of milk. He poured a mug for he and Emily to share.

After eating, Emily wanted to see the animals. Michael had put a rope railing along the cabin and storage bin for her to use. Getting to the front of the boat was no problem. They were riding smoothly along with the current. She held onto the rope and counted livestock. Three horses, three cows and a bull, none lost.

When she returned to the rocking chair Matthew noticed the look of pain on her face. He knew her arm was bothering her. "Is you ready for a dose of laudanum, sweetie?"

"Not just yet. I want to wait until sunset, if I can," she answered.

She sat down, drank her milk and enjoyed the mid-day sun on her face. She watched the shore, looking for animals, waterfalls, rivers, whatever. She liked watching Matthew at work, his two faithful dogs at his feet. It was good to be home.

She occasionally walked the length of the boat and noticed little differences in the repacking. The cattle were restless, as it was their first day back on a barge. They had been on dry land for a week and needed to readjust their balance sensors.

When she passed the geese, she remembered why there was only two. The white thing that jumped out at the cattle had been a goose! She didn't know why there was only two left but imagined the missing geese had been killed in the accident that caused her injuries. She hadn't seen the goose that hit Hetterschmidt's horse so was unaware that was what caused her mishap. She now understood why Michael had apologized. He had been driving the wagon holding the crates of fowl. He would have discovered the missing crates when the wagon and barge had stopped.

At sunset they tied up to the shoreline on the north side of the river. Matthew and Jerome took the dogs for a run. Michael made a pot of coffee to wash down potatoes, sweet corn, tomatoes and ham. Emily asked him to just heat her up a bowl of soup.

"It was a goose," Emily said simply, talking to Michael's back. "The white thing that jumped out at us was a goose."

Michael froze in position. "I know. The crate must not have been tied on tight enough. I should have double checked it," he said without looking at her. His voice carried incredible sorrow.

"Yes. The private should have made sure everything was tied down good. Yes, you should have double checked," she said.

He turned to face her. She was walking away.

"There's no way I can express how sorry I am, ma'am," he said to her retreating back.

Emily went to her cabin and took a dose of laudanum. She struggled out of her new clothes and into her nightgown before the drug overcame her. She was sound asleep when Matthew checked on her.

The men ate alone. After dinner Michael brought out his cigars and gave one to each man. They had been a parting gift from the lieutenant. Matthew and Michael talked about the lieutenant's desire to have his family move to Fort Louisville and his wife's unwillingness to expose her children or herself to the dangers of the wilderness. Being a soldier was hard on families.

Matthew spent more than an hour telling Jerome and Michael about Meriwether Lewis and William Clark. He was careful to include the details about Clark's Negro slave, York, and the Native girl, Sacagawea. York was six-foot-two-inches tall, knew French and worked as a translator for the Corps of Discovery. He was a man of great strength and a good hunter. The Native men called him "Great Medicine" and the Indian women fought over him. Sacagawea was a Mandan Indian who was married to a Frenchman named Charbonneau. She was an interpreter and knew the mid-west area well. She taught Lewis and Clark much about the animals, plants, and customs of the natives.

Matthew was preparing Jerome for a stopover that could be troublesome. He wanted to spend a day in Paducah, Kentucky. The town had been settled by George Rogers Clark, the military man and laid out by William Clark, the explorer and Matthew hoped to learn new stories about the latter. After hearing the tales of William Clark and Meriwether Lewis, Jerome decided he wanted to see Paducah, himself.

The morning air was surprisingly crisp and cool when they arrived at Paducah wharf. The town was quiet, as it was seven-thirty on Sunday morning.

Matthew and his crew were dressed their best. They felt this was almost a sacred stop on their journey. If they were going to represent the citizens that were fans of the explorer, they wanted to make a good impression.

Matthew and Michael went ashore alone. They found three fisher-men mending nets on the wharf and chatted with them for a few minutes. Matthew asked if his barge would be in their way. They barely glanced up but indicated there was no problem.

Matthew casually mentioned that his wife and a friend were tending the barge. He told the men that if anyone objected to the location of the barge, his friend, a black man named Jerome, would move the boat.

"Your nigger knows how to steer a barge?" inquired the man closest to Matthew.

"Jerome is a fine sailor but he's not my slave. He's a free man," that was the opening Matthew hoped for.

"That so," a second man said. "My wife's brother has got a black friend that can steer a boat on the ocean by looking at the stars. Claims he came from some island off of Floridy with nothing to guide him but sun 'n stars. Purdy smart feller, I reckon."

"Getting from Floridy to Kintuck without getting shot be the hard part, I reckon," the third fisherman added.

No one laughed. It wasn't meant to be a joke. The men told Matthew where he could find an old timer that would be more than willing to share his stories about the town.

The fishermen agreed to keep an eye on the barge and animals so all occupants could go listen to the stories. They walked into town to a house where the fishermen had directed them. There they met one of the first settlers, now an ancient man with poor eyesight and almost no hearing left. He welcomed the strangers onto his porch and spun his story as though told a thousand times before.

Homer Howard built a cabin near the mouth of the Tennessee River in 1825. Two years later, William Clark laid out the streets of the town. The early settlement was known as Pekin. William Clark selected the name Paducah but Homer didn't know if it was to honor the Chickasaw Indian leader, Chief Paduke or whether Mr. Clark was trying to name it after the Comanche tribe known as the Padoucas. At any rate Paducah became the county seat in 1832 when it was moved from Wilmington. The place had been growing ever since and now had several hundred folks, mostly farm people.

Homer invited them to join he and his wife for breakfast but they had eaten and declined. He told them there would be a church service at nine o'clock in case they were interested in meeting the rest of the folks in town. Emily entreated Matthew to stay for church; it had been awhile since they had been in a house of God. The Baptist service was standard and the singing fair. Jerome was the only black man in attendance and drew several quizzical looks.

The parishioners wanted to meet the new comers after service. They were hungry for stories themselves and wanted to hear about the plans of the westward bound travelers. The congregation lingered under the elms and listened to Matthew's dreams of farming in rich soil surrounded by towering mountains. For vacations he would take his family to the Pacific Ocean. On the way west he was looking forward to joining a buffalo hunt with soldiers from one of the outposts. He told about herds of animals that stretched from horizon to horizon. He had read that in his father's book on the Corps of Discovery. The townsfolk nodded as they had read the same stories or had been told them by the Rogers brothers themselves.

Michael told of his plans to search for gold in the Sierra foothills. His dreams of splendor consisted of becoming rich in a year's time and returning to his hometown of Philadelphia to build a mansion, marry a socialite and live happily ever after.

Emily hoped to open a hospital in the Willamette Valley and tend the indigenous Americans. When she related her story, she heard a hiss from the back of the crowd. These people had too recently suffered from Indian warfare to care if any Natives were saved from pain and suffering. A woman came forward and suggested Emily build a hospital in Paducah and help "her own kind." The woman's husband immediately said he could show Matthew some fine acreage for planting - course, it needed to be cleared first. Matthew and Emily declined the invitations. They wanted to see the country before settling down.

The churchgoers weren't interested in Jerome's reason for traveling with the pioneers. They ignored his presence among them. He was not extended an invitation to settle in the area.

By noon, the foursome was waving goodbye to the dozen or so people standing on the wharf wishing them Godspeed. Emily was grasping a beanbag given her by a woman who had used it as physical therapy to regain use of her hand after breaking her wrist. The woman had given Emily some homemade ointment and instructions on exercises. For the first time since the accident, someone had given Emily positive information and assurance that she could use her arm again.

Jerome had been uneasy the whole time he was on Kentucky soil and was glad to be underway again.

Chapter 26

The group camped at the confluence of the Ohio and Mississippi Rivers. Matthew and Michael rode their horses north from the campsite to familiarize themselves with the mile wide river. The hounds raced and chased each other along the shore as the men rode. Paddle-wheelers plied the waterway leaving barge-rocking wakes behind. Traffic was brisk; two passenger laden boats had gone north and one south during the hour of the men's ride.

When they returned to the barge, they reported their findings to Jerome and Emily.

"We have a hard day's work ahead of us tomorrow, better turn in early," suggested Michael.

Matthew received information on the river before leaving home by talking to travelers at Fort Harmar. He had a general idea where the strong southward currents were and where the waters flowed gently. He had a hand-drawn map marking islands and sandbars. The map had asterisks where known settlements were located.

He had been wise enough to purchase the ropes used to guide the barge through the Louisville Falls. They would come in handy along this river. He felt two men on horseback and one man on the rudder could get the barge through areas of strong southerly currents. They would tether the cattle to trees and return for them when they had the boat secured at the end of the run.

Matthew figured it would take three days to get to St. Louis. All he asked of Emily was that she take extra care not to stumble or jolt her injuries. The next week would be critical in her healing process; he didn't want any setbacks. He tried to talk her into staying in bed while they were underway. He knew there was little chance that would happen.

Emily lay in bed listening to Matthew's gentle snore. He had no problem getting to sleep on the sheepskin. Emily pondered her uselessness. She wondered what she could do to help the men during the next few days. Cooking on a rocking boat was out of the question with only one arm. They had food prepared anyhow. She couldn't keep her balance and hold the rudder. She certainly couldn't pole. It really wasn't safe for her to stand on the front of the boat and watch for debris. Wait, that was it! She could watch for debris! She worked out a plan and fell asleep.

She dressed as quickly as possible the next morning. When she alighted on deck, the men were involved in their tasks. Matthew was feeding animals, Michael was cleaning cages, Jerome was preparing breakfast and lunch.

She kissed Matthew good morning, extended a cool, polite greeting to Michael and joined Jerome at the stove. She quickly explained her plan to Jerome, begged for his help and received reluctant concession.

At seven thirty, Matthew asked, "Is everybody ready for this?"

"Not quite," Emily said. "Jerome is going to secure the rocker on top of the storage container. I'm going to sit up there so I can watch for submerged debris and sand bars."

"What?" Matthew exclaimed. "You most certainly ain't going to do no such thing."

He glared first at Emily then at Jerome.

"You lost your mind, man?" he turned his anger on Jerome. "Did you think afore you agreed to this scheme? What if the barge starts rocking in a big wake?" he was animated and stood over the seated Jerome in an intimidating manner.

Jerome stood up, knocking over this stool in the process. He deliberately put his face two inches from Matt's nose. Matthew took a step backwards and found boxes prevented any further movement.

"I ain't going to do nothing to hurt Missus Kilkenny and you knows it," he fairly shouted.

Matthew was taken aback. He never heard Jerome assert himself before.

"I'm going to make sure the chair is tied down tight and she's tied to it so she won't fall over. She'll be safe as you and me," he turned and walked away.

Matthew was dumbfounded. He turned to scold Emily. The triumphant smile on her face told him it would be a waste of time.

Michael double checked to make sure the articles on the boat were secured for turbulent water. Jerome fixed the rocker in a forward position on top of the permanent storage structure. It looked like it was in the middle of a giant spider web with all the ropes holding it in place. So much for using the ropes to pull the barge via horsepower.

Jerome helped Emily into her throne. He showed her his quick release knot on the rope across her lap and she pulled it twice to prove she understood. She had a loop on her right side to hang onto during the rocking in the wakes. She wore her sunbonnet to shade her eyes and was delighted at how far in front of the boat she could see. She hardly noticed the mild throbbing in her left arm.

Matthew climbed onto the storage box to double check Jerome's work. He was satisfied Emily was safe though he knew she would feel the rocking motion of the boat more than the men on the deck.

He kissed her and said, "If you get kilt, don't blame me."

"Matthew, I have to help. We're in this together," she returned his kiss.

"If you see anything, call out to Michael. He's closest to you. We already have signals worked out in case he sees danger ahead. He'll let Jerome and me know."

Emily looked at the man holding the ropes ready to cast off and nodded. Michael tipped his hat to her.

Emily noted the position of Jerome on the outside of the boat and a bit behind her. Matthew was on the rudder at the rear and had the most restricted vision. It would be almost impossible for her to turn and look at him let alone shout a warning he could understand and react to. Michael was the logical person for her to communicate with. She smiled weakly at him.

"Ready?" he asked.

"Yes," said Emily.

"Yep," said Jerome.

"Let's go," Matthew said.

Michael shoved the front of the barge and adeptly swung aboard. He dropped the rope to the deck and grabbed his pole. He shoved it into the river bottom on the side nearest shore moving them into the stream. Once underway the rope was retrieved and a coil wound between palm and elbow with each stroke of the pole. Michael looked like he had been doing this all his life.

Matthew let out a war whoop, "We're really on our way, folks. Oregon, here we come!"

Michael laughed and started a song with a cadence that worked in with rhythmic poling strokes. Jerome soon picked up the tune and sang along. Matthew joined in at the chorus. Emily relaxed and watched the water.

The river was so big. She hadn't conceived the idea that it would be wider than the Ohio. She thought about the little Hocking River where she and Matt grew up. Water flowed through their lives like blood through their veins. She wondered what it would be like to stand on the shore of the vast Pacific Ocean. Someday she would know.

"Sandbar on the right, a hundred yards ahead," she called out to Michael.

Michael stopped singing, whistled shrilly and made a hand motion over his head then pointed to his right with his right hand.

"Gotcha," called Matthew and Jerome in unison.

Emily did not return Michael's smile and he looked away from her and back at the shoreline.

The men held their positions on the barge for two hours. When they were ready to change, Jerome asked Emily if she wanted to come down and stretch her legs. The offer was enticing but she knew Matthew would insist on docking the boat before she negotiated her descent.

"I'm fine. I'll stay put until the next changeover," she smiled and hoped her tiredness didn't show.

The motion of the boat had intensified her pain. She would love to take some laudanum and sleep for a couple of hours. Matthew had been right, of course. She had no business sitting up there in the sun with her broken ribs continually swaying back and forth with the water's motion. Maybe she would concede defeat at lunchtime and lie in the cabin where she belonged.

"Tree! Submerged tree on the left, fifty yards ahead," she shouted.

Jerome was in the forward position now. He whistled and motioned with his left-hand then pointed left with the same hand.

"Gotcha," Matthew and Michael called out.

Matthew turned the rudder a little and they started moving to the right.

"The log's floating to the right," Emily shouted and tried to give directions at the same time. "Pull left! Pull left! Hurry!"

Jerome whistled and motioned with his left arm ending with a fast circular movement.

The barge appeared sluggish when it turned left. Emily was sure they were going to get entangled in tree roots. She put her feet flat on the storage container, grabbed the rope loop and braced for a collision.

Michael was suddenly in front of her at the center of the barge. His pole poised. He drove the pole into the tree and shoved hard. Jerome joined Michael in the bow and pushed his pole into the tree base. The barge squealed as the tree slid harmlessly along its side.

The dogs reacted instantly and ran about Jerome's legs barking at the offending tree. The geese squawked loudly, the ducks quacked and the chickens cackled. The tree continued southward and the barge gently rocked in place.

When the animals relaxed, Matthew called out, "Nice going, Mrs. K. You saved the day."

Michael and Jerome saluted her and she smiled in return, "Thanks gentlemen. Just doing my job."

Emily didn't notice her pain or tiredness for an hour thanks to the adrenaline rush. Then she started noticing the number of lovely, shady spots they could have tied up for lunch.

By the time Jerome called out, "Change over," she felt like her bladder would burst, her ribs hurt from the irritating movement and her arm was unbearable.

"Let's stop for awhile," Matthew called. "I need a break."

They tied up to shore in a park like setting. Weeping willows graced the banks and foot deep grass waved in the breeze behind the trees.

Emily pulled the quick release knot. She had six hands reaching up to help her down. Her legs felt numb and she thought she might need all three men.

"Hang on honey, don't stand up," Matthew climbed up on the storage box.

He braced himself between boxes and took hold of Emily's rope loop with his right hand.

"Now put your hand behind my neck and I'll pull you out of the chair. You'll be a bit dizzy from sitting in the sun," Matthew spoke softly as though telling a secret. "Don't try to walk for a couple minutes."

"Okay," she whispered back. "Let's go."

He was right (again), she was dizzy and his free arm encircled her waist. The dizziness subsided but her legs still felt rubbery.

"I'm going to turn sideways so you can lower yourself. Get to your knees first. I won't let you fall," Matthew was reassuring. She did as she was told.

Matthew held onto her good arm, "Now, sit down and swing your legs over the side."

Michael startled her by putting his hands on her hips, "Put your hand on my shoulder and I'll lift you down to the floor."

She hesitated until Matthew said, "Go on. It'll hurt your ribs for a minute but it's the best way."

Emily obeyed. A pain shot through her rib cage as she was lowered. Michael kept his hands tightly on her waist until Matthew jumped down and took over.

He picked Emily up in his arms and carried her to the cabin and put her on the bed.

"You earned the afternoon off," Matthew said. "I'll bring you some milk and food in a couple of minutes."

"Wait. I need to use the chamber pot first and I don't know if my legs will support me," she said embarrassed.

"I knew you'd need me for something, some day," Matthew said with a grin.

"Don't make me laugh. You'll have a mess to clean up, if you do," she retorted.

A few minutes later, Jerome handed Matthew a tea towel covered board. It held a bowl of soup, cup of milk and a small bouquet of wild flowers in a bottle.

"Perfect, thanks men," Matthew nodded to both men as he took the improvised tray.

Emily had washed her face and hands with Jerome's soap and was lying on the bed.

"Try to eat a few bites before you go to sleep," Matthew said putting the tray down on the edge of the bed.

She rolled her head to the side, "Flowers! Who had time to pick flowers?"

"Well, it twas either Ole Blue or Michael. That'd be my guess," Matthew said.

Emily blushed slightly.

"Hey, you're not going sweet on another man is you?" Matthew put his eyebrows together.

"No. No, of course not. It's just that I did some thinking while I was sitting up top. I owe Michael an apology," she admitted.

"Oh?" Matthew formed the expression as a question.

"I accused him of being responsible for my accident. He wasn't. I was," she said quietly.

"Well, you eat a bit. Drink some milk, take a nap and we'll talk later. You're too weak 'n tired for a good argument right now," he said and kissed her cheek.

He propped her up on a pillow and the folded sheepskin.

"Boy, am I glad I was clever enough to trick you into marrying me, Matthew Kilkenny. I sure do love you," Emily said with mock seriousness.

Chapter 27

*E*mily was not "good as new" when they arrived in St. Louis. She required one dose of laudanum to make it through a twenty-four hour period. She took that at bedtime hoping a restful night would heal her arm. It throbbed by noon the following day and she bore the pain by distracting herself. Each day she tried to be more independent than the day before. She faithfully did the finger exercises the Paducah woman had suggested. Her arm was still encased in gauze so she couldn't use the ointment for stimulating muscles.

She sat in her lookout perch each morning. Emily observed passing scenery as well as debris in the water and waved to other boats' passengers. She drew a map noting tributaries, sand bars and islands then compared it to the one Matthew carried. Emily's was more accurate but she had no names to put on the map. She wrote little notes about distinguishing features of each location. This became entertaining; she decided to do it all the way across country. She would buy a journal in St. Louis and keep a record of their travels. Maybe someday school children would learn about Lewis, Clark, Sacagawea and Emily Kilkenny.

In the afternoon she lay in bed and read medical books or Matthew's new book on range cattle. Reading put her to sleep, she napped at least two hours. A lack of stamina was something new to her and she found it frustrating.

In St Louis, she went to the hospital to have a doctor check her arm and ribs. He found the surgery to be well done. There was no sign of infection. He congratulated her on avoiding amputation. Her brain did not register good fortune at having a useless appendage hanging from her shoulder. She wanted to know when she would have full use of her arm.

"Never," was the doctor's brutal answer.

That was not what she wanted to hear so she reworded her question. What could she do to regain control of her muscles? The doctor knew of nothing.

"Maybe fancy doctors in Boston or New York know something I don't," he answered.

Emily could feel panic rising in her throat. She wasn't quite nineteen and this man was telling her one accident ruined her for life.

"Do you know anyone who specializes in muscles and tendons in St. Louis?" she asked trying to keep her voice calm.

"No. Our specialties run more to gunshot wounds, stabbings, Indian torture, stuff like that. This is a frontier town. People stop by on their way to somewhere else. They just want to be patched up well enough to get where they're going. If you want a miracle worker, go to Paris, London or New York," the tired doctor said.

He left the room. A woman came in to help Emily dress. The new bandage freed her arm from her rib cage. With difficulty, the assistant got the arm into a sleeve and then pulled the dress over Emily's head. She put her good arm through the other sleeve last. The weight of her injured arm hanging freely was painful for the shoulder. A sling was provided and Emily asked to be left alone in the room a few minutes.

The thoughtful assistant, in her mid-forties, wiped Emily's sweating face with a damp cloth. "Okay honey, but keep in mind, there's a lot more hurt folks waiting to see the doctor. Don't be too long," she patted Emily's good arm and left the room.

Two minutes later Emily emerged into the waiting room with a big smile on her face.

"Good news," she told Matthew, "there's no infection. I'll be right as rain in no time."

"I knew you was faking it all along," Matthew said, squeezing her hand. "You're just too lazy to pole the boat. Leastwise you get to wear your arm on the outside of your clothes, now."

"I got some good news myself," Matthew continued. "Got to talking to this here feller and he's heading for N'awlins. That's down at the bottom of the Mississippi."

"You mean it's on the bottom of the river? Underwater?" Emily teased, trying to hide her broken heart.

Matthew laughed, "It's downstream beyond the Ohio River. Anyhow, he's going to come over tonight and see about buying our barge."

"Our beautiful barge. I hate to leave it," she said sadly.

Matthew helped her into the hired surrey and took her to the little farmhouse where they were staying. It was actually a one-room cabin sitting on two acres of land. The men had carried their belongings to the cabin in a rented wagon and the livestock were enclosed with a split rail fence.

Michael O'Brien slept in a tent behind the cabin and looked after the animals when Matthew and Emily were away. He was developing an attachment to the two playful bloodhounds and enjoyed exercising them with the duck decoy. He had added a straw stuffed raccoon skin to their toys and would tie the dogs up while he hid the toy and then turn the dogs loose to find it. They were happy with a reward of affectionate words and praise accompanied with lots of ear scratching.

When the Kilkennys were at home, Michael went into town to see outfitters, talk to wagon train masters, gather information on Indian activities and visit saloons to get the latest gossip from the gold fields. It looked like gold was being discovered in the Sierra from south of Sutter's Sawmill all the way up into the Cascade ranges of Oregon. He would have his choice of where to make his fortune.

Chapter 28

*J*erome stayed on the barge at night. He moved his belongings inside the cabin and bought a lock for the door. The barge was moored two miles downstream from the busy St. Louis wharf. Jerome wished it were further away.

He walked into town each morning trying to decide what to do with the rest of his life. He took the ferry across to East St. Louis, Illinois. Illinois had no slaves. He could live there and read and write to his heart's content.

Missouri was settled by New Englanders on the east and by Southerners on the west. They were in a great deal of turmoil over the slavery issue. Some people owned one or two slaves as household help. Farmers had six to ten slaves and worked side by side with the slaves to get the ground to pay them a living. There were a few free Negroes but they constantly lived in jeopardy of being mistaken as slaves. Jerome didn't want to live in Missouri.

St. Louis was a major stop for people heading for New Orleans to work in the fishing or shipping industry. Educated southerners were going east to New York, Philadelphia or Boston. Laborers were trying to get to Chicago where industry was just establishing a foothold. A few were run-away slaves, uneducated, and with little hope for good paying jobs. Many men talked of going to the gold fields of California or Colorado. St. Louis brimmed with excitement. People had high hopes that wherever they were going was better than where they'd been.

Jerome tried to find employment in East St. Louis. He found he could work for pennies helping people prepare for departure to points west, east, south, or north but permanent employment was scarce.

The population was overwhelmingly male, young, and white. There were scattered settlements of Negroes in East St. Louis and Jerome wandered toward those. He found the only difference was the color of the people's skin and perhaps the amount of capital they had. Indigent whites lived in poorly constructed shanties and did menial labor along side black men.

A few people wanted to settle in East St. Louis, there was the occasional entrepreneur from New York, Philadelphia or other eastern cities setting up shop. Jerome tried getting a job in those stores or restaurants. He tried to get a job in carpentry as the building industry was booming. He thought of getting a job on a paddle wheeler and filed that option away for future reference. He sat on the wharf trying to think of what type of place would use the skills he had.

"Excuse me mister. Can you tell me how to get to this here place?" a black youth about fourteen held out a piece of paper with a name and address on it.

Jerome looked at the paper, "It says, 'Jones and Sons, Outfitters, 238 Main Street, East Saint Louis.' You're off to a good start. This here is East St. Louis."

The youth smiled, "Now comes the hard part, eh? Where's Main Street?"

"Plumb in the middle a town be my guess. I ain't got nothing better to do. I'll help you find it," Jerome stood up.

"Can you read, boy?" Jerome asked.

"No sir, not yet," he answered.

"You going to learn soon?" Jerome was just making conversation as they walked along.

"If I can. This here's my uncle," he said holding out the slip of paper. "My mama is hoping he'll take me in and send me to school."

"Where's your mama?" Jerome asked.

The boy didn't answer. At the first cross street, he looked at a street sign, "Does that say 'Main Street?'"

"Nah, that's Water Street," Jerome looked to see where the most traffic was then walked that direction.

"This here is Main Street," he said looking at a painted board. "It's only a short street so let's walk along and see if we can find 'Jones and Sons'."

147

There were no numbers on the buildings so Jerome had no idea if he was walking toward the store or away from it. Some properties had no names and potential customers were peering in the windows to see what type of goods was carried.

Jerome had no idea what an "outfitter" would carry so didn't bother looking in unnamed stores.

"There's Aunt Beulah!" the teenager exclaimed.

Jerome looked the direction the boy was pointing and saw three women carrying baskets of groceries.

"Come on," he called to Jerome as he started across the street.

Jerome was ready to take his leave when the women turned as the boy called out, "Aunt Beulah!"

A middle-aged woman of generous proportions headed toward the boy with her arms open wide. She had a broad smile on her face and was crying out, "My baby, my baby boy!"

The youth was embarrassed and at the same time elated to see his aunt. She threw her arms around him, smacking him on the back with her basket.

"You gone and got all growed up! Let's look at you," she held him at arm's length for a couple of seconds then clasped him to her breast again.

She turned to her smiling friends, "Looky who's here! This is Charlie's sister's boy! He was just a tyke when we left home. Glad your mama got word to us you was coming. I sure wouldn't have knowed you," she gave him a hug with one ample arm almost knocking the boy off his feet.

Jerome left the family reunion and started back toward the waterfront. A farmer walked out of the feed store and bumped into him.

"Sorry," he said and turned to walk away mumbling to himself lost in thought.

"Excuse me, sir," Jerome said. "Does you know about any jobs for a grown man here abouts?"

The man stopped in his tracks.

"I'm looking for some help right now. Does you know anything about hogs?" he inquired.

"They are good eating," Jerome said.

The man laughed. "I think you're just the feller I was looking for. I'll give you a dollar, cash money, to help me get my hogs to the wharf," the man seemed desperate.

"I'm looking for steady work, not a day job. Thanks just the same," the thought of walking hogs through town to the wharf was most certainly not what Jerome wanted to do. He turned back toward the water.

"Okay, okay, make it two dollars. I can't afford no more than that," the farmer entreated.

The man had a hold on Jerome's sleeve, his eyes pleading, "I'm going to miss the boat if I don't get some help purdy quick."

Jerome hesitated a moment longer then conceded. He didn't know anyone in town. Why did he care if folks laughed at him?

He followed the farmer almost a mile before coming to a makeshift pen with nearly a hundred swine in it.

"Holy cow!" Jerome exclaimed in surprise. He was expecting half a dozen, more or less.

"Nah, them's hogs. Cows is taller," the farmer laughed.

Two boys about eight and ten-years old were walking around the pen poking sticks at the animals that were trying to root their way under the enclosure perimeter.

The farmer introduced his sons then realized he didn't know Jerome's name.

"We have got an hour to get these here hogs to the wharf. I sold them to a man that's taking them north for butchering."

"That's not much time for herding all these critters through town," Jerome said, wishing he was up wind from the smelly lot.

"You telling me! If you can help me get them all there on time, I'll give you a two-bit bonus," the farmer was afraid Jerome would back out.

"Tell me what to do and let's get going," Jerome answered the relieved farmer.

"Get a big stick and whack them if they try to go anywhere but down the road," the farmer gave the simple instruction.

"You boys get on one side, Mister Jerome will take the other and I'll walk behind them," the farmer was already dismantling part of the enclosure to make a gate.

"Sooooeeeee, soooeee, soooooeeee," he called out. A few pigs rushed toward him.

"These guys is the leaders," he said heading them toward town.

Jerome felt the thirty dollars Matthew had paid him in the soles of his shoes and wondered why he was bothering with this aggravation but knew it wasn't for money.

Pigs rushed through the opening shoving, grunting, and squealing. They were off down the road behind the leaders. One pig dashed behind the boys heading off across the open field. The youths were after her immediately. The older boy ran up beside her head and waved his arms. She turned away from him. He tricked her into running right back into the group. She trotted along with the crowd showing no further sign of wanting to escape.

Jerome pulled a six-foot long branch from the pigsty and used it to wave at pigs that thought of running off on his side of the road. When all the pigs were trotting down the road they covered a space of thirty yards. Jerome wondered how they could ever get a parade like this through town where there were pedestrians, horses, wagons, surreys and Conestogas all vying for the same space.

When all seemed to be calm and regimented, he called back to the farmer, "Does you do this often?"

"First time. It's taken me five years to get this lot together. I saved five good sows and a boar at home so I can start over again," the proud farmer replied.

"I hope you got somewhere to put these critters at the wharf," Jerome stated.

"I do. There's a pen waiting outside the loading platform," the farmer replied.

Jerome thought of the dock area and all the traffic. The loading platform had a glut of freight on, under and around it. There were four boats loading and unloading goods at any one time. Passengers and their luggage were intermingled with supplies. Ferries made a continual circuit between St. Louis and East St. Louis from dawn until dusk.

Jerome looked at the two youngsters bouncing along the other side of the road. There was no way two men and two boys could get all these hogs in a pen at a busy wharf. He dreaded the work and humiliation that lay before him.

The town was just ahead. They could see traffic on Main Street and the farmer called out to his younger son, "Moses, you run on ahead and shout out to the folks that we is coming. Go on now, you run real fast."

The lad took off fast as his short legs and bare feet would carry him. He started shouting as soon as he got to the edge of town. Jerome was amazed. The horses and wagons pulled to the side of the road and stopped. Pedestrians stood in doorways. A wide path was cleared.

"You heard tell of Moses parting the water, ain't you? My Moses can part people and horses," the jovial farmer said half-heartedly smacking a pig that had stopped moving.

"Aaron, you mosey up to Wharf Street and turn these animals toward the water when they get to you. Get now, catch up with your brother," the farmer ordered.

Jerome, you come back toward me a bit so that you can help keep them moving. They may want to duck under wagons 'n such. Got your stick? Good, you will need it now," the farmer seemed to have a plan in mind.

Jerome wished they had a least four more men to help them. Just as the thought crossed his mind, the nephew of Beulah Jones, waved to him. The boy had a companion about fifteen-years old, "Can we help? Where you headed?"

"Sure can. Glad to have you. We're going down Wharf Street," the farmer said.

The boy looked at Jerome questioningly.

"That's the one we walked up to Main Street," Jerome said.

The boy nodded and took a position on the far side of the hogs from Jerome. His acquaintance was a bit further toward the front of the animals ready to help turn them. The farmer's two little boys were in the center of Main Street at the corner of Wharf dancing around in anticipation.

"By golly! We are going to make it just fine," Jerome said aloud.

The farmer beamed, "We better wait until we got these here beasts inside the pen afore we celebrate."

There was an occasional errant pig under a wagon or on the boardwalk, but mostly they traveled right down the center of Main Street and, upon encouragement from the four lads, turned onto Wharf Street.

Jerome breathed a sigh of relief when they had all turned the corner. He looked down Main Street and all was back in motion again. He had just learned that animals have the right of way on the streets of East St. Louis.

Suddenly he heard a terrible crash. People screamed and ran. Horses reared and stampeded through the streets pulling wagons, carts and riders with them. Pigs ran every which way. Pandemonium reigned.

Jerome grabbed a child off the sidewalk and shoved him into the arms of a woman standing in a doorway. He tried to take cover himself and threw his arms over his head and stood with his face flat against the wall of a store.

The noise continued, it was coming from the wharf. One crash followed another. The air was filled with the sounds of splintering wood and shattering glass. The loading docks collapsed under the weight of all the freight.

Boxes, crates, barrels, hogsheads, and sacks came down.   The contents mingled in one vast morass of incongruous muck.   Sugar, salt, molasses, beans, flour, whiskey and brandy flowed in sluices from the broken platform.

The pigs squealed with delight as the aroma hit their nostrils. They ran as one to the swill. They ate, drank, waded and rooted in the mess. Another hog farmer arrived on the scene with nearly as many pigs as Jerome's employer.

The swine intermingled, partied, got drunk and fought. They reeled, tumbled, grunted, and squealed. They staggered, fell, slept and snored.

The townsfolk and boat passengers watched the hilarious sight for nearly two hours. They would tell their children and grandchildren about the day that they saw nearly two hundred hogs get drunk in East St. Louis.

Chapter 29

The farm family from Pittsburgh came to the cabin about five o'clock. They were eager to be on their way down river. They had inherited a cotton plantation near New Orleans and hoped that someday they would be wealthy and able to ride on a fine paddle wheeler. Right now they were looking for an inexpensive way to get their belongings to their new home.

Matthew took them to the dock to see the barge. It was cleaned and freshly painted. The cabin had Jerome's belongings in it but the rest of the barge was empty.

Family members started claiming different areas as their own. The parents would have the cabin, the boys would share a livestock pen, the second pen could hold farm implements and the built-in storage container would hold their household goods.

Yes, they wanted the barge. A price was agreed upon. Then the man announced he would have the money just as soon as he sold his Conestoga and team of oxen.

Matthew asked if a trade was possible. He had never considered oxen but was open minded. The farmer was willing to consider a trade.

"What's the difference between a Conestoga and a wagon?" Matthew inquired.

"A Conestoga is bigger. It's named after Conestoga, Lancaster County, Pennsylvania, where they were first made," the knowledgeable farmer remarked. "They are sturdier than farm wagons. Got wider wheels, which is important in soft dirt, sand and such."

The family returned to their campsite with Matthew and Emily. Matthew liked the extras the man had added to the covered wagon. The well-built wagon was in good condition considering the number of miles it had carried the family. Pittsburgh was six hundred miles east of St. Louis. The family had been enroute over a month. They had been stalled by the army because of marauding Indians in Indiana.

Matthew inquired if the fighting was still going on near the Wabash River.

"Far as I know. The soldiers thought they had things under control then a wagon train was ambushed. We had to circle way north out of our way," the father replied.

Matthew said they were traveling with a retired soldier from Fort Louisville, Kentucky. His fort had been supplying men for the skirmishes.

"He may have gotten out just in time. Some areas are having real problems with the redskins. Hope you don't have trouble going west," the mother said. She wondered how safe travel on the Mississippi was for her own family.

Emily wanted to get more information on traveling with oxen before they committed to a trade for their barge. The men set up an appointment in two days' time to render a decision.

The next day, Matthew went into St. Louis to talk to outfitters and get a general idea on the value of a Conestoga with a pair of oxen. He talked to a man recently back from the Colorado Rockies. The mountaineer said Natives were more apt to kill pioneers for their horses than oxen. The man said he didn't know of any families that had successfully taken livestock over the Rockies and the Sierras. He suggested the southern route for such a venture. He warned of Apaches, Mexican bandits, and days without water or food on that route.

Matthew tried to discern whether this bearer of gloom and doom was a negative person, trying to persuade travelers not to make the trip, or genuinely concerned. He decided to check the information elsewhere. He went to the army fort, which was humming with activity.

A wagon train was departing for the Bozeman Trail in the morning. Matthew tried to talk to a scout but had no luck. He bought copies of maps to study various trails and was persistent in finding someone who would give him advice on which trail to take. A wagon train was scheduled to leave for Santa Fe, New Mexico in ten days. That would suit Matthew, if Emily was well enough to travel. A few other people had taken cattle along that trail so it seemed reasonable they could too. If the route over the mountains was too rough for cows, he could sell them to an army fort before starting up the range.

He'd considered staying in St. Louis until next spring. That would give Emily a chance to heal and be close to a doctor. She had rejected that notion saying she was practically well now. He knew better.

After an extensive day of research in St. Louis, Matthew convinced Emily oxen and a Conestoga would be an acceptable way to get to Oregon. She agreed with his assessment and a trade of Conestoga for barge was made the following day.

Matthew went to the barge and helped the family load their goods. With no animals and few barrels of supplies, the barge seemed enormous and luxurious. Matthew wondered how on earth they would ever get their supplies on the Conestoga.

He arrived at the cabin shortly after noon and found Emily waiting for him at the front gate. He knew the noise of the Conestoga could be heard quite a ways off. There was no sense trying to surprise her. She wanted to start loading the wagon right away that day. Matthew wanted to do it more methodically. He told her he would draw up plans so that their unneeded items could be stored in hard to access places and their everyday needs would be at easy to reach spots. It made sense.

The roof was twenty-eight feet long; the ends slanted outward from the bottom. The covering then provided more protection from rain and the cargo space was slightly larger than a farm wagon. The floor of the Conestoga was curved so that the load wouldn't shift and it could carry 5000 pounds. It came apart into three sections - the cover, the wagon box, and the undercarriage and running gear. The back wheels were larger than the front wheels and the outer rims were iron over wood. It was constructed of various types of wood; hickory was used for the tongue and the bows; spokes were made of oak.

Matthew and Jerome built oak boxes with wheels and axles on the bottom that could be rolled under the benches lining either side of the interior.

They installed a wall three feet high on either side with pegs and hooks for hanging items.

There was already a box on the outside of the wagon that held cooking utensils and food. Matthew created a "refrigerated" container by buying two clay pots of different sizes. He packed sand between the two and on the bottom. He would put the food in the inner pot and then pour water on the sand. As the water evaporated, it drew warm air away from the inner pot. He had learned this trick from a Negro in Ohio who said that's the way people in Africa kept their goat's milk cool.

The previous owner had an extra wheel, axle and several spokes attached to the bottom of the wagon along with tools for replacing a wheel or shrinking the iron. Sometimes the wood shrank as it dried out and then the iron "tire" would also have to be shrunk.

Matthew put hinges on the boards at either end of the wagon so they could be lowered horizontally. That way the two front boxes and two rear boxes under the benches could be accessed from outside the wagon. That also made a handy table for food preparation.

To enter the center boxes, barrels would have to be unloaded from the wagon. That is where they would put things not needed until they were "home." He had thought of putting exterior doors on the sides of the wagon to get to the center boxes but decided against it. That might weaken the integrity of the vehicle while traversing rough terrain.

The six barrels would go on the floor inside the wagon. Boards and the mattress from the hospital bed would be put on top of the barrels as their sleeping quarters. Their maximum weight was reached; he hoped the oxen could bear the load.

Emily arranged belongings in numbered piles in the cabin. She put numbers on the rolling boxes and kept a list of what she had put in each box. They wouldn't have to search the whole wagon each time they needed an article.

All this work burned up three days of precious time. They would still be ready to leave with the train headed for Santa Fe. Matthew signed up and paid the wagon master.

The time schedule suited Michael O'Brien and he agreed to accompany the train. He bought a pack mule, which was capable of pulling a small wagon. Emily humbly requested he accept responsibility of getting the crates of fowl out west. He accepted.

The four barge occupants had discussed the Louisville Falls accident at length and realized Emily's injuries and the loss of fowl were due to a series of unfortunate incidents. No blame was assigned any one person. All were sorry it had happened and wanted to do as much as possible to make it right.

When Michael returned from St. Louis two days before departure, he had the mule and wagon in tow. Inside the wagon were two crates. He had been able to find a farmer willing to sell him ducks and geese. He bought a goose and a gander, a drake and two ducks. Emily was ecstatic, her full complement of fowl was replaced. She offered payment to Michael who thought the idea of her paying was absurd. Then he'd have to pay her for her contributions, Jerome for his, and Matthew for his. He said if they started paying each other, they might as well take a single dollar bill and hand it to each other while they stood in a circle. Matthew was delighted to see Emily and Michael laughing together when he walked into the yard.

Chapter 30

*J*erome had done a lot of soul searching. He queried several people on life in the west and on the trip itself. He heard horror stories about uprisings in western Missouri. Indigenous people weren't involved. There were battles between emigrants from Kentucky, Tennessee, Virginia and North Carolina who had brought their slaves to Missouri. The established abolitionist in the area let them know in no uncertain terms that they were unwelcome.

In that year, 1853, a male Negro, twenty-two years old brought $1000.00 on the Missouri market. The hemp industry was thriving and many white men refused the hot, strenuous, dirty work.

Northern migrants worked with free black people and others from neighboring states on the Underground Railroad. The two factions were attacking, and killing each other at an alarming rate. Farm buildings were burned to the ground and crops destroyed.

Jerome had no desire to become embroiled in controversy over slavery. Under no circumstances did he want to bring trouble to Matthew and Emily. He decided to stay in East St. Louis, Illinois. He accepted Matthew's offer to live in the cabin for the balance of the month. Matthew had paid the rent for that long. They left him the hospital bed frame and made a mattress of dried grass. They also left him food, a small selection of medicines and bandages, and a new outfit of clothes.

He needed little else as he spent his days looking for work. He was hired for a week to erect a new loading platform at the docks in East St. Louis. There were twenty men on the project and it went quickly. Freight was backing up on either side of the river and speed was a necessity.

One morning he came across two men unloading a wagon of building supplies not far from the corner of Whaft and Main Streets in East St. Louis.

"Morning gents," he called.

Two black men in their early thirties returned his salutation.

"You building a house?" he asked.

"Nah, it's going be a school," one man said.

"Is you the boss of this here project?" Jerome inquired.

"Could be. What's the problem?" a friendly looking man said as he set down a keg of nails.

"I'm lookin for steady carpentry work. You got any openings?" Jerome held his hat in his hands gripping the brim.

"Could be. You done any building in the area afore?" the man came toward Jerome wiping his hands on his trousers.

"Not exactly, well excepting the new loading dock at the wharf. I helped build a barge what's sitting in the river. We built it back in Marietta and floated it here," Jerome explained.

"Marietta? That's in Ohio ain't it? Must be a fair builder if the barge floated that far. My name's Bill. Bill Ethridge," the man held out his hand to Jerome.

"Jerome. Jerome Jeffers. It's a good barge. If you want to see it, you have to be quick. Folks that bought it are fixing to leave for N'awlins any day now."

"That so. You wouldn't happen to have any references, I suppose?" Bill queried.

"References? No, but I got a letter from the owner of the barge and my emancipation papers. You want to see them?" Jerome asked.

Bill Ethridge studied the papers. Jerome could tell he was having a hard time reading the note Matthew had written and the papers from Mr. Jeffers.

"By the sounds of these papers, you should be wearing a halo," Bill said handing them back to Jerome.

"How much money you need and when can you start?" Bill asked.

Jerome was elated, "I don't know how much money the job's worth. You just be fair. I can start right now."

"Okay, Jim, come meet your new partner," Bill turned to the younger man who had continued to unload the wagon.

Jim smiled as he came forward, his sweaty hand outstretched, "Jim Saunders is the name. What you call yourself?"

"Jerome Jeffers, pleased to meet you," the two shook hands.

"I'll pay you the same as Jim so there is no squabbling over money. I give Jim five dollars a week. You can work for a week and I'll see how you do. If you is good as the letters say, you got a steady job. If not, out you go. Fair enough?" Bill set down the ground rules and Jerome accepted them.

He helped the two men unload the balance of the wood.

"Jim and I will go get the next load. You get started sawing the footings," Bill announced when the wagon was empty.

Bill gave Jerome a saw and pointed to a stack of twelve-inch diameter logs. He told Jerome how long he wanted them and handed Jerome a wooden yardstick.

After the men were gone, Jerome began to work. He was on his third log when he heard a woman's voice behind him.

"Excuse me. Are you the man building the new school house?" she asked.

Jerome turned to find a short, chubby, brown woman in her mid-twenties. She had her hair pulled back in a bun and carried a parasol with one hand and a stack of books with the other.

Her dress could not have been more plain. It was gray in color with no collar or cuffs. There was a single row of gray buttons that went from her chin to her toes. Jerome found her beautiful.

"Yes, ma'am. I'm one of the men what's building the school."

"Well, I want big windows, you hear? I don't want any pokey little windows. The children need lots of light to see by. Can't expect them to read and write, if they can't see," she was obviously used to being in control of the situation.

"I don't know what kind of windows Mr. Ethridge got planned. I'll pass on your message. I surely will," Jerome tried to be agreeable.

"Whose Mr. Ethridge? I thought you said you were building the school house," she demanded.

"I'm one of the men. Don't rightly know how many there is altogether. Maybe just three of us. Mr. Bill Ethridge is the boss. Jim Saunders is helping us, too," Jerome tried to be more clear.

"Oh well, tell Mr. Ethridge that Miss Simmons wants big windows and plenty of them. Also, I want the wood stove up front, not in the back of the room. I don't want any children getting burned while my back is turned," she stated.

"Yes, ma'am. I'll tell him. Is there anything else you want?" Jerome could see she was ready to leave and he wanted to detain her.

"Are you being smart with me, Mister, Mister.......?" she narrowed her eyes.

"Oh, no ma'am. I trying to get the message straight in my head - big windows 'n lots of them and the stove at the front of the room. I got it," he tipped his hat to her.

"Just to make sure I got it straight, you better come back tomorrow and check," Jerome put his eyebrows together and tried to keep a straight face.

"There are just two things, Mister... What is your name sir?" She asked in frustration.

"Jeffers. Jerome Jeffers at your service," he bowed.

"Mr. Jeffers, I'm sure you can remember two items. However, if I think of anything more, I'll see Mr. Ethridge," she turned and left.

"I do like a sassy woman," he said to himself smiling as she primly marched down Main Street.

Jerome finished eight footings before the wagon reappeared. He told Bill about Miss Simmons requests while the three men unloaded it. Then to Jerome's surprise, they unhitched the horses and tethered them to a tree. Bill was camping at the site.

"Don't want my supplies to walk off during the night. You got a place to stay Jerome?" Bill asked.

"I'm sort of twixt 'n tween," Jerome answered. "I'm staying in Matthew's cabin next week. After that, I got to find a new place in East St. Louie."

"Say, that might work out with my plans, if you're interested," Jim spoke up. "I'm staying at Beulah and Charlie Jones's boarding house until a week from Saturday. I'm getting married and moving to a cabin down from my wife's folks. You want to come see the boarding house?"

Jerome set up an appointment to visit the boarding house on Sunday afternoon. He felt sweaty and dirty at the moment and wanted a bath and a meal. Jim agreed to inform the Joneses of the potential boarder.

"Fine, I'll put in a good word for you. Mrs. Jones, Beulah is a bit fussy who she takes in cause her family lives there, too. Nice folks, real nice folks, though," Jim said.

Jerome's spirits were high as he walked back to the barge. Things were falling into place. He had been depressed over the loss of his friends, Matthew and Emily. Now a new life was unfolding in front of him.

He worked on the school for the next two days. The men worked from seven a.m. until six p.m. Sunday was their day off. Bill paid the two men in cash on Saturday and intimated he wanted both of them to return on Monday morning. Jerome asked for Monday off work to take care of some important business.

Bill said, "Well then, I hope you show up Tuesday. We need your help."

Jim and Jerome walked together until they got to Wharf Street. Jerome turned toward the ferry and Jim walked up tree lined Elm Street.

Jerome went to the cabin where Matthew, Emily and Michael were loading the Conestoga. The married couple planned on sleeping in it for two nights before they left. That way they were more apt to notice changes they wanted to make.

Emily greeted Jerome with a smile, "Special dinner tonight. We have lots of celebrating to do."

The meal looked like Christmas dinner. Matthew roasted a turkey with dressing. Michael made a cherry pie and an apple pie. Emily fixed roasted vegetables and misshapen biscuits with her one good arm.

Jerome was glad he had stopped on the way home and bought two bottles of wine. He had some celebrating of his own to share with the Kilkennys and Michael. Several toasts were called for before and during the meal. The group was a bit tiddly and giggly by the time dessert was over. The final toast surprised everyone including the initiator.

Jerome said, "Let's drink to my wedding. I met the woman I'm going to marry."

Emily squealed with delight. Matthew clasped Jerome's hand, "Tell us about her. Where'd you meet her? Do we get to meet her afore we leave on Monday?"

Jerome felt silly, partly from the wine, an unaccustomed beverage, partly from thinking of his potential intended. "Her name's Miss Simmons and she's the school marm. I met her once and I don't know where she lives yet, but she's the woman for me," his face and neck felt warm but he was sure of himself.

"It might take you a little while to woo her," Emily said. "But I have no doubt you'll win her heart."

"Somehow we have got to exchange addresses so you can write and let us know when you get married," Matthew said.

"General delivery," Michael said. "We can write you care of General Delivery of East St. Louis and you can get the letter at the post office. We can give you our addresses when we get settled but in the meantime, you could write to us at forts along our route."

"If all goes well, I'll be living in a boarding house on Elm Street in East St. Louis in two weeks' time," Jerome explained about the Jones' boarding house.

"We'll give you a ride over there in our surrey tomorrow. That way you'll arrive fresh and clean to meet Mr. and Mrs. Jones. We can give you a reference. It might help."

Jerome told them Bill Etheridge would be happy to see he had a reference also.

The four people worked together cleaning up the dinner mess. Then they sat outside under the stars and talked until they were melancholy over the prospective separation.

Michael announced he was going to bed before the tears started. The party broke up and all retired.

Chapter 31

*J*erome was grateful he hadn't thrown away the suit of clothes Mr. Jeffers bought him. Now he had two to choose from. The one Matthew and Emily gave him would be nice for work and the one from Mr. Jeffers could be used for going to church and for courting Miss Simmons. He felt quite spiffy dressed for his visit with Mr. and Mrs. Jones.

Michael suggested Emily and Matthew join him and Jerome for church services. It might be a long time before the three of them saw the inside of a church again. The Kilkennys agreed.

The Kilkennys took the surrey and Michael rode his horse. The ferry ride across the Mississippi was short but gave Matthew and Emily time to bid farewell to the waterway. They pointed out recognized landmarks and said they were glad they were on solid ground again. Emily suspected Matthew might be telling an untruth, she knew she was. They arrived at East St. Louis Baptist Church in time for the ten o'clock service.

The congregation was entirely Negro. It was Emily and Matthew's turn to feel awkward. They were greeted warmly by the white-robed minister and found their way to seats midway down the aisle. People turned to look at the white folks, smiled and nodded. There was an occasional, "Welcome brothers, welcome sister." Jerome proudly shook every hand offered.

Matthew held Emily's hand for ten minutes into the service then he released it so he could join the congregation clapping hands. Michael joined the joyous celebration of the existence of Jesus Christ, the Savior by clapping and singing the rhythmic hymns. He loved any excuse to sing. His baritone voice rang out among the bass and sopranos of the other people and he was one with them. Emily couldn't clap her hands and was self-conscious about singing among strangers. She extended her good arm heavenward and swayed to the music as many in the group were doing.

The sermon started out slow and the soft-spoken minister enticed new comers to introduce themselves. After each person announced their name, a parishioner would say, "Praise the Lord," or "Praise God."

The sermon gained in momentum and people spoke out loud asking forgiveness for their sins. The minister was booming by the time he accused the audience of working their way to hell unless they mended their way. Emily was intimidated and slightly embarrassed by the emotions expressed around her. The memory would last a lifetime.

People filed out of the church at the end of the service and clasped and hugged each other. Jerome heard a familiar voice.

"Hello there, friend," it was Beulah Jones' nephew. "Say, if we are going to keep meeting up, we should know each other's name. Mine's Ephraim Jones. What's yours?"

"Jerome Jeffers. Guess we would have met today anyhow. We are coming to your uncle's house after we find some lunch."

Jerome introduced Ephraim to his companions. No sooner was that done than Mr. and Mrs. Charles Jones joined them and the process started all over again.

Mrs. Jones insisted they all come to her house for Sunday dinner. She claimed there wasn't a restaurant in town that served better food than she did.

The procession of carriages and horse riders went down Main Street and turned onto Elm.

"Oh, Matthew isn't this a lovely place. It reminds me of Athens," Emily exclaimed.

The Victorian houses were painted white with green trim. Children played on shady lawns and parents fanned themselves on porch swings or chairs. Several called out greetings to the passing parade.

Jerome thought it was similar to Lexington. There was one difference - more than half the residents were Negroes. For the first time in his life, Jerome was proud of his race. These people were successful landowners, not slaves of another race. He saw a new goal to attain; he wanted to own a house on Elm Street one day.

They arrived at the Jones' home and alighted. The front door flew open. Jerome gasped and grabbed Matthew's arm.

"That's her! That's my future wife!" he whispered.

Miss Simmons showed no sign of recognition. She greeted the Joneses and announced she had just returned from her Methodist Church not one minute before they arrived.

She wore her hair in a bun as before and the same style dress though this time it was a soft blue.

Introductions were made once more. Miss Beth Simmons was a boarder in the home. She politely greeted each of the white people showing no sign of surprise that Mrs. Jones had invited them to dinner the first time she saw them.

When she was introduced to Jerome, she said, "Have we met? You seem familiar to me."

Jerome astounded everyone when he answered, "Yes, ma'am. We have met. I'm your future husband."

Miss Simmons took a step backwards. A gasp or two was heard from other people.

Mrs. Jones saved the day by laughing heartily, "Well, before we start making wedding plans, why don't we have dinner? You girls come help me set the table. You men get some extra chairs out of the boarders' rooms."

As soon as the kitchen door swung closed, the women all talked at once.

"Who is he?" asked Beth Simmons. "He's so handsome."

"He's a good man, a very good man," Emily said.

"Don't waste no time with frills does he?" laughed Beulah.

"Wait! Start over. Where have I met him?" asked Beth.

"He's helping build the new school house. Just started that job a couple of days ago. Are you the teacher?" Emily said.

"You mean that raggedy, sweaty, smelly carpenter at the school house looks this good when he's cleaned up? Hmmm hmmm." Beth was smiling.

"I do declare! You are putting me in a real spot of bother, girl," Beulah said.

"How's that?" asked Beth.

"Why he's come here to interview for a vacancy when Jim moves out next Saturday. He's a fine, hardworking, Christian-Baptist at that. I want him to stay. BUT, that's a big 'but' I doesn't want no hanky-panky going on in my home," Beulah shook a spatula at Beth.

"I don't even know the man! I'm sure not going to be sparking with a stranger. I rarely keep company with a gentleman. You already have me hopping into bed with this fellow," Beth giggled like a fifteen-year-old.

Beulah put one arm around Beth and one around Emily and they all laughed.

The kitchen door swung open.

"We put the extra leaf in the table and have enough chairs for everybody. Now all we need is some food," Charles Jones said as though it was perfectly normal to find three women hugging and laughing in his kitchen.

The table was set for twelve people. The youth that helped Ephraim and Jerome herd pigs was the Jones' son, Ephraim's cousin. There were two boarders the company had not yet met-one man, one woman. There was enough fried chicken, mashed potatoes, gravy, coleslaw and peach cobbler to feed twenty people. Charles commented that his wife frequently brought guests home to show off her cooking.

She said she wanted extra in case the boarders wanted it for lunch on Monday. The meal was consumed among familiarity and good cheer. Nothing further was said about Jerome's faux pas.

Charlie spoke to Jerome as they went for an after dinner walk alone. The interview was short and a decision was made.

"You is welcome to stay in my home as long as you behave yourself and pay your room and board fee on time. No gambling, no drinking, no cussing on the property. If you get out of line with the ladies, you are on the street. No second chances. Understand?" he asked.

"Yes sir. I've only had wine a couple of times, I don't gamble and rarily ever cuss. I'll behave like a gentleman for sure. Maybe you got an idea how I can win Miss Simmons heart. I'm aiming to marry her and I'm getting older by the minute, don't have a lot of time to waste," Jerome said.

Chapter 32

Emily was the first patient to be seen for the day. She arrived at the hospital waiting room an hour before the doctor. Matthew dropped her off on his way to return the rented surrey. He had Emily's mare tethered to the surrey. His stallion pulled the buggy.

Michael followed them into town with the Conestoga being pulled by the oxen. He had his horse and mule tied to the rear of the wagon. The mule was pulling a cart packed with Michael's gear and three crates of fowl. The crates were secured with a spider web of ropes, the same ropes that were used to guide the barge through the Louisville Falls.

Jerome had taken the day off work to help his friends get underway. He herded the cattle on foot behind the covered wagon.

The doctor was rested from Sunday off work and in a friendlier mood on this visit. His hectic week was just beginning. He examined Emily's wounds. The ribs were a bit sore but healing nicely. He re-wrapped the rib cage with wide strips of cotton material and told Emily she could remove the wrapping at night. The doctor thought it best to keep the rib cage tightly wrapped while riding in the wagon or on horseback for another month.

The arm incision had closed and there was no further worry of infection. No bandage was needed. It was to be kept in a sling to prevent tension on the upper arm. The inner workings were not completely healed. He told Emily the muscles were foreshortened because of being in one position for so long. She would have an arm that hung bent at the elbow the rest of her life.

He approved the bean bag exercises and said she may regain the use of her fingers and wrists, eventually. The physician gave her an elixir to restore her stamina. She took a dose in his office and felt a tingling sensation in her throat, when the fluid reached her stomach, it created a warm feeling. She asked what the contents were.

He said, "Iron, zinc, manganese, potassium iodide and a slug of alcohol."

She made a mental note not to take the elixir in conjunction with laudanum.

Matthew was waiting with their horses in front of the hospital. Emily needed to step onto a box to comfortably mount her horse. She told her version of her medical condition to Matthew as they rode to Fort St. Louis to join the wagon train.

Michael had secured the fourth position in a train of eight wagons. Twenty people were on horseback. Matthew and Emily joined Michael and Jerome among the confused throng. Last minute preparations were under way; people were dashing about on foot and on horses. Six soldiers patiently waited for the signal to leave.

The wagon master whistled and made a wide circling motion with his hat in his hand, then he pointed at the fort gate. They were underway by eleven o'clock. Spirits were high and people enthusiastically waved and called out to strangers as the procession made its way through a residential section outside the fort. The parade stretched out over a mile long. Emily and Matthew had quite an entourage themselves.

Jerome chose to stay with them until they made their first stop five miles from the fort. He drove the oxen team and chatted with Emily and Matthew who were on horseback. They were keeping their cattle in line in front of the oxen. The cattle weren't used to all the commotion and wanted to wander into the pastures along the trail.

Michael brought up the rear riding his horse and leading the mule with the cart. He passed the time getting acquainted with the soldiers that were constantly riding up and down the column. Each time an unknown soldier passed, Michael called out to him, introduced himself and told of his history in the army. The guards gladly gave their military background and then went about their business. Michael knew all six soldier's names by the first stop.

Matthew, Emily and Jerome had an emotional farewell. Promises were exchanged and awkward hugs shared. Emily showed Jerome where she had written down the address of the boarding house. She assured him she would write soon and often. Surprise gifts were produced. Jerome and Matthew walked together back towards St. Louis until they reached the end of the wagon train. One last handshake and the separation was made.

Jerome chose to run the first half-mile until he reached a copse of trees. Hidden in the trees he turned to watch the wagon train until it was out of sight.

Chapter 33

*S*oldiers taught the pioneers how to circle the wagons when they arrived at Fort St. Charles that first evening. The livestock were turned loose inside the circle. Cooking fires and tents were also inside the circle. The wagons would be used as shields in case of attack. Mass confusion ensued as people organized an evening meal and sleeping arrangements. To make matters worse, a drizzling rain started.

Michael started a fire in front of his lean-to beside the Kilkenny wagon while Emily poured a container of soup into a cast iron pot. She sliced bread, standing under the overhang at the rear of the wagon. The bowls and spoons were in the exterior box next to the water barrel.

Matthew unhitched and fed the oxen, fed and watered the fowl, and settled all the animals. The horses, cattle and oxen were tethered to a rope stretched between the rear of the Kilkenny Conestoga and Michael's cart. He lectured the dogs on staying under the wagon and was ready to eat by the time the soup was hot. The three ate in peace under the shelter of the lean-to that was to be Michael's bedroom. They listened to the arguments going on in camp.

"I'm glad we took time to organize afore we left the cabin," Matthew said. "These poor folks may not find what they need to make a meal afore we get to Kansas."

They knew it would be awhile before it was quiet enough to sleep. After supper implements were cleaned and stored, Michael brought out a harmonica. Emily wanted to lie in bed so excused herself from sitting in the lean-to. She listened to the melodic sounds and was soon asleep.

Michael and Matthew sat with a dog on either side. Ole Blue and Betsy were not about to stay under the wagon when their master was in view. The music had drawn a group of listeners from wagons on either side of the Kilkennys. They stood in the rain holding coats over their heads. Someone threw a log on the cooking fire indicating they planned on staying awhile.

A soldier broke up the concert at eight-thirty, "We want wagons ready to roll by seven in the morning. Better turn in. We'll be ringing the wake-up bell about four-thirty."

People disbursed. Matthew put a bowl of dinner scraps and an old blanket under the wagon. The dogs knew it was their assigned sleeping place by the familiar smell of the blanket.

Michael rolled out his bed in the lean-to ready to retire. By ten o'clock the camp had settled down and he fell asleep. Matthew lay awake worrying. It seemed daunting when he counted the things that could go wrong. Did he have the right to expose Emily to the dangers that lie ahead? It was his dream not hers. He turned his head to study her profile in the dying firelight.

Four-thirty arrived way too soon. Matthew wanted to sleep for a couple more hours.

Emily was bright and cheerful, "Come on sleepy head. It's a new day. I can hardly wait to see what new experiences we have."

She stood in the small square of floor space at the foot of their bed and used cold water from a canvas bag for the wash basin. She was dressed and ready to descend from the wagon before Matthew crawled out of bed. Michael restarted the dead campfire before he untethered the oxen and lead them to the yokes lying at the front of the Conestoga.

Emily had coffee made, ham and bread sliced, and Michael had the oxen hitched by the time Matthew joined them. At breakfast Michael hinted that they needed to make a schedule of chores for mornings and evenings so they would have a known routine. Otherwise they might end up like their agitated neighbors who started the day with more arguments. The whole camp appeared to be in turmoil.

The first wagon belonged to the wagon master. It was pulled by six mules. Katie and Sam McCafferty worked together to harness and hitch their team. Mrs. McCafferty drove the team. Their wagon pulled out of the circle and advanced a hundred yards. Mr. McCafferty helped the people from the second wagon. They had a dozen head of cattle. Two youngsters, a man and a dog were trying to separate their cows from others and get them to congregate in front of the second wagon. A woman was preparing breakfast and re-packing her food and cooking utensils into more accessible places. Sam McCafferty got the family's animals organized and told the people to pull forward behind his wagon before eating their breakfast.

Two men, who were trying to control four sleek, spirited horses occupied the third wagon. The animals were not happy with the prospect of pulling the wagon again. They were not dray animals but young riding horses. Mr. McCafferty suggested the owners exchange them for mules, dray horses, or oxen at the first opportunity.

By the time the third wagon pulled into line, Matthew and Michael had their animals under control, the wagon packed and all three stood beside the wagon to await instructions. They were sure Mr. McCafferty would compliment their efforts.

"That wagon behind the mule won't make the trip. Better plan on getting rid of the fowl and wagon in Jefferson City. Your Conestoga's packed too heavy. Think about what you want to eliminate," he told them. Then he directed them to pull forward behind the forming procession.

When the wagon master's back was turned, Emily made a face at him and stuck out her tongue. Only Matthew saw her, "Well, Miss Sunshine. How do you like your new experiences so far today?"

"I'm not getting rid of the fowl. They're important. They'll supply the train with fresh eggs and roasted birds for holidays," she said pouting.

"We'll work it out," he answered. "I'm going to walk the first couple of miles. Want to keep me company?"

She nodded, still pouting over the prospect of losing her feathered friends.

Michael climbed aboard the wagon seat and picked up the reins. They were ready to move out. Not so with the rest of the pioneers.

It was another hour before the wagons were lined up. It was after eight o'clock and the sun was already drawing moisture from the rich soil and turning it into humidity. By noon the walkers, including Matthew and Emily, were drenched in perspiration. The animals as well as the people eyed the inviting waters of the Missouri River.

"You know what we forgot to bring?" asked Emily.

"What?" Matthew couldn't imagine packing another item into their wagon.

"A bath tub," Emily said.

"When we stop for the night, I'll dump a bucket of water over your head," Matthew teased.

"That sounds good," she was beginning to weave from weariness.

Michael stopped their oxen and Matthew helped Emily climb aboard. He brought her a drink of water from the barrel. He had a drink himself and poured the second cup of water over his head. The soaking shirt felt good for a few minutes. Then the sun turned the moisture to steam.

He plodded along the next hour until the wagon master allowed a short lunch break. Some people ran to the river for a quick dip. Some brought pails of water to their animals. Matthew fetched water to the oxen. Michael walked the cattle, horses and mule to the river downstream from the swimmers. Emily gave the fowl containers of cool river water. She emptied the pan of dirty water the ducks had been sitting in and gave them clean water. They splashed her for her efforts and she laughed.

She collected eggs and made an omelet for lunch. Emily spread a blanket under a large oak tree and carried the food and eating utensils there. She was asleep on the blanket when the men found her.

The afternoon was hot and humid but the terrain was level and they made good time. By sunset, they were ready to stop near the settlement of Washington. They circled the wagons on the banks of the river fifty miles from St. Louis.

A soldier came by to talk to Michael. He joined the group for supper. He and Matthew became fast friends when the soldier mentioned he studied the findings of the Corps of Discovery. The young corporal said Washington, Missouri had a handful of settlers when Lewis and Clark stopped there in 1804. On their return trip in 1806, several families had arrived from the southern states. People were now at odds with each other over the slavery issue. There had been a few farms burned out. The soldiers would patrol the wagon train area to keep the travelers safe during the night. The last train through had been attacked as a free black man had been traveling with the group. Matthew and Emily exchanged a knowing look. They were glad Jerome was safe in Illinois.

Chapter 34

The wagon train followed the trail beside the Missouri River. It stopped near the settlements of New Haven and Hermann, as did the Corps of Discovery. Hermann was populated with German and Russian immigrants who introduced red winter wheat to America. The farmers on the train bought barrels of the wheat seed to take west.

When the train stopped for a three-day break near the growing capital of Missouri, Jefferson City, Emily knew she had to make a decision about her ducks, geese and chickens. No one had mentioned the matter since the wagon master made his suggestion. She was very quiet that evening and Matthew knew what was on her mind.

Some wagons already needed repairs. Replacement parts could be bought in Jefferson City. The two men traveling in front of the Kilkennys planned to sell or trade their horses for dray animals. Other people had medical needs to be met. Everyone had laundry and mending to do. Some of the walkers had worn their shoe soles through and needed replacements.

Emily was the first one to arise the following morning. The coffee was made and the fowl cages cleaned by the time Michael and Matthew stirred. At breakfast she sadly asked the men to take her fowl to town to sell. She decided she would rather give them to people now than have them die of heat in the desert or freeze in the mountains that lie ahead.

The trio looked for ways to lighten their load. Michael said he was selling the cart in town, if it was no longer needed to carry the fowl cages. His mule could carry his supplies in saddlebags. Matthew said he was selling his mining tools so that he wouldn't be tempted to go back into mining when they reached their destination. It seemed ridiculous to travel over two thousand miles to do the same job he had left. Emily agreed to leave many of her beloved books behind.

Matthew sold his equipment to an enthusiastic Welshman in Jefferson City. The man was on his way to Leadville, Colorado, high in the Rockies. He would be much more apt to find a profitable job in the silver, lead, zinc mines if he came equipped with his own tools.

Michael sold the cart and bought packs to be used on the back of a mule. He surprised everyone when he arrived back at camp with those packs full. He was carrying two barrels. He had previously gotten permission from the wagon master to bring a keg of German beer to camp. The second barrel contained sauerkraut and sausages. Two gentlemen in a surrey carrying strange looking musical instruments accompanied him. Word of a party spread quickly in camp. Women prepared dishes to compliment the sauerkraut and dug out their finery. Men used their farming tools to cut grass and level a smooth spot of ground to be used as a dance floor.

Matthew arrived at camp at five o'clock and presented Emily with a green and white dress with an embroidered bodice hand made by German lady artisans. He had green ribbons to be used as a sash and to tie up her auburn curls.

She was just removing a German chocolate cake from the Dutch oven when he arrived and was hot and sweaty. She accepted his gift with gratitude for his thoughtfulness but didn't feel like dressing up for the party. Emily was still depressed about losing her beloved fowl.

She looked south when she heard the rumbling of wheels and bouncing metal. The men who had bought Michael's cart were using it to bring a wash tub for her to take a bath. It was just a loan but she was so happy about taking a proper bath and dressing in a beautiful new dress, she forgot all about losing her feathered friends - for awhile anyhow.

Matthew and Michael set up a private enclosure using the canvas from Michael's lean-to. Water was heated and Jerome's soap brought out from her trousseau. She happily dug out clean underwear including stockings and a camisole.

She luxuriated in the warm water and scrubbed every inch of her being. It felt so good to shampoo her hair. Matthew did that chore with pleasure.

He scrubbed the curls into a mound of bubbles, then held his hand against her forehead as he poured pitcher after pitcher of warm, clear water over her head. Matthew helped her get into the confining clothes, which felt very strange indeed. She had gone with no underwear except pantaloons for so long. The stockings were awkward for Matthew to manipulate but he eventually got them to her satisfaction. The final touch to her outfit was a sling made of the green ribbon matching the one tying up her hair. Her adrenaline was pumping with excitement and she rejected his suggestion that she lie down to rest while he bathed and dressed. Instead she sat in her rocker in the shade and watched the party preparations take shape.

"Oh Michael, what a wonderful idea! Thank you for arranging all this," she exclaimed.

He stood under the tree with her, waiting his turn in the bathtub. "I just brought the beer and musicians. Other folks took over from there."

It was true. People were getting acquainted for the first time on the trip. Women were working together sharing recipes and ingredients for food, helping bathe and dress children and trading items of clothing so that each one had a complete party outfit to wear. Men were setting up tables and chairs around the newly constructed dance floor. Michael's old cart was to be used as a stage for the musicians. By late afternoon all was ready. The musicians ate first, the adults sampled the German beer, and kids played around and under the tables.

The accordions were brought out and the air filled with a strange new music while the pioneers enjoyed the feast and tapped their toes. The musicians' wives rode up in a surrey and were introduced. They were going to teach the pioneers to polka. What a party it was! There was music, dancing, singing - some folks even tried to imitate the German words - and camaraderie reigned until after midnight.

As Emily drifted off to sleep, she commented, "Doesn't it just make you wonder what new experience we will have tomorrow?"

Chapter 35

The next morning the pioneers reluctantly bid farewell to the musicians and their wives as the German immigrants bounced off in their surreys and cart. The vehicles were filled with gifts from the grateful pioneers. Evidently, the wagon master had told more than one person to lighten their load.

Emily packed the new dress in her trousseau chest after airing it out most of the morning.

She talked to the woman in the fifth wagon about helping her start a women's group saying she wanted to continue the camaraderie that was started the evening before. They conceived a plan to get together once a week to exchange ideas for adaptation to trail travel and settlement in the wilderness. The women's meetings would be informal and the times unspecified since neither Emily nor her neighbor knew when, where, or for how long the travel stops would be. The train would be back on the trail the next day so they chose to have their first meeting that evening. The neighbor thought it best to take turns having the meeting at different wagons. The first would take place at the Kilkenny's at seven o'clock.

There were eight women, six married and two single ones. All eight women showed up for the meeting. Some had children with them. It was too early to send older kids to bed and younger ones were tired and grouchy. The mothers requested future meetings take place soon after lunch while the little ones were napping and older ones were busy at play or doing chores, or have it an hour later in the evening after the little ones were down for the night.

A lady with four children excused herself early as her children were so distracting. After she was gone, one of the single women suggested activities should be planned to keep the children occupied during the meetings. This woman, about twenty years old, was going west to teach school. She accepted the responsibility of organizing games for any youngsters who showed up.

Katie McCafferty, wife of the wagon master informed the group the next multiple night stay was planned for West Port, Missouri in six days. It was agreed to meet after lunch at the McCafferty wagon on the first full day in camp at West Port. The subject for discussion would be food preservation and food preparation. Some people were having trouble cooking the amount needed for multiple meals and storing it without spoilage taking place.

The first meeting broke up and women walked back to their wagons chatting as they went.

An excited Emily told Matthew about the planned meetings.

"Sounds boring to me," he said.

"Maybe so, but meetings could be helpful. I think the men should do the same thing. Some men have more experience caring for wagons than others. Some know more about hunting, or fishing. You could learn from each other," Emily talked while doing her exercises.

Each day she tried to straighten her arm a bit further and to lift it a bit higher. She painfully moved it back and forth. She could already grasp things with her fingers and twist her wrist a short distance. Little by little she was regaining movement.

Soon after dark, Michael walked up to the wagon with six fish he had caught in the Missouri. The corporal with him had caught three. The soldier said he would clean all the fish if Emily would fry them up in the morning and invite him to breakfast.

Next morning Emily fried enough bacon to make sandwiches for lunch. She dipped the fish in a bowl of whipped eggs and milk then into a bowl of cornmeal seasoned with freshly picked dill weed before dropping them into the hot bacon grease.

Matthew sliced the oranges he had bought in Jefferson City, and Michael made cornbread in the Dutch oven. The cooperating trio had prepared another delicious meal. The corporal commented on how well the three worked together and said they could give lessons. A few single men wandered by the wagon drawn by the aromas. They hoped to be invited to breakfast. Emily extended an offer for future meals to each that caught enough fish to share. Emily missed the fresh eggs her chickens had provided. She was down to her last few eggs and wasn't about to offer to share them.

The rest of the travelers were busy packing for the day's trip.

The summer heat took its toll the next few days. Sam McCafferty rode up and down the column encouraging people to drink plenty of water, dress as cool as possible, but to make sure their skin was shaded. No children were allowed to go shirtless.

The people walked in the shade of their wagons whenever possible. The noon break was extended after people agreed to break camp at six o'clock instead of seven in the morning. The distances made were short. Overnight stops were made at Marion, Boonville, Arrow Rock and Glasgow.

A cheer went up when McCafferty announced they would be pulling into West Port, three and a half miles south of the junction of the Kansas and Missouri Rivers. He planned another three-night stay at that location. He cautioned each party not to take more than was needed when they passed that point. He assured the farmers seeds would be available at Fort Vancouver in Oregon territory. The wagons should be kept as light as possible for the dray animals sake as well as to prevent bogging down in wet conditions.

After a rejuvenating stay in West Port, a change of plans was announced. McCafferty said Apaches were on the warpath along the Santa Fe Trail and the wagon train would proceed along the northern route following the same basic trail taken by Lewis and Clark. Matthew was probably the only person glad to hear that news. The others were concerned about the stories of sky scraping mountains to cross and raging rivers.

There were several trails leading out of West Port and they were occupied with freight trains or troops marching off to Indian skirmishes. McCafferty chose the route to Gardner south of the Kansas River.

The livestock benefited from his choice. They feasted in the seven-foot high grasses. Blue stem, buffalo grass, and other varieties made the stock fat and healthy. Horsemen followed the wandering herd to make sure none were stolen or lost. The cattle were out of view when they walked more than ten yards from the trail. The branded cattle were all kept in one herd now instead of each owner trying to take care of his own animals.

The dray horses, mules and oxen had developed a trail mentality and followed the wagon in front of them. Children as young as six were given the position as drivers while their parents walked or rode horse.

Sam McCafferty assigned various men to act as scouts. Michael and Matthew were frequently chosen to accompany a soldier.

Emily occupied herself with physical therapy as she walked during the day. She was frustrated with her slow progress. She could move her arm any direction a couple of inches but she had no strength and couldn't hold so much as a coffee cup with that hand. At the women's meeting in West Port, she learned one of the husbands was a doctor. Emily wanted to offer her assistance to him but hesitated because of her condition. She told his wife of her knowledge, but cautioned the woman to be sure to tell the doctor of her limitations.

Matthew returned from scouting duty with something draped over the haunches of his horse. People gathered to see the strange animal. The beautiful beige and white creature was a pronghorn he had shot.

"Thought you might enjoy some fresh meat," he said lowering himself to the ground. "Purdy animal, ain't it? Can run faster than a horse, too. Joel's going to show me how to tan the skin so we can use it for a blanket or something. He used to skin rabbits, squirrels, coons and such back in Kentucky."

"Indian women make dresses out of skins. Did you know that?" Emily asked.

"Yep. Learned it from Sacagawea who traveled with the Corps of Discovery. Also those shoes I got you in Louisville was made by Indians out of skins."

"Right now we'll worry about how to prepare and store the meat," Emily said.

"I'm sharing with the other three scouts so we only got a quarter to fiddle with," Matthew replied.

"If each scout shares his quarter with one other wagon, every wagon owner will get some meat," Emily said.

That was done and the wagon owners cooked their meat and shared with the outriders. It was decided pronghorn was a worthwhile meat to be hunted and processed for future use. Sam McCafferty told the people the pronghorn was called an antelope although it was really a member of the deer family. It got the name antelope from mountain men that had seen the game in Africa run.

A hunting party was assembled and men started out ahead of the wagons in the morning. Matthew led the group, showing them where he found the original animal. The hunting dogs sniffed the hide and crisscrossed the flat plains looking for a similar scent. It wasn't long before they were on the trail of a herd. Unfortunately, the dogs loud bragging of success scared the antelope off and the hunters searched all day for the herd. They went back to camp empty-handed.

A new plan was formed and the dogs were tied securely to the wagon before Matthew and the men started their second day of hunting. It was more successful. Four pronghorns were shot, skinned and butchered before noon. The meat was distributed among the pioneers and frames were erected for smoking and drying meat into thin strips. Roasts were cooked with vegetables for the evening meal and leftovers stored for the next day's midday meal.

The south wind came up that night and brought thunder, lightning and rain with it. The following morning the troop marched along through the wet grass following a well-marked path. Women commented that they were glad the meals had been cooked the day before, as it would be hard to start a fire in the rain.

The rain continued intermittently over the next week and the wagons were mired in sticky clay. Some days only five to ten miles forward were accomplished. Wind continued day and night and tempers began to fray. Arguments broke out and children whined and fought. Everyone was tired of the continually wet, windy conditions. Men without wagons were finding it hard to sleep and were complaining of sickness. McCafferty was blamed for the weather and mutiny was in the making. People were sure the weather would have been fine, if they had traveled further south.

Scouts were sent out to look for the best path to follow. The high ground was chosen and they walked along the ridge of the Platte River. Indians were sighted but the neophyte scouts were unsure of their tribe and didn't know if they were friendly or not. A state of alert was called; a defense plan was practiced.

Chapter 36

By the end of the second rainy week, the train was traveling knee deep in mud and water. Every horse rider worked beside wagon owners pushing and pulling the contraptions a few feet further. At times only two or three miles was covered after an exhaustive day's work.

The only dry wood was the small amounts carried in the wagons. Katie McCafferty suggested groups of about ten people share a single pot of soup or stew to ration the wood.

The wagons were double-teamed using the mounted men's animals. The train managed to make six miles one day and was in sight of a stand of timber. After camp was set up, men and mules went to the trees to gather bundles of dead wood. People huddled around blazing fires to dry clothes and hung bedding on meat drying scaffolds.

The rains let up for one night but the south winds howled tormenting people with continually flapping canvas. In the morning a discouraged farmer called for a vote on continuing. A spirited debate ensued for thirty minutes. Two families could go no further. The entire train was saddened to leave them camped beside the road. McCafferty assigned two soldiers to wait with the families for armed escorts to arrive. He knew the road was well traveled by soldiers between Fort Atkinson and Fort Laramie. The cavalrymen were to return to McCafferty's train once the settlers were safely in the hands of other military men.

Grumbling about hiring a new wagon master once the train arrived at Fort Laramie was heard but not openly discussed. Only a mile had been covered when one wagon was so badly bogged it had to be off loaded. The wagon was dug out of the sticky clay and reloaded under the scrutiny of McCafferty.

All the women shared the owner's grief at leaving furniture and books sitting in the mud beside the trail.

Spirits were lifted when the rain let up and rainbows shimmered across the watery plains. A scout returned saying he found a field of wild strawberries near a stand of fine black oak. The strawberry patch was three miles ahead. It became a goal to be won at all cost. Trunks of clothing were left by the wayside along with farm implements and barrels of unknown contents.

Emily and Matthew took inventory to see if they could part with any more equipment. The only furniture they had was the rocking chair. They decided it would be senseless to leave such a light item behind. Neither wanted to dispose of this reminder of a dear friend. Emily was horrified that Matthew would even suggest the trousseau or medical equipment might be excess baggage. She childishly claimed they probably really didn't need the farm tools or so much ammunition. A truce was called and nothing was left behind.

The party was within a mile of the treasure when they had to stop because of darkness. Only two short miles had been crossed in the entire day. The main topic at dinner was recipes calling for fresh strawberries. There was only enough firewood for two fires; Sam suggested one for the evening meal shared by the entire group and one for cooking coffee and porridge in the morning.

A giant pot of Indian stew was made for dinner. It started with contributions of meat or vegetables put in boiling water until the pot was full. That was cooked for an hour. The children were fed and more contributions refilled the pot. That was done until everyone had a bowl of food to eat. McCafferty said a typical Indian dish was to keep a pot of food heating on a fire twenty-four hours a day, as some food was used, new items were added.

Michael's bedroll was soaked through. The small fire wasn't sufficient to dry it. Matthew loaned him the sheepskin while he and Emily shared their bed covered with a cotton sheet.

"Our love will keep us snug and comfortable," Emily said curling up against Matthew's back. She had no way of knowing Michael was sharing the sheepskin with the schoolteacher, Deborah Dawkins. The woman who had been creating games and amusement to entertain the children during the women's meetings had caught the attention of Michael early in the passage. All four slept well and content.

The wind became still overnight. The rain abated. The eerie silence woke some people. They wondered if this was the calm before a vicious onslaught. The morning bell rung by Sam or Katie McCafferty sounded different to Emily. It was muffled and further away than usual. That seemed especially strange now that the circle only contained six wagons. She lifted the end flap and found a sheet of dense white fog shrouding the environment. She could barely make out the wagon parked ten yards away.

"Matthew, Matthew, look at this weather!" she exclaimed.

Matthew shook himself awake and lifted his head.

"Hmmm, looks like our new experience for today will be crawling on our hands 'n knees looking for the trail," he said sleepily.

McCafferty went from wagon to wagon telling people he planned to wait until the fog lifted a bit before moving out. He forecast it would be clear enough to see the trail between ten and twelve o'clock. In the meantime he wanted the men to meet at his Conestoga in an hour with any leather straps not in use.

The community campfire was lit and people brought their coffeepots and brewed the strong elixir required to make them alert and ready to face the new day. Then a single pot of porridge was made for all to share. By the time it was ready to eat, the embers were mostly ash.

At the men's meeting, Joel, the young farmer from Kentucky told of his childhood when his parents were too poor to afford both a plow animal and a milk cow. They made a harness for the milk cow and she doubled as a dray animal.

The men passed suggestions from one to the other as they made harnesses to enlist the beef cattle into the job of pulling the wagons. By ten o'clock the six wagons were lined up, each pulled by a team of six animals. The parade looked strange indeed with two mules and four beef cattle lined up in front of some wagons. Others had six horses or a mixture of horses and mules. Matthew and the two hounds sat behind their pair of oxen and four calves.

Michael had his normal riding horse and pack mule and rode on one side of the fidgeting cattle. Emily rode her mare on the opposite side leading Matthew's stallion that was a bit skittish at the unfamiliar feel of barrels resting on his ribs. Matthew occasionally flicked a cow on the nose with the leather whip to keep it from chewing its way free from the harness.

The day was a long stressful one with cattle trying to break loose from their confines, pulling their partners off balance. When a cow fell, it panicked kicking at air trying to regain a standing position. Sometimes it took a dozen or more men to get the team of beasts calmed and progressing forward. To add to the confusion, two rain swollen streams had to be crossed. The four soldiers and all out riders rode beside fearful cattle and every wagon attained solid ground safely.

After six tiresome hours, the party reached the strawberry field. To their surprise it was occupied by Shawnee women and children. They were harvesting their crop of fruit. McCafferty communicated with the women that the settlers would like to spend the night in the vicinity and share the fruit. One woman, who spoke English, told the wagon master they would have to get permission from the chief. She sent two children to fetch some men from the village hidden in the black oak forest.

The handsome warriors arrived on Appaloosa ponies and escorted the bedraggled pioneers to their village. The pioneers unfamiliar with Indians feared for their lives but Sam assured them the Shawnee were peaceful. The entire village turned out to watch the strange procession stagger into camp.

Some of the Indian men had been to the Methodist Mission School and spoke English. They had learned white man's ways and were now farmers rather than hunters/gatherers. They invited the white people to feast on their potatoes, corn, beans, and blessed strawberries. After dinner, a group of men from the train met with the chief and his advisers. The whites were asked to stay over a few days and recover from their rain soaked condition.

Three educational days were shared with the friendly nation. The south wind blew almost continually and occasional showers interrupted plans to unload, clean and repair wagons. Eventually, the travelers were ready to continue their westward migration. Dr. Brian Jamison and his wife, Jesse left one cow with the Shawnee farmers as an expression of gratitude. The meat would be welcome in the village during the long, cold winter ahead.

Chapter 37

*E*mily was delighted with the tanned beige and white pronghorn dress. A Shawnee had shown Matthew how to work the material for maximum softness. The pieces from two deer were fitted together for maximum coverage but the dress didn't reach Emily's knees, so she wore Matthew's cut down trousers underneath. The bits of left over material were turned into a new pair of moccasins to match the simple, practical dress. She wore the outfit as they left the village and wished her mother and mother-in-law could see the unique style of attaching one piece of fabric to another with leather thongs. She thought of her beautiful wedding dress, which had been built by a committee of women and was now carefully stored in her mother's cedar chest for future use by her sister, Jenny.

The train followed the north fork of the Platte River. The route had taken the troop onto a high flat prairie littered with prairie dog homes. The tiny animals amused everyone until they were told they created holes in the ground that could be disastrous for moving cattle and horses. One misstep and the large animal could break a leg. McCafferty skirted the rodent village taking the train along limestone cliffs nearly a hundred feet high. The wind had carved weird and wonderful shapes of all sizes into the perpendicular walls. The pioneers were entertained by giving names to the formations.

Toward evening the limestone cliffs nearly disappeared and were replaced by clay and sand bluffs and hills. A herd of buffalo was grazing in the distance unconcerned with the passing train.

Shawnee braves had warned the soldiers that they would be traveling within two easy day's ride of Kaw Indian villages. The Kaw were not a friendly nation. Fortunately the soldiers that had stayed behind with the dropouts returned to their post with the train so they had a full contingent for protection. The soldiers reported that the families had been escorted to their destination by a military troop traveling east from Fort Laramie. The pioneers had chosen to return to Jefferson City and settle there. The thought of the polka party held near that city brought smiles to many faces.

Two soldiers and two volunteers were posted to guard duty. The guards were relieved of duty after four hours. The watch was set up from seven p.m. to seven a.m. Feeling secure, the cotillion slept well in their clean dry beds.

At noon the next day, four dirty, unkempt Kaw Indians approached the train begging for food and ammunition. No ammunition was supplied but they were given five pounds of flour and five pounds of pinto beans in exchange for information about their villages and the Kaw intentions toward passing pioneers. McCafferty was assured the villages were well away from the path taken by the white man and the poor Indians had no ill feelings toward those looking for a better life well west of Kaw homeland. The Indians left the group with smiles and good wishes.

A thunderstorm came up in the late afternoon. Flashes of lightning struck a small stand of timber frightening animals into running helter skelter and bringing the train to a halt for almost two hours. When the weather cleared six animals were missing. Two horses and four cows were unaccounted for. A search party was organized and began looking for the strays. Animal tracks found a short distance away suggested they were traveling with four unshod horses. Foul play was suspected and the search party returned and asked the soldiers to accompany them. It was nearing sunset so the search was postponed until first light.

The following morning Michael joined soldiers and volunteers searching for the missing livestock. In the evening he told Matthew they lost the animals' trail somewhere along the rocky shore of the Platte. They found where the animals entered the water but not where they left it.

Emily consoled herself with the proclimation that the Kaw were well away from the train and would cause no further damage. Men nodded at Emily's statement but no one believed it.

Few people slept well the second night after the livestock went missing. Wolves howled intermittently as though to reinforce the knowledge the pioneers were out of their element. Lightning flashed in the distance and thunder sounded. The rain didn't reach the trail but the wind rattled wagons and tents all night.

In the morning, Sam ordered the uneasy travelers to proceed along the washed out trail. One soldier accompanied three scouts. The soldier was familiar with Kaw culture and a veteran of three skirmishes with other Indian tribes. The pioneers hoped his expertise wouldn't be required.

Michael joined a second soldier and two other volunteers to search once more for the lost animals. The men complained that they needed the Kaw expert with them as they were most likely to encounter the savages.

Michael's mule and Emily's mare were tethered to the wagon, which she drove. Matthew rode horseback, he didn't want to be encumbered by leading the mule and mare in case he needed to move swiftly in an attack. He didn't stray far from his wife during the day's travel.

There were few conversations taking place. The whole train tensely proceeded expecting trouble around every bend. At noon McCafferty called for an hour's halt but wanted the wagons circled and the dray animals kept in their harnesses.

People took care of necessities and some reclined for a few minutes rest. Even the children were unusually subdued. There were six children and six women left in the train after the two families returned to Jefferson City.

The party trudged on after lunch and walked nearly eight miles before sunset. Camp was set up on a ridge with good views in all directions. They could even see Chimney Rock off in the distance.

Shortly after dark, whoops and hollers were heard a short distance off. The train members scurried into defensive positions. A lone rider was heard riding toward camp shouting, "Don't shoot, it's Michael O'Brien. Don't shoot!"

"We have the lost animals. We're bringing them in," he continued to yell.

Michael rode up to Sam and made a quick report. The wagon master told men to move one of the wagons so the livestock could be brought inside the circle.

When all were secured, people gathered around to hear the story of the brave searchers. McCafferty announced he wanted the number of men on watch doubled to eight immediately. The guards could hear the story later. The Kaw may have followed the retrieved livestock.

The animals had been found outside a filthy, stinking lodge where several Kaw were having a drunken party. The white men moved the animals away without the knowledge of the redskins. The soldier told of sending the volunteers ahead with the livestock on the return trip. At a couple of key locations he secreted himself in the rocks and watched for anyone who might be following. No one was spotted.

McCafferty wanted eight more volunteers to relieve the guards during the night watch and he wanted to be on the move at first light. He told the people they were about a hundred miles from Fort Laramie and he wanted to get there as soon as possible. Sam said he would send a couple of soldiers on ahead in the morning to notify the fort of their position and ask for reinforcements to escort the train to the fort. It wouldn't take the Kaw long to trace their lost treasure - once they sobered up.

Michael told Emily and Matthew the search party had more concern with wolf packs than Indians. The wolves threatened them several times on the return trip. Fort Laramie was offering a bounty of a dollar fifty per skin for wolves. They had become a plague to ranchers establishing homesteads around the fort.

A misting rain fell throughout the night. The wolves howled and growled close to camp. A shot rang out twice during the night as a guard spotted a wolf trying to make off with a calf.

The train rolled out as soon as it was light enough to spot hazards like prairie dog holes. People were quiet again today. Only the noises of animals and rolling wagons were heard. Everyone watched the horizon for signs of Indians.

The morning was cool after the rain. The scenery was monotonous; the one high point in view was Chimney Rock. It appeared as a beacon and the wagons rolled toward it all day long. The level prairie made travel easier and the changing shape of Chimney Rock gave the travelers something other than potential danger to think about. Four hours later the pillar appeared as a single round pillar with rubble at its base.

The train camped near the base of the rock. Sam told his followers it would take the soldiers three days to get to Fort Laramie and it would be a week before the escort would join them. For that reason he wanted eight men per shift to rotate guard duty each night. He also wanted four volunteers to follow a mile or so behind the train to watch for signs of Indians approaching. That was the most hazardous of the jobs and Emily cautioned Matthew not to volunteer. He wanted to stay near his wife so chose one of the night watch jobs. Four single men were assigned rear duty the next day and four different men volunteered to scout ahead. That left the four soldiers with the pioneers. The march went without incident during the day.

The outriders slept under wagons or pitched their tents between the wagons. Michael relieved Matthew of his night watch after sleeping for a few hours. The two hounds slept in the tiny square of floor space at the bottom of the bed. No one could sneak into the wagon without being spotted. Emily felt well loved, well protected and irritated with her dependency.

Chapter 38

*D*awn arrived bright and clear. The wagons were already underway when the sun made its appearance. The ground was dry and the double and triple-teaming was no longer required. The cattle enjoyed their freedom by trotting along quickly in front of the train. Scotts Bluff was clearly in view standing sentinel like a fortified castle.

Spirits were high since no Indians had been spotted in the three days since the recovery of the animals. McCafferty warned the guards not to get complacent; that might be just what the Kaw were waiting for.

Emily noted in her journal how different the landscape was from Athens, Ohio. The botany consisted of sparsely treed hills in the distant west. Rivers could be seen as long, wide, straight paths across the plains. Grass was shorter now than it had been a week before, and more yellow than green. The bluffs were yellow, tan, white and rust colored. Athens would be lush green now in late summer with the Hocking River running clear and full after summer rains. She felt slightly melancholy as she thought about the family and friends she might never see again. She quickly recovered and wrote about her plans for visits from various family members when she and Matthew were established in a lovely valley homestead at the base of a towering mountain.

The train left the mile-wide Platte River and went fourteen miles to the base of Scotts Bluff. They were happy to make so much progress in one day. The grass was sparse and dry. It looked like no rain had fallen in this area for several days. The cliffs blocked the south wind and people noticed the dry heat as they set up camp.

There was a cool spring in a ravine with wild currants and chokecherries growing beside it. The camp was surrounded on three sides by impassable high clay walls. The guards only had to watch for intruders from the east.

The women and children bathed in the pool after everyone had gathered drinking water. Emily stayed in the shallows with the children. She longed to dive and play with the two single women in the deeper water but dared not. She noticed the motion of her handicapped arm seemed easier in the water and spent several minutes manipulating it.

The teacher, Miss Deborah Dawkins offered to shampoo Emily's hair. What a treat! Emily readily agreed. The two women chatted amiably while Deborah scrubbed. Emily liked this bright, cheerful young woman. They discussed books they had read and found they shared a love of classical music. When Emily returned to her wagon, she told Matthew she felt like she had been on a week's vacation.

Matthew had venison steaks and rice cooked for dinner. Michael walked up with a pot of beans on one arm and Deborah on the other. Emily was surprised and pleased that the couple joined them. Emily and Matthew had surmised Michael was spending most of his time with the soldiers. That had been a false assumption.

After dinner, Michael and Matthew went for a dip at the spring while the women cleared away the dinner gear. In the course of conversation, Deborah said Michael had proposed marriage. She was considering a wedding at Fort Laramie. One thing worried her about their future together. Her teaching contract was for a school in Beaver Valley on the Scott River in northern California. Michael wanted to search for gold in the Sierra foothills at a place called Hangtown near Sutter's Fort a week's travel south of Beaver Valley.

When the men returned from the river, a bottle of Paugh wine was brought out and congratulatory toasts were drunk. The married couple passed on sage advice for a happy, healthy married life.

"Don't ever tickle your wife's feet when she's under water," Emily said.

"I'll drink to that," Matthew laughed.

Their party was short lived. McCafferty announced that tomorrow would be their most critical day for a possible attack from the Kaw. He felt, if they were going to attack, it would be before the soldiers could arrive from Fort Laramie. Tomorrow was their last chance. He asked that the wagon's contents be secured for traveling fast over rough ground, all guns were to be cleaned, loaded and tested before departure.

When the wagon master left the Kilkenny wagon, the foursome finished their wine in silence and bid each other good night and went to their sleeping accommodations.

"The families with children must be scared to death over the prospect of having their children endure a fight," Deborah said as Michael walked her to her wagon.

"Well, there's six kids and six wagons. You might talk to the parents and see if they want to put one child in each wagon," Michael responded. "It sounds harsh but that way they would be less apt to lose their whole family if a wagon is destroyed and the inhabitants killed."

Deborah was silent. Finally she agreed to think about the suggestion. The two kissed and parted company.

Matthew had first watch so he had left for his post when Michael returned to his lean-to beside the Kilkenny wagon. He asked Emily if she needed anything before he retired and she replied in the negative. He bedded the dogs under the wagon. Made sure they had food and water then retired. He removed his boots and belt and left the rest of his clothes intact. Michael made sure his rifle was ready to fire and laid it beside his blankets.

He lay back and closed his eyes. Camp was relatively quiet. He could hear the livestock settling in and a dog barking at shadows. There were a couple of people securing their belongings. Something was missing. He listened and tried to discern what was different.

"There's no wind and no wolves!" he thought as he dropped off into a deep, dreamless sleep.

It seemed like only a matter of minutes passed before Matthew was shaking his foot. "Hey, ole man. It is your turn."

Michael wanted to ignore Matthew. It was so long since he had a full, uninterrupted night's sleep. Michael rolled and groaned. When his arm came down it landed on his rifle.

"I thought I'd get more sleep if I retired from the army," he moaned. "Now, I'm waking up in the middle of the night to work and not even getting paid for it."

"Tomorrow night the uniforms can take over and we'll all sleep good," Matthew said tiredly.

Michael held his boots upside down and banged on the heels. He wanted to check for scorpions before slipping his feet inside. When his boots were in place, he stood with the rifle in one hand and his belt in the other.

Matthew offered him a cup of lukewarm leftover coffee. Michael downed it in three gulps. He splashed cold water on his face, put on his hat and belt and started walking. Matthew showed him their assigned lookout position and pointed out the other guards.

There was a general flurry of activity as guards were replaced. The light from the moon cast a silvery glow over the prairie, escarpment and camp. It was a peaceful scene.

Matthew headed for his wagon and Michael settled in trying to memorize the landmarks he saw and noting where shadows fell naturally. A volunteer struck a match to light a cigarette and was immediately reprimanded with loud growling voices. Michael thought he saw a quick flash of light on the distant eastern horizon. It happened so quickly and only once. He decided his mind was playing tricks on him.

The night became quiet. The guards were noiseless except for the one heard snoring softly. There were few animals about. The time passed slowly. At three a.m. the flurry of guard changing took place. As Michael left his post, he made a mental note of the volunteer that lit the cigarette.

The next day, the train started out over the dry, sparsely grassed prairie. Pronghorn and buffalo were seen but not pursued. A black tailed deer buck was shot at dawn and quickly butchered. The hunters decided that was one way to test their weapons. They promised to share the meat at evening meal.

Deborah Dawkins, Michael's girlfriend, showed up at the Kilkenny's with a four-year old girl named Marie Jackson. Deborah explained that one family wanted to spread their children out among the wagons in case of attack

The child sat on the seat of the wagon next to Emily and chatted cheerily about all manner of things in her young life. Her pigtails bounced with the bumps. She was wearing a miniature version of Emily's sunbonnet, which restricted her vision. She saw only what was right in front of her and didn't notice activity around the wagon. Little Marie played with a neckerchief making it into imaginary friends. Emily enjoyed the distraction as they rolled along under the hot dry sky. She wondered how many children she and Matthew would have and she prayed she didn't fall pregnant until they were safely settled.

Michael rode up beside Matthew. They had a quiet conversation and Matthew dropped back behind the wagon. Michael never looked at the wagon as Emily tried to get his attention. He concentrated on the eastern horizon and Emily followed his line of sight. Her hand tightened on the reins when she saw the cloud of dust.

Emily swiveled on her seat trying to find Matthew. He wasn't in sight. She noticed there were several men missing from the column including the four soldiers. She froze. McCafferty rode by and told her to pick up speed. She smacked the oxen with the reins and they trotted a degree or two faster. Emily asked Marie to climb into the wagon and sit on the floor. The child wanted an explanation. She was at that stage where every command was responded to with a "why?"

Emily felt panic mounting. She had the urge to shout at the child but restrained herself.

"I want to race that wagon up front. I'll go very fast and if you sit on the floor, we might beat them," she said smiling at the child.

In two quick bounds, the youngster was among the wagon belongings. She sat on the floor beaming up at Emily. Emily put her pistol on the seat with the butt tucked under her buckskin dress. She held the reins in the fingers of her useless hand and cracked the whip loudly over the heads of the oxen with her good arm. The startled beasts stepped up smartly.

All the wagons were moving out at double speed. No pedestrians were on the ground; everyone was either on horseback or in a wagon. People gripped handles wherever they found them in the bouncing wagons. Alarm showed on everyone's face.

Michael passed the Kilkenny wagon and Emily shouted, "Where's Matthew?"

"Rear guard," Michael answered and raced off.

Emily was third in line among the six wagons. She glanced back at the smiling child.

"Are we winning?" Marie asked.

"So far," Emily said cracking the whip over the oxen's heads again. The animals speeded up a bit more and the hounds raced beside them barking approval.

Cattle, cattle dogs, Michael and a couple other horsemen led the train. The wagons were in close pursuit with outriders flanking their sides. The riders had rifles in hand. McCafferty raced from wagon to wagon shouting one phrase, "Get ready to circle when we get to that rise."

He pointed to a hill that looked several miles away. Actually, it was only about one mile away but would test the ability of the cattle and dray animals to their limit. None were used to traveling any distance at a fast speed.

Emily hit a ditch and screamed as she bounced off her seat and onto her knees. Her pistol hit the floor. Michael was at her side instantly.

"I'm okay, it just scared me," she yelled.

"I'm coming aboard, move over," he yelled back.

"I'm okay!" she repeated with emphasis.

He was riding stride for stride with the oxen standing in his stirrups, his rifle in his left hand. Emily's heart was pounding wildly as she envisioned another accident. She scooted quickly to the side of the seat away from Michael. He grabbed the frame of the wagon cover with his right hand and jumped. His feet hit the side of the wagon and his torso pivoted toward her. She turned her face away as she saw the rifle headed her direction.

Michael was lying face down across her lap. He put his rifle on the floor and righted himself on the seat. He took the reins from her and grinned.

"I won't tell, if you won't," he said mischievously.

"Not a pretty picture but it worked," she smiled back.

Emily held the canvas frame with her good right arm but didn't feel the least bit secure with all the bouncing.

Michael looked around the left side of the wagon to see what happened to his horse and mule. He was relieved to see an outrider was leading them. He saluted the man and then realized it was the one who had lit the cigarette while on guard duty. Michael's relief turned to a sinking feeling of impending doom.

They were climbing the rise and the livestock were lathering and foaming at the mouth. The horsemen turned the cattle and the train made a large jelly roll movement until all wagons were in place with cattle inside the circle. The animals slowed to a stop.

Marie screamed, "Yea! We win! We win!"

Michael was surprised to discover the passenger but reacted quickly. He jumped off the wagon and held up his hands telling Emily to jump. She did. He ran to the back of the wagon and got the child. He carried Marie to Emily and told them to lie down under the wagon. Michael and another man took barrels from the wagon and put them as a barrier in front of the woman and child.

Shots rang out a short distance away. The rear guard was engaged in battle with the advancing Kaw. Approximately twenty Indians mounted on U.S. Army horses were riding fast toward the rear guard. An assortment of weapons was wielded.

Matthew and nine other men were prostrate on the ground using anything available to shield themselves. They were about two hundred yards from the circled wagons. Two horses had been shot and Matthew was lying behind one dead animal aiming his rifle at a Native.

Michael fell to the ground and rolled under the Kilkenny wagon. Emily was lying on her stomach with her pistol in hand peering around the right side of a barrel. Michael pulled up on the left side of the second barrel cocking his rifle.

Marie sat between the two, "Are the people mad at us because we beat them?" she inquired innocently.

"No, honey. Some bad guys are trying to hurt us. You lie down and put your face on your hands. Put your hands on the ground like this," Emily indicated with the palm of her left hand.

"Your arm looks funny," Marie said.

"Lie down, now!" Michael shouted and the startled child flew into position with her face turned toward Emily. Tears welled in her eyes but no one saw them. Michael and Emily were watching the Kaw braves who were within twenty yards of the rear guard and aiming their weapons.

Michael's horse and mule dashed past the Kilkenny wagon accompanied by a rider on a second horse. Michael knew where they were headed and took careful aim at the back of the rider. He pulled the trigger and the cowboy slumped and slid to the ground.

"Michael! You killed one of our people!" Emily yelled. "You shot him in the back!"

Marie started to cry out loud. Emily swung her pistol around aiming it at Michael.

"Who are you? What are you doing?" she asked in a state of shock.

"He was a traitor, Emily. I saw him signal the Kaw our position when I was on guard duty last night," Michael had dropped his rifle and had his hands up in the air.

"Honest. I told Sam about it. Ask him," Michael was afraid to move for fear the shocked woman would shoot him.

"He was taking my horse and mule to join the Kaw. You notice he didn't have a weapon out shooting at them," Michael said.

Emily turned to look at the fallen rider. What she saw was even more astounding. The Kaw had turned and were riding away as fast as they could go. Matthew was looking toward the wagon train with a big smile on his face. Emily wasn't aware that her mouth was hanging open or that Michael had turned the barrel of her pistol up to a harmless position. She was watching the mounted cavalry from Fort Laramie chase the Kaw Indians down the rise and across the flat prairie. Michael gently straightened her trigger finger and removed the pistol from her hand.

Marie had her face buried in the palms of her hands and was sobbing. Michael gently patted her and assured her everything was all right. The bad guys had gone away. She didn't believe him. He was the bad guy.

Emily regained her composure and consoled the child. She was aware for the first time that she no longer held a gun.

Michael crawled out from under the wagon and went to check on his victim. The man was not dead but was in a great deal of pain and breathing laboriously. Michael rolled him onto his back. The man's hat came off and long straight black hair fell out.

"When did you join our train?" McCafferty asked as he walked up beside Michael.

The Native didn't speak. He coughed. Blood oozed out the corner of his mouth. He groaned, coughed again and died. Emily joined Michael and McCafferty and looked at the dark skinned man prostrate on the ground.

"When did you know he was a traitor?" she asked McCafferty.

"I didn't know he was among us until Michael told me this morning," the wagon master answered. He must have joined us during the evening while men were bathing."

Matthew walked up and put his arm around his wife, "That bathing stuff is dangerous. Glad to see you in one piece, Mrs. Kilkenny."

"We do need to work out a better strategy for the rear guard," McCafferty said. "Hoping the enemy kills our horses so we'll have someplace to shield ourselves don't seem too practical."

"Well, this is our first try at combat," Matthew intoned. "Bet you the rear guard wasn't the only ones what made a mistake or two."

"Quite possibly," said Michael grinning at Emily. "Quite possibly."

Deborah joined them and Michael hugged her. "How'd you fare? Did you see any scared, irrational people back your end of the line?" he asked.

"Heck no! All professional Indian fighters down at our end," she laughed. "Crying and screaming doesn't count, does it?"

Chapter 39

Wheels needed to be repaired or replaced. An axle was broken. Two horses came up lame and were shot. Three men had been wounded and the doctor needed time to attend them. McCafferty announced they would stay put until the following morning.

Matthew and Emily checked the contents of their wagon. No major damage was done. Michael and Matthew reloaded the two barrels and replaced cracked spokes.

Michael's horse was injured in the fray and was put down. He decided to tether his mule to the Deborah Dawkin's wagon and take turns driving with her. They both liked to walk several miles a day so riding was merely a rest period.

The afternoon went quickly with all the work to be done. The sun was about to set when the military returned. They were invited to dine on venison stew and side dishes prepared by various cooks. It was obvious with the thirty or so extra men, that there wasn't enough meat to offer steaks or roasts. The soldiers claimed venison stew sounded much better than hard tack. With biscuits and beans cooked with bacon added to the menu everyone ate heartily.

The soldiers related what happened after they rode by the wagon train. The Kaw were deliberately chased for more than two miles to get them away from the pioneers. Then the cavalry split into two sections riding on the flanks of the Natives. The crack riflemen shot horses at the beginning of the Kaw troop. The Kaw fell or slowed to get around the prostrate animals. The military charged into the disorganized group and hand to hand combat ensued. In the end three Kaw were killed including the leader. As soon as he fell, the others tried to escape. They had four mounted braves and the rest ran on foot. The soldiers picked up their own wounded and the stolen horses the Natives had been riding and retreated a half a mile, giving the Kaw space to come back and get their own wounded and dead.

The lieutenant in command told his men to let the Kaw have the four horses still in their possession to transport their wounded and dead the long distance home. Soldiers followed the retreating Kaw for three miles. When they set up camp, the military men turned westward. No soldiers or pioneers were killed and few were injured.

"You won't be bothered by that mob anymore. They don't usually come this far west anyhow and now that you are nearing Fort Laramie, they won't follow," the lieutenant said. "With only four horses it would be impossible for them to accomplish more than steal a few head of cattle."

"That's what started the fracas," Michael told him. He talked to the lieutenant about strategy and past experiences for awhile during dinner.

After dinner McCafferty announced the military was going to escort the train into Fort Laramie. They would be taking guard duty for the next few nights. A cheer went up from the tired pioneers.

Deborah brought Marie to the Kilkenny wagon after dinner. She was supposed to thank Emily for taking her in the Conestoga. Marie became tongue-tied and hid behind Deborah's skirt as soon as she saw Michael. Michael squatted and spoke to the child very quietly. He apologized for yelling at her and scaring her. He promised to never do it again.

The child responded by sticking out her bottom lip and moving as far away as she could get and still hang onto Deborah. No amount of talk from either woman could convince Marie that Michael was a good guy.

He tried another tactic. He played his harmonica softly. Marie had to come around Deborah's skirt enough to find out how he was making the music.

When Michael played, "Oh, Susannah," the adults clapped and sang. By the end of the song the child was clapping along. He next played "Turkey in the Straw" and Deborah danced with Marie while Matthew danced with Emily. That did it. By the end of that song, Marie ran up to Michael and begged for more music. He played his own version of "Brahm's Lullaby."

Matthew picked up the child and rocked her in his arms. Michael promised to play more music for her at a later date but said he needed to go to sleep now. Marie thanked him profusely and threw her arms around his leg in an embrace. Deborah blew Michael a kiss and took the child back to Marie's waiting parents.

The next morning, the military escort rode single file on either side of the train. The spare horses were tethered one behind the other and led by the rear guard. Two scouts left at sunrise and reported back to their commander and the wagon master that the route ahead was clear.

After seeing almost nothing but dried grass for a few days, the travelers were glad to see the fine stands of cottonwoods in the river bottoms and on sandbars. There would be plenty of wood for camp fires the next two nights. Flocks of wild ducks and geese covered the sandbars and a hunting party set out with instructions to bring back enough for two meals. Matthew and his dogs were in their element. The party of six hunters brought thirty ducks and seven geese back. They were cleaned and cooked. Children made war bonnets from the feathers. Women gathered duck eggs and made noodles to be dried for future use. So far, one problem the train had not suffered was hunger.

Chapter 40

The train approached Fort Laramie. The white battlements of that fort and its twin, Fort Platte, were surrounded by Shoshone and Arapaho lodges. The travelers crossed the clear stream of the Laramie River, which was about forty feet wide and two feet deep. The outer banks showed that at times the river was twice that size.

McCafferty said the train would be staying at least three days. He wanted hunting parties to bring in a winter supply of buffalo and suggested they use Shoshone guides.

The first day in the fort was used for the usual flurry of blacksmith work, carpentry, laundry and restocking staples. The second day a party of twenty men including four Shoshone left on a buffalo hunt. The remaining men cut down trees and built racks for stretching skins and drying meat. Some women learned lessons from the Indians on preserving the skins.

Emily and Deborah made friends with two shy middle aged Shoshone women. The older women knew much about survival under hardship conditions. The young white women wanted to learn as much as possible. Emily was astonished to learn that of all the tents in the area, she had chosen the one belonging to the medicine woman as her stopping place. The Shoshone medicine woman and Emily traded ideas on medical care and the use of herbs. Most of what the Shoshone told Emily was completely foreign. She wished Dr. Six from Athens was here to enjoy the education. The medicine woman knew next to nothing of surgery and was fascinated when Emily described some of the procedures used to help injured miners.

The dark skinned woman named Red Sky asked the obvious question. Why hadn't Emily cured herself? Emily explained that she was working on it but it would take a long time. The reverend healer asked if she could try. Emily asked questions about the procedure. It was a sacred ceremony known only to healers; it couldn't be revealed to anyone else. Red Sky told Emily she would be put to sleep with a cup of tea and wake up with the use of her arm. It sounded too good to be true. Emily wanted to talk to Matthew before submitting for treatment.

Matthew was skeptical and more than a little afraid of the "put to sleep" part. The two of them paid a visit to the army doctor. The doctor said from what he knew of Shoshone medicine, most of it worked through "mind over matter." They usually put people to sleep through hypnosis and did a lot of chanting and drum beating.

Emily slept little that night. She read medical books, she prayed, she thought. By morning, she was worn out and wearily told Matthew she decided to try it. She felt that the worst that could happen would be no change.

"No, babe. The worst that could happen is you go to sleep and never wake up," he said.

Silence ensued, both parties deep in thought.

"Go with me and talk to Red Sky. Hear her out. Help me make the final decision," Emily pleaded.

"You couldn't keep me away. I want to be beside you every minute," he answered.

"If we accept, it's a secret ceremony, she won't let you inside the tent during the procedure," Emily replied.

"Don't go, Em. You is fine just like you is. I can help you do anything you can't do alone," he pleaded.

"What if she could help me and we didn't try? Someday we'll have children. I want to hold them in my arms. Maybe Red Sky can give me that power," she entreated. "I want to help cure other people. I can't do that with one arm. I'm afraid to do it and I'm afraid to miss the opportunity."

In the end the two young people went to Red Sky, medicine woman for the Wind River Shoshone Nation. Matthew found the woman intelligent, sensible, sincere and safety conscious. They came to an agreement to do the procedure. Emily would spend the night, he asked to sleep outside the healing tent. His request was granted.

At dinnertime they ate with the medicine woman and her two assistants. Emily was only permitted to drink a broth. After her serving was dished up, cooked vegetables, meat and spices were added for the others. Matthew noticed the medicine woman didn't eat anything.

After dinner, the five people spoke amicably of many things. The upcoming ceremony was never mentioned. As soon as the moon became visible, the healer said it was time to begin. By now Emily was a nervous wreck. She kissed Matthew as he held her tightly.

"It is not too late to say no," he whispered.

She shook her head and went inside the tent. Matthew sat back down beside the glowing embers of the dinner fire.

Inside the tent was a small fire with a pungent fluid simmering. There were three bowls of oil with wicks, and an assortment of gourds and animal skins. Vessels made from animal organs hung from a horizontal stick of shiny wood.

Red Sky told Emily to undress so she could be bathed. She did as told. An assistant took the clothes out of the tent and handed them to Matthew. Red Sky lit one of the oil lamps and sat cross-legged in front of it. She bowed her head in prayer, reciting poetic sounding verses over and over.

One assistant removed the simmering fluid from the fire and added something from two of the bladders hanging grotesquely behind Emily. The second assistant told Emily to stand on the deerskin with her right arm hanging at her side and to close her eyes. She mixed the simmering liquid with some cool water and poured it over Emily's head. She lathered the hair and rinsed it with clear water. Then she put more of the liquid on a soft rabbit skin and washed Emily head to foot. The first assistant rubbed the cleansed body with a rough cloth. Emily felt tingly all over after the bath. She was then sponged with a harsh smelling liquid and put into an incredibly soft gown covering all of her body except her head and affected left arm. Emily noticed the top of the garment had a drawstring so it could be placed up over her right shoulder after being tucked in under her left arm.

Red Sky never looked up during the preceding actions. She was pleading fervently for blessings upon her patient and herself. Her eyes were still lowered but her hands were raised in supplication.

Emily was seated on a clean dry deerskin and given a cup of tea. The sweet, minty odor barely disguised the familiar scent of laudanum. She sipped the warm tea as the assistants disposed of the bathing equipment and laid out clean rabbit skins, gourds, bones shaped into tools and a container of incense. The last item was set afire, as were the remaining two oil lamps.

The air was becoming stifling and Emily felt perspiration forming on her face. Her tea was finished and she was drowsy but fighting off sleep. Suddenly the praying stopped. Emily was having a hard time keeping her eyes open. The assistants gently laid her down on the rabbit skins and the last thing she remembered was seeing Red Sky stripped to the waist and washing herself with the pungent fluid.

Matthew watched the tent and listened to the chanting for ten minutes. Then he stood and paced back and forth for fifteen minutes. All went quiet inside the tent and he rushed to the door ready to spring at the first sound of pain or alarm. He heard nothing. After five minutes he relaxed and decided to lay out his bedroll.

An older man came by and smiled knowingly. He clasped the startled Matthew on the shoulder. "May you have baby boy. Big strong boy," he said then walked off.

The chanting started inside the tent again and grew in volume. It came from three voices now instead of one. He thought he heard Emily groaning but wasn't sure. He sat on the bedroll so close to the tent, he touched it.

It was a groan! He was sure now. Should he burst in and rescue her? She promised to call out his name anytime she felt she needed help. She hadn't done that. Maybe they had gagged her. No, he was being ridiculous. What possible motive could they have to harm her? They were obviously friendly toward whites. They lived with them and depended on protection from the military post. Matthew lay back on his bed with his head next to the tent.

Red Sky rubbed ointments and liquids made from plants and animals into the arm. The recipes had been in her family for three generations. She manipulated the elbow and shoulder. Each time she did so, she dug her fingers deeper into the frozen joints. When her massaging reached the wrist, she pulled on the arm. At first the joints didn't move at all. Little by little throughout the night they moved a fraction of an inch further. She administered more laudanum laced tea with a teaspoon sized indented bone when Emily stirred and showed signs of wakefulness.

The assistants bathed Emily's face with cool water, listened closely to her breathing, felt her heartbeat, fanned both Emily and Red Sky and prayed. They bathed Red Sky's face, gave her sips of herbal tea for strength, and kept the gourds of ointment and fermented liquid full.

As daylight appeared on the eastern horizon, Red Sky sat beside Emily and placed one foot on her ribs and one on her head. She held Emily's wrist and pulled with all her strength. The arm straightened from shoulder to wrist. Red Sky held it out straight and twisted it palm up, then palm down. She lay the arm down at Emily's side and manipulated the elbow and shoulder joints one more time.

Exhausted, Red Sky lay beside Emily and slept. The assistants cleaned away all medical appurtenances. They bathed Emily's perspiring body with soap weed and water and put a clean gown on her. This gown had normal sleeves and her arms were repositioned lying at her sides. Emily slept soundly while being dressed.

Two hours later, Red Sky emerged from the tent and told Matthew he could see his sleeping wife. She said Emily was to stay in the tent with her assistants for one day and one night. Then she could return to the fort. Red Sky turned and walked away.

Matthew entered the tent and knelt beside his unconscious wife. Both her arms lay at her sides. Matthew smiled gratefully. The procedure worked, Emily would be able to hold her babies, their babies. He bent down and kissed her, listened to her regular breathing, rose and left the tent. He returned to his wagon and crawled into bed and slept.

Chapter 41

Emily floated in and out of consciousness during the day. She dreamed of smoky caves and growling animals. She fought the animals waving her arms and brandishing a rifle. When she awoke she thought wryly how strange that she saw herself with a moveable arm and holding a rifle.

She attempted to lift her arms to prove to herself how foolish the dream was. Both arms extended into the air over her head. She stared in astonishment. She put her arms down and wept for joy.

As the day went on the fog cleared in her mind. Each time she woke she put her arms up to see if she could still move her left arm. It became progressively more sore as the laudanum wore off. But it did move.

In the afternoon she awoke to find Matthew sitting beside her. She touched him with her left hand. He lifted her hand and kissed it. She tried to sit up and found she had a pounding headache.

"It is the smoke and fumes," Matthew said. "The place still reeks of medicine and smoke. You'll feel better when you get fresh air."

"Where's Red Sky? Where are the assistants? I want to thank them," Emily said with a thick tongue.

"They come 'n go. They want you to stay in here tonight. I'll come and get you in the morning. You got to sleep off the medicine," Matthew explained.

"Laudanum. Their medicine was laudanum, same thing we use in Ohio. I'll be okay, Matt," she said with a thick tongue as she curled up and went back to sleep.

Matthew sat watching his wife sleep for a few minutes. Then he went to find Red Sky. He walked around the tents taking in the sights, sounds and smells.

"Shoshone is just folks like the rest of us. They's trying to make a living and raise kids like any white man," he concluded.

He stopped to watch a group of men making tools from animal bones, obsidian, and wood. They spoke their Native language and a man or two glanced at Matthew. Self-conscious, he started to move away then stopped and turned back.

"Can you speak American?" he asked.

"Yes," one man responded after a short silence.

"Can I watch you make tools? I'd like to learn how," he said sincerely.

Two men moved over to make room for him to sit between them. He watched and asked questions until sunset. The men packed up their belongings ready to quit for the day. Matthew shook hands all around and thanked the men for allowing him to join them.

Matthew decided it was too late to look for Red Sky anymore that evening. He walked back to the fort wondering how he could ever repay Red Sky for the medical miracle.

He met Michael and Deborah coming out of the chapel. They greeted him with the news of their impending wedding. They were getting married in two days. Mathew hugged Deborah and shook hands with Michael.

"Course, I want you to be my witness," Michael said.

"Glad to do the job. You're getting a good woman. Nothing better for a man than a good woman," Matthew said.

"Speaking of good women, where's Emily? I haven't seen her all day," Deborah asked.

Matthew explained the incredible experience. In the end another round of handshakes and hugs took place. The three returned to the Kilkenny wagon and finished off the bottle of wine opened at the announcement of the betrothed couple. Then they retired.

Matthew thought the bed felt way too large and slept restlessly. He dreamed of chasing buffalo. He was riding bareback and shooting with a bow (a weapon he'd never touched in real life), using arrows tipped with obsidian. He woke early and prepared a pot of coffee. How lonely it was without Emily. How did he ever manage to live without her? He didn't feel like eating anything. He sat dejected staring into his coffee cup.

Little Marie walked up and said, "Don't be sad. You can hold my doll, she'll make you feel better."

Matthew looked up to see the child holding her brand new store bought doll out toward him. He smiled. "That's a mighty purdy baby you got. You must be a special girl to get a nice doll baby like that."

"Mr. O'Brien and Miss Dawkins gave it to me. If you hold her close, she'll make you feel happy inside," the child pushed the doll toward Matthew's hand.

He took the doll uncertain how she wanted him to hold it. He held the coffee in one hand and the doll in the other and smiled at Marie.

"No, you have to hold her against your heart," the child demonstrated with the doll cuddled in her arms like a mother with a real baby. Then she handed it back to Matthew.

He obediently sat his coffee down and held the doll to his chest. The child beamed. That in itself made Matthew feel better.

"Can Miss Emily come out to play with my new baby doll?" Marie asked.

"She's not feeling good right now. Maybe when we're back on the trail you can ride in our wagon and she can hold your baby," Matthew explained.

The child happily skipped off looking elsewhere for a playmate. Matthew watched her go.

Funny thing, I do feel better. Maybe I better get me a doll or better yet a little girl, he thought.

Now in good spirits, he walked to the blacksmith to borrow or rent a surrey for an hour. The blacksmith harnessed the Kilkenny's stallion to a surrey. Matt made his way to the Shoshone medicine woman's tent. He walked inside with Emily's clothes draped over his arm.

Red Sky and Emily were having tea. Emily was a bit groggy but obviously happy. She told Matthew her arm would be sore for a few days but should be fully mobile.

"Oh Matthew! Isn't it wonderful? I'm so happy. I want to pay Red Sky by giving her something really special. Her people travel twice a year and she has to walk and carry her belongings. I want to give her my mare," Emily said matter-of-factly.

Matthew was shocked. He too wanted to give Red Sky something special but certainly hadn't considered anything as valuable as a horse. He smiled wryly at Red Sky but her eyes were downcast and she didn't see the expression.

"Can we talk about payment after I get you home?" Matthew tried to sound casual.

Red Sky and Emily finished their tea and spoke of exercises Emily would need to perform. Matthew waited outside the tent while Emily dressed. He helped her into the surrey and could tell her arm hurt badly. The laudanum was wearing off.

They rode the short distance to their Conestoga and Matthew helped her into bed. The sheepskin was folded up as a backrest and she lay back against it. Deborah called from outside and wanted to know if it was convenient to visit. She brought chicken soup and fresh bread.

Matthew excused himself and returned the surrey. He wanted to give the two women time to talk privately so walked around looking for work to be done. He checked on their animals grazing in a field along with all the other livestock from their train. Two of the men from the train rode their horses around the perimeter of the field watching for wolves or any other problems.

His hunting dogs were under Deborah's wagon sleeping while Michael greased the axles. Matthew asked if he could help. Michael told him to check the wagon for any needed repairs. Matthew checked the wheels and spokes. He lifted the tongue and looked for cracks or signs of wear. He looked over the canvas cover, checking for tears or worn spots that might leak. The wagon was in good condition.

He greeted Deborah's lifelong friend and traveling partner, Katherine Reed. She was sitting on a box working on a hastily prepared wedding gown.

"Good day, Mr. Kilkenny. How are you two faring the trip so far?" she asked.

"Em's had medical treatment on her arm and it's a bit sore. But she can move it now so everything's rosy at our place," he replied.

The woman nodded and went back to her needlework. Matthew could think of nothing further to say so stooped to watch Michael.

"Fixing up your wagon for a wedding night trip?"

"Not your usual honeymoon cabin, is it? We're trying to buy our own wagon and team before we leave the fort. We want to make sure Katherine's is in good condition before we send her off on her own," Michael explained.

"Anything I can do to help?" Matthew asked.

Michael replied in the negative and Matthew was glad when he spotted Deborah heading his way. That meant he could go back to his own wagon. He said good-bye to Michael and Katherine and whistled for his dogs. The three of them walked briskly toward the Kilkenny wagon. He tipped his hat to Deborah as they passed.

At the wagon he fed and watered the dogs to their delight. They were used to being fed after the humans finished dinner in the evening. He climbed aboard and sat down beside his wife. She was reading a novel and laid it aside.

"It's hard to focus on the words when you have drugs in your system," she said. "I guess you want to know why I'm giving away my precious horse. Well, I tried to think of the most valuable possessions I have. I wanted to give Red Sky something I loved. Then I eliminated the things that would be more burdensome to her than a pleasure-like the rocker. She would have to carry it each season when they moved. I thought of my medicines and equipment and decided they might be harmful without the education on their use. She would have no use for the linens in my trousseau. My horse was the logical solution."

"And what are you going to ride when we get to Oregon? What about the horse breeding we talked about? What about two good horses for pulling farming implements?" Matthew asked.

"I'll ride in the wagon or walk from here to Oregon. We can trade the wagon for a horse when we get there and keep the oxen for farm implement drayage," Emily had evidently thought the situation through.

Matthew sat quietly thinking of the ramifications of having one horse. Their farm stock was dwindling and he seemed powerless to stop the drain.

"Please, Matthew. Say it's okay. I won't do it, if you say not to," Emily said.

"I don't know what else we could do for her to say thanks. She probably don't need money," he said. "It just seems like a mighty big doctor bill."

"She gave me back my life, Matthew," Emily said quietly.

There was silence in the wagon for a few minutes.

"I'll take her the mare this afternoon," Matthew said just as quietly.

Chapter 42

Michael and Deborah were behind Matthew and Emily as the train left Fort Laramie. They drove a converted farm wagon pulled by two mules. One was Michael's original pack animal; the second was purchased from the army. The blacksmith had converted the wagon into a covered vehicle. Katherine and Deborah split their supplies so both wagons were now loaded lightly.

Emily found the Shoshone used clay pots and Matthew was able to buy two sizes to make Michael and Deborah a cooler for their meats and dairy products. That was their wedding gift from the Kilkennys.

Emily felt bad that she hadn't been well enough to cook a feast or do anything special for the wedding. She attended the ceremony along with other members of the train and a few soldiers from the fort. She used the occasion to wear her German made dress. Cake and coffee were served at the rear of the church after the service.

"At least there was music. I'm glad the captain's wife could play that little organ during the ceremony," Emily told Matthew.

"Not everyone gets a big blowout for a wedding like you had Mrs. Kilkenny," Matthew said.

"Oh Matt, wasn't our wedding party perfect? And the ceremony! I loved it all. It was a dream come true," she reminisced.

"Yeah, especially when you admitted you wasn't good enough for me," he teased.

Emily blushed at the memory, "You are a special man. I still feel the same way, I'm not half as good a person as you are. I'm so glad you married me. I would have been a spinster for sure, if it wasn't for you."

"I reckon I got a purdy good deal myself. Not many women willing to give up a comfortable home, family, friends, and a medical practice to go traipsing off into the wilderness with a poorly educated, out-a-work miner," Matthew admitted.

They rode side by side on the seat. Matthew's horse was tied to the rear of the wagon. Emily held Matthew's right hand with her left, just because she could.

The cattle were scattered loosely in front of the train and along the sides of the wagons. Cattle dogs barked at any that wandered too far away, bringing them back into the fold. Matthew's bloodhounds liked that game and joined their comrades chasing and barking at cows.

Matthew watched the white painted mud walls of Fort Laramie and Fort Platte disappear behind them. The land was chalky white, gray and beige. The grass was yellow or brown. A few people could be seen on horseback or riding in a wagon. Some were settlers, some soldiers and some Natives.

"What wide open spaces. You can see for miles and miles," Michael said riding up beside Matthew.

Emily and Matthew nodded looking around.

"Trees are pretty scarce except for the cottonwoods. Reckon we better gather extra firewood when we stop tonight," Michael continued.

Emily and Matthew nodded again. Michael cleared his throat and said, "Well, I just wanted to let you know I'll still help care for the livestock or drive the wagon or help anyway I can. Marriage didn't change our agreement."

"I reckon it did," Matthew said.

Michael looked surprised, "How's that?"

"I'll help you and your missus, if you need anything. Now, we is equal friends," Matthew smiled.

The two men touched the brim of their hats in farewell and Michael rode off after a straying cow. The dogs gleefully followed him.

"Those two dogs don't know who their master is anymore," Emily said.

"I don't care. Just as long as you remember who yours is," Matthew said putting his arm around her shoulders. Life was good. They had their love and their health, the sun was shining and they were seeing new country.

The train rattled along the plains beside the Platte. The immigrants admired the formations in the marbleized bluffs. The ground was powdery white limestone and sandstone which made easy traveling. They enjoyed seeing herds of antelope, buffalo, deer and occasional elk. They knew wolves, coyotes, grizzlies, and rattlesnakes were out there somewhere but chose not to think of them when things were going so well.

"Two men stayed behind at Fort Laramie to become wolf hunters," Michael said the first evening in camp. "Figured they'd catch another train west next spring. The government's paying a dollar fifty per head for wolves."

"I'd like to go on one or two wolf hunts but not make a living doing it," Matthew replied.

"The buffalo hunt was really something to see. Got scary when all those enormous beasts were running beside us. They looked so wild-eyed. I got one of the skins. Mangy looking but it'll be warm this winter," Michael said. "McCafferty said we might go on one more hunt just before we start up into the Rockies. You'll have to go on it with us. Maybe you can bag yourself a skin. We share the meat, as you know, but the skin goes to the shooter."

The previous hunt was the day after Emily's medical procedure and Matthew was asleep in his wagon.

"We've got lots of dried meat now. Where would we put more?" Emily asked.

"Sam asked us to take a couple of barrels of dried meat in our wagon and a couple in Katherine's. He doesn't want to run short in case we get caught in an early snow going over the mountains," Michael told her.

"That means we'll be stopping long enough to dry the meat and tan the hides," Emily was excited. "I could fix a proper banquet as a wedding celebration."

"That's a nice thought but unnecessary. Deborah and I feel very happily married now. We don't need anymore public celebrations," Michael said deflating Emily.

"I know. I just wanted to do something special for you. You have been so good to us the past several weeks. You're a good friend. I hope Deborah and I will become longtime friends," Emily tried to explain her motives.

"I'm sure you will. You can help us pan gold while Matthew is plow-ing his fields," Michael laughed. He was glad Emily hadn't said he'd been a friend since causing her accident and hoped those thoughts were well and truly buried.

Chapter 42

Deborah convinced Emily that she really didn't want a wedding party. It would be too sad to have such an affair without Michael's family or her own in attendance. Deborah had written to both families before leaving Fort Laramie and that would have to suffice. She didn't want wedding gifts from the fellow travelers, as they would have to take something from their meager belongings to give to the newlyweds.

"Well, okay then, no party," Emily said, "but if you need anything, please come to us first."

Katherine walked with the younger women for a couple of hours each day. She told Emily her reason for traveling west after Emily was sworn to secrecy. Katherine had answered an ad in the newspaper in her hometown. She was going to a town called Rough 'n Ready to become the bride of a saw mill worker in a newly established supply center. Rough 'n Ready was located in a valley surrounded by snow tinged mountains most of the year. The mountains on the western side of Beaver Valley were covered with pine trees and the sawmill worked round the clock supplying gold mines and mining towns with lumber. Katherine's intended had two children aged seven and nine who were motherless. He was looking for a mature woman to take on the responsibility of homemaker and mother to a ready-made family.

Katherine was looking forward to this new experience. She had spent the previous ten years taking care of her aging parents. When they passed away, she realized, as a thirty-year old, she was too mature for regular suitors looking for prime young women to bear them many children but she longed for a family to call her own. She expected her dream to become reality when she reached the little settlement.

Katherine was breathing hard by the time she came to the end of her tale. The reason was that the train was climbing a ridge covered with a scattering of pines. At the top, McCafferty called a stop for lunch.

The three women, Matthew and Michael ate quickly so they could walk from point to point admiring the beauty around them. The immediate country was dry rolling hills. To the south and east the immense prairie, a sea way seventy million years earlier was in constant movement. The wind blew the tall, golden grass in waves; herds of buffalo and pronghorn could be seen mowing down that grass as they progressed across the plains. To the west was the roughest range of mountains any of them had ever seen. The ragged, sharp pinnacles protruded above shear granite cliffs. High in the mountains, crevices filled with ice forewarned the pioneers not to tarry too long before ascending the awesome barrier. To the north there were valleys and rounded knobs stretching to the horizon.

Directly overhead, cumulus clouds were beginning to form. They encased the peaks sucking out water in preparation for a downfall of rain.

McCafferty announced he would like to travel for another few hours before the rain started. The pioneers were now experienced in making a quick job of eating and moving on.

The party was enroute within minutes heading north toward Horseshoe Creek. Travel went smoothly for two hours with six miles crossed. Then the land became sandy and horses and wagons bogged down. It took four hours to make the next mile.

The rain started with huge flat splats and the tired, dusty people stood with their faces heavenward drinking in the needed moisture. The momentum built and the volume of water drenched everyone to the skin. They scurried to shelter and tied the end flaps of the wagons down to protect their belongings. Men without wagons ducked under the Conestogas of their friends or wrapped up in tarps. Dogs dashed for the same cover as the single men. The livestock turned its back to the wind that was gusting violently.

Emily and Matthew got inside their Conestoga just before the hail started pelting the canvas. The noise was intense and Emily sat on the bed holding her ears. Matthew bounced from place to place holding the canvas against the wind's force. The wagon rocked with gusts hitting it from various angles. The ice pellets hit the taut canvas with a ringing sound and bounced off.

The torrent lasted less than fifteen minutes then went in search of new victims. People emerged from their shelters to investigate the damage. Animals were bleeding from skin punctures. Some wagons suffered a rip or two. Katherine's cover was ripped beyond repair. Haggard faces expressed the unspoken question, "What next?"

McCafferty treated the storm as a routine experience. He said the train would move on to higher ground despite the diminishing light. He told them to leave the animals untreated and march out immediately. The first person to object was shouted down, "That's an order! Move out now!"

The last wagon was pried out of sandy clay in the gully and pulled to the top of a knoll when they heard the thunder in the distance. The roar didn't stop it grew in intensity. It made the weak hearted clasp each other in fear. Strong-hearted people grasped reins of animals to steady them and prayed.

The deafening sound grew nearer. One person thought it was a tornado and hugged a tree; others thought it was an avalanche.

A ten-foot wall of water gushed down the gully where the wagons had been sitting. It thundered past the startled people in a maddening rush to the valley floor. The roar lessened and fast flowing water carried trees, rocks and mud downstream.

"Flash floods are common in the plains and desert near mountains, remember that," Sam McCafferty said. "Now we can circle the wagons and take care of our animals. Be sure to put salve on any open wounds to keep flies out."

Marie brought Katherine to Michael and Matthew and said, "These men can make you all better. Don't cry any more. I gave Miss Katherine my doll to make her feel better but that didn't work. So I told her I knew two grown men that can fix anything."

Michael assured Katherine she could use his previously occupied lean-to until they could get her a new canvas top. Deborah had a different plan. Michael was to occupy his old tent and Katherine would share the wagon with her.

That settled, the women went to see what could be salvaged from the devastated wagon. Michael went to plead with McCafferty to send his fastest horseman back to Fort Laramie for a replacement cover.

The bridegroom had the wagon master's sympathy but he wouldn't agree to send a soldier back to Laramie. His reason for the refusal was that it would take seven or eight days for him to make the round trip. The train was only seven or eight days east of Fort Bridger. He didn't tell Michael he wanted soldiers on alert in case of an attack by Natives. He also didn't mention that they were entering grizzly country and experienced marksmen might be needed for protection.

It was midnight before the wounded animals had been doused down with salves. Enough dry wood had been found to make it through dinner but most of the animal treatment was done with light from kerosene lanterns. Wet clothes and bedding were hung on meat-drying scaffolds. Dry blankets and tarps were shared among the increasingly close knit group.

Marie snuggled down to sleep in the warmth between Emily and Matthew. She clung to her precious doll and smiled at her two friends.

"Isn't this fun? Can I sleep with you every night?" She asked.

Emily returned her smile, "We'll talk about it in the morning."

Chapter 43

The train now consisted of seven wagons, ten outriders, and four soldiers. There were six women, all married except for Katherine Reed. Marie Jackson had three siblings and there were two adolescents in Brian and Jesse Jamison's wagon. There were twenty-one grown men. They would need more meat to supply those numbers with food, if stuck in the mountains over the winter.

McCafferty organized a buffalo hunt the morning after the storm. He would take ten or twelve men on the hunt to increase their chances for an element of surprise. The four soldiers were to stay behind for the protection of the women and children. Michael and four other men volunteered to stay behind since they had been on the first hunt.

McCafferty would lead the hunt jointly with a Shoshone guide he had hired at Fort Laramie. Matthew was delighted with the opportunity to experience a buffalo hunt and hoped to win a nice warm skin for the coming winter. He was told to report to the Shoshone, Brown Eagle.

Brown Eagle told the four men under his charge to take two cleaned and loaded guns—one rifle and one pistol. They were also to take a sheathed hunting knife and large saddlebags for the meat. He told them to double check buckles and belts on their tack. A saddle coming loose during the hunt was certain death.

Matthew felt his adrenaline mounting as he prepared his gear. He barely heard the safety lecture Emily was reciting. Ole Blue and Betsy sensed his activity meant an imminent hunt and sniffed the bags, guns and equipment before chasing each other excitably around and under the wagon.

"Them dogs got to be tied up. They can't follow me this time. The buffalo would hear us coming a mile away," Matthew said to no one in particular.

Michael took the dogs to Katherine's wagon where he would be working. He tied them to a wheel and placed a pan of water and two large bones under the wagon. The dogs were immediately distracted by the bones and forgot about Matthew's activity.

Michael returned to share a couple of hints he had picked up on his earlier hunt.

"You'll notice the bulls and mothers with calves are the most apt to charge your horse," he told Matthew. "Stay a distance from the herd so your horse doesn't get gored. Wear your neckerchief over your mouth and nose so you don't choke on dust."

"Yeah, good idea, Michael," Emily agreed. "And pull your hat down tight before the run starts so you're not blinded by the sun. Take a canteen of water. You'll need it as soon as the run is over."

"The head's the hardest part of the animal," Michael recited. "Don't bother aiming at the head."

"Brown Eagle approached the trio smiling. "Sounds like you two are after my job. 'Bout ready, Matthew? We want to get started as soon as possible."

Emily was stunned into silence by the man's well-spoken English. She looked at the bare chested man with her mouth hanging open.

"I attended the Methodist Mission School in Shawnee, Kansas for six years, ma'am," he answered her unasked question.

Emily blushed and tried to think of some quip to show she wasn't surprised by his manner of speech. None came to mind so she smiled and nodded.

"Me takem good care of white hunter boy," Brown Eagle jested.

"Thank you," Emily said meekly. "I need him back safe and sound much more than I need buffalo meat."

Most of the pioneers stood on the ridge and watched the hunters find their way northeast off the knoll. A large herd of bison could be seen in the distance, probably two miles away. The hunters descended the knoll slowly letting the horses choose the way. Once on the prairie, the horses were brought to a trot and then a canter.

When the horses could no longer be distinguished one from another, Emily, Deborah, Michael and Katherine returned to the work at hand.

Emily cleaned and reapplied salve to the hail wounds of all their animals except Matthew's horse, which was in use. She saw no signs of fly blown infection on the cattle or oxen and was thankful for that. Emily and Deborah worked together on the O'Brien's and Katherine's animals.

Michael and Katherine transferred perishable goods from her wagon to his own. To make room for her clothes, books, and linens he had to carry barrels of beans, dried buffalo, and flour to her wagon from his. Fortunately, an outrider helped him. The torn canvas was removed and salvageable pieces were used to repair other wagons. The sewing was man's work because of the strength needed to pull the curved needles through the heavy material. Katie McCafferty supplied the heavy cotton thread and curved needles and showed the men the best technique to prevent leaking around the patchwork.

One soldier took three outriders and the Jamison boys to find ample wood for drying the buffalo meat.

A fire was built and water brought from the stream to boil for laundry. The rain from the previous evening muddied the outrider's supplies plus the clothes the wagon owners were wearing before they sought shelter. The torrent was now an icy cold, swift moving creek about a foot deep.

The cattle were kept inside the circle at Sam's orders and had little grass to graze on so laid in the shade and chewed their cud. Sam had ridden around the wagons several times making sure they were as secure from attack as possible. He was worried because of the loss of manpower while the hunters were gone.

Deborah took the opportunity to school the four Jackson children. She was teaching four-year-old Marie and her six-year-old sister, Rebecca to count and say the alphabet. The two older children were given reading, writing and arithmetic assignments. That left Hester and Elijah Jackson, the parents, free to minister to their wounded animals, do laundry and make wagon and harness repairs.

It was a busy camp and no one was concerned about Natives or wild animals. They felt secure under the watchful eyes of the soldiers. One soldier sat on a rock overlooking the camp and surrounding countryside. Two soldiers rode their mounts around the perimeter of the camp going in opposite directions. They were about a quarter of a mile out from the wagons. There was little possibility Natives, wolves, bears or mountain lions could sneak into camp.

Brown Eagle and McCafferty split into two groups when they were about a half-mile behind the herd of bison. The hunters received complete instructions from their leaders. They proceeded single file with hats pulled down, neckerchiefs placed over noses, loaded rifles across their thighs. The horses moved at a canter on the perimeter of the cloud of dust. As the men reached the rear of the herd, they moved to the side putting a distance of about a hundred and fifty feet between them and the bison and galloped at a speed slightly faster than the lowing brown mass of fur.

When they were half way up the herd, Brown Eagle and McCafferty gave a signal – the hunters moved in closer to the bison, cocked their guns, aimed at spots just behind the forward legs of young cows and pulled their triggers.

There was instant panic. The herd began to run and men had all they could do to stay out of the way of charging horns and trampling feet. The dust became blinding within seconds as the sharp hooves dug into the dry soil. Most of the bison ran as a compact unit. A few wild-eyed beasts skirted the mob looking for free space to run faster.

Matthew was riding his mount at the same speed as the herd. He had no idea how far ahead or how far behind the other hunters were. He concentrated on keeping his distance from the animals.

He found it impossible to pour gun powder down the barrel while riding so pulled away from the herd and stopped his horse. The loading procedure took about a minute, then he raced back into position and aimed at a young cow. He fired and saw the cow stumble but keep on moving. He felt sure he had hit her and tried to keep an eye on her.

He was now dependent on his horse to keep the pace and watch for hazards. Matthew's heart was racing, his mount darted around rocks and animals. Matthew dug his knees into his horse to keep his balance. He placed the rifle into the scabbard hanging from his saddle and withdrew his pistol from the holster. He was ready to shoot again.

He searched the sides of the nearby animals but saw no blood. Where was his wounded cow? He thought she might be dropping back in the herd so slowed his horse a bit. He searched in vain.

A shot rang out. A cow directly behind his horse stumbled and fell. She somersaulted barely missing Matthew's horse with her flying hooves.

Matthew kicked his horse with his heels and headed ninety degrees away from the herd. His quick thinking saved his life as bison raced around the fallen animal. Some didn't see the victim in time and fell themselves. That created an expanding hazard for the following animals that were stampeding.

Other shots rang out and the bison scattered running pell-mell in all directions. As the melee continued, buffalo were following Matthew's horse. Fortunately, the horse was faster and he emerged from the dust and spotted an enormous erratic block about a hundred yards away.

Matthew raced toward the rock giving his horse time to make the turn and come to a stop on the far side. Matthew dismounted and held the reins of his frightened mount so the animal couldn't back away from the boulder. The herd flowed around either side and disappeared in a cloud of dust.

Matthew stood still until his heart was beating regularly. He stroked his horse's head and neck until the animal was calm. Then Matt untied the canteen of water and drank thirstily.

"Thanks for nagging, Em," he saluted the knoll in the distance with his half empty canteen.

Matthew shook dust from his neckerchief and wet it. The cool cloth felt like heaven on his dirt encrusted eyelids. When he finished washing his face, he reloaded both guns, replaced the neckerchief and rode slowly back toward the fallen animals.

The herd had passed; the dust lingered just above ground level for as far as the eye could see. Dead and injured bison lay scattered on the terrain. Some were still pawing the air. He rode up to one of those and pulled the trigger of his rifle. The animal heaved a sigh and lay still.

Matthew surveyed the scene. A group of hunters were congregated in one spot, some kneeling, some standing. He ignored them for the time being and looked for other wounded bison. He saw a calf in the distance limping on three legs. Its head hung low in a weakened state.

Matthew rode toward it and the calf made no effort to escape. When he got closer, he could see multiple wounds. The animal had been trampled. Matthew took his pistol out and put the calf out of its misery.

McCafferty and two hunters were riding toward him and he went to meet them.

"How many you reckon we got?" Matthew asked.

"I count twelve animals down and one man lost," McCafferty sadly related.

Matthew was surprised. Then he recalled the group of men he had seen.

"Who was kilt?" Matthew asked.

"Fellow name of Johnson, one of the outriders on his way to the gold fields," McCafferty said. "His luck ran out before he even got to Californy."

"He was following you. He shot the cow behind your horse and in front of his own. He got tangled in the stampede around the fallen cow," another hunter said. "I was behind him but further away from the herd."

"Lack of experience," a grizzled older man said. "He should have never shot an animal in front of his mount. Always shoot to the side."

The man spit a shot of tobacco juice at the ground and shook his head in disbelief. He pulled his tattered buffalo cape over his shoulders and led them to the group of men around their fallen comrade.

Chapter 44

"We've got way more meat than we can eat," Sam McCafferty said looking around the prairie. "I was hoping to get about four cows. Brown Eagle, do you know of any Native settlements near here that would take the meat?"

"I'm sure the Absaroka would be glad to have it this winter. They have an encampment on Boxwood Creek a day's ride west," Brown Eagle answered.

"Why don't you and Matthew ride over there an offer them eight of these animals," Sam suggested.

"I'll do that. We'll stop back at camp and get a bedroll and some grub," Brown Eagle replied. "Do you want me to send a wagon down to haul back what you butcher?"

"Good idea. Send the supply wagon and a couple men," Sam ordered.

"Where you want to bury Johnson?" an outrider called from the somber group around the mangled corpse.

"Send a couple of shovels back with the supply wagon," McCafferty called after the retreating figures.

"We'll bury him where he fell. If someone wants, they can make a marker. Here's my saddle rug. Wrap him up in this," Sam tossed the blanket to the nearest man.

"The rest of you follow me. We got to start skinning and butchering before the flies carry off our kill," McCafferty showed little compassion for his fallen rider. He knew loss of life or limb was the price paid for a careless moment in the wilderness.

One man stayed behind to wrap Johnson's remains in the blanket and carve his name and death date in a limestone rock. Since he found the rock fairly soft for carving, he added the words, "kilt whilst hunting buffalo."

Brown Eagle and Matthew reached camp as people were sitting down to their noon meal. A crowd gathered around the duo and the news was broadcast.

There were no ministers in the group but a short memorial service was planned. Johnson's two closest companions volunteered for the burial. They took the emptied army supply wagon, shovels, tarps to put over the buffalo meat, a clean sheet to wrap the body in and a bible and went to the scene of the accident.

Matthew and Brown Eagle packed a bag of dried meat, biscuits, water, and two bedrolls and headed out for the Boxwood Creek encampment.

They were still in the valley of the Platte River as they had been since leaving Fort Laramie. Perhaps because of his mining background, Matthew was interested in geology and the lay of the land. He noticed the gray granite hills, rounded on top by wind and weather that ran parallel to the river. The mountains in the background were approximately four thousand feet higher. They contrasted to the foothills by being extremely rugged and steep. In some places the cliffs were nearly perpendicular to the valley.

They crossed several small streams flowing from the recent rain. As the sun was setting the men came to a canyon with sheer red cliffs. They followed along the eastern side of the arroyo until it was too dark for sure footing. They had covered nearly eighteen miles since leaving camp.

Matthew built a fire and set up a lean-to of canvas while Brown Eagle tethered and stripped the horses of their gear. The animals were able to graze on the dry grass and had been watered at the creek.

Brown eagle propped his bedroll against his saddle and the two men ate in silence. They let the fire die down after coffee was made and settled back to listen to night sounds and look at the stars. In comfortable companionship the two soon drifted off to sleep.

Brown Eagle was up well before dawn and had a fire started. Left over coffee was reheated and biscuits consumed. They were back on the trail at first light. Five hours later they were met on the trail by four Crow braves. Brown Eagle knew the Hokan-Siouan language and was able to communicate with the young men. The Shoshone and white man were escorted to the village.

Along the way, Brown Eagle explained some history to Matthew. The Crow were now part of the Absaroka tribe. They used to be part of the Shoshone tribe called Hidatsa. A dispute caused the Crow to split off from their old nation and move west to the valley of the Yellowstone River. They were friendly toward whites in general although there had been a couple of unpleasant incidences, possibly instigated by the whites. The enemy of the Crow was the Sioux.

Once at the village, Brown Eagle spoke to the council of elders that was assembled tending other business. He explained that the white men had hoped to kill four buffalo for their meat supply. In the stampede twelve animals had gone down. The white leader invited the Absaroka people to share their good fortune.

A party of Absaroka men with portable travoises for carrying meat was soon on their way back through the valley with Brown Eagle and Matthew.

Matthew's winning ways soon earned him new friends among the braves. Brown Eagle interpreted and the men traded hunting stories and fish tales. Matthew told about his former job, which sounded unbelievable to the Natives. They never went underground because that was home to some of their early ancestors. The ancestors wouldn't appreciate the intrusion.

Matthew told of his river trip on the Ohio and Mississippi and the Indians told of trips they had made in their bullboats. The river rapids in the stories got bigger as the day wore on.

The afternoon and evening sped by as they journeyed. When they settled for a night's rest, one Crow suggested Matthew trade him food so they could try something new. Matthew agreed and dug out a couple of hard biscuits and some dried buffalo beef. The Crow laughed heartily when handed the food. He regained his composure and brought forth his dinner. He gave Matthew some hard flat bread and dried buffalo beef. The coffee with sugar was a treat to all of them. Since there were only two tin mugs, each man took a sip and passed the mug to the man sitting next to him. Two pots of coffee were consumed by the brotherhood.

The Indians spread out on the bare ground or straw mats to sleep. Matthew felt his wool bedroll was decadent and made no effort to set up the lean-to.

Brown Eagle was the first to arise in the morning and had a pot of coffee brewing by the time the others stirred. Breakfast was a duplicate of dinner and the party was enroute early.

When they arrived at the hunting ground they were met with a surprise. The camp had been moved to the area. All twelve buffalo were butchered. People were cutting the meat into strips and placing it on scaffolds. The skins had been rolled in salt but not cleaned due to the lack of time. It had been more important to get the meat preserved before it went bad in the late summer heat.

Emily hurried to Matthew's side, "I was so worried. We didn't know if the Natives were friendly or not. Also a soldier told Michael we're in grizzly country."

"Wow! Where's my gal that wanted new experiences every day?" Matthew grinned. "I had a grand time. We shared stories about hunting 'n fishing like I used to do with my brothers. The Absaroka are as friendly as the Coakleys."

"I sure don't butcher buffalo everyday," Emily replied with a smile on her blood smeared face. "That's my new experience for today. I'm glad to hear you had a nice vacation. Now get to work."

Emily still had problems with her arm because of the loss of strength. She had been cutting meat for a couple of hours and was ready for a break. She and Matthew retired to their wagon, washed and changed clothes. She dropped their soiled clothes in a pot of hot soapy water.

"I'm letting our clothes soak. Let's have a cup of coffee. I want to hear about the hunt and your trip," Emily suggested.

Neither wanted to eat in the presence of so much blood. They sat on the ground and rested against a wagon wheel while Matthew related the highlights of the previous two days.

"We all attended Johnson's burial," Emily said as a prelude to her report. "Dr. Jamison read some passages from a bible and his wife sang a hymn. One of Johnson's friends told us a bit about the man. It's a shame we didn't get to know him until he died. He was only twenty-two and sounded like a fine young man."

"Maybe we ought to start sharing dinner with different outriders so that we can get to know more about them," Matthew suggested.

"Good idea, Matt. Our next best friend might be riding with us and we don't know him yet."

"Huh?" Matt looked at her puzzled.

"Never mind," she laughed and slapped his knee. "We better get back to work. McCafferty wants all the meat drying or roasting by sunset."

"What a slave driver! Never a moment's rest," Matthew said forcing himself off the ground.

Chapter 45

The Absaroka used their obsidian scrapers to clean the buffalo skins. There was no meat or loose fuzz on the skins when they finished. One especially large bull skin was requested as a gift to their chief. The pioneers agreed and watched with fascination as the warriors cleaned the interior of the head. They then scraped, pounded and brushed the fur. When the men finished the skin could be used as a robe or costume with enough room for a man to put his head into the skull of the animal. The slightly opened mouth would be used for sight and breathing by the wearer.

Other skins were cleaned but the heads removed. These skins could be used as blankets, robes or carpets. Each of the hunters hoped he would be awarded a skin.

A campfire meeting was held where red and white men shared equal voting power. McCafferty conducted the meeting offering options for the distribution of the skins. Suggestions were accepted from the group. There were two men who had gotten skins from the earlier hunt. They abstained from the current distribution. That left eleven skins to be distributed among eighteen white men and thirteen red men. The hunters agreed that it was impossible to know if their shot was responsible for the death of a particular animal. A few buffalo had been killed in the stampede.

Some skins were in better condition than others. Some were larger. Some were thicker. The solution agreed upon was that each skin would be numbered one through eleven. Thirty-one slips of paper would be put in a hat. Each man drew out one slip. The numbered slips entitled the bearer to the skin with the corresponding number. Some slips had no numbers meaning the bearer didn't get a skin.

Marie, being the youngest person in camp, held the hat. The first drawing was the placement in line of the hunters. Numbers one through ten were drawn; Matthew was fifth in line. Then the numbers eleven through thirty-one were put in the hat and the balance of men drew for their spot in line. The men lined up and were ready for the skin lottery. There was a friendly atmosphere of jostling and joking.

Emily knew how valuable a heavy blanket would be in the winter ahead. She hoped to get one and felt selfish because of her desire. She felt the Jacksons would need the warmth for their children, or the outriders who slept on the ground.

Finally, the drawing for the skins started. McCafferty was first in line and drew a numbered slip. The cheering in the crowd drowned out the few hisses. He walked to the skins and picked up the tattered calfskin with the corresponding number of his slip of paper. There was laughter from Sam and his wife as well as a few others.

"Oh, well," Katie McCafferty laughed, "I hate to cut arm holes."

She wrapped the fur around herself and displayed two gaps in the sides where her arms could protrude. The other women cheered her good humor.

Sam said he would use it as a saddle blanket as his had been buried with the unlucky Johnson.

Brown Eagle was second in line. He drew a blank slip and Matthew, Emily and a few other people groaned disappointment. Some people held him responsible for Johnson's death, others didn't like Natives and most didn't know the man at all.

The next hunter drew a blank and groans were heard from his comrades. The fourth man pulled a numbered slip and performed a victory dance on his way to the skins. With a great dramatic gesture, he swung the prize in an arc up over his head and brought it down around his body as a full cape.

The audience cheered his bravado, clapped and whistled. Marie seeing all the attention the man received and aware her friend was next in line tried a dance of her own.

"Whooo, whooo. Mr. Kilkenny, yea, yea, yea!" she cheered as she twirled her body around holding the hat well above her head. Some of the pieces of paper blew out and were picked up by the breeze.

Marie was immediately embarrassed and clasped the hat to her chest. Her brothers caught the escaped papers and took them back to the child.

"I don't want to play anymore," she said pouting.

Mrs. Jackson coaxed the upset child to no avail; the men in line were growing impatient with the delay so Sam interceded.

"Okay, okay. Let's change hat holders. We'll go from the youngest person in camp to the oldest. That's probably me. Is anyone willing to admit being over forty-four?"

Everyone laughed. The grizzled outrider said he was a "mite bit" older but was smart enough to avoid volunteering. The tension was broken and Matthew stepped forward to draw from the stirred slips in the hat held by the wagon master.

Emily closed her eyes and said a little prayer. It was to no avail, Matthew drew a blank piece of paper from the hat. Emily let out a sigh but didn't know if it was from gratitude or disappointment. Groans and words of consolation were heard from onlookers. Matthew was becoming well known and appreciated among the pioneers.

The drawing went on and Matthew sat on the ground beside Emily and cheered for each winner or groaned for each loser. When the procedure was finished, four skins were taken by the Absaroka and eight by the wagon train. Hunters held four, probably the same number as animals actually killed by gunshot.

The visiting Crow Indians felt it was their responsibility to guard the drying meat from carnivores during the night. There were twelve scaffolds; one guard was posted at each.

Four fires were cooking roasts and stews to be shared over the next two or three days. Other fires were boiling water for bathing and laundry. People wandered to their own campsite to wash and rest from the bloodiest day of their journey.

Chapter 46

*T*he meat took two days and three nights to dry. Each night the Indians stood guard. In the morning they retreated to a wooded area on one of the knolls to sleep for a few hours.

When work was finished for the day, the men assembled for sporting competitions. There was spear throwing, archery, shooting, racing, weight lifting and wrestling. Matthew's upper body strength from years of mining made him the champion in the spear throwing for distance, the weight lifting and wrestling. Michael tied with an active soldier for first place in target shooting.

Emily was proud of Matthew though she felt the competitions were a bit silly and childish. She had no brothers of her own and her father rarely spoke of his youth. Her family was close to the Kilkennys but the boys had become men at an early age due to the death of their father. They went to work in the coal mines before becoming teenagers. They occasionally went hunting or fishing but she wasn't aware of contests they entered. She didn't say anything aloud as her young marriage had taught her men took their sporting abilities very seriously.

She spent her free time helping Hester Jackson make a blanket out of her newly acquired buffalo skin. They scraped and pounded the skin until it was pliant and smooth. They brushed the fur over and over until the loose bits were detached. The last step was to clean it with soap and water and let it blow dry in the afternoon breeze. That got rid of most of the gamey odor.

Brown Eagle introduced the pioneers to buffalo dung as fuel for campfires. Wood was going to be scarce in the near future and dung was plentiful at their current campsite. He recommended they store some dried patties for future use. The first evening dung was used it was discovered that it repelled the clouds of mosquitoes that had plagued the troop since the last rain.

Two Crow braves took a small group to search for wild onions, carrots and seasoning for buffalo stew. They found enough to flavor two pots of stew so everyone got a taste of the wild vegetables. They also found chokecherries, which were sugared and eaten for desert.

The morning of departure dawned bright and clear as usual in this high, dry prairie. The meat was divided and stored. Farewells were made and the settlers parted company from the Absaroka, both richer from the shared experience.

Now fully loaded with meat, the train headed into some of those silver crowned mountains Matthew had dreamed of seeing. He wasn't disappointed. The slow uphill grade had walkers panting. They noticed the difference in their breathing ability and the older folks tired quickly. The animals plodded onward and upward working up a sweat. South Pass was twenty to thirty miles wide at an elevation of eight thousand feet.

Matthew pointed out one remarkable sight after another.

"Look Em, the hills are black as coal!"

"Did you ever think we'd see so many beaver dams in one day?"

"September and the tops are white as an old man's head."

"Look at that waterfall; it must be a mile high!"

"You can't see the tops of the mountains for the clouds!"

Herds of pronghorn showed little concern with the train. They stopped munching on the bitter sagebrush long enough to show mild curiosity, then went back to work.

The scraggily bearded mountain man traveling with the train rode ahead with the scouts and set beaver traps. The following day he returned to the sites and retrieved his catch. He claimed beaver was good eating but only a few train members ate the fatty meat. The season wasn't right to get the beautiful thick pelts but any skins were usable when tanned properly. When he got sixteen furs, he gave up his project.

In the evening he told stories about "the good ole days" in the 1830s when he traveled with Ashley, Sublette, Clyman and Smith. They trapped beaver throughout the Rockies. He told of rendezvous when no children or ladies were within hearing range. Rendezvous were wild parties of heavy drinking, gambling, and womanizing with squaws. The mountain men had been out on their own all winter and they brought their pelts to rendezvous to trade for necessities to do it all again for another year.

The whole time he told his stories, he worked his skins. After a couple of weeks it became obvious he was making jackets. This was curious to the onlookers who watched him. The hunter wore grease stained buckskins from head to toe and had a winter coat made of buffalo hide.

His gruff exterior evidently hid a kind heart. When the project was complete, he presented the jackets to the Jackson and Jamison youngsters. He was embarrassed by the gratitude of the youngsters. They hugged him and thanked him for making them feel like real westerners.

"Shucks, dain't nothing. Everyone needs skins to wear out here. This'll get you started," he said quietly. "Hey, has anybody noticed where the cows are?"

Hester Jackson recognized his deliberate trick to detract attention from himself. "They are wandering further and further away looking for forage," she said. "There's been no rain since the torrent. We better get to grass soon."

The thirsty dry earth had soaked that water up in a matter of hours. Then it had returned to its natural state of dusty limestone soil. There were myriad streams and along their banks green grass and shrubs survived. There were even a few willow trees but nothing substantial for the animals to eat.

Matthew and four other men kept track of the livestock. The dogs enjoyed their daily romps over new terrain. They helped keep the cattle from straying up ravines or down canyons. They chased the deer for sport but the agile animals bounded out of range quickly. The dogs were becoming more cattle dogs than hunters.

The men discouraged their dogs from chasing black bears, which were seen regularly. The bears took flight, running and bawling into the high country. The worry was that the dogs would choose the wrong adversary. If they decided to have sport with a grizzly, it would not turn and run away.

Matthew was having the time of his life. He was awake before daylight and eager to experience another day. Emily enjoyed his enthusiasm as he related his day to her.

"Some of the mountains look like they just blew out of the volcano last week," he said. "Michael calls it vitrified, I call it glassy. Glassy mountains, just imagine. Wish my pa could of seen this place."

"Others are old, worn down smooth granite with thick dirt patches where the wind blew it against a barrier," he continued. "Did you notice how much colder the wind is getting? Winter's coming."

"I'm sure glad Uncle William gave us that nice warm sheepskin. It feels good at nighttime now. It'll be a life saver in another month," Emily remarked.

Matthew checked Emily's face to see if she meant she wished he had gotten a buffalo skin. He saw no sign of hidden meanings.

"If you get a chance, would you bag a couple of grouse?" Emily said one morning. "It would make a nice change from buffalo. I hear there are still a few about."

Matthew and the dogs left Emily cleaning up breakfast fixings. He cleared an opening behind their wagon so the lowing cattle could escape the circled wagons. Other men joined him and rode along behind the livestock, which headed for a nearby stream. They would clear out the vegetation before the train was on the move.

Matthew and Michael chopped up clumps of brush and carried it back to the dray animals. They dumped the dried plants in front of the hitched oxen and mules and returned to the stream for water.

"This water is so clear and clean compared to streams back east," Michael said. "If the train tarries for awhile, I think I'll do some fishing. Want to join me?"

"Nope. Not this morning. The hounds and me are going to scare up some grouse. Em's getting tired of buffalo. I'll get an extra bird for you, if you will catch a couple of trout for us."

"Deal," Michael replied. "Too bad Em's tired of buffalo, that will be our staple food for a month or so. When we drop down west of the ranges, we'll be in desert."

"Desert! I thought we'd have mountains most a the way now," Matthew was surprised at this new information. "Seems like McCafferty's not keeping us all told of what to expect."

"He's going to have a meeting when we get to Bridger and let the folks decide if they want to go south by the Salt Lake or north to Fort Hall," Michael reported.

"I'll start studying my maps. Right now I better go look for some birds," Matt grinned.

Wagon owners were gathering forage and water for the dray animals already yoked in place for the day's travel to begin. An outrider was circling the cattle keeping an eye open for snakes and carnivores. There was little problem keeping track of the cattle as long as they had green grass along the stream to eat.

Matthew and his dogs headed westward in search of a herd of prong-horn. Deer were the only animals beside grouse that would eat the bitter sage. Matthew felt if he found one, he would find the other. They had traveled less than two miles before Matt saw a herd of approximately twenty pronghorns.

He checked the direction of the wind and smiled when he realized it was blowing from the west. The deer wouldn't smell him coming. He dismounted and put the horse's reins under a rock to keep it in place. He commanded the dogs to "heel."

Ole Blue and Betsy fell in behind Matt and he approached the herd slowly staying behind boulders as much as possible. When he was fifty yards away, he could see the grouse pecking the ground around the legs of the pronghorn.

"Quiet dogs," he demanded and squeezed their muzzles gently.

Now the dogs knew a hunt was imminent and wagged their tails with joy. Blue let out a little "yip" of excitement. Betsy and Matthew both growled at him. He momentarily lowered his head in remorse but couldn't contain his excitement. He was right back in place ready for the next command from his master.

Matthew carefully felt his way along the glaciated rubble until he and the dogs were twenty yards away. He cocked his gun and stood to take aim. He chose a grouse slightly away from the deer. He didn't want to take a chance on wounding an ungulate. He gently squeezed the trigger.

The blast startled all the animals and they scrambled to escape. The dogs jumped from behind the rock and chased the pronghorn.

"You guys need more training," Matthew said as he walked over and picked up his downed bird.

The dog soon realized they couldn't catch the speedy pronghorn and turned to look for their master. They caught sight of Matthew walking back to his horse. They ran up to him and sniffed the bird in his hand.

Matthew tied the bird to his saddle and took a drink of water. He watched the deer to see where they would settle next. They stopped running within half a mile and went back to grazing. Once they felt secure in their new location, the birds joined them.

Matthew spotted a gully east of where the animals stopped. He walked his horse and dogs down the deepest part of the gully until he felt he was parallel to the herd. He tethered the horse once more and ordered the dogs to "stay." Blue whined in disappointment and Betsy nipped him on the nose.

Matthew crawled up the hill with his reloaded rifle. At the top he found the deer had moved his direction and were almost on top of him. He aimed at a nearby grouse.

"Blam!" the shot rang out.

Simultaneously both dogs were at his side.

"Fetch," he said quietly.

Ole Blue got to the fallen bird first and gently picked it up. Neither dog paid any attention to the bounding ruminants.

"Good dogs," Matt said scratching their ears. He let Ole Blue carry the prize back to the horse.

Matthew mounted his horse and headed for the cloud of dust that told him the train was underway.

Chapter 47

The train traveled south of the Wind River Range. The pioneers delighted in views of perpendicular cliffs and granite mountain peaks. As they came out of the range on the western side, they caught glimpses of the Uinta Mountains covered with snow. They were in awe of the splendor surrounding them. They crossed the parched soil in relative comfort as the days were cooler now and they weren't concerned with rain or mud.

The pioneers may have been more comfortable but their animals suffered from the lack of nourishing food. All that grew on the pass was sage, prairie thorn, and a few other stunted plants. The men went up river and down looking for food for the animals when they camped on the Big Sandy River. Very little was found. At least water was plentiful. They crossed four or five streams each day.

Emily made three meals from the fresh grouse. The second bird was traded to Michael for two Brown Trout. It was almost a week before they had to eat buffalo again.

"I wonder how long it will be before we have fresh fruit and vegetables again," Emily commented to Deborah.

"Probably not until we reach California or Oregon," Deborah replied as they walked side by side. "Have you thought anymore about my suggestion of looking at Beaver Valley in California?"

"Matthew has to pick the spot we live. This is his dream we're fulfilling."

"I know, but I'm just hoping you will look at the place before you settle down," Deborah had developed a fondness for her smart, strong willed friend.

Hester Jackson approached the younger women. "Are you going to work on the quilt this evening?" she asked.

"I'd like to," Emily replied. "Making quilts from our worn clothes seems like a useful skill to learn."

"Count me in," Deborah responded. "Michael's going fishing again. I won't see him 'til after dark."

"Good. I'll check with Katherine and Katie. Jesse Jamison already agreed to come," Hester said as she headed up the line of wagons.

"Your women's get together is popular. That was a good idea, Em," Deborah said.

"Look at all the good ideas we've shared? It's worked out great," Emily smiled. "Too bad the men don't do the same. They meet out of necessity or when ordered to by Sam."

"My mother used to braid scraps of material into rugs. I could teach that some time," Katherine said joining Deborah and Emily.

"Sounds good to me. None of us will be in any position to waste things for awhile—if ever," Deborah sighed.

"Now, now, think positive. We'll all be in the clover in a couple of years. Katherine with her rich husband, Michael will find tons of gold, and Matt will be a cattle baron before he's twenty-five," Emily said cheerily.

"I'm for that, Mrs. K." Matt said from inside their wagon.

"Hey, I thought you were asleep," Emily giggled.

"How's a man supposed to sleep with all that chatter going on outside," Matt said.

"Okay, we'll leave. Meet you at the Jackson's at seven o'clock," Deborah said.

Katherine followed Deborah's lead and dropped back beside her own wagon. Josiah Jamison, the doctor's son, was driving it. A short time later McCafferty called for the wagons to circle for the night. Emily climbed into her wagon to get her sewing equipment ready. Matthew was lying on the bed with his hands behind his head.

"So what's the story on Beaver Valley?" he asked.

"Deborah wants us to see the place she, Michael and Katherine will be living before we settle in," Emily answered.

"I got that part. What did she tell you about the place?"

"It's newly settled. Stephen Meek was the first white man in the valley in 1835. He was looking for beaver and found plenty there. A man named John Scott took a group of men over the mountains from Fort Read and found gold in 1851. He's got a river named after him for his trouble as well as finding a bit of the yellow rocks," Emily repeated what she'd heard.

"The gold rush at Sutter's lumber mill encouraged Hudson Bay Company and other merchants to put in a trail from the Willamette Valley to Sutter's Fort to haul supplies. The trail goes through a range called the Siskiyous. Beaver Valley is over those mountains, and then over another lower mountain beside the trail. The valley is completely surrounded by mountains. The grass grows well and is green most of the year. The old beaver ponds have been drained and the soil is rich for growing crops," Emily paused for breath.

"Sounds okay but don't sound no better than the Willamette. We'll look at both places. See where we can get the best land for our money," Matthew said holding up his arms for a hug.

"You sure you want to go quilt a blanket?" he asked wiggling his eyebrows suggestively.

Emily laughed, "You're supposed to be asleep. You have guard duty in just four hours. How do you expect women and children to sleep knowing we have a groggy guard on duty."

She lay on top of him and kissed his cheeks and mouth.

When she started to get up, he said, "You are getting to be a cold, cruel woman." He pulled her down for one more prolonged kiss before releasing her.

"We'll talk to Michael and Deborah tomorrow and see if we can find out more about that valley," Matthew rolled toward the canvas as Emily picked up her sewing kit.

"See you in the morning, my love," she whispered.

Emily sat down between Jesse Jamison and Deborah O'Brien. Six women sat around the edge of a tattered blanket. Each had a sewing basket and some scraps of material.

Most had worn the same two or three outfits day in and day out for the previous three months. They were worn out in some spots and still good in others.

Jesse Jamison and Hester Jackson had made makeshift shirts for their children from salvageable parts of their dresses combined with their husbands worn shirts. The material they donated to the quilt came from worn children's clothes.

Each woman cut her used clothes into pieces and shared them with the others. The odd shapes were put together to form squares. The quilt had started with a central square and four more squares added to the sides. None of the squares were the same size so artistic creativity came into play for the balance of the blanket. The hodgepodge was now approximately three feet by four feet in size. The goal was to get a finished quilt about six feet wide by eight feet long. Most of the beds inside the wagons were three to four feet wide and seven feet long. They would have a drawing to see who got the quilt when it was finished. In the meantime, it was used as an excuse to share gossip, ideas and camaraderie.

The younger Jackson children were settled into bed when Emily arrived. She peeked inside the wagon and blew Marie a kiss. The child responded with a duplicate gesture. Deborah taught the older children how to play pick up sticks and they had their own campfire near the center of the circle. That way, their giggles and chatter wouldn't bother men working or resting in the wagons or in their tents.

Emily struck up a conversation with Jesse, "My arm is getting stronger every day. If some medical problem arises, please tell Dr. Jamison I would be willing to assist."

"So far, we've been pretty lucky. He's treated some for sunburn, scrapes and bruises but that is about all since the Kaw attack. He could've used your help that day."

"Believe me, I wanted to help," Emily said.

"You're more brave than me. I tried to help with a birthing once and passed out," Jesse laughed. "Guess it was because I knew how much pain the poor woman was in."

"Could be. I know I have some fear of having children. Course I will, God willing, but I'm nervous about the delivery," Emily admitted. "Guess I must have helped Dr. Six with a couple dozen deliveries. None of the mothers looked like they were having fun."

"Ah, but the rewards are great," Hester chimed in.

"Most of the time," Jesse said. "There are days when I'd gladly give my boys to the nearest person that wanted them."

"Teenagers. Learning to be independent and still follow parents' rules isn't easy on parents or children," Katherine added. "At least you had the chance to know and love your children before they became troublesome."

Only Deborah understood Katherine's consternation about the family awaiting her arrival.

"Oh, yes. Most days I look at those young men and remember the pet snakes and frogs we've had in the house. Or think about the homemade gifts they've given me for Christmas," Jesse said. "Sometimes, when I'm feeling poorly, all it takes is a hug or a kind word of appreciation from one of them to lift my spirits."

"They're good boys," Emily said. "They work as hard as grown men. They hunt, fish, make repairs, chase stray cows."

"They're entertaining, too," Deborah added. "I love their unique ideas when I'm giving them lessons."

"Guess I'll keep them," Jesse chuckled.

"Well, until some pretty young thing catches their eye," Katie joined the conversation.

"Just as my son got old enough to carry on a decent conversation, he was spirited away by the love bug," she said. "Don't get me wrong. My daughter-in-law is a sweet, pious girl. I just wish she hadn't come along for a couple more years."

"How old was your son when he married?" asked Deborah.

"Twenty-four," Katie McCafferty responded.

Emily looked at Deborah in surprise. No one said what was on her mind. The needles and thread went in and out of multicolored material; arms went up and down and work progressed.

"How does your daughter like the blanket we knitted?" Katherine asked Hester in reference to the last completed project.

"She loves it! That reminds me of a point I wanted to bring up," Hester said. "I'm not going to be in the drawing for the quilt. I feel our family is receiving too much from the train members."

"See, it pays to have cute little tykes," Deborah smiled.

"We have the coats from the mountain man, the doll from you and Michael, the buffalo hide and the knitted blanket. That's enough. It's not fair for us to receive any more gifts."

"Michael and I wanted to give Marie the doll. We adore her," Deborah said in surprise.

"Everyone had an equal chance to get a buffalo skin," Emily added.

"The old man wanted to show off his ability when he caught the beaver and made the jackets," Jesse said. "My kids got coats, too."

"Well, I was glad that Rebecca got the blanket after Marie got the doll, but still fair is fair. Our family won't be in the drawing," Hester said with a stubborn look on her face.

"We should have the quilt finished in a couple of weeks, if we keep going. Good thing Sam kept those feathers from the ducks the men killed awhile back. They'll make good ticking," Katie McCafferty said.

"I have a bolt of muslin. We can use that for the under covering," Emily added.

"Katherine, was there enough canvas left from your disaster to make something? A canvas coat would keep the rain and snow off someone," Hester asked.

"It was all used to make repairs on other wagons," Katherine said. "When I get to Beaver Valley, I'll donate the new canvas to someone traveling further. I won't need it."

"Beaver Valley, how on earth did you pick that place to stop?" Katie asked.

"Why do you say that? Do you know something bad about the place?" Katherine hedged.

"No, never been there. Don't know anything about it. Where is it anyhow?" Katie asked.

"Near Klamath Lake in Oregon," Katherine answered trying to think of a way to change the subject.

"That's wild country. Hope you have a big strong gold miner waiting for you there," Katie said.

"Yeah, one that has already found a mother lode," Hester added.

"What's a mother lode?" Jesse asked.

"Why that's what's right in the middle of the claim I'm going to file," Michael said walking up to the group.

"Hello, sweetie, are we having fish for breakfast?" Deborah asked.

"Yep. I've got four. I came down to see if you wanted to keep them all or give away a couple," Michael said.

"There isn't enough to share with everyone so we'll keep them," Deborah said embarrassed, as she was sure some of the ladies would have enjoyed a change from their buffalo diet. "I'll leave you ladies now. See you in the morning."

"I'd better get my youngsters in bed," Hester said and started gathering up her work.

"Me, too," agreed Jesse.

The sewing circle broke up to Katherine's relief. She vowed to watch what she said more closely. She didn't want to be teased about marrying a stranger.

Chapter 48

The troop followed the Green River, known as the Seetskadee to the Indians. It was nearly one hundred yards wide and a yard deep in most places. It ran through a parched land with nothing but scraggily cottonwoods along its banks.

The train crossed the river and followed its valley about six miles then turned south and went onward to Blacks Fork Creek. They followed Blacks Fork over granite gravel and made almost thirty miles for the day. That was one of the longest rides covered in one day. The foot sore walkers were glad to cool off in the river after drinking water was removed. The water was noticeably cooler than their last bath.

"The warm days are melting the early snow fall on the peaks," Sam remarked. "The nights are cooler because we're at a higher elevation. It all adds up to cold bath water."

"Right now I'm more concerned with food for my livestock," Matthew said. "We've been lucky to have water most of the way. When're we getting to good grass again?"

"Tomorrow with any luck," Sam replied. "Once we cross Hams Fork, we should start seeing grass."

"None too soon. My cattle are getting so weak, they don't want to walk," Elijah Jackson said.

"We can stop there tomorrow and let the livestock get a good feed," Sam said. "But we're only two days out of Fort Bridger, if we keep 'em moving."

"Maybe the outriders want to hurry on to the fort. Those of us with livestock could stay behind an extra day," Elijah suggested.

"I don't like to split up. It makes us more vulnerable to Indian attack," Sam said. "We'll talk it over and take a vote after supper."

"Sounds fair, I'll spread the word," Elijah said.

Sam turned to Brown Eagle, "Would you and another scout head out at first light and make sure I'm not lying? Don't want the folks tearing my hide off if there's no grass in the valley."

"Sure. We'll check it out. You'll be underway before we can report back. Better hope for the best," the Shoshone replied.

The sound of hoof beats as the scouts left camp at four a.m. woke up Matthew. He couldn't get back to sleep so slipped out of the wagon quietly with his fishing tackle in hand. As soon as his feet hit the ground, his dogs were beside him. The sentries had a small campfire going and a pot of coffee sitting beside it. Matthew picked up his mug and headed that way.

He roused a neighbor's dog who growled a quiet warning, "It's just me, Fred. It's okay, go back to sleep boy."

The dog made no more noise and Matthew walked over to the campfire unimpeded. He saw no sentries nearby and assumed they were on patrol. He helped himself to a cup of coffee and sat down beside the fire. The dogs lay down beside him.

As soon as the sky was light enough for him to walk the unfamiliar ground safely, he arose. The sentries approached on horseback, arriving from different directions.

"Morning men. Hope you don't mind, I helped myself to your coffee," Matthew greeted them.

"Did you leave us a cup?" one young soldier asked.

"Yep. Pot's half full," Matthew answered.

"That's all right then," the boy said.

"If I get a mess of fish, I'll have my wife fry us up some fish and potatoes for breakfast," Matthew added as he went toward the stream.

"We get off duty at seven. We'll take you up on the offer," the second soldier said. "Watch out for rattlesnakes. It's time for them to be getting their morning drink. They don't take kindly to intruders."

"Rattlesnakes, eh. Do they look like the ones in the hills of southern Ohio?" Matthew asked.

"Don't know, never been to Ohio. These fellers got diamonds on their backs and a rattle on their tail. They coil up and then spring at you."

"They good eating?" Matthew asked.

"I ain't that hungry. Your Indian friend might want one with his beans when he gets back from scouting," the younger soldier said.

Matthew knew the sentries were aware of people coming to and going from the camp. He went off to the river, the dogs ran in front of him and assumed they were meant to play in the water. They ran into the stream barking and jumping about. They swam to the far side, chased each other on the shore for awhile and then splashed back to Matthew. Ole Blue ran up to the man shaking water as he came. He expected to receive praise and affection but didn't get any.

"So much for catching fish. They are probably in the next country after all your splashing about," Matthew said.

He picked up a piece of cottonwood and threw it into the water. Both dogs raced toward the floating stick.

Matthew sat on the bank and watched them frolic. Thirty minutes later, the dogs were worn out and ready to rest. Matt heard people moving about in camp, picked up his unused rod and returned to his wagon.

Emily was making coffee, "Ah, do we have fish for breakfast or beans and buffalo?"

"How about some hound dog 'n beans?" he smiled. "Darn dogs scared the fish clean back to the Mississippi with all their thrashing about."

He kissed Emily's hair then her neck. "You smell mighty nice. Did you wash up with Jerome's soap?"

"Yes, it's a special occasion so I treated myself," she said.

"What's the occasion?" Matthew asked.

"My birthday. I'm nineteen years old today," Emily grinned. "Forgot didn't you?"

"Sorry, Em. I don't know what day of the week it is, let alone what date," Matthew said turning Emily around for a hug and proper kiss. "Happy birthday, honey."

"When you newlyweds get finished greeting the day, would you join Katie and me?" Sam asked.

"Yep. We could do that," Matthew said. "What's wrong?"

"Not much," Sam said walking away.

Matthew went inside their wagon, washed up and put on a clean shirt.

He and Emily walked hand in hand to Sam and Katie McCafferty's wagon.

"Something sure smells good—like real bacon instead of salt pork," Emily said.

Katie laid down the spatula she was holding and hugged Emily, "Happy birthday Mrs. Kilkenny. Won't you join us for breakfast?"

Emily was surprised. She had no idea Katie kept a record of all the train members' birthdays. She and Sam invited each person to share a meal with them on their birthday.

Katie had fixed bacon, pancakes with strawberry preserves, canned peaches, and coffee. The board used as a table had calico on it and sprigs of cottonwood in a glass jar of water. Emily ate slowly letting each spoonful of peaches sit in her mouth for few seconds before chewing and swallowing.

"I want to savor every bite. How did you know I was longing for fruit?" Emily asked.

"Just about everyone is," Katie laughed. "Sam wanted me to leave my canned goods beside the road when we were in the boggy area. I wouldn't do it."

"Contrary woman. She's supposed to set an example for others. She won't mind me either," Sam said rocking back on his barrel with a toothpick in his hand.

"The meal was delicious. Thank you very much," Emily said. "I'll help you clean up. Don't want your husband grousing on you for taking too long."

The wagon train was underway thirty minutes later. Emily rode in the wagon with Marie and Rebecca Jackson. They took turns holding Marie's doll wrapped in Rebecca's knitted blanket. Emily taught the girls a lullaby to sing to the doll.

Matthew rode up beside his wagon and saw the homey scene. "Mrs. Kilkenny, what you think of raising a houseful of little girls when we get settled?"

"I think that's a fine idea, Mr. Kilkenny," Emily smiled at her beloved.

Chapter 48

rown Eagle, acting as scout for the wagon train, returned with the news that the valley beyond Hams Fork was knee deep in grass. Sam passed the word that the train would spend a down day there tomorrow. When they arrived, camp was set up and the cattle, horses, mules, and oxen were set free to graze. It was shortly after noon so they had a day and a half to fill their bellies.

"Our cows are looking mighty puny. We'd have to stay here a week to get them in good condition," Matthew said.

"Do you think any will die?" Emily asked concerned.

"Maybe, can't say. They are wobbly for dang sure," Matthew replied. "Since we stopped early, did you want to do something special for your birthday? Like take a swim?"

"Let's walk upstream and see if we can find a pool with no hazards."

They walked along the shore. Matthew told her to watch for rattlers sunning themselves on the rocks. She jumped back thinking he had seen one. He laughed at her and explained that he meant "when walking in general." No snakes were seen. They went about a mile and didn't find an acceptable place for a good dip. The water was too shallow, there were too many weeds, or the site was too public. Something was wrong with each site Matthew suggested. They headed back to their wagon.

Emily saw something shiny on the ground a short distance from their path. It was an anthill filled with tiny pieces of broken glass and beads. She picked beads out of the sand pile until she had about twenty. She grew tired of brushing off the ants, which fought to retain their personal treasure. She later asked Brown Eagle if they were Indian beads. He confirmed her suspicions.

Natives traded white men animal skins for glass beads then decorated hides with beads. A women's group must have been sitting near the river working on skins and dropped beads. The ants found them and carried them home.

She picked flowers as they walked and Matthew pulled up tubers he thought looked similar to ones the Crow Indians had shown them. He planned on asking Brown Eagle if they were edible before tossing them in the evening stew.

Neither noticed the buildup of clouds and they were a quarter mile from camp when the rain started.

"Looks like I'm getting a bath for my birthday after all," Emily said as she started walking faster.

The ground was uneven and rocky so they made no attempt to run. Their clothes were soaked through by the time they reached their wagon.

"Brrr. What a cold rain!" Emily said stripping off her dress. "I'm shaking all over. Bet the river is cold too. Just as well we didn't jump in."

The rain was short lived. When the clouds blew away, a new dusting of snow was seen on the Uinta peaks.

"Wow! I do love mountains? Aren't they the purtiest things you ever seen?" Matthew exclaimed.

"They are beautiful. I hope we don't have to climb them to get to Oregon," Emily answered.

"Sam is supposed to have a meeting when we get to Bridger. He wants to find out, do we want to go north along the Snake River which is the short way to Willamette. Or should we go south through the desert below the Salt Lake and into Sacramento Valley then north to Oregon," Matthew told Emily.

"What does that mean? Is one way mountains and the other desert? Have you studied the mountain man's maps? Would it be safer to go south? What about Indian attacks?" Emily queried.

"I studied Lewis 'n Clark's maps. I want to go north. I'm in a hurry to get there," Matthew answered. "I figure north cuts off a month's worth of travel. We'll see. I won't put you in danger of freezing. If the weather holds, I want to keep moving toward Oregon," Matthew had made up his mind. Now he hoped the majority of train travelers voted his way.

The down day was spent as usual with hunters and fishermen looking for variety for their diet, women did laundry, children played with the dogs or in the edge of the water. Wheels were removed from wagons and axles greased, spokes replaced if need be, leather was mended. The livestock luxuriated in tall grass. Men cut grass to carry with them for the lean days ahead.

The following day the troop arrived at Fort Bridger, a minor fort mainly for trading with the Shoshone and Ute nations. Natives and unkempt white men greeted the wagons with their wares. There was livestock available at the fort; some worn out mules were traded for fresh ones. Katherine got new canvas for her wagon much to Michael and Deborah's delight. A bit of horse-trading went on though the Indian ponies didn't appear tame. Things made of leather were available and pioneers loaded up. Every buckskin dress and shirt was bought. Moccasins with fur linings and tops reaching the knees went quickly, and buffalo skin blankets were snatched up.

Emily and Matthew went shopping individually without the other's knowledge. Matthew traded a keg of brandy for a buffalo blanket and a new outfit for Emily. Emily traded a small bottle of laudanum, a bottle of horse lineament and a roll of gauze for a heavy winter jacket and knee-high moccasins for Matthew. They approached Deborah and Michael at separate times and asked the newlyweds to hide their purchases. Matthew put the buffalo blanket in his own wagon as it was too bulky to hide.

Jim Bridger and Louis Vasquez had recently sold the trading post to Mormons. The Latter Day Saints planned on stocking it for family trade. They had acquired a few vegetables from Indians that were farming in the fertile valley. That evening the regular fare of beans and buffalo was flavored with carrots and onions; bread was made with fresh flour and coffee beans were added to chicory.

Michael played his harmonica and by the time he was on his third song, a fiddler from the fort joined him. Women donned new buckskins and moccasins. Emily wore her Paducah Sunday-go-to-meeting dress. She piled her hair on top of her head and held it there with pins borrowed from Katherine. She was a feast for the eyes of the beaver and buffalo hunters.

Matthew noticed the men looking longingly at his wife and stood close to her side. One of the cleaner looking men asked her to dance and she politely declined saying she was recovering from a trail injury. Matthew breathed a sigh of relief.

"I can see you are the belle-of-the-ball. I was afeared you'd be passed around dancing all night and I wouldn't get a chance to hold you in my arms," Matthew whispered.

"Now that I've admitted to being a cripple, we don't dare dance. You'll have to figure out another way to get your arms around me," she whispered back.

Matthew's only response was heightened color creeping up his neck and across his cheeks.

"You look like you just swallowed a canary, Matthew. Am I intruding?" Deborah asked.

"No, you're just in time. I was looking for a dance partner for Matthew. I don't feel like dancing this evening," Emily gave Matthew a little shove toward the dance area.

"I'm sorry Deb. My wife's teasing, I don't feel like dancing tonight, neither," Matthew said stepping back to put his arm around his wife.

Michael walked up with an anxious look on his face, "Brown Eagle just told me that Joe Yellowtop told him that Everett said you're feeling poorly, Emily. Are you okay? Is your arm bothering you?"

"Oh my goodness! Michael go play your music. Nothing's wrong that won't be cured in the morning. Matthew dance with Deborah. I'm going to sit in my rocker and enjoy all this attention," Emily laughed.

Emily turned toward their wagon to get her rocker and saw Katie and Sam coming toward her with concern written all over their faces.

"Are you all right?" Katie asked. "We just learned you were injured. Did you fall down in the rain yesterday?"

Sam took her elbow to help her back to her wagon. "Do you need to lie down?" he asked.

Emily had a hard time keeping a straight face. "Sam would you please bring my rocker over here. I'll be all right tomorrow."

"Sure, no problem," the wagon master said. He put Katie's hand under Emily's elbow to make sure she didn't fall while he was gone.

Katie put her arm around Emily's waist to support her.

Emily whispered into Katie's ear, "I'm just suffering from a jealous husband who's afraid of all those love starved men devouring his wife."

"Well, I can understand that. You look pretty as a rose," Katie replied.

Sam returned within two minutes and had the rocker and one of Katie's shawls. He helped settle Emily into the chair and asked Katie to "wrap her up."

"Maybe it would help if I threw the shawl over your head," Katie intimated.

Instead, she put it over Emily's knees and tucked her in like an aging cripple.

A look of relief crossed Matthew's face when he saw Katie and Sam standing guard over his bewitching wife.

All the women except Emily danced with several different partners. Katherine was the most popular when it was learned she was single. Men danced jigs with other men and no one thought they looked strange. There simply weren't enough women to go around.

As the party broke up, Sam let it be known there would be a meeting at his wagon at 6:30 a.m. He had told several people during the previous week what the meeting would be about. Word had spread to all wagons and every outrider. Each man had a chance to consider his options.

Matthew spent a restless night thinking about the morning meeting. He wished he had done more campaigning for the northern route. Emily got very little sleep because of Matthew's movement in the small bed. They were both groggy and edgy when they got up before dawn.

Matthew checked the animals by lantern light and found them contentedly lying on the grassy plain. Emily fixed breakfast and lunch, bathed and dressed in her Fort Louisville buckskin dress and moccasins. She stuffed new pieces of canvas into her moccasins, which had worn through on the soles. She regretted not getting new shoes. They were sold out by the time she'd finished trading for Matthew's surprise. She smiled when she thought of how delighted he would be with the practical presents.

Matthew returned from the pasture and poured himself a cup of coffee. He stood beside her not saying anything, just staring into the camp fire.

"You seem distracted this morning. What's on your mind? Why were you so restless last night?" she asked.

"I'm worried about this morning's vote. If we got to go south, I think we'll lose the cattle to the desert," he said.

Matthew had no reason for concern. The meeting took less than fifteen minutes. Sam explained the options, voiced his preference and took a vote. Two thirds of the people chose the northern route. Sam bowed to majority rule.

The wagons rolled by eight o'clock. There were a few more outriders as mountain men joined the group. Gold in California and Oregon sounded more promising than beaver or buffalo skins from the Wind River or Uinta ranges.

The trip between Fort Bridger and Fort Hall on the Snake River was almost completely devoid of forage. The cattle and horses suffered from lack of food. They ignored the bits of dried sage and were sustained on grass gathered by wise travelers at Fort Bridger, cottonwood leaves, or what little oats were left. Drinking water was plentiful in the area between the Green River and Bear River. Streams flowed into the gravelly valley from mountain snow run off. Occasional stands of cedar trees were found and fire wood gathered.

Buffalo had not been seen for several days. A few lucky hunters supplemented their larder with grouse or rabbits. Matthew and his dogs brought in a pair of rabbits one day. He and Emily were becoming good at tanning furs and turned the skins into mittens for the impending winter.

The third day out from Fort Bridger the train followed a ravine up the east side of a valley and found fine groves of aspen trees. Their leaves were golden and fluttered in the steady breeze. The ground was steep and required constant attention so the travelers were unable to do much sightseeing. There was some stunted grass browning under the autumn colored trees.

At the end of the day, the pioneers were rewarded with fine camping facilities in a broad grassy valley on the Bear River. They had steep volcanic debris on two sides of the camp but the valley itself was a perfect place for grazing. Matthew walked to the McCafferty wagon to ask for a two-day lay over for the animal's sake.

"I feel like a dinosaur might come strolling by any minute," he said opening the conversation. "Don't you feel like we've walked back in time?"

"It's something different. That's for sure," Sam responded admiring the vitrified mountain slopes.

They discussed geology for a few minutes before Matthew brought up his request. Sam rejected the idea of staying over an extra day saying they needed to keep moving to get across or around the Cascade mountain range before winter snowfall.

Matthew returned to his wagon still admiring his surroundings. He repeated the dinosaur theory to Emily.

"I hadn't thought of it that way. It's sure different than Ohio," she said. "I've never seen black boulders on black gravel that wasn't coal. These rocks look like sea shells when you break them open."

"What you talking about? How could a rock look like shell?" Matthew asked.

Emily broke a round rock and showed Matthew the conchoidal marks on the inside. "It looks like a glass shell."

The night was cold at this elevation and people retired to huddle under blankets or buffalo robes as soon as dinner was cleared away. Matthew presented the buffalo blanket to a delighted Emily. Matthew was glad they had it. They slept warmly with the sheepskin on the bottom and the buffalo over top.

The result of the early retirement was that they were awake before dawn. The troop was ready to roll as soon as it was light enough to pick out a trail.

A week out of Fort Bridger the train arrived at Soda Springs where hunters from Fort Hall greeted them. The men had killed some deer and elk and were drying the meat. People got acquainted and gleaned information from each other.

Water bubbled from the ground. Around the springs and geysers the ground was salt covered clay. Emily drank from the cup of water offered her by a new acquaintance. The strong soda content took her breath away. She gasped and coughed until she could breathe normally again. The hunter told her people took the water in barrels on the trail and found it beneficial for gastric distress. She had Matthew fill a water barrel with the liquid.

Another hunter showed Michael and Deborah a hot spring. The water boiled out of the ground too hot to touch but it ran into a cold stream a short distance away and the water was perfect temperature for bathing. The balance of the afternoon and evening was spent there. Makeshift tarps were erected and the women and children scrubbed each other's scalps and backs in privacy. Cares of the trail floated downstream with the rinse water and spirits were high. The men eagerly awaited their turn at the bath water. Razors were brought out and two-week old beards removed. Lice inhabited scalps were scrubbed and some bodies washed fully clothed. Men didn't like to do laundry.

"Saves one step," said the mountain man as he climbed from the pool dripping in his wet buckskins.

Ropes were strung between wagons and laundry hung. Outriders scrubbed their bedding that was infested with lice and ticks and they took advantage of the free flowing hot water to clean everything they could.

"Did you notice how soft the water felt?" Matthew asked Emily. "You don't need soap to feel clean. We could sell this stuff back home. My ma would love it."

This was the first time Matthew had mentioned his family in a month's time. Emily wondered if he too was homesick. All the wonders in the world hadn't alleviated Emily's desire to see and talk to her family and in-laws.

Chapter 49

It was another three days of fatiguing travel over cinders and chasms of volcanic rock before the party came to the broad verdant valley of the Snake River. The valley was crisscrossed with cold, fast moving streams. Matthew and Michael joined other men on fishing expeditions, large trout were caught in abundance, and many were smoked and dried for future use.

Women searched for wild vegetables and found it was too late in the season to find anything useable except gourds. Brown Eagle declared them edible and a pumpkin-like soup was made. A few of the gourds with thicker skins were taken to be dried and used as storage vessels.

About suppertime the train's scouts returned from a visit to Fort Hall. They brought good news of a well-stocked supply station. There were fresh horses and cattle for anyone who wanted an exchange. Flour, wheat, rice and beans were available as well as a limited supply of potatoes. The potatoes were grown locally and were of exceptional quality.

By noon the following day the white washed walls of Fort Hall came into view. They stood out starkly against the rocky brown and black background of the Wind River Range.

Emily told Matthew, "I want to get to the fort early to get some new moccasins before they are sold out. I'm not comfortable in the worn, leather, boy's shoes from Athens and my moccasins are no longer useable."

Matthew confessed, "I bought you a new buckskin outfit including moccasins at Fort Bridger. I've been keeping it in Deborah's care in case you had a spell of depression due to the hardships of climbing the ranges."

Emily laughed and said, "Deborah is hiding a surprise for you also. And for the same reason."

"There's just too much to see and do to take time out for depression," Emily said. "I do miss my family, but I also enjoy the new friendships we've shared and am fascinated with the landscape. Some of it is hard walking, for sure, and I feel sorry for the dray animals, but all-in-all, it has been the experience of a lifetime."

Sam McCafferty walked out of Fort Hall with a knowing smile on his face. He had a pleasant surprise for some members of his train—mail. Sam approached Matthew.

"Say there Matt, you interested in reading some news from Mr. and Mrs. Caleb Fitzgerald or John Kilkenny?"

"Missus Caleb Fitzgerald! I'm right curious who that might be. Caleb is an old bachelor friend of my pa," Matthew responded with surprise.

"Emily! Em, we got mail," he shouted at Emily who was putting on her new clothes in Deborah's wagon.

She stuck her head out the front opening, "From whom? I hope it isn't a bill," she laughed.

"Come see. We got two letters," Matthew said walking toward her. "You open one, I'll open the other."

Emily jumped down from the wagon bare footed and instantly regretted it. "Ouch! That gravel is sharp as glass."

"It is glass according to Sam, volcano baked glass," Matt said.

She traded Matthew a buffalo-skin jacket for the letter.

"Nice jacket, honey. Thanks. That'll be perfect the next couple a months on the trail and the next few winters at our homestead," Matthew said putting on his new coat.

Emily was already opening the letter from Mr. and Mrs. Caleb Fitzgerald. Matthew opened John's letter and said, "Son of a gun!"

When he looked up he saw that Emily had blanched white. He knew why. Emily finished her letter first and stood looking at Matthew with her mouth open. Matthew chuckled a nervous little laugh. Then he burst out with a joyous whoop, grabbed Emily and swung her off the ground.

"Do you want to trade letters or talk about what we've read?" Emily asked.

"Trade letters first" he answered.

They did that. Emily read a few seconds and exclaimed, "Oh, my gosh! Matthew! Matthew!"

"Quick, Deborah, toss me some moccasins. I want to dance!" Emily shouted louder than was necessary for her friend to hear her through the canvas wall.

Michael walked up to the wagon with the dogs on his heels, "What's all the commotion?"

"My ma got married!" Matthew said.

"And they're coming to Oregon!" Emily added.

Emily and Matthew were both talking at once. Deborah alighted from the wagon with shoes in hand and gave them to the gesticulating girl.

"Oh, Matthew, congratulations! That's wonderful!" Deborah said. "When will they arrive?"

"Their booked on a steamship leaving Philadelphia the first of March. They'll be in San Francisco by June," he announced.

Emily had donned her moccasins and was dancing around Matthew, "Oh, Matt! We'll be a family again."

"With three extra men and a woman, I got to get us a big farm," Matthew said.

"Whoa! You're mom's marrying three men? Wow! Ohio has some strange laws I didn't know about," Deborah said.

Matthew calmed down enough to speak logically. "Ma married a family friend, Caleb. He came to America with my pa years ago. They are coming west with my two brothers, John and Luke."

"I'm so glad you're brothers are getting out of the mines," Emily hugged Matthew.

"I'm sure happy we came the north trail. I might not have gotten these letters if we went south from Bridger."

"We have to write to them. We'll leave the letter here for delivery back east. Hopefully they'll receive it by Christmas," Emily was too keyed-up to stand still.

Matthew and Emily spent the balance of the day in a state of excitement. They did have presence of mind to replenish supplies. They were able to get twenty pounds of potatoes and ten pounds of onions. They looked at the fort's supply of livestock fattened on the valley of grass but decided to keep the younger ones they brought west with them.

Their cattle, oxen, and horse were thin but muscular; they knew they were free from disease. If they traded for the fat stock, they would have an unknown element. Perhaps the new cattle had been left at the fort because they were diseased.

Fort Hall had chickens for sale also. Matthew bought a couple to cook and eat. No one suggested taking any on the trail.

The Kilkennys, O'Briens and the McCafferty's shared a dinner of fried chicken, mashed potatoes and gravy, canned green beans, and canned peaches along with a bottle of Paugh wine. They called it a wedding celebration and discussed Caleb as a new member of the family.

"We'll have music in the house!" Emily cried. "Caleb's a wonderful singer and Lydia plays the violin."

"Don't know how I'll take to it, if he threatens to strap me," Matthew said with mock seriousness. "I'm bigger than my new pa."

Matthew told the others of his youth when Ian, his father, and Caleb had taken the Kilkenny boys fishing or hunting. Ian had died when Matthew was only four so most memories of his father were limited to stories he'd heard from his mother, brothers and Caleb. One exception to that was when Ian read aloud the adventures of Lewis and Clark. As a toddler, Matthew requested his father read that book over and over. His father's enthusiasm for the explorers was transferred to Matthew early in life.

Caleb had been moral support for Matthew's mother and a male influence on her sons after Ian died in a mine accident. They all liked and respected the man. He'd be a welcome addition to the family.

John and Luke were twenty-two and twenty-four years old respectively and would be able to help establish a Kilkenny homestead for future generations. Matthew's plans expanded by the hour that day. He had no idea whether his brothers were interested in farming but that didn't deter his dreams.

Emily liked the idea of having grandparents for her children. She wanted her little ones to know the love of a large family. She had grown up without grandparents and envied her schoolmates that spoke of being spoiled by granny's attention.

A thought crossed her mind—how lonely her own mother would be without the support of Lydia. Emily had a sudden flush of guilt for reveling in the thought that Lydia was coming to live with them. It was momentary. She was soon back to planning matching rockers, rooms for John and Luke, and how big a kitchen they would need.

Sam told Matthew about the Donation Land Claim Act of September 1850. Matthew was entitled to three hundred twenty acres of land in Oregon as a married man, so was Caleb. John and Luke would be entitled to one hundred sixty acres each. That was a sizeable chunk of land to establish. He also told him about Willamette Cattle Company where cows were sold for eight dollars apiece. Matthew could buy good starter stock. Fort Ross, on the California coast sold horses, pigs and chickens. All it took to become a land baron was money and hard work.

"Well, we can do the hard work part. The men, all being miners, are bringing muscles to the west," Matthew settled back against his wagon wheel content in his dreams.

Chapter 50

Two days later two outriders plus the two single men traveling in a wagon separated from the group and headed south toward the Humboldt River. They planned on following that route to the gold fields in the Sierra Nevada Mountains east of Sutter's Fort. They had hired a scout at Fort Hall. The parting was amiable with good wishes for all.

Michael, Deborah and Katherine had to make a decision about which party to join. The distance to Beaver Valley was about equal so, after a lengthy discussion, they chose to stay with the known leader.

"I'm glad you're going the northern route," Emily told Deborah and Katherine. "Matthew's talking of traveling straight through to Willamette. I'm afraid we're going to be caught in winter weather."

"Sam said we probably wouldn't have to worry about that for another month. His main concern is forage for the animals," Katherine said.

"Our next fort is Boise and that's about two weeks away," Deborah said. "We can decide then whether to go on. It should be safe, weather wise, for two weeks.

The three women walked beside the Kilkenny wagon. The trail was hard on the feet of humans and animals alike. The valley of the Snake River was littered with sharp obsidian. The lava had seeped up through great chasms in the earth's mantle rather than being the result from a cataclysmic explosion.

When she saw the roughness of the trail ahead, Emily traded her moccasins and buckskin dress for one of Matthew's old shirts and the worn boy's boots. Deborah wore a pair of Michael's army pants with the legs rolled up to fit her shorter legs, but had no shoes fit for such a trail so made do with her leather lady's shoes.

Katie McCafferty was the only person who commented aloud about the ladies wearing men's clothes. "Wish I had your gumption girls. I envy you wearing those trousers. My legs are bleeding almost to my knees from prickly sage."

"Wrap your legs in a couple of those tanned rabbit skins Sam made," Katherine suggested.

"I'll do that! Why didn't I think of that?"

Michael walked by leading his horse.

"How's your arm coming along?" he asked when he saw Emily doing her stretching exercises as she walked.

"I'm pleased with the progress. My goal is to be back to normal strength when we reach Fort Vancouver," Emily replied.

"Seems like you're doing more chores all the time," Michael said. "I thought you were back to full health now."

"Not quite. I notice the strain when I lift a pail of water or full pot of coffee. Sure glad the lady in Paducah gave me the bean bags to squeeze," Emily said. "I would never have thought of something so simple to strengthen muscles."

Michael rode away from the ladies and joined Matthew at the head of the column. Riders were coming toward the train. They were still quite a distance away but Sam and the soldiers were preparing for an unpleasant encounter.

"You ladies get in your wagons. Keep the wagons close together. Make sure your guns are loaded and within reach," a soldier told the trio.

Men brought the cattle in close to the train and tied loose horses to the wagons. Matthew jumped on the back of his wagon and tethered his horse. He joined Emily on the seat.

"Brown Eagle says he thinks they're Nez Perce," he commented as he put his rifle in the rack in front of his knees.

"Friendly, but they'll steal horses if given the chance. We don't want another Kaw adventure," he continued.

"This ground is too rough to speed up. We couldn't make a run for it. Our animals are getting damaged hooves now," Emily noted. "Why don't we circle the wagons?"

"Cause Sam don't want to look like we don't trust them," Matthew smiled. "Course, we don't."

The Indian party approached slowly. When they were a quarter mile away, they sent one brave toward the train alone. He spoke to Brown Eagle, assuming the Shoshone knew the Sahaptin language. A few minutes later Brown Eagle told Sam the Indians wanted to trade smoked salmon for dried buffalo. The people who heard this conversation passed the word the Indians were friendly. Sam cautioned his wards to be wary of theft.

The Nez Perce stayed through the noon break trading with individuals. They were on their way from the Salmon River to Fort Hall on a trading expedition. Brown Eagle brought a Native to Emily and Matthew's wagon. The Indian had two horses with large woven baskets on either side of their backs.

"What you got here?" Matthew asked the Nez Perce approaching him with an extended hand.

They shook hands as Brown Eagle introduced them. The Indian shook hands with Emily and she noticed his firm grip and callused hand. He was used to physical work.

"Grass. I cut grass for horses. You trade?" the Indian asked.

Matthew looked at the grass and found it to be reasonable quality hay.

"I'd sure like to have that for my critters. What you looking to trade for?" Matthew said.

"Guns," the answer surprised Matthew.

"I don't have no extra guns. How about beans. I could spare a couple pounds of beans," Matthew replied.

The Indian turned to walk away.

"Wait," Emily called. "Look at our fine cloth for making clothes. Have you got a woman?"

The Indian stopped and turned back. He didn't know what "cloth" was and wanted to find out.

Emily climbed inside the wagon and brought out a bolt of calico cotton. She took a corner and rubbed it against her face to show how smooth the cloth was. Then she unrolled it a ways and wrapped it around her body.

The Indian's face lit up. He approached to touch the cloth. Brown Eagle stepped between Emily and the Nez Perce. They engaged in an animated conversation. The Nez Perce turned away. As he reached for the reins of his horse, Brown Eagle made a guttural sound. The Nez Perce faced the white couple, smiled and nodded once.

"Give him enough to make one dress," Brown Eagle said. "And two pounds of beans."

The deal was consummated. Now Matthew had to figure out where to put the hay the Indian was dumping on the ground. Brown Eagle grabbed a basket and gestured. The Nez Perce shook his head violently.

"I'll give him enough calico for two dresses if he gives us the baskets," Emily interrupted.

The trader wanted ammunition and he, Matthew and Brown Eagle exchanged another heated conversation. In the end Matthew had the baskets and grass and Emily cut off six yards of material. Hand shaking was performed all around and the Indians went on their way.

Brown Eagle and a soldier followed the Nez Perce for two hours. A second cavalryman and the mountain man rode ahead of the train as scouts. The party progressed northwestward following the Snake River valley. The next morning, Brown Eagle and the corporal returned. The Nez Perce had shown no interest in returning to the wagon train to steal horses or goods.

The scouts returned with the news that there was no grazing grass for the next thirty miles at least. That was as far as they had ridden. They saw no signs of more Indians or hazards other than a lack of fresh food for the animals.

Matthew rationed the four baskets of hay. He gave each of his four cows, two oxen and horse one large handful of hay and a cup of oats each morning and evening. They supplemented the meager feeding with stunted desert weeds.

The Jacksons had two nursing calves born on the trail. The mother's milk dried up and the calves became too weak to walk. The calves were strapped over the mules' backs and carted along the trail. The mules staggered under the added weight and began to fall behind. Elijah Jackson realized his only option was to kill the calves. Hester Jackson cooked as much meat as her family could eat in a week's time. The excess veal was distributed to travelers according to need. Emily and Matthew had enough dried buffalo and smoked fish to last another month so rejected the offer of fresh meat.

The youthful outriders were most needy. They hadn't brought trade goods or allocated their spending money wisely enough and were running short on food. Their horses were existing on sage and water and were suffering from malnutrition. They were a sad looking lot that staggered into Fort Boise on October 1.

Chapter 51

ort Boise was a dreary place. It did offer shelter and protection; there was a small contingent of soldiers, a sawmill, a sutler's store, a blacksmith, and little else. The train members who chose to wait out the winter at Fort Boise did so reluctantly. They knew it would be a long seven months before they could proceed west. There was hay stored for livestock as neighboring Cayuse Indians had farms. They also supplied the fort with a variety of vegetables including corn, squash, beans and potatoes.

Three outriders hired on as laborers for the army. They knew their horses would take them no further. They would earn their room and board plus a stipend by felling trees from the Sawtooth Mountains and cutting it into lumber.

The Jacksons were afraid to attempt the completion of the trip to Willamette before winter. Their animals were in poor shape; the people were tired of traveling, and the past week of frosty nights had been considered a forewarning of dangers ahead. The train participants understood Elijah Jackson's concerns but knew they were losing valuable morale boosters in the children. An emotional farewell was bid with repeated hugs and promises.

By the end of the week following the stop at Fort Boise, other pioneers considered the Jacksons wise. The trail didn't improve. The train traveled north beside the Burnt River through mountains. The few remaining outriders contributed their horses to help weakened dray animals. All personnel walked. Every able bodied man and woman pushed wagons on steep grades.

The arduous journey to the Powder River took longer than expected. They covered only ten to twelve miles per day. Downhill was as hard as uphill, trees were tied to the backs of wagons for extra weight to keep them from sliding out of control. The final precipitous grade brought them into Grande Ronde River valley.

The animals were given respite, as brown winter grass grew thick along the river. All members of the party took turns with scythes and sickles cutting grass for future use. The animals were well fed for a few days. They crawled over the dry landscape of the Blue Mountains and descended into the Umatilla River area. The high desert offered no vegetation but wild bunch grass, and most of that had been eaten by Cayuse livestock. The grass from the Grande Ronde River valley was rationed. The Jamisons still lost one cow to starvation.

Scrubby cottonwood and sage was gathered for cooking fires. The nights were bitterly cold but the days warmed to comfortable walking weather.

Spirits lifted when a scout returned with the news that the Columbia River was less than a day away. They also reported four Walla Walla Indians were making their way to the train with potatoes, corn and squash.

Emily told Matthew her mouth watered at the thought of having corn and squash but they had nothing left to trade. She later learned the Indians were looking for clothes. She was able to trade her green and white dress for a bushel of vegetables.

"I feel like I'm giving away apiece of my life," Emily remarked. "The only thing I will have to remind me of our German encounter is the notes in my journal."

"That was a grand party, heh, hon?" Matthew consoled her. "I'll have the thought of you doing the polka in your purdy dress in my head forever."

Tears involuntarily rolled down Emily's cheeks. For all the wonder they had experienced, the hardships were taking their toll. Emily felt old and tired. She looked at her rough, dried hands and knew they would never again be soft and delicate. She tried to concentrate on pleasant thoughts of seeing Matthew's family next year or of a warm home nestled in a lush valley.

Katie noticed her mood swings and attributed it to traveling conditions.

"The trail getting to you, Em? We are all tired. Just hold on for another month. You can do it," Katie encouraged.

"That warm jacket you got me has been a blessing," Matthew said trying to change the subject.

He chatted cheerfully as he chopped the squash into small pieces for fast cooking. He added some dried buffalo, potato, and onion to the pot.

Emily gouged a hole in the sandy gravel about a foot in diameter and a foot deep. They had learned that rocks lining such a hole could help cook food after the sage had burned out.

Katherine asked to share their fire. She had a pot that held two cups of beans and a small piece of salt pork for her dinner.

"Yes, sure," Matthew said. "That little pot don't take up more room than a minute."

"I got some dried corn from the Walla Walla, but it will have to soak before I can cook it," Katherine said. "Did you get any vegetables?"

"Yes, we got a bushel of mixed squash and corn," Matthew replied. "But it was awful expensive. Cost Emily her German dress."

"Sorry to hear that Emily. You'll be dressed in silk and lace a year from now. Don't fret," Katherine tried to cheer the sad woman.

"You mean I'll be down to wearing my under garments for daily chores?" Emily pouted.

"Silk underwear under men's clothes! Ain't you the fancy one," Katherine teased. "You've been a bit testy the past few days, Em. Do you feel okay?" the older woman asked putting her arm around Emily's shoulders.

"I'm not testy. It's the ground we're going over that's testy. Did you ever imagine such a miserable trail?" Emily dumped an armload of brush beside the fire pit.

"Yeah, I guess we're all feeling the strain, especially the animals," Katherine responded. "I dried some mint leaves found outside of Bridger. If we can keep the fire going after the food cooks, maybe we could have a nice hot cup of tea."

"Sounds great," Emily muttered.

Matthew fed and watered the animals while the women gathered more sage and cooked the meal. They said little as they worked.

"One more day to the Columbia," Matthew said when he returned. "We're almost there once we reach that river."

They arrived at the great river in midafternoon. The river ran through sandy plains and had rocky banks. Timber was still nearly non-existent with occasional sightings of small willows. Any driftwood found on the banks was salvaged.

The group passed Walla Walla Indian encampments on sandbars and all gazed at each other out of curiosity. The Natives were clad in western wear due to their trading habits.

McCafferty commented that it was strange to see the camps on the river at this time of year. The salmon weren't good eating, they were in such poor condition from being in fresh water too long. Most salmon were taken in June when they began their swim upstream from the ocean.

Emily noted the fast current of the river. She knew they had another flat-boat ride ahead of them shortly. The thought made her nauseous.

They made camp against a pumice outcrop blocking the cold wind blowing from the west. McCafferty suggested building one campfire to be shared by everyone. All the firewood and sage that had been gathered throughout the day was piled in one spot. A depression was dug in the sand and lined with rocks. People prepared their pots of food before the fire was lit. Sam sparked his flint against a piece of cotton wool. The cotton smoldered then caught fire. Sage burst into flame and shortly the driftwood was burning. Once the fire had died down enough for cooking, all pots were put in place.

Michael brought out his harmonica and played campfire favorites while the food cooked. As soon as the sun set, the chill night air descended. People wrapped up in an assortment of skins obtained along the trail. Dr. Jamison produced some whiskey and people drank a bit to warm their blood.

Soon after dinner, the pioneers sought the warmth of their beds. The fire had lasted only a short time and gave little radiant heat.

"Now I'm wishing we had taken the longer route going south," Emily said snuggling up to Matthew's warm back. "The Columbia looks none too friendly."

"The flat-boats take one family at a time if they have livestock and a wagon," Matthew said. "We'll watch a couple of days and see how professional the sailors are. That way we'll know if we want to take a boat or try to cross the mountains."

"We can't cross the mountains alone!" Emily was startled by the suggestion.

"It'll all work out. Try to get some sleep. You'll feel better in the morning," Matthew said.

But she didn't feel better in the morning. As soon as she stood up, she was nauseated. "I'm not used to drinking whiskey, I feel a bit queasy."

She sat on the edge of the bed waiting for her stomach to settle. Matthew brought her a cup of coffee before he went to the men's morning meeting. She looked at the hot brew for a full minute before jumping to the back flap of the wagon.

She emptied her stomach, which left a foul taste in her mouth. She bathed, cleaned her teeth, dressed, and washed off the rear of the wagon. Emily looked around to see if anyone was watching her. Matthew and Michael stood at the bluff overlooking the river. Men were pointing different directions. They were obviously too engrossed in the business of the day to pay any attention to her.

Katherine was scrubbing clothes on a washboard. Katie was harnessing the McCafferty's team. Jesse and Deborah were cooking breakfast. Emily sighed in relief.

Her stomach was still a bit unsettled as she prepared for the day. She avoided fixing food. Matthew was surprised when he returned from the meeting to find no breakfast.

"We having breakfast this morning?" he asked.

"Could we just have hardtack and dried buffalo, please?" Emily entreated.

Matthew shrugged and took some jerky from the barrel.

"We'll be walking west another day or two 'til we get to the mission," he said between bites. "There's five or six families waiting their turn on the barges at the mission."

The group walked along the narrow banks of the churning river. The black rocks were perpendicular on the canyon walls. Occasionally they came to deep sandy patches, which were tiresome for walkers and animals. The animals sank in the sand to their knees before hitting the obsidian hidden underneath. There was no space between cliff and water to walk around the sand.

"I don't know which is worse, cliffs along a swift river or sand," Jesse complained.

"Every inch of the trail has been bad for miles and miles. I wonder if the other group is in Sacramento Valley yet? Sure wish Michael had chosen that direction," Deborah whispered to Jesse.

They finally arrived at the Methodist Mission at The Dalles. Indians solicited their services as guides across the Cascade Range. The travelers rejected their offers. The snow-capped mountains with Mount Hood's crown lost in the clouds had bolstered flagging spirits. They knew they were approaching their final destination. Just a day's ride on the Columbia and they would be at Fort Vancouver, the northern point of the Willamette Valley.

Emily felt fine after walking a few miles and returned to her normal cheerful demeanor. She chatted with Matthew, Michael, and the women, and teased the two Jamison boys.

She could hear the roar of the river as they neared the mission. While others were checking the supplies of the store, she and Matthew walked to the river. Whirlpools swirled violently among rocks as though the water was desperate to find a way past. The wind blew foam onto obsidian banks making them glisten in the sun. Their sparkle taunted the prospective travelers, as if no harm could come to someone willing to come closer and admire their beauty.

"Matthew, good heavens, does anyone survive that?" Emily yelled above the noise.

She gripped Matthew's arm tightly. He patted her wrist with his free hand and tried to think of something positive to say. He was too frightened at the thought of submitting his wife, himself and all their worldly possessions to the devil before him to say anything.

"Let's go talk to the boat people, Matthew. I doubt if this is where they put the flat-boats into the river," Emily suggested.

She turned away from the raging water, fear filling her heart.

"Maybe we portage around this part," Matthew said.

"Portage! The mountains come right down to the water's edge," Emily stammered. "Let's hope the boatmen have some plan we don't know about."

The boatmen were not encouraging. "The water's fast but much safer and more manageable in the spring when it's deep enough to float over the rocks. It's powerful dangerous this time of year," the manager said. "We'll take you, if you really, really want to go that way. You got a wagon?"

"Yeah," said Matthew. "And four cows 'n two oxen 'n two dogs 'n a horse."

"Can't help you," the manager shook his head. "Don't want the responsibility. I'm just taking men with one or two horses. Don't like taking women but do it if there's enough men to control the skiff. Need very strong men to help maneuver the boat through the rapids. Won't take wagons or unnecessary animals."

"What would you suggest we do?" Emily asked. "Are the guides taking people across the mountains reliable? Could we get a wagon over the trail? Could we make it before winter sets in?"

"Whoa, lady! I ain't God. I don't know what he has planned for weather. He doesn't consult me. The trail is a hard one but people are making it all the time. Probably thirty or forty wagons this year. Indian guides are just folks. There's good ones and bad ones. Some are reliable and some ain't."

"If we was to wait for the high water of spring, where could we live?" Matthew was getting concerned he wouldn't make the final leg of the trip.

"Well, you could check with the Methodist pastor. He might need some workers. Outside of that, you're on your own. You could stay in your wagon with six or seven months' worth of food and your own fuel for fires," the boat manager wasn't sparing them any despair.

"Thanks for the information. We've got some idea what we're up against now," Emily said turning to leave.

"One more thing," Matthew said. "Do you happen to know how long it takes a wagon to get over the range?"

"It's eighty or ninety miles across. Probably average ten miles a day," the boatman replied.

Back at camp Emily and Matthew drank coffee and talked about the options. They knew others from the train must be pondering the same things. They went to McCafferty to see if he was willing to take the train across the mountains. A meeting was held that evening.

The soldiers were scheduled to return east, they were only contracted to take the wagon train to The Dalles as it was assumed the pioneers would get on a boat and be at Fort Vancouver in one day's time.

One outrider had gotten a job at the mission and would wait out the winter. The remaining outriders decided to attempt the river.

The McCaffertys, O'Briens, Jamisons, Kilkennys, Katherine Reed and Brown Eagle would hire a Walla Walla guide and cross the ominous Cascade Range.

"I sure wish there weren't thirteen of us in the party. We need all the luck we can muster," Matthew told Michael after the meeting.

Chapter 52

A handsome Walla Walla brave about twenty-five years old was hired as scout. Ceantoan appeared with his wife, Shinnay on the morning the train was ready to leave. They rode into camp on sturdy, well fed pinto ponies, which were a noticeable contrast to the pioneers scraggily looking livestock.

"How'd they do that?" Matthew asked.

"Do what?" Emily watched the approaching Indians.

"Get their ponies fat."

"Maybe they feed them salmon," Emily jested.

Matthew told Emily he was glad to see the fourteenth person join the party. Now he was sure they would have nothing but good fortune for the final leg of the journey. The traveling women felt more comfortable when they saw the stranger had brought a wife with him. Surely he would do nothing to endanger his pretty squaw.

Katie and Katherine introduced themselves to Shinnay, a shy girl of about eighteen. Shinnay stared at the gesturing white women and made no move to descend from her pony. Brown Eagle explained to the young squaw that the women were inviting her to have a cup of coffee before departure. Shinnay ignored Brown Eagle and followed her husband.

The rejected women weren't deterred, "We'll wait until she gets a bit used to us before we invite her to join us again."

The women took their places beside the lead animals pulling their wagons. The train crossed four branches off the Deschutes River the first day and was seven miles from The Dalles by evening.

One of the branches had been too deep to ford and wagons were floated across on water-tight boxes. The horses were walked into the water's edge and air-tight boxes places under the wagon beds. Horses were unhitched and wagon beds removed from undercarriages and left sitting on top of the boxes. Cattle pulled the empty undercarriages across as they swam the river. The wagons were dragged into the water by harnessed horses. The other end of the ropes were secured to the floating boxes. Two ropes were tied to the rear of the wagon and around the boxes and men held onto them while the horses pulled the wagon across the river. It was the men's job to keep the wagon from floating downstream. People not tending ropes clung to animals. Such a crossing took two to three hours even though there were only five wagons.

As they were settling in for the night, a pair of riders approached camp. Sam McCafferty and Dr. Brian Jamison, who were on guard duty, stopped the men on the outskirts of the circled wagons. The new arrivals delivered bad news. The outriders from the train that were on the first flat boat down the cascades of the Columbia had crashed. Four men were swept into whirlpools and not seen again. Sam was given the names of his former wards.

Word of the accident spread quickly through camp and a somber group held an impromptu memorial service for their lost companions. All joined in the prayer group except Ceantoan and Shinnay.

The Indians had gone for a walk in the moonlight. They found a quiet pool in the stream. Although the water was cold, they stripped and swam in the pool for several minutes. Shinnay climbed out shivering from head to toe. She was soon enclosed in the warmth of loving arms. The Walla Wallas had been united as husband and wife less than a week. Lost in the happiness of their love, they neither knew nor cared about the sadness of their employers. They strolled back to camp about ten o'clock and found it quiet. The only person awake was Brian Jamison, who was on watch. Ceantoan and Shinnay snuggled together under their Hudson's Bay Company blankets.

At first light the party continued their trek south in the Tygh Valley. They came to the intersection where travelers from the east had made a path known as the Barlow Road Cutoff.

"Now, why didn't we take that road?" Michael asked McCafferty.

"Truth is, I didn't know about it," Sam answered honestly. "It wasn't there when I came this way in '46."

"I've taken two trains the southern route out of Bridger since then," Sam continued. "It was hot and dusty. We lost one man to the heat and two animals. I hoped this way would be easier."

Michael asked Ceantoan about the cutoff through their interpreter, Brown Eagle.

"It is called Road in Ravine. It turns off white man's trail at top of hill west of John Day River, goes southwest to valley of rye grass at Nish, above Hay Canyon. Then it goes southwest to the ridge below Finnegan Canyon and Buck Hollow. The trail climbs the ridge to Tygh Valley at Wamic after going across River of Falls (Deschutes)," the brave recited the geography where he'd been guiding emigrants for three years.

No one felt worse about the mistake than McCafferty, "those boys lost on the river would be alive today, if I'd known about the cut-off."

"I knew about Barlow's toll road," he sighed, "but hoped to avoid it because of the cost. It's steep to the summit and I feel they charge too much."

Emily noticed how old and tired Sam appeared and wondered if he was well.

The party had their noon break at the intersection and talked about the road ahead. Sam told them the toll price was five dollars per wagon and ten cents per animal.

"Are they going to charge ten cents for them worthless hounds?" Matthew asked.

A couple people laughed knowing the hunting dogs were like children to Matthew. Michael and Deborah automatically looked at the dogs. The Jamison cattle dogs and the Kilkenny bloodhounds were having a tug-of-war with Josiah and Robert Jamison. The boys were holding buffalo bones and the dogs were trying to wrest them free.

"Yep," Sam said, "they charge for every critter. The road gets rough in spots but can't be any worse than what we've already encountered. We'll try to make it to the gate this afternoon if you all want to go that way."

He spent the next half-hour looking at maps with Ceantoan and Brown Eagle. The women checked supplies.

"The cooler you gave us as a wedding gift has been a blessing. We've had fresh meat and fish for a week longer than other folks," Deborah told Emily as they did a food inventory.

"The fish sure makes the clay smell bad," Emily replied. "Have you found anything to get rid of the odor?"

"The water at the soda springs worked well," Deborah answered. "Now if we could just find hot soda springs every hundred miles, we'd be in good shape."

"Don't make me think about bathing," Emily smiled. "Sometimes I dream I'm sitting in hot water next to ma's cook stove at home. We had good mother-daughter talks during bath time at home."

"What did you talk about? My mother never talked to me, just yelled at me," Deborah confessed.

"Oh, mostly Ma would talk about when she was a young girl. Her elderly aunt and uncle and their daughter raised her. Their daughter is Matthew's mother, Lydia Coakley Kilkenny Fitzgerald," Emily smiled at the thought of Lydia's new surname.

"What? You married your cousin!" Deborah exclaimed.

"I don't know, maybe. My grandfather and Matthew's mother were brother and sister. Relatives get married in Appalachia," Emily said unconcerned.

"Well, if it suits you, it tickles me plum to death," Deborah shrugged.

"Looks like the men are ready to move out. Are you walking or riding?" Katie interrupted the conversation.

"Walking," Deborah and Emily answered in unison.

The women went to their lead animals and got the procession started. Once all the vehicles were moving, the animals followed the wagon in front of them. The women clustered together to discuss their opinions.

"Poor Sam, he feels so bad about those young men dying in the river," Katie started. "I don't believe he slept a wink last night."

"Everyone who joined the wagon train in St Louis knew the trip was going to be dangerous," Deborah voiced her thoughts. "They chose to go on the river although we could all see it was impassable."

"I'm sorry we never got to know the outriders better," Emily said. "Matthew and I discussed having them to dinner individually so we could get to know them. We never got around to doing that. Do you suppose anyone will notify their families back east?"

"Sam's going to do that. He told me so this morning. He had addresses for their families. Course some folks are going west to run away from something. The addresses of next of kin could be false," Katie sighed.

The friends walked on in silence, each lost in her own thoughts.

Josiah and Robert Jamison ran past them in a race to their father's position at the head of the train.

"Now what?" Katie thought aloud. "Not more bad news, I hope."

"Pa, pa," the boys yelled as they ran. Brian turned in his saddle when he heard them.

The women watched the animated duo and deduced from their excitement that it was a boyish matter on their minds. Josiah and Robert trotted beside their dad's horse as he caught up with Sam.

The boys repeated their story to Sam who shook his head three times, listened to more entreaty then nodded in assent. The boys clasp each other in jubilation.

"Sam just lost an argument…again," Katie laughed. "I'm sure we'll hear the whole story shortly."

The route was becoming more arduous as they traveled. The weak dray animals were slipping from time to time as they struggled with their loads.

Sam called the train to a halt and assigned jobs. The women were to walk in front of the train removing boulders and fallen limbs of trees. The men were to push the wagons or help the women where needed. The riding horses were called into action as dray animals once more. Ceantoan and Shinnay would keep their horses for scouting and keeping tabs on the cattle.

People and animals alike worked up a sweat as they fought for every foot of road gained. The horses foamed at the mouth, the people panted heavily. They reached the top exhausted, drenched in their own perspiration.

Ceantoan spoke to Brown Eagle who was sitting on a fallen tree trunk breathing hard. Brown Eagle relayed the message to the Jamison boys who were lying on the roadway beside their wagon.

The boy's jumped to their feet and ran from wagon to wagon with the news.

"There's a cascade of cool spring water a quarter mile off to the north," Robert reported to Emily and Deborah. "It ain't so fast as to be dangerous. There's a pool at the bottom. Sam says we can all go swimming."

"Oh lordy! I can't turn that down," Deborah was on her feet. "I'll get some soap. Come on Em, let's go."

Emily couldn't resist. She pushed sticky hair from her face.

"What are you going to wear?" she called after Deborah.

"Just what I have on," Deborah called back.

Emily looked at her worn out trousers and shirt, "Why not?"

Matthew led the oxen onto a knoll beside the trail and tied them to a Douglas Fir tree. He released the stallion and bull that had been harnessed to the wagon along with the oxen. They grazed on the sparse grass.

Matthew found his most worn clothes and changed into them. By the time he joined the others at the hidden playground, they were in the water. Men and women washed, splashed and played. The wall of the cascade was made of granite worn smooth by water. The wide sloping bedrock had depressions washed out like giant pockmarks filled with clear water. Some were five feet deep, most were two to three feet deep.

Jesse Jamison lay fully clothed in a shallow pool. She reclined and let the flowing water wash over her tired body. Her eyes were closed to the troubles of the world. Her husband sat next to her vigorously scrubbing his scalp and full beard with soap weed.

The Jamison boys and outriders that had rejoined the group after their comrades drowned, rode the water down the rock base. The total length of the cascade was about fifty to sixty feet with a drop of ten feet. Robert rolled over and over on this way down the marble-like surface. Josiah floated on his stomach with his hands out in front of him. He let out a war whoop of exhilaration as he went past his parents. They ignored him, lost in their own enjoyment.

Emily shared a pond on the upper level with Deborah and Katherine. Katherine laughed for the first time in several days. Her calico skirt filled with air and ballooned up under her chin. She punched the air out and the skirt immediately refilled with bubbles.

Deborah scooted down until she was submerged and blew bubbles. She came up for air and repeated the action again and again. Emily rubbed soap on her clothes and skin happy with the feeling of cleanliness. She observed the beautiful surroundings. Trees taller than any she'd seen before waved their tops gently in the breeze. Glorious dark-blue and black birds named Stellers Jays called raucously to one another. A delicate gray and white bird called a Nuthatch ran up the bark of a trunk looking for hidden insects. Squirrels went back and forth along the limbs chirping alarm, warning others of the intruders. A hundred feet away the water fell from a higher elevation in a shimmering curtain down to the sparkling stream feeding the cascades. Emily tried to memorize every detail. She took a deep breath filling her lungs with a pine scented fragrance. The sun warmed her face as she squinted at the deep azure blue of the sky overhead.

Matthew decided the boys and young outriders were having the most fun so frolicked with them.

"Where's Katie?" Emily asked.

"She, Sam and Brown Eagle stayed with the wagons. Sam wanted to write some letters," Katherine answered.

Emily wished she hadn't been reminded of the accident just when she was enjoying this moment of bliss.

"Michael, Ceantoan and Shinnay are scouting the road ahead. Hopefully it has a more gradual angle," Katherine said.

Chapter 52

*M*ichael reported on the descent from the ridge. It was as steep as the ascent. Sam ordered large pine trees tied to the back of the wagons. He told each woman to double-check the contents of their wagons.

"Make sure they're secured," he said. "It looks like a bumpy ride ahead. You can ride down the hill to add weight to your wagon, but I want a man handling the reins."

Brown Eagle climbed onto the seat beside Katherine. "It'll take some muscle to keep the animals from going too fast. You being delicate, I better handle the critters."

Katherine blushed. She was a strong farm-woman used to carrying her parents from room to room in their declining years and doing the chores normally handled by her father. No man had ever considered her "delicate."

Once they began the descent behind Ceantoan's lead, she was glad she wasn't in control of the rolling wagon. She grabbed the board in front of her to keep from sliding off the seat.

Emily hung onto the back of her seat and tried to identify the sounds emanating from the wagon. She was afraid to look and see what was sliding. Matthew had tied the rocker to the cross members of the canvas so sliding barrels wouldn't break it. What had they forgotten to tie down?

"Those ropes from Louisville Falls sure come in handy," Matthew said leaning all his weight on the brakes.

Emily nodded agreement, "It takes some nerve to charge people to use this route."

"At least they cut the trees and pulled the stumps out. Would be nice if they moved the boulders out of the way," Matthew said standing for more leverage on the reins.

An outrider had problems with his fully loaded mules. One animal pitched his load over his head and ran down the hill disappearing into dense timber. His lost load was distributed to other complaining animals that were dancing around on the unstable ground.

All made it to the bottom in good time and reasonable condition. The land became an uneven plain covered thickly with fir trees, pines, and deciduous oaks.

"No problem finding fire wood here," Michael called out on his way after a cow heading into the thicket.

They crossed a cold stream that was chalky white.

"Matthew, what makes the water so thick?" Josiah asked his friend.

"Danged if I know," Matthew responded cupping his hands to dish up the milky liquid. "It feels gritty like sand."

Brown Eagle saw Matthew and the boys pondering the water.

"It's called 'glacial silt'," he told them. "It comes from the glacier up on the mountain."

The boys looked the direction Brown Eagle pointed but Mt. Hood was hidden behind the towering trees.

"What's a glacier?" eleven year old Robert asked.

"Frozen snow. It's there all year 'round. Each winter it grows and in the summer it melts back a bit but never goes away. The water that drains out under the snow is this ground up gravel," Brown Eagle filled his palm with stream water.

"You learn that in the Methodist school in Kansas?" Matthew asked.

"No, I learned it from my grandfather who lived in the Rocky Mountains way north of South Pass," Brown Eagle said.

"Can we drink it?" Matthew asked.

"Won't hurt you but it won't taste good," Brown Eagle answered.

The troop crossed three more silted streams before they halted for the day. They pulled off into a meadow left behind when beaver dams filled lake beds with sediment. The grass was waist high and the starving animals ate throughout much of the night.

In the morning, Matthew, Michael and Brown Eagle went hunting. Ole Blue and Betsy bounded off zig-zagging across the valley ever alert for bird or beast.

291

Ole Blue scared up two pheasants. Brown Eagle shot one and Matthew the other. The men reloaded their guns while waiting for the dogs to retrieve their kill.

"That'll make a tasty dinner. Let's see if we can find a couple more," Michael suggested.

The dogs returned with the fine fat birds and gladly accepted their praise. Betsy, filled with self-confidence, went back to work. Blue was sure he would find more birds before his mate and leaped from spot to spot startling field mice, marmots and Clark's Nutcrackers. The delicate gray colored birds flew to tall trees surrounding the meadow and the four-legged animals ducked into their burrows.

It wasn't long before Betsy found her quarry; two more colorful pheasants took to the air. They were downed immediately by the waiting hunters.

"There's eighteen people in the train. If we find two more birds, we'll have enough for a feast. If not, these birds will do for everyone to have a piece or two," Michael said.

They walked about following the dogs for another thirty minutes before giving up. When they returned, they found the dray animals harnessed and the train ready to leave.

Women cleaned the birds while the hunters ate breakfast.

"Let's make our stale bread into stuffing for these birds tonight," Deborah suggested. "Does anyone have any onions left?"

"I have four or five," Emily said. "What about sage, we could sprinkle that on the roasting birds."

"I dried plenty of sage coming across that dusty plain," Katherine volunteered.

Other recipes were planned and Katie offered the last of her canned green beans for the occasion.

Jesse conspired with her boys to provide entertainment. Looking forward to the evening made the day's march go faster. As people came up with plans to make the evening special, they passed the idea onto others. Even the shy Shinnay caught the enthusiasm. She whispered a plan to Ceantoan for entertaining the white people.

Katie suggested they have the drawing for the rag-rug the women's group had recently finished. Michael, of course, agreed to play his harmonica and sing. Matthew jokingly said he would dance a jig.

"Not a bad idea, Mr. Kilkenny. I seem to remember sitting out the last dance we had," Emily laughed. "I'll let you make it up to me tonight."

The train passed by Barlow's toll gate about ten o'clock and were stopped there for half an hour while the accounting was done.

The gatekeeper was an elderly cripple who looked like he would be unable to stop anyone who wanted to sneak through without paying.

"Why you suppose Barlow would hire an old man like that?" Matthew asked Brown Eagle. "He couldn't stop a chipmunk from going through without paying. Looks like he's just waiting to get robbed."

Brown Eagle pointed out two sharp shooters lounging against the rocks on either side of the road a short distance in front of the train. They were blocked from obvious view by the timber.

"I'd think twice before I'd take on the old boy," Brown Eagle said. "Ceantoan tells me the gent is Barlow's uncle who was looking for a way to occupy his time. He used to be a buffalo hunter 'til he lost a leg."

Sam spoke to the old man after Ceantoan returned from scouting the road ahead. An argument ensued and the watchmen immediately became alert. One man took up a shooting position behind a boulder. The other cocked his rifle and walked toward the gate.

"Suppose we ought to support Sam?" Matthew asked Brown Eagle.

"Let's wait a minute. They're hassling over money. They'll come to an agreement."

By the time the gunman joined the gatekeeper, the argument was over. The gatekeeper handed Sam some money and hobbled toward the gate. He swung it open and indicated the first driver should proceed.

Sam handed a dollar to each wagon owner.

"What's this for?" Emily asked.

"Ceantoan tells me there's been a forest fire up ahead and we'll have a rough time getting around downed logs," Sam reported. "I talked the gate-keeper into a discount for our trouble.

"Maybe, if we give those fellers the extra dollar, they'll clear the way for us," Emily replied indicating the gunmen.

Ceantoan smiled for the first time on the trip, "Not likely, ma'am."

Chapter 53

The train made its way across the devastated land. The fire was recent, some stumps still smoldered. They stopped frequently while mules pulled burned trees off the track. Ropes broke under the strain and were replaced by leather straps. A wagon wide path was cleared.

"Glad the weather is cooler," Deborah said wiping her face on her sleeve. "Imagine doing this a month ago."

The blackened women put their weight against a two-foot diameter limb attached to a tree being pulled by the mules. The tree gave way and moved a few inches. Renewed efforts moved it a bit more. The Jamison boys joined the women and gradually the tree was moved far enough to get the wagons past. The men cut fallen giants with whipsaws and axes. They made moveable size pieces out of the barricades.

The group moved only five miles during the tiring day. A wide sandy creek had stopped the path of the fire. The train spent the night beside that creek. People washed up before sunset. Night brought the cold air.

A bonfire was built in addition to a cooking fire. A festive atmosphere revived the tired travelers. The pheasants were put on spits to be roasted. Stuffing was cooked in a Dutch oven, the last of the potatoes were roasted. While the food cooked, Michael played his harmonica. The Jamisons acted out a skit written by Josiah. Shinnay and Ceantoan chanted and danced a ceremonial dance, which they later admitted was part of a rain dance.

"Oh no, I hope it only brings a sprinkle," Emily whispered to Matthew.

The roasted birds and side dishes were relished and compliments were passed to all the cooks. People attempted to stay outside visiting for awhile after supper. The cold air eventually drove all of them to the warmth of their beds.

Morning brought frost-covered ground. The temperatures remained cold until the sun creeped over the peaks. By that time, the train had progressed four hours further west. The day was an easy one. The road was clear and relatively smooth through a long flat valley. People walked briskly in the cool autumn air. The skies were clear and bright. Mt. Hood, Mt. Jefferson and other Cascade crests sparkled in the sun. The valley ground was covered with ferns. It was a perfect day to be walking across Oregon Territory.

In the evening Sam McCafferty made the announcement everyone anticipated for so long. "Ceantoan tells me that after we cross that ridge tomorrow we drop down into the Willamette Valley."

A whoop went up among the pioneers. Matthew grabbed Emily and swung her in a circle. They hugged, cheered and laughed. Emily exchanged hugs with Deborah, Katherine and Michael. Matthew embraced the women. He and Michael shook hands and slapped each other's backs simultaneously.

"We made it, ole boy! We made it!" Matthew said.

"Deborah and I have another fearsome range to cross before we'll be home in Beaver Valley, but I think we'll rest awhile in the Willamette—a week or so, anyhow," Michael said.

Four Walla Walla Indians came into view. They were returning from trading in the valley. The Indians spent the night with the pioneers. Brown eagle was the busiest person in camp. Everyone had questions for the traders. He was the only person in the train that spoke both Walla Walla and English though Ceantoan was learning a bit on each trip.

"Where's the nearest town?"

"Where can we find out about the Donation Land Act?"

"Where's the trail to California?"

On and on questions were asked and answered throughout the evening. By midnight the camp was finally quiet.

In the morning, spirits were high. The last ridge, which was strewn with remnants of a fire was a minor detriment.

People worked happily, sawing, cutting, and breaking trees apart. By late afternoon they reached the summit of the ridge and wanted to go further.

Sam argued with some over the potential hazards of going on that evening. Common sense prevailed. A halt was called and people reluctantly unhitched wagons and prepared for another night on the trail. Smoke curled from a chimney in the distance. The sight drew the pioneers attention as much as any awesome scenery they had seen along the way.

Katie voiced the women's thoughts, "Just think, there's probably a woman in that cabin fixing supper. She has a sink, water pump, table, cook stove, and all kinds of conveniences to do her job."

"And when they eat, they'll sit on real chairs at a real table, and have serving bowls and pitchers of cold milk and eat off real dishes," Jesse added.

"She might even have a table cloth, napkins, and flowers on the table," Katherine said dreamily.

"Food. Should we mention things like apple pie, sliced tomatoes, crispy lettuce, cherries, buttermilk, butter," Emily moaned.

"No. No, whatever you do, don't start talking about food. We won't be able to choke down our dried buffalo and beans tonight," Deborah said laughing.

"I hates to break up this dreaming session," Matthew said, "but it might be a month or more afore any of you get to have such modern niceties."

"That's right," Sam put in. "Most of us aren't going to stop and take up residence tomorrow."

"I'm going up to Fort Vancouver and see about land for sale," Matthew said.

"I'm going to the nearest town and rent a hotel room until I can get information on gold fields," an outrider joined the group. "At least I'll sleep in a real bed in the hotel."

"Looks like we'll be splitting up," Sam said. "Think I'll break out some whiskey to propose some toasts."

Men thought that was a good idea and followed Sam to his wagon. The women dug out their iron pots and heated the beans one more time. They at least had left over pheasant to go with the beans. Sam toasted everyone and everything. Brian, Matthew and Michael discussed their plans for the near future. The Kilkennys and Jamisons were going to Fort Vancouver to see about land. The O'Briens and Katherine Reed were heading south over the southern Cascades and then over the Siskiyous. Two outriders would go that far with them, but were headed down the Sacramento Valley to Hangtown near Sutter's sawmill to take up a mining claim. Much to Jesse's distress, the Jamison boys wanted to accompany the outriders. Brown Eagle was going to look for a job with the army as a scout and interpreter. Ceantoan and Shinnay were returning to their people near The Dalles.

It started to rain and the party broke up. "That rain dance really worked!" Emily whispered to Matthew. "It just took a little bit of time."

Men staggered to their quarters and collapsed into sleep.

Women lay awake fantasizing about china cups filled with sweetened tea, hot bath water, soft chairs, eating fruits, vegetables, and fresh dairy products. Jesse thought of a vase filled with flowers on a checkered tablecloth, of wearing cotton clothes, and high buttoned shoes. Eventually, they too succumbed to sleep.

A steady drizzle fell from the sky in the morning. Men with hangovers attempted to corral and harness animals. Sleepy women cooked coffee under the shelter of a canvas tarp and shared what cooked food they had.

It was almost nine o'clock before the wagons rolled out. The road was slippery. Wagons slid sideways on descending slopes. The Jamison vehicle slid toward an embankment. A boulder prevented it from going over the edge and dragging the mules with it. The wagon tipped over as it hit the rock.

Two hours were lost while the wagon was unloaded, righted and reloaded. Jesse cried over dishes carried across country only to be broken on the edge of the Willamette. She was inconsolable. Brian, her husband tried to tell her they could get new dishes. How could new dishes replace ones that had belonged to her mother. Jesse continued to sob after they were in motion. Katie asked her if she was really crying about the dishes. Jesse shot Katie a strange look but nothing was said for several minutes.

"I'm so tired. I laid awake all night worrying about my three men," Jesse started. "What if they can't settle down? Brian says this trip has been the best part of his life. He would like to go on and on."

A fresh flow of tears rolled down her cheeks. She blew her nose on the corner of her apron.

Katie put her arm around the despondent woman's shoulders, "It'll be all right. Once he has a place to call his own, he'll settle in."

"And the boys? They've matured so much on the crossing. They're talking about striking out for the gold fields. Robert's only eleven! He can't leave home. Good heavens, Josiah is only fourteen, they're mere babies in men's bodies."

Jesse sank onto a stump and shook with despair, "Not only have I lost my mother's dishes, I've lost my family."

Emily patted Jesse on the shoulder and told her to drink the proffered medicine.

"I'm not sick," Jesse wailed.

"I know, I know. This will just make you feel a bit better. It will warm your insides. This rain has made us all feel cold and empty inside."

"Exactly! I feel cold and empty inside," Jesse said and drank the brandy down in one gulp.

She hiccupped and said, "Well that did warm me up a bit. I think I need some more to fill that empty spot."

Emily could hear her hiccupping as a second shot was drawn from their barrel. Jesse smiled weakly as Emily handed her the tin mug.

"Drink slower this time," Emily said too late to do any good.

Jesse felt the glow trickle down her esophagus and warm her stomach. She said nothing but handed Emily the mug and started walking briskly to catch up with the rest of the party.

Emily smiled, "Another miracle performed. A temporary miracle but none the less, the patient does feel better at the moment."

Emily tossed the mug in the rear of her moving home. "Even the wagon looks tired," she thought.

She pulled on the rope holding the canvas tied together at the rear. The rope was frayed from wear. "It wouldn't hold up through a good wind storm."

She trotted beside the wagons until she was beside Matthew. He was wearing his new coat as protection from the cold rain.

"You look like a true mountain man, my dear," she said taking his hand. "Tell me. Have you enjoyed the crossing?"

"Mostly. Felt miserable 'bout your injuries. Was sorry we lost animals. Really liked Jerome, floating on the rivers, being in the mountains, hunting buffalo. Why you asking? You ready to walk back to Athens?"

"Not quite. Let me rest a week first," she said smiling.

"When do you want to go to Fort Vancouver to see about land?" she asked.

"Don't know. I'll try to get the story on land when we stop in Oregon City. Vancouver is only a day's ride from there."

"Katie says we'll be in Oregon City tomorrow night. They're going to spend one night with us on the Abernethy Green before going to their own home. They own a boarding house in Oregon City."

The rain let up soon after noon and spirits improved. No one wanted to stop for lunch break. "We're like horses getting close to the barn after a day's work. Everyone's focused on getting to Oregon City as soon as possible," Deborah said.

They pulled into the meadow behind Governor George Abernethy's home near six o'clock that evening. There were wagons scattered around the acreage. Some looked like they had been there for some time.

"Mr. Abernethy is a merchant and miller in town. He got his land from the Donation Land Claim. Smart feller. He lets immigrants park on his land when they arrive from the Barlow Road. They end up buying supplies from his store," McCafferty explained. "He became the Provisional Governor of Oregon from 1845 to 1849 because he was so popular with earlier immigrants."

"Enterprising gent," Michael said. "Would he be the one to see about a trail to Beaver Valley?"

"I imagine he's pretty busy, but someone in his store will send you down the right path," Sam answered. "When you leaving to go south?"

"Pretty quick, maybe three or four days. Don't want to get stuck in snow going over the mountains."

"I thought we were staying in Oregon City a week," Deborah said surprised.

"Maybe. We'll see. The rain made me want to keep moving before the snow starts," Michael replied. "It'll be November in a couple of days."

"I want to clean out the wagon and replenish our staples. Don't know what kind of stores they have in Rough and Ready. It's just a little mining town. Bet prices will be high, too," Deborah told him.

The wagons were parked in close proximity to each other but not in a circle; no one was worried about an attack this close to town.

The pioneers wandered about trying to decide what to do first. The Jamison boys wanted to see the town, the women wanted to get clean and dressed presentable before appearing in public. The men wanted to get the news.

Matthew, Michael, the Jamison men, and Brown Eagle went into town. It was twilight and they carried two lanterns with them for the return trip.

Sam and Ceantoan built a shelter of canvas to be used as a bath house. The women gathered wood and started water heating.

"The ground is muddy from the rain. There's no way we're going to stay clean," Katherine said.

"At least we'll smell better," Katie said smiling.

Jesse was inside her wagon where she had been since arrival. Emily decided to check on her.

"Jesse, are you okay? Come join us for a cup of coffee," she called by the back flap of the Jamison wagon.

There was no response.

"Jesse, Jesse, are you okay?" Emily called out in vain.

She peeked inside the flap and saw Jesse curled up on a bed apparently asleep.

Emily left her and went back to preparing for a bath. She looked at her supply of clothes and realized she had nothing to wear except one city dress she had worn in Paducah. She didn't want to wear cut off trousers or soiled buckskins to town.

"I'll have to make some new dresses as soon as we settle in," she told Deborah.

"We're all in the same fix. We should have been making new clothes on the trail instead of blankets," Deborah muttered.

"I was worried about spending winter on the trail. I never thought about being presentable to city folks," Emily decided on her cleaner buckskin dress for the evening. She would wear her Sunday dress to town whenever she went. "Oh, my gosh! I have to wear fur-lined moccasins with my church dress. I don't have any shoes!" she exclaimed.

Chapter 54

The men made their way toward Oregon City on a road following the Clackamas River. Adrenaline was flowing and the excited group became boisterous as they rode.

A surrey pulled by a fine, well-groomed horse came toward them. The lanterns on either side bobbed merrily along until the wagon was about a hundred feet away from the pioneers.

Matthew called out to the occupants, "Helloooo there. Hold up."

He meant to stop the wagon long enough to ask a question or two. Instead the expression "hold up" scared the couple into speedy flight. The driver whipped his horse again and again until the surrey was well away from the scroungy looking men.

"I hope you don't plan on becoming a politician here abouts," Michael said. "You'd never get those two to vote for you."

Matthew sat on his horse in a state of confusion, "Might bit unfriendly 'round here. I wondered how far it was to town."

Brian Jamison laughed, "We look like bandits with our dirty clothes and scraggy beards. When you shouted 'hold up,' that confirmed the folks' fears."

Matthew joined the others in a good laugh, "Yep, especially Robert, he's one scary looking critter."

They rode on into the darkness. Two miles further they met some men on horseback that said the town was just a short distance ahead.

"Falls of Willamette, we old timers call the place. Politicians thought up the fancy name of Oregon City," the older man said. "You look like you could stand a drink. Just arrived, would be my guess."

"You're a good guesser," Matthew said. "We're hoping to find Governor Abernethy."

"Fancy folks don't go outside after dark," the man informed them. "You'll have to come back in the morning."

"Thank you for the advice. We'll go on to refresh our memory of what a town looks like," Matthew tipped his hat and kicked his horse gently in the ribs.

They rode a bit faster now knowing they were close to town. Brian had a hard time keeping Josiah and Robert from riding ahead.

"Aw, Pop, can't we meet you at the store," Robert pleaded. "We want to see lights and hear real music and ….."

"Hey! You mean you didn't like my harmonica playing?" Michael pretended to be offended.

"Oh yeah, sure. It was great," Robert said apologetically. "I mean we want to hear a piano playing the latest tunes."

"We want to see if they have any young folks," Josiah added.

"You mean young women?" his father asked.

"Nah, we don't care nothing about girls. We want to know about gold digging, and can young men go to the fields," Robert replied.

"We're almost there," Brian said. "You two reign in your spirits for a few more minutes."

Five minutes later, they heard the sound of horses, wagons, and humans. They rounded a bend and there was Oregon City, Falls of the Willamette, in all its splendor.

Men were lounging against hitching posts or darkened buildings. Many were smoking hand rolled cigarettes and talking to acquaintances.

Two men were tossing a third one into the bed of a wagon. A woman leaned out a second story window and yelled, "Take his clothes too. And when he comes to, tell him not to bother Sally again." She threw a shirt and trousers into the wagon.

Coarse female laughter followed her retreating figure. A woman standing in the doorway on the porch called to the pioneers, "You boys looking for a bit of fun?"

"No. Thank you, ma'am," Michael said. "We don't need any fun."

Michael tipped his hat to the woman and noticed Josiah and Robert did the same.

"You boys look for Mr. Abernethy's store," Brian said trying to place himself between the boys and the woman.

Brown Eagle chuckled, "When the boys are ready, neither man nor beast will keep them away from women."

"That times a long way off, Brown Eagle," Brian said. "Jesse would skin me alive if she knew the boys even looked at a woman of the night."

"It looks like the store is closed up tighter than a bank safe," Matthew said pointing to a shuttered store window.

"I see two houses of pleasure and the sheriff's office open for business," Brian said.

"Let's find a saloon and have a beer. The boys could have a sarsaparilla and listen to music. Maybe we can pick up some gold field news," Michael said.

"I'm not game to take the boys into a saloon. Robert's only eleven," Brian said.

"Aw Pop, come on. I'll just listen to the music. Nothing bad is going to happen," Robert begged.

"I said 'no' boy. We'll go talk to the sheriff," Brian was emphatic. "We'll meet you three out here in an hour."

"Can I go with them?" Josiah asked. "I want to find out about the gold fields."

Brian was getting agitated so Michael spoke up, "Not this time, Josiah. We'll tell you everything we hear. We need you to find out from the sheriff if the fields are close to Oregon City, or do we have to go all the way to California. We'll trade information in an hour."

Brian nodded to Michael in gratitude. He knew Josiah looked up to the former soldier. The group split up. The Jamisons went to the sheriff's office.

Michael, Matthew, and Brown Eagle looked unsuccessfully for a saloon. They rode the length of town and then came back to the sheriff's office to join Brian.

"We can't find a saloon!" Michael said to Brian.

"That's cause Oregon's a dry state. No alcohol supposed to be sold in the territory," the sheriff replied.

"Son of a gun, I sure didn't know that!" Michael said. "Where can we find out some information on what's happening in the gold fields.

"There's a group of miners outside of town at a campsite about a mile north. They're on their way to Fort Vancouver to catch a boat back to the states," the sheriff pointed toward the north end of town.

"Okay, we'll go up there and meet you three back here in an hour," Brown Eagle said.

That was agreeable to everyone and Michael, Matthew, and Brown Eagle mounted their horses and turned them north.

They rode into the rowdy camp and made their presence known. The sound of poker chips falling on a pile, talking, laughing, and clinking tin mugs came to a halt.

In the silence a burly miner scraped back his empty barrel from the contrived poker table and stood up. He unbuttoned his jacket revealing a gun in his waistband.

"What the hell are you doing here?" he asked drunkenly.

Chapter 55

The angry man tipped over the poker table, mugs and pitchers crashed to the ground among playing cards and chips. Men dived for the nearest hiding place. A woman screamed.

Brown Eagle stood between Michael and Matthew and stared at the offensive miner. He saw the man reach for the pistol sitting in his belt.

Brown Eagle doubled up his fist and swung. He hit Matthew on the side of his jaw and knocked him off his feet. Matthew flew backward knocking over two men. They stumbled into other men who jumped to their feet and swung at imaginary foes, accidentally connecting with men trying to move out of the way.

Chaos ensued. Everyone tried to slug someone. Debris flew. Bodies swiveled and swayed, fell and were kicked out of the way.

Matthew found himself pinned to the ground with a heavy body on his chest. He managed to free his arm and felt his jaw. It was painful but didn't feel broken. He rolled the inert body off and got to his knees.

A large man picked Matthew up by the shirt and the seat of his pants and slid him along the ground. He felt like a rag doll tossed aside by a careless child. Brown Eagle stopped his slide.

Matthew clenched a handful of Brown Eagle's long black hair on the way to his feet and swung with his free hand. He landed the blow on Brown Eagle's cheek just below the eye. Brown Eagle's head bobbed backwards and he lost his grip on Matthew's shirt. The two men fell, arms and legs entwined.

"Let's get out of here before the shooting starts," Brown Eagle shouted above the hubbub.

Matthew was dazed but managed to crawl to a large tree. Just as he was about to escape, someone grabbed his moccasin and dragged him back into the melee. He fell on his stomach and caught hold of a tree root. The man dragging him let go and found a different target to pummel. Matthew looked around the crowd; he recognized Michael's army shirt lying under a table and crawled toward his friend. A shot rang out. He dived behind a log. Two more shots were heard, then silence.

"If anyone draws a gun, I'll shoot him dead," the sheriff boomed.

Matthew turned toward the voice. The sheriff and two deputies stood with two drawn pistols each. None of the fighters drew a gun. One by one they stood with their hands in the air.

Matthew rolled toward the blue army shirt. It hadn't moved. Panic constricted his throat, he couldn't get his breath.

Brown Eagle stood beside the sheriff, "Excuse me, can I get to my friends?"

"Stay where you are," the sheriff told him without taking his eyes off the men.

"It looks like one is bad hurt," Brown Eagle said.

"Is he unconscious?" the sheriff asked.

"I hope that's all it is. He hasn't moved since you walked in," Brown Eagle answered.

"Okay, check it out. The rest of you get your stuff and get out of here. You hear me? Go somewhere else, camp by yourself or with one other person, not in gangs. Don't, I say DO NOT wait in the dark to carry on the fight. Get out of here. My jail's not big enough to hold all of you so I might have to kill a few," the gravelly paternal voice had men filing past with their heads bowed in embarrassment. They went to their bedrolls and tack and loaded up their horses.

Brown Eagle joined Matthew at the table where Michael lay.

"Is he breathing?" he asked.

Matthew put the back of his hand under Michael's nostrils and nodded.

"Should we roll him over?" Matthew asked.

"No! Don't move him," Dr. Jamison was suddenly on his knees beside the fallen man.

"Let me check his neck. If it's broken we can't turn him over," he said.

Brown Eagle's eye was swollen shut. There was a cut on his cheek. Outside of that he was okay so stood and moved the table out of the doctor's way.

Matthew's jaw was blue and swollen, his neck hurt, his head hurt, his shirt was torn, and he was missing a moccasin.

"Why'd you hit me?" he asked Brown Eagle.

"To keep you from being shot," Brown Eagle answered. "I saw the mad man looking at us. He was reaching for his gun; I wanted to knock you out of his way. I didn't know which one of us he intended to shoot. Thought it was best to distract him."

"My teeth are loose," Matthew said after running his tongue around his mouth. "Next time you want to distract someone, warn me so I can duck."

"How's Michael, doc?" Brown Eagle asked.

"His neck's all right. He has a nasty bump on his head. Either he hit the table leg or someone hit him with something hard–like a whisky bottle," Dr. Jamison said checking for broken ribs.

Michael stirred slightly.

"That's a good sign," Brian said. "Would you see if they have a hospital in town, Matthew?"

Matthew headed toward a deputy, one of the few people left in the area.

"'Excuse me. You got a hospital here abouts?" he asked. "My friend has a head bump."

"No hospital. Dr. Forbes has an office in the front part of his house. Take your friend down there," the deputy answered pointing toward town.

Brian sent his sons to get a board on which to carry the injured man. The boys returned almost immediately with a board from a wagon. Michael was wrapped in a bedroll. Brian held Michael's head while the others lifted his body onto the board. He was carried to Dr. Forbes home in a miner's wagon.

Robert rode his horse to Dr. Forbes' ahead of the party to alert the doctor of an incoming patient. There was a lighted lantern hanging from a post near the front door. Evidently the doctor was used to night visitors.

When they arrived, the doctor was in pajamas and a robe. He had his medical supplies ready to attend the wounded man and motioned the group into his surgery. The patient was deposited on a long, narrow table covered with a clean, white sheet. Michael was disrobed and covered with a second sheet. His friends then left the room.

Brown Eagle, Matthew, Josiah, and Robert sat quietly on Dr. Forbes front porch while the two doctors worked on Michael.

"Where's your shirt sleeve, Brown Eagle?" Robert asked.

"Don't know, maybe someone else wore it home," he answered.

"You want me to go look for it," Josiah asked. "I could look for Matthew's shoe at the same time."

For the first time Matthew realized he was missing a moccasin.

"Can you do that without getting into trouble? Your ma would kill us all if she knew we let you go alone," Matthew said.

Josiah promised to speak to no one on his way to or from the improvised gambling site. The boy rode his horse up the street. He managed to find a moccasin but no shirtsleeve. The campsite was empty except for some broken barrels and boards.

An hour later Brian came out from the clinic.

"I'm going to spend the night here with Michael. It's best if the four of you go on back to the wagons. The women folk will be worried."

"Will he be all right?" Brown Eagle asked.

"We won't know for a few days. He has a fractured skull. We've done all we can tonight."

They stared at the doctor not comprehending what a fractured skull meant.

"Should we report this to the sheriff?" Brown Eagle asked.

"Why don't you stop by and tell him you'll be back to make a report tomorrow," Brian suggested.

The tired men walked into the jail. There were a dozen men in the two cells. They were asleep, sprawled on the bunks available and spilling over onto the floor.

"Too drunk to make it home tonight," the sheriff indicated with his thumb pointing at the cells.

"What about the man that started the trouble? Where's he?" Brown Eagle asked.

"You mean the one that looks like a lumberjack? Joe's his name. I heard the story. He lit out. We'll pick him up tomorrow, if he doesn't come in on his own. We know where he lives," the sheriff said.

He listened to Matthew tell of Michael's condition, sighed and said, "You boys get back to camp. I'll have a deputy ride with you just in case someone's laying for you. We'll take care of police business tomorrow," the sheriff seemed as tired and depressed as the pioneers.

Chapter 56

*I*t was after midnight when the men arrived in camp. A campfire was blazing. Jesse, Emily, Deborah, and Katherine sat near it talking quietly.

"Something's wrong," Jesse jumped up when she saw the figures approaching. "Two horses don't have riders."

Emily gasped and ran toward the men.

"Matthew, Matthew," she called into the dim light.

"I'm here, babe," he answered. "I'm okay."

He dismounted and hugged his wife.

"Michael's hurt. Is Deborah awake?"

"Yes. What happened?" she touched his swollen jaw.

"Let's go back by the fire. Is Jesse awake?" he asked.

"Oh, dear God," she shuddered when she saw Brian Jamison and Michael O'Brien both missing and a stranger with the boys.

The other women stood in front of the fire watching the sad parade. Jesse cried out when she saw her sons. They dismounted and hugged their mother.

"Where's your father? Is he dead?" she wailed.

"No, Ma! No! Pop's okay. Mom calm down," Josiah held his mother tightly. He was the protector consoling the weak.

"Sit down ladies. We'll explain everything as best we can," Brown Eagle sighed.

He walked to Deborah and took her hand. She let out a low groan.

"Michael? Is he...? Is he okay?" she whispered gently touching Brown Eagle's swollen eye.

"No, ma'am. He's been injured. Brian and another doctor are taking care of him. He got hit on the head and is unconscious. We'll know more tomorrow," Brown Eagle sounded like a very old man.

"Who are you?" Katherine asked the stranger.

"I'm Deputy Hinkley, ma'am," the policeman dismounted and walked to the fire.

"Brown Eagle, would you please tell the good women folk what happened, then I'll explain what I know," the deputy said.

"We went to a campground of miners who were drinking and playing poker..." Brown Eagle started and stopped when he heard Jesse gasp.

"No, no. I mean Matthew, Michael, and I went to the campground to get information on the gold fields," he restarted.

"The first place you went in town was where a bunch of men were drinking and playing cards, Matthew?" Emily had her hands on her hips demanding an explanation.

"No! Listen! I was just starting at the point where Michael got hurt," Brown Eagle tried to explain.

"Michael got hurt!" Emily almost shouted. "Your eye is swollen shut. Your cheek is cut. Matthew's jaw is twice normal size. And Michael's being attended by two doctors. Did you walk into an ambush of Kaw Indians in that campground?"

"Let that be a lesson to you boys," Jesse interrupted. "Stay out of saloons, gambling houses, or anywhere men are drinking or playing poker. Drinkers are violent people."

"No! No! Brown Eagle hit me," Matthew explained. "Not the drunks."

"What?" Emily slapped Brown Eagle hard on his uninjured cheek before she thought what she was doing.

"It's okay, Matthew hit me back," Brown Eagle retaliated as he clutched his sore face.

"Oh my heavens!" Katherine said. "Don't little boys ever grow up?"

"Stop! Stop! Just stop it," Deborah said through her tears. "We know what you're saying. Or trying to say. You got drunk, got into a fist fight,

Michael tried to stop it, and you both hit him until he was unconscious," she turned toward her wagon.

"No!" several men's voices called out at once.

Sam and Katie arrived at the fire in nightclothes.

"Good grief! What happened? Did Indians attack you?"

"NO!!!!" they all shouted at once.

The two outriders, Ceantoan and Shinnay were suddenly beside the fire as were a couple of strangers from other wagons that had arrived at Governor Abernethy's Green.

"What's going on?" an outrider asked wiping sleep from his eyes.

"Oh, it's simple," Deborah said. "Matthew hit Brown Eagle, Brown Eagle hit Matthew. They both beat up Michael. Just a typical drunken brawl."

Deborah sank to the ground sobbing. Katherine and Emily knelt to console her.

"I hope one of you outriders has a spare bedroll," Emily said. "Matthew is going to need it tonight."

Brown Eagle burst out laughing. "Now I remember why I never married. Let's go to bed and talk tomorrow."

No one moved.

"Okay," Deputy Hinkley said. "Let me explain what I know."

Everyone turned toward him.

"Joe Aster was at Dr. Marcus Whitman's place, Waiilatpu, in November 1847 when the Cayuse attacked. He ain't been right in the head ever since he witnessed the massacre," the deputy began.

"That's too bad. I'll see you folks in the morning," an outrider turned to leave.

"I mean that's why he wanted to kill Brown Eagle," the deputy continued.

The outrider stopped in his tracks. "Brown Eagle was involved in a massacre of white people?"

"No! Now everyone just shut up and let me talk. No interruptions," the deputy ordered.

"Joe hates Injuns, all Injuns. He saw the Cayuse kill men, rape women, and steal children in 1847. Course they did that cause of the measles epidemic the white folks brought that killed off their families," Deputy Hinkley went on.

"Jo Lewis told the Cayuse that Doc Whitman was poisoning them, that's what caused the measles. Jo was a half-breed troublemaker and spread his lies smoother than fresh whipped butter. He said the poison was causing the Cayuse to die. They didn't know what caused measles and believed Jo. Jo said Doc Whitman, a truly good and holy man that worked as a missionary in Oregon Territory for years, wanted the Cayuse farm land for his friends that was coming in the future."

"Well, the Cayuse wouldn't stand for that. No sirree. They came and killed poor saintly Doc Whitman, his good wife, and a passel of mission helpers. Joe Aster saw it all from his hiding place. It drove him crazy."

"Soldiers found Joe Aster wandering in the desert near the mission and brought him to Oregon City. Dr. Forbes fixed up his body but couldn't do much with his brain. Joe's okay until he sees a Native. Then he goes crazy and tries to kill them," the deputy finished.

Everyone was silent, waiting for more. Finally Emily asked, "Did poor old Joe Aster make Matthew hit Brown Eagle? Or was Matthew drunk?"

"We didn't have nary a drop of alcohol," Matthew said in frustration.

Now Emily and the others were ready to hear the story of how Joe Aster created all the havoc.

No one left before Matthew told the whole story. When he finished, Emily said, "I'm sorry I slapped you Brown Eagle."

"Thank goodness you don't hit as hard as Matthew," Brown Eagle gave her a twisted grin. "I'd be blind in both eyes."

"Now, can we go to bed?" asked a very tired Robert.

"Everyone say a prayer for Michael before you go to sleep," Deborah said as she slumped off to her wagon.

Brown Eagle settled into his bedroll just as Matthew arrived with a raw venison steak.

"What on earth? Surely you don't want to eat at this time of morning," the Native exclaimed.

Matthew explained the steak was for Brown Eagle's eye, Emily sent it over. He finished by saying, "Believe me, it's easier to wear raw meat on your face than it is to argue with Emily."

The next day Emily checked on the results.

"Are you sure you wore the steak all night?" she inquired screwing up her face.

"Yes, ma'am," he said.

"I don't believe you. The swelling hasn't gone down. It's so hard to get you savages to accept modern medicine," Emily said scrutinizing the wound.

"Yes, ma'am," Brown Eagle laughed. "Maybe we should put leeches under the steak next time. How about you, Mrs. Kilkenny, would you accept some tea for morning sickness from an old savage?"

She sucked in her breath, "What makes you think I'm in a family way?"

"I have eyes," he said.

"Does Matthew know?" she asked.

"Doesn't he?" Brown Eagle asked surprised.

Chapter 57

*K*atie and Sam McCafferty packed their belongings and bid farewell to the train members not going to town. Emily and Deborah rode in the McCafferty wagon with Katie. Sam, Matthew, Brown Eagle, and Deputy Hinkley rode their own horses. Brian's and Michael's horses were tethered to McCaffery's wagon for Brian and the ladies to use for their return. Matthew and Emily planned to ride double. No one thought Michael would be returning to camp that day.

The entourage stopped at Dr. Forbes office. Brian greeted them somberly.

"No change. He didn't wake up," Brian sighed tiredly. "Dr. Forbes thinks there's pressure on the brain from the blood build up. When the blood drains away, Michael will wake up."

"Can I see him?" Deborah asked.

"Yes, but be prepared, he looks real bad right now."

Deborah wasn't prepared for how badly her husband would look. Only his face showed from the massive bandages wrapped around his head. His face was the color of ashes. He lay in bed with his arms folded across his chest, the common position of a body in a casket. Deborah kissed his face and wept openly. She took his hands, one at a time and massaged color into them. Emily kept her arm around Deborah's shoulders until the wave of tears had subsided.

Matthew and Brown Eagle stood uncomfortably at the foot of the bed. They twisted their hats and tried to think of something consoling to say.

Sam and Katie stood by the door unsure of what was expected of them.

Dr. Forbes entered the room.

"What's this? A party? Everyone get out except the wife," he said sure of his authority.

"I'll be right outside, if you need me," Emily kissed Deborah lightly on the cheek.

Matthew hugged her firmly, "He's strong. He'll be all right in a few days."

Katie and Sam hugged Deborah and gave her the address of their boarding house.

"You come stay with us until Michael's ready to return to camp with you," Katie said.

Deborah nodded never letting go of Michael's hand.

"How is he doctor? Will he recover? How long will he sleep?" she asked.

"Has Brian explained the situation?"

"Yes, a bit, something about blood on the brain. What does that mean?" Deborah asked.

"His skull was fractured, probably with a bottle. Anyhow, he was hit on the head and the bone broke. That caused bleeding under the skull. I did surgery to release the pressure. Now, all we can do is wait and pray" Dr. Forbes said gently.

"Can I stay with him? Or does he need to be moved somewhere else?" she asked.

"I don't want him moved for a few days. That is, I don't want his head moved. It would be good if you could stay and help take care of him. I don't have an assistant right now. I'll teach you what to do. Do you have a place to stay in town?"

"I can stay at Sam and Katie McCafferty's boarding house," Deborah pulled the slip of paper from her pocket and showed him the address.

The doctor's eyebrows shot up with surprise when he saw the address. Then he regained his composure and said, "Good. That's walking distance. You'll need to get away a few times during the day. I don't want you staying here at night. You'll get worn out fast in your condition."

Deborah looked at him puzzled, "I'm not ill. I probably look terrible because I didn't get much sleep last night. I can stay here at night and ask my friend, Emily to stay with Michael a few hours during the day while I sleep. She has medical training."

"We'll work it out. Emily might be just the person we need. I'll talk to her. Sorry about the rude remark. I thought you were six or eight weeks pregnant," he said.

Deborah inhaled deeply, "Really! What makes you think that?"

"Practiced eye. I'm getting old. Could be mistaken," he smiled.

"That would explain some strange feelings I've had. My womanly misery has never been regular, so I didn't think anything about missing last month," Deborah felt herself blushing. A quiet feeling of bliss enveloped her. She leaned over and kissed Michael on the lips.

"You just have to be all right, Michael. You're going to be a father," she smiled through tears of happiness.

"Is Emily one of the ladies outside?" Dr. Forbes asked.

Deborah nodded and he continued, "Why don't you bring Emily in here. I'll go over instructions with both of you at the same time."

Deborah wiped her face on the hem of her dress and went to the door, "Em, please come in here."

Emily and Matthew both jumped to their feet and headed toward the door.

"What's wrong?" Matthew asked.

"No change. We need to talk to Emily alone right now. You can come in later," Deborah said.

"You look like you have good news," Emily said.

"I do. I'll tell you about that later. Right now I need to know if you'll help Dr. Forbes and me take care of Michael while he's unconscious," she looked at Emily quizzically.

"Yes, Of course. What do you want me to do, doctor?" Emily's color heightened with excitement at the prospect of practicing medicine.

Dr. Forbes went over the details of working with an unconscious person. They would have to spoon feed him water every few minutes, change his diaper two or three times a day, exercise his arms and legs and wash him each day.

If Michael developed bedsores, the doctor would show them how to deal with that problem. Dr. Forbes said Michael would probably be up and about before sores developed. Michael was propped up on pillows to encourage the blood to drain away from his brain so there was very little potential of him choking on the water they fed him.

A schedule was agreed upon. Emily would be there from noon until sunset. Dr. Forbes would relieve Deborah at other times during the night and morning. His office was open from ten until four. He made house calls from eight until ten in the morning and from four until eight in the evening. That varied according to how many people needed him, so he could periodically minister to Michael while Deborah took care of her own needs.

Emily opened the front door and found Brown Eagle and Matthew standing there waiting to enter. Brian was asleep in a chair on the front porch. Katie and Sam were walking around the front yard admiring the flowers.

"Why don't you two men come in for a few minutes. Emily and Deborah probably have things to discuss," said Dr. Forbes.

The men entered and Dr. Forbes gave them his prognosis, which was neither encouraging nor discouraging. It was a wait and see situation. Paralysis was a possibility he discussed with the men that he hadn't mentioned it to the women.

Deborah made arrangements to room at the boarding house. Brian agreed to bring the O'Brien's wagon to the house the next day. Deborah told Emily to use Michael's horse to get to and from town.

"We'll keep your mules pastured with our livestock after Brian delivers your wagon to McCafferty's," Emily said.

Deborah wiped her forehead with the back of her hand. There were so many details to think of.

"Listen ladies, I have an idea. Now just say 'no' if you want to. You two are going to be busy the next few days. Could you trust me to buy you a couple of city dresses and a pair of shoes?" Katie asked.

"Oh, that would be wonderful! What a great idea! I feel so dirty in these buckskins," Deborah said. "I'm sure I'd feel better in a nice, clean, plain dress. I'll get the money out of the wagon tomorrow when Brian brings it to town."

Emily agreed. She didn't want to take the time to shop but felt she shouldn't wear her grubby clothes around someone with an open wound.

"I'll write down sizes and get you some money when I get back to our wagon," Emily said.

"By the way, I don't want a dress with an attached belt. I want something that hangs loose," Deborah said. "Also, I want sensible low heeled shoes for everyday wear."

"Me too," Emily said.

The two young women looked at each other questioningly. Deborah smiled and shrugged her shoulders. Emily felt her neck get warm and turned toward the doctor's house. Matthew and Brown Eagle were emerging as she reached the porch.

"We have a lot to do today, Matt," she said. "We'd better get moving."

They hugged Deborah again and said good bye. Brian joined Matthew, Brown Eagle, and Emily as they walked to the sheriff's office.

Chapter 58

"What you want from us? Do we file a complaint, give you a report, or what?" Matthew asked the sheriff.

"Why don't you tell Hinkley your version of what happened. He'll write it all down and you can sign it," the sheriff responded.

"Then you'll arrest the man or men responsible?" Emily asked.

"Have to see if any laws were broken before I arrest anyone, ma'am," he answered.

"There's a man lying over at Doctor Forbes' house...," Emily started but the sheriff interrupted her.

"Just tell the deputy what you know to be true, what happened to you personally. I'll do my job if any laws were broken," the sheriff said laconically.

"Look at these men! They were almost killed! One man is clinging...," she started again.

"Ma'am, please. If you were involved, tell your story to Hinkley. If not, please don't say anything," the sheriff rose from his chair making him more intimidating.

Emily, Matthew, and Brian sat on a hard bench against the wall while Hinkley took Brown Eagle to another room to give his deposition.

Matthew picked up Emily's hand and squeezed it.

"Brian, why don't you go second? I know you're tired and want to get back to your wagon and family," Matthew said.

"Thanks, I would like to get back to Jesse. She's gone funny on us this past week or so. I'm worried about her," Brian said.

"Jesse's worried about where her family is going from here," Emily said. "She's scared. She needs to know you're all going to settle down here in the valley."

Brian didn't respond. The trio sat quietly for a few minutes.

"When are you going to Fort Vancouver to find out about land, Matt?" she asked her husband.

"I want to stay close by until Michael's out of the woods. Deborah needs us," he answered.

"I'll be here. Katie and Sam will be here. I think, if you and Brian left for Fort Vancouver day after tomorrow...," she said.

"I don't want to commit to the Willamette Valley just yet," Brian interrupted. "Maybe next week, or the week after that, I'll go to Vancouver."

"Yeah, me too," Matthew said.

"Matthew," Emily said exasperated. "I thought you were in a big hurry to get here so you could find out about land before snowfall began."

"I was," Matthew tried to explain. "But that was afore Michael got hurt. He's my friend. If he's paralyzed I want to..."

"What?" Emily was on her feet. "What do you mean, 'paralyzed'? What is this all about Brian? How sick is Michael?"

Emily could feel her heart pounding, "Oh, dear God. No. Not paralyzed. From a stupid fight. Brian tell me what you know."

"He's in the Lord's hands. Nobody knows if he suffered permanent brain damage. If his brain is injured it could mean deafness, blindness, paralyzation, loss of memory, most anything," Brian heaved a deep sigh.

"Of course, I knew that. I just didn't want to think about it when a friend was involved," Emily collapsed back onto the bench. They sat in silence until the door swung open.

A tall, muscular, unshaven man with dirty, long hair walked in with his eyes squinted adjusting to the dim light in the room. He looked at each person.

"Hello, Joe. Take a seat. We'll get your statement as quick as possible. These folks are ahead of you," the sheriff barely looked up from his paperwork.

"Joe Aster?" Emily asked.

"Yes, ma'am. Do I know you?" he quickly removed his hat and stood like a schoolboy before her.

Emily sat very still staring up at the huge man. Her hands were on the bench beside her hips. Matthew felt the tension building. He lifted his arm intending to put it around Emily's shoulders and restrain her. At the same moment she sprang from her seat. She pummeled the man on his chest and stomach. She put her right arm back ready to swing her mightiest blow to his face. Matthew grabbed her wrist. The action caused her to lose her balance and she stumbled. Joe Aster caught her before she fell.

"Sorry, ma'am. I know I shouldn't touch you, but I didn't want you to fall down. Sorry," he said and released her. He didn't seem aware she had been beating on him with the intention of inflicting pain.

The sheriff was at her side, "Ma'am, would you step outside with me, please."

Her anger was just below the surface. She wrenched free from Matthew's grip and gave him a look that warned never do that again.

Emily turned back to Joe Aster ready to strike him with a verbal diatribe.

"Ma'am. Outside. Now!" the sheriff emphasized the urgency.

Emily straightened her buckskin and brushed imaginary crumbs from the front before turning to follow the sheriff. Her head held high, her arms folded across her chest.

"Do you think he'll be all right out there by himself," Brian asked Matthew.

"Yeah, he's got a gun," Matthew replied. "I do love a sassy woman."

The phrase immediately made Matthew think of Jerome. He wondered if Jerome and Beth were married yet. Matthew reflected on the black man that had been a good friend. He hoped his life in Illinois was going well.

"I know you," Joe Aster recognized Matthew. "You're that Injun lover what came into the campground last night."

Joe's demeanor changed. He was no longer the humble little boy standing before a respected teacher. His eyes sparked, he reached for the front of Matthew's shirt.

Matthew grabbed Joe's wrist as he stood up. One fast movement and he had the taller man in a hammerlock. He pushed the arm until the man fell to his knees.

Brian took Joe's gun from his belt and retreated to the far side of the room.

"The sheriff said to sit down and wait your turn to tell your story. Now, is you going to do that?" Matthew asked giving the arm a jerk upwards.

Joe fell forward catching himself with his unrestrained hand.

The sheriff walked through the door alone.

"Oh, for heaven's sake. Can't I leave you people alone for a minute," the sheriff drawled. "I hope you aren't thinking of settling in Oregon City."

He took the gun away from Brian and tossed it in a desk drawer.

Matthew released his hold on Joe and everyone sat down on the benches. Brian and Matthew sat facing Joe Aster.

"Where's my wife?" Matthew asked.

"She chose to wait outside rather than be arrested for disturbing the peace," the sheriff sighed.

Matthew grinned at Brian. Brian shook his head then chuckled.

Joe glared at the two men. He was trying to sort out Brian's connection to the "Injun lover."

Brown Eagle emerged from Hinkley's office. Matthew sat ready to spring on Joe if need be. Joe tensed and watched his hated adversary intently Brown Eagle shook hands with the sheriff and told Matthew he was returning to Dr. Forbes'.

"Take Emily with you. Maybe she can help Deborah. She's outside," Matthew said never taking his eyes off Joe.

Brian arose and walked toward Deputy Hinkley.

"This shouldn't take long. My story's pretty short," he said as he left the room.

Joe looked from Hinkley's door to the office exit. He still couldn't connect the three men together.

"You hire some other Injun lover to back up your story?" he asked Matthew.

Matthew ignored him.

"Lying bastard. How much you have to pay him?" Joe asked.

"Shut up, Joe," the sheriff said quietly.

Chapter 59

The depositions were all taken. A dozen men gave their versions of the campsite brawl. The only person that came close to being arrested was Emily. She was incensed that Joe Aster wasn't behind bars. According to the statements of eleven other people, all he did was say, "What are you doing here?" That was not a crime.

A fellow card player said he saw Joe reach for his gun and he kicked Joe's barrel out from under him. Therefore he never drew on, or threatened anyone. It was not against the law to carry or wear a gun. This was the wilderness. Many people carried guns for protection.

Brown Eagle admitted to hitting his friend, Matthew. There was no law against protecting your friend from a perceived danger. Matthew had made no complaint against Brown Eagle so there was no charge.

Matthew admitted he hit Brown Eagle, but a man was allowed to protect himself if he thought someone was attacking. Brown Eagle filed no complaint, so no blame could be laid.

Emily stood in front of the sheriff resting her palms on his desk and yelling in his face. Calling a sheriff a nincompoop and threatening the delicacy of his eardrums was disturbing the peace of his office. When Hinkley put her in handcuffs and turned her toward a cell filled with smiling drunks, she became truly penitent and saw the error of her ways. Fortunately, the sheriff was lenient and let her off with a warning.

Emily rode Michael's horse back to camp in a subdued mood. She was so sorry Michael had been injured. It seemed unfair to avoid the hazards of the trail only to be struck down by a whiskey bottle when you reached your destination.

Jesse had sent her sons to town with a grocery list. They returned in time for her to fix a banquet. Jesse and Katherine spent the afternoon baking pies and bread, roasting chicken, baking potatoes, and steaming peas and carrots. Robert had put the milk containers in the Clackamas River sand to make it icy cold.

Boards were set up on barrels and Katherine produced a roll of gingham to be used as a tablecloth. Jesse brought out the remnants of her mother's china and supplemented it with the usual tin plates and mugs. At least there was enough china for the three women.

Emily showered at the canvas enclosure set up by the men. She changed into her Paducah church dress and helped herself to a glass of medicinal brandy from their keg. She felt much better by the time she made it to the dinner table.

Matthew showed up at dinner with two bottles of his uncle's wine. He toasted Oregon – "land of green valleys and shining mountains."

Emily drank her first glass of wine too fast and needed a second glass to toast Katherine and Jesse, cooks extraordinaire. She still had half a glass left when Brian toasted all the friends made along the trail. Jesse wanted to toast Deborah and Michael and all the friends missing from the meal. Of course, Emily had to drink to them. With the last half of her third glass of wine she stood and held her glass aloft.

"Here's to our coming child. May she grow strong, beautiful, and smart; may she always love her home in the shiny mountains."

People cheered and clapped. Emily promptly passed out. Matthew carried her to the wagon and Katherine helped get her dress off.

"I hope the gravy stain comes out," Katherine said. She took it to her wash tub to soak.

Emily stirred and Matthew cradled his groggy wife in his arms, "And may she grow up to be strong spirited and temperamental like the most beautiful woman in the world."

Emily smiled and snuggled against his chest.

"Das not 'ow ah meant ta tell ya 'bout da baby," she slurred.

"I love you, Mrs. Kilkenny," Matthew kissed her gently. She was already asleep.

Brown Eagle called out cheerily, "Come on Matt. There's plenty of food left."

"Congratulations!" Jesse said. "You'll make a fine father. With a big farm, you'll need some sons to help you."

"Here, here," Brian said. "Let's toast your future sons with a glass of fresh milk."

"I'll drink to that," Katherine said returning from her washtub.

"Did Ceantoan and Shinnay get an early start towards home?" Brown Eagle asked.

"Must have, they were gone when I woke up," Josiah said.

"What does that prove?" Jesse laughed. "Yes, they did get out of here before eleven o'clock this morning. I had my daily chores done before you got up son. They left before any of us were awake."

She nudged her older son and ran her fingers through his hair. Brian smiled to see his wife acting normal. He didn't think to attribute her actions to the wine.

The meal was cheery with teasing and storytelling. As soon as dishes were cleared away the mood changed. Plans were made for taking care of Deborah and Michael's needs.

"Em's not going to be in any condition to help Deborah tomorrow," Matt said. "We'll stay in camp and keep an eye on everyone's belongings."

"I'll drive O'Brien's wagon to town and take Jesse and Katherine. They can help Deborah and do some shopping," Brian said. "I'll bring the O'Brien mules back here in the afternoon."

"Take Michael's horse and mine for the ladies to ride home," Matthew suggested.

"I'll go along to help Brian get the wagon situated and carry Deborah's things into McCafferty's rooming house," Brown Eagle said. "Then we can find out where to go to get land information and I'll find out about joining the army as a scout."

Katherine heard Jesse give a sigh of relief. She was glad someone was pushing Brian into taking action on settling down.

"We haven't seen the outriders all day. Maybe they took off for the gold fields without us," Robert said.

Jesse's peace was short lived, "You're not going to the gold fields. You're too young."

Before Robert could argue, Josiah said, "Nah, they left their stuff over there."

Josiah pointed to two tents with a cooking kettle and coffeepot.

"They'll be back," Brian said. "They're getting rid of some rust in their pipes."

Jesse tsked and Josiah snickered. Robert was puzzled and changed the subject.

"Can Josiah and I go into town to look around? We want to find young people."

"I think that's okay, don't you, Mother?" Brian took Jesse's hand and squeezed it. Jesse gripped her husband's hand hard.

"Will you promise not to go to saloons or gambling houses?" she asked.

"Sure," Robert said. "We just wanted to go last night to hear music. We know how dangerous it is to be around drunks. There aren't any saloons in Oregon Territory, Ma. It's against the law to sell liquor here."

Jesse looked directly into Josiah's eyes, "Do you promise me young man? No gambling and no going anywhere people are drinking alcohol."

"Yeah, sure. I'm more interested in high school. Do you think they have a high school where we're going to settle? I'd like to go back to school."

Brian felt his wife relax, her hand melted. The boy couldn't have said anything more pleasing to his mother.

"Yes, of course, you can go to town," she cooed.

Chapter 60

Emily was lying on her bed wishing she didn't have to move.

"Want some coffee afore you get up?" Matthew asked.

"No. I don't want to see, hear, or smell anything that's supposed to go into my mouth," she growled.

"Wine doesn't usually make you sick. Must be the baby," Matthew tried to console his wife.

"I wish you hadn't said the word 'sick'," she said. "Go away, leave me alone."

She was nauseated and her bladder was full. She knew she needed to get up very soon but procrastinated.

Matthew took the dogs and his gun and headed toward the woods. He was on foot and planned to hunt small animals.

"Maybe we'll have grouse or rabbit for dinner," he called over his shoulder.

That did it. Emily bounded out of bed and barely made it to the back flap before vomiting.

Matthew wisely chose to ignore the sound and kept walking away from camp.

"Darn, darn, darn," Emily said.

Matthew had put her to bed in her camisole and pantaloons. Now they were wet and nasty. She looked about for something to put on. Her head hurt, her mouth tasted terrible, her stomach was upset. She was a mess. She wanted to cry but knew that would just make her head hurt worse.

She climbed down from the wagon and emptied her bladder. She cleaned up the outside of the wagon and threw two buckets of water on the ground to wash away the mess behind the wagon. Emily got a pair of Matthew's

trousers that were threadbare and a ragged shirt and headed for the community shower. The bucket of water hanging overhead had been sitting overnight and was icy cold when it fell on her; she squealed.

Now she was shaking with cold and had brought no towel with her. She
pulled the trousers up her wet legs and quickly put the shirt on. Her hair
dampened the shirt immediately. She was so cold.

Emily gathered up the soiled clothes and dashed barefooted back to her
wagon. She held the clothes as far from her body as she could and dropped
them on the ground before climbing back into the wagon.

Her feet were muddy but she didn't care at the moment. She got back in
bed and pulled the buffalo robe over herself. She lay in a coiled position until
she stopped shivering. Her stomach felt less queasy now, but her head hurt
when she moved.

"I'm never, never going to drink alcohol again," she vowed disgusted with
herself.

She dozed off to sleep and dreamed of rocking an infant in the chair from
Jerome. Jerome and Beth were in the dream as well as her sister, Jenny. They
were admiring her beautiful new daughter. Emily slept soundly for over an
hour.

She was awakened when the dogs returned howling and barking. She lay
there listening to Matthew talk to his dogs. He was working on something,
she could hear metal clinking.

"Now when my son goes hunting with us, you dogs will have to scare up
twice as many animals, got that?"

He was scratching the dogs' ears, she could tell from the low groaning
sound the dogs were making. She smiled, what a good man he is.

She sat on the edge of the bed waiting for the wave of nausea to leave. Her
head felt better. She looked at the mud on the floor, lifted the buffalo skin and
clucked her tongue at the mess she had made. There was a lot of laundry to do.

Emily wiped off her feet and pulled on her moccasins. She brushed her
hair and cleaned her teeth. By that time she decided she was going to live
after all. She gathered their soiled clothes and a washboard. Once outside she
smiled weakly at Matthew.

"Maybe, I'll try some coffee now, and some toast or a biscuit."

Matthew was cleaning two rabbits and pointed with his bloodied knife toward the coffeepot sitting beside the hot coals. Emily thought she would vomit again when she saw the knife. She turned away and swallowed several times.

"How come I don't look sexy when I wear those clothes?" he said grinning.

"You do," she smiled back. "I sure don't feel sexy. Don't get any ideas. I've got to get the laundry done, so I can take care of Michael this afternoon," the thought brought her back to reality.

"Hey, where is everyone?" Emily asked.

"In town. Katherine and Jesse are going to help Deborah. Brian and Brown Eagle are going to find out where to get papers for claiming land. Josiah and Robert are doing boy stuff, and we're supposed to keep tract of livestock and belongings in the camp," he answered.

"Oh," she sat eating the dry biscuit and sipping lukewarm coffee.

"I'm glad you're having my baby," he said. "When'll he be here?"

"About the first week of June," she answered "I'm glad too, but I hoped SHE wouldn't arrive until we had a house."

"We ain't going to have a house this winter. I'll be traipsing around looking at land. Figured it'd be next April afore I could look at Beaver Valley," he said cleaning his skinning tools in a pot of hot soapy water.

"The baby's due the same time you'll be in San Francisco meeting the family," she commented.

Matthew didn't respond. He wrapped the cleaned rabbits in cheesecloth and put them in the meat cooler. The skins were cleaned and put on a wooden frame to dry. The dogs cleaned up the offal.

Matthew sat down beside her and poured a cup of coffee.

"What do you think? What do you want to do? Go over the Siskiyous and wait out the winter in San Francisco? When's the last you can travel?"

"I'm sorry. I wanted to wait to get in the family way. Wait 'til we were settled in," she said.

"Would you stop saying you're sorry. Neither of us is sorry to be having our own baby. I know I been looking forward to taking George Washington Kilkenny hunting," he leaned over and kissed her hair.

"Well, Julia Marie Kilkenny has decided she wants to be born in late May or early June," Emily grinned at her husband.

"It'll take all winter to check out the Willamette Valley land. You'll look at Beaver Valley next April, make a decision and put in the paper work. Your land, your family, and your daughter will all need your attention on June 1," Emily sighed.

"I asked what you want to do," Matthew reminded her.

"Get a room with Katie and Sam and stay there until the baby is old enough to travel," she said.

Matthew rubbed her back. He realized she had no underwear on and was immediately aroused. He pulled her into his arms.

"Been a long time since we was all alone," he reached under the shirt and rubbed the bare skin of her back.

"Matt! Be serious," she said but didn't move away from him. She set her coffee mug on the table and put both arms around her husband. She had her head on his chest and felt his heart pounding against her cheek.

Chapter 61

Deborah was giving Michael a spoonful of water when Katherine walked into the tiny well-lit bedroom off the surgery.

"How is he?" she asked.

"No change. The only movement I've seen is his Adam's apple when he swallows. Thank goodness, he's swallowing the water," the tired woman answered.

"What should I do? Emily couldn't make it today," Katherine said.

"Oh? Is she all right?" Deborah asked.

"She'll be fine, just under the weather this morning. Did you know she was expecting?" Katherine asked.

Deborah smiled, "Realized it yesterday when she and I both ordered dresses without belts."

"Deborah! Deborah! What're you saying? Are you in the family way, too?" Katherine grasped Deborah's arm.

Deborah nodded.

Katherine spun her around and hugged her, "Oh, honey! I'm so happy for you. Does Michael know?"

"I told him several times last night but don't know if he heard me," Deborah said wiping Michael's face with a damp washcloth.

"Here, I'll show you how to exercise his arms and legs. You have to do this every hour. And also give him a spoonful of water every ten or fifteen minutes," Deborah manipulated her husband's arm, wrist, and fingers. She went through the whole procedure one time then asked Katherine to take over so she could get some sleep.

"I'll be back in about four hours. Dr. Forbes will check in with you before he opens his office for appointments. He's making house calls right now," Deborah explained.

"Jesse's going to help also. She wanted to shop this morning. We're all so tired of our raggedy clothes. You can sleep eight hours, if you want. Jesse and I will take turns today," Katherine told her friend.

"I'll try. I had nightmares as soon as I fell asleep yesterday. Then I lay awake for hours. I only slept a couple hours. Wake me up if he comes to, of course," Deborah started for the door.

"Wait! Where will you be?" Katherine asked.

Deborah wrote down the address and directions to Katie and Sam's boarding house.

Katherine was settling into the routine when the door opened and Dr. Forbes, Brown Eagle, and Brian walked in.

"Oh hello. Who are you?" asked the doctor.

Katherine explained her presence without saying anything about Emily's drinking to excess the evening before.

Dr. Forbes gave the three of them an update on Michael's condition.

"I'm afraid, if he doesn't regain consciousness today, he may have severe brain damage. He may be just as you see him until he starves to death," the doctor's statement shocked the trio.

"Isn't there anything you can do? More surgery? Leeches? Something," Katherine pleaded. "He's going to be a father soon."

"No. I've done all I can. It's out of my hands," the doctor lifted Michael's eyelid and peered into a glazed, staring, non-responsive eye.

"Now, who is going to stay here and exercise him while his wife catches up on a bit of sleep?" Dr. Forbes asked.

"I am," Katherine answered. "You men go about your business looking into the Donation Land Claims."

"The courthouse down at the end of Main Street should be your first stop," Dr. Forbes said. "They have copies of the survey in the General Land Office."

The two men walked their horses to the courthouse.

"Babies seem to be contagious. You better watch out, Brian," Brown Eagle said.

"I wouldn't mind a dainty little creature like Marie or Rebecca around. They don't stay little for long, though. On the other hand, I'd hate to raise a girl in these times. Seems like morality is on the decline," Brian surprised Brown Eagle with his answer and he thought it best to change the subject.

"Did you want to take the O'Brien's mules back to camp after we finish at the land office?" he asked.

"I'll go back to Sam's and get the mules just before we leave town this evening," Brian said. "Sam has two acres of grass behind his house. That should keep them and Michael's horse occupied for one day."

It took the land clerk and hour to lay out the maps, surveys, and paper work, and explain what each sheet represented. He was bald on top and the hair around the bottom was worn shoulder length. He had on a tiny pair of glasses, which he used for reading. He looked over top the glasses to talk to people. He reminded Brian of pictures he'd seen of Benjamin Franklin, which gave Brian an initial feeling of respect for the man.

"Before you get engrossed in picking out your homestead let me tell you the qualifications. You have to be white, male, and an American citizen over the age of eighteen."

Brian jotted that information into a notebook.

"I'm qualified, I'm over eighteen," Brian said smiling.

"I don't understand why Natives don't qualify. It was their land to begin with," Brown Eagle said.

The clerk immediately got defensive. "They weren't cultivating the land. They didn't have permanent wooden or brick homes on it. It was unclaimed wilderness that they just wandered around on while hunting and fishing," he said crossing his arms.

"The Cayuse and some other tribes are farmers. Many tribes have permanent structures for homes. The Mandans have stockaded villages of permanent structures. They are farmers just like white men. A lot of the land the wagon train passed over couldn't be cultivated to raise a bushel of hay. But it still belonged to the Natives living there," Brown Eagle said.

"Wait a minute. We didn't come here to talk politics. If I get involved in another fight, Jesse will leave me for sure," Brian said.

"You're right. Okay, I don't want your land, or my peoples' land back, whatever. You keep this land that the Hudson's Bay Company, the English, the local Natives, and half a dozen other groups think is theirs, and give it to my pure white Euro-American friends," Brown Eagle said bitterly.

Brian felt a pang of guilt.

The clerk cleared his throat. When he spoke it was directed toward Brian. He stood with his back to Brown Eagle. "You can locate on any vacant, unreserved, non-mineral public land in the Oregon Territory," he intoned as if he made the same statement ten times a day. "The good bottom land of the Willamette, Umpqua, and Rogue Rivers has already been claimed. You can look at the land around the edge, in the foothills," he told the doctor.

"You can claim 160 acres for yourself and 160 acres in your wife's name. You did say you were married Mr... What's your name, sir?" the clerk looked intently at Brian.

"I was married when I left the wagon this morning. If our boys don't get into trouble today, I'll probably still be married tonight," Brian said.

"And your name, sir," the clerk stood with a pencil poised over a logbook.

"Dr. Brian Jamison. My wife is Jesse Jamison and our sons are...," Brian said before being interrupted.

"Are the boys eighteen or over?" the clerk asked.

"No," Brian answered.

"I don't need their names. Dr. and Mrs. Brian Jamison, right. I have you down now," the clerk said. "Your wife's given name isn't important."

"It is to her," Brian said taking a distinct dislike to this officious man. He questioned his respect for the man solely on the clerk's looks.

"The blocks of land are rectangular. See the Willamette Meridians?" the clerk pointed to two dark lines forming a tee with each end at a cardinal point. The longer line went north and south through the Willamette Valley. The shorter line went east and west just below the Columbia River.

"Out from those lines are the rectangular blocks. Some aren't rectangular because that land was claimed before the surveys started in 1850. Anyhow, you have to pick the land with the co-ordinates shown here, cultivate it, and claim it," the clerk recited. "Now the land that is left is here, here, and here. Choose your land from those areas, have a surveyor make a field map, plant crops, and file your claim within three months. Then it's all yours. It's that simple."

"Sounds complicated to me but will be worth the effort if we get a decent homestead," Brian shook hands and gathered up an armload of papers.

Brown Eagle had been waiting at the door and Brian turned toward him.

"One more thing," the clerk said. "Bring your field map and fee here to Surveyor General John B. Preston within three months from your survey."

"Wow, that was confusing. I hope you understood it," Brown Eagle said when they were on the busy street.

"I understood the part that all the good land had been taken," Brian answered. "I want to put these papers somewhere safe. Would you mind going to Sam's house before we look for someone to induct you into the army?"

When they arrived at the boarding house a commotion was going on. Katie swung a broom at a man exiting the house with stacks of clothes and parcels.

"Get out you rascal," swat, swat went the broom. "Don't you ever come back here again."

"He didn't pay his bill," Brian said.

Katie turned on her heels and marched up the porch steps.

"Katie," Brown Eagle called. "Is Sam around?"

Katie McCafferty turned toward the approaching men. It was obvious she was still steaming.

"He went up to Fort Vancouver this morning. Please come in and help me," she opened the front door.

They followed her into the house and up the stairs.

"That terrible man was renting two connecting bedrooms. He has been here a year! A whole year, mind you," she opened the bedroom door wide.

Brian gasped, Brown Eagle laughed.

"It's not funny, young man," she said blowing a wisp of hair out of her eye. "Look at this place! He was running a, a, a... you know. Help me get this garbage out of here."

338

She stripped satin sheets off the bed while Brown Eagle took down red lacy curtains. Brian was looking for somewhere safe to put his papers.

"Can I leave these papers in the parlor downstairs until this evening?" Brian asked.

"Help yourself. They should be all right on that table in the corner. No one uses that," Katie said tearing a picture of a nude woman off the wall.

"I'll be back in a minute," Brian said excusing himself from the bedroom.

Brian put the papers on the table as suggested and returned to the garishly decorated room. Brown Eagle was stuffing lengths of lace and silk into a pillowcase and Katie cleared a dressing table covered with perfume bottles, creams and lotions with one sweep. The bottles crashed into a wooden crate.

"Here Brian, take this box to the back yard and burn it," Katie said shoving the box into his arms.

The box was leaking and Brian still reeked of cheap perfume two hours later when he and Brown Eagle escaped Katie's forced labor.

"Think Jesse will believe you?" Brown Eagle asked.

"No, of course not. We have to fabricate a fantastic story she'll believe," Brian groaned.

"Why don't you just buy new clothes and have the store burn the old ones? You were going to get new clothes anyhow," Brown Eagle suggested.

"Good idea! Where's the dry goods store," Brian felt better already.

Everyone they passed on the elevated wooden sidewalk turned to look at the flowery smelling couple. Brian and Brown Eagle didn't take notice. They were single minded-get new clothes before they met someone who knew them.

They made it safely to the store and were attired in completely new outfits within thirty minutes. Brian gave the clerk an extra dollar to burn their old clothes.

Back on the street, they marched confidently toward Dr. Forbes office. Josiah and Robert saw them and ran to greet them. Josiah stopped in his tracks ten feet from his father.

"Pop! Did you visit Yvonne, too?" the boy asked with a startled expression on his face. Josiah shot his father a hate filled look, turned and ran away.

"What's his problem?" Brian asked Robert. "Who's Yvonne?"

"She's a fancy lady he went to see this morning. You smell just like her," Robert explained.

"How do you know about 'fancy' ladies, young man? Oh, never mind, I don't want to hear it," Brian said exasperated.

"Now what?" Brown Eagle asked.

"Robert, go find your brother. Tell him he's needed at Sam's house immediately. Go. Go on boy, do as you're told," Brian waved his hand indicating he wanted Robert to follow Josiah quickly.

"Brown Eagle would you please go to the doctor's office and ask Jesse to meet me at Sam's house as soon as possible?" Brian asked.

"Now that's a good idea," Brown Eagle said and walked briskly away.

The family met on McCafferty's front porch and Katie explained why Brian smelled of cheap perfume.

"You could have told me yourself, Brian," Jesse said smiling. "I would've believed you, of course. Now Josiah, why don't you tell us about your new little friend, Yvonne?"

Chapter 62

*D*eborah walked slowly along the residential street. She wanted to observe living conditions as she thought she'd be here for a long time, maybe forever. Most of the houses were cheap construction. They looked temporary. She saw a woman taking laundry from a clothesline and waved. The woman nodded but didn't stop her work. Two houses had covered wagons sitting in the back yard. The canvas was frayed and weeds grew around the wheels.

A cold breeze caught her hat and she grabbed it before it could escape. She drew her shawl closer around her shoulders. The autumn rain could be seen in the mountains.

It'll be raining here before nightfall, she thought and walked a bit faster.

The clinic was empty when she arrived and a sign on the front door said Dr. Forbes was on his rounds and would return at six p.m.

"What a lonely life Dr. Forbes has," Deborah said to Jesse who was ministering to Michael. "He doesn't seem to have a life away from work."

"Brian worked long hours when we were back east. He left at seven o'clock in the morning and usually got home about seven in the evening. At least he ate dinner with us most evenings and spent Sunday with his family," Jesse said massaging Michael's feet and moving the toes.

"I could tell when a troublesome patient had taken a turn for the worse or better by his mood when he walked through the door," she went on. "I hope Brian and I can spend more time together out here. I wish he'd go into farming instead of medicine. I could work beside him then. There's no place for women in medicine."

"Where's Brian now?" Deborah asked.

"He and Brown Eagle went to a fort somewhere, an outpost anyhow. Brown Eagle wants to be a scout for the army," she clucked her tongue. "Why would anyone want to travel back and forth across country? Once was enough for me."

"I agree with you. I sure wouldn't want to do it for a living. Is Katherine shopping?"

"Yes. She wants some pretty dresses to impress her gentleman in Rough and Ready. I've only been here about three hours. You can go get yourself a new dress if you like. I'll stay with Michael," Jesse offered.

"I gave Katie money to buy me a couple of dresses and a pair of shoes. She'll probably do that tomorrow," Deborah said taking up the glass of water and spoon.

"In that case, I'll turn Michael's care over to your capable hands and make my way to Katie's house. Brian's going to meet me there to go back to camp. I don't want to be walking the streets after dark," Jesse picked up the packages from her morning shopping.

"Thank you so much for helping out. Thank God for good friends," Deborah gave Jesse an awkward hug across a hatbox and shopping basket.

"You'd do the same for us. I feel like we're family. All we have is each other out here in this wild place," Jesse headed out the door eager to be on her way.

Deborah put a teaspoon of water in Michael's mouth by squeezing his lips on the sides until they formed a funnel. She watched his Adam's apple so she'd know when he swallowed.

"How are you this evening, my darling? Are you warm enough? It's getting chilly outside. It's going to rain soon," she tried to sound cheery just in case he could hear her.

She gave Michael three spoons of water, washed his face being careful not to get the bandage wet, and began exercising his left arm. She kept up a banter of lively conversation for several minutes. She told him about Katie's evicted tenant and about Brian obtaining a passel of maps and papers to start his search for land. Then she discussed potential names for their child.

While she was bending his right arm up and down at the elbow, she held his hand. She felt movement in his fingers, knew she was just imagining it, and went on with her list of names.

"Katherine has been like a big sister to me since I left home at fourteen. She took me in so I could finish high school and get my teacher's certificate. I was thinking of naming a daughter after her. Is that all right with you? Maybe call our daughter Mary Katherine. That's a fine sounding Irish name to go with O'Brien."

There it was again, a slight pressure on her fingers! Maybe she hadn't imagined it before.

"Of course, Erin or Kathleen are nice also. Maybe we could name her after your mother or sister. Would you like that?"

The finger definitely moved. She kissed his hand, "Oh Michael, please come back. I need you so. Please, please be well again."

An hour later, Dr. Forbes entered the room to find Michael's eyes open staring at the ceiling. Deborah was chatting away as she lay on the bed snuggled against Michael.

"What's this? Is our patient awake? Hallelujah!" the doctor walked quickly to the bedside.

"Can you hear me, Michael?" he asked.

Michael blinked as his only response.

"Can you see me?" Dr. Forbes leaned above Michael's face.

There was no response.

"He can move his fingers," Deborah said. "That's a good sign isn't it doctor? He's going to get well, isn't he?"

"There's a good chance he will. There's a good chance," Dr. Forbes said absently holding a lantern beside Michael's face. "It may take all winter but we'll take it one step at a time."

The Jamisons, Katherine, and Brown Eagle weren't aware of Michael's progress. They were on their way back to camp when Michael made his first movement.

Emily had done laundry most of the day so it was Matthew that cooked dinner. He had the two rabbits on a spit, roasted potatoes and pumpkin in a cast-iron kettle and baked cornbread in the Dutch oven. He'd made enough for a dozen people just in case someone else wanted to eat with them. The hot meal was enjoyed by the whole group while Brian explained what he'd learned about free land.

Matthew told of his plans. "Just as soon as we know about Michael, I'll start exploring the possibility of a homestead. I want to get somewhere off the beaten path so my brothers and stepdad can get plots nearby."

"I think I'll start looking tomorrow," Brian said. "Robert and Josiah, I want you boys to go with me. The place I pick will be your spread someday."

"I want to help Deborah, so I'll stay behind," Jesse said.

"I'll be here, if you want to go with your family," Emily was pouring a second helping of milk into a mug as she spoke.

"I know you will, but he may need to be lifted out of bed to change the sheets. You girls shouldn't be lifting a full grown man in your condition," Jesse explained.

"Oh, so Deborah is expecting also," Emily smiled. "I thought she might be."

Katherine had been very quiet during dinner. Now she spoke up and her statement surprised everyone. "I'm glad you two are here to help Deborah," she mumbled. "I'm leaving tomorrow."

"Leaving! Where you going?" Robert was the first to mouth the question.

"The outriders offered to escort me to Rough and Ready, if I'd leave tomorrow," she said quietly. Katherine knew the train occupants thought she'd stay with Deborah for as long as needed.

"My gentleman's expecting me before winter. I need to get over the Cascades and Siskiyous as soon as possible," she looked around at the surprised faces. "If I wait two weeks, I may be stuck here until spring."

"I want to go with the outriders," Robert said. "I want to be a gold miner. Can I go with you Katherine?"

Katherine didn't reply. Both parents did.

"No, young man. You'll stay with us until you're sixteen," Brian said with authority. "Then you can make your own decisions."

"Sixteen! Five whole years! All the gold will be gone by then," Robert slammed his mug onto the table.

"Sixteen! You mean I've got to hang around for two more years?" Josiah got into the family discussion.

"Yes," both parents answered simultaneously.

"Can we discuss this matter privately," Jesse said looking embarrassed.

"Just let me say this," Katherine stood up. "Neither the outriders nor I want the responsibility of taking you boys along."

The boys were stunned silent for a minute. Josiah regained his voice first.

"But Bill's my friend," he said. "He's the one that gave me the money to visit Yvonne."

Now Jesse was on her feet, "That settles it then. Neither of you boys are going. You're not to have anything more to do with Bill or the other man, whatever his name is."

The boys left the table and walked off into the dark arguing. "Dummy. What did you say that for?" Robert asked. "I almost had them talked into letting us go."

Emily, Matthew, and Brown Eagle watched the embers die out in the fire. It was five minutes after the rest of the party left before anyone spoke.

"Peaceful out here in the evening," Brown Eagle said quietly.

"Yeah, it fools you into thinking the whole world's just fine," Matthew said picking at his teeth with a stick.

It started to sprinkle and the three of them began putting food away.

"Not many leftovers. At least we can have cornbread and gravy for breakfast," Emily said. "Good dinner, Matt. Thanks for cooking it."

"Right. Thanks, Matt," Brown Eagle said as he hurried off to his tent.

Matthew lit the lantern inside their wagon, "The heat from the light will warm up the air in here whilst you get ready for bed."

Emily poured some water into the wash basin and tied up her hair.

"Thanks, honey. I'm just going to wash my face and hands tonight. I took a cold shower this morning."

"Tomorrow we'll go talk to Sam and Katie and see if they'll put us up for the winter. Agreed?" Matthew reiterated their earlier conversation.

"Yes, we could do that," she said. "Or I could while you go look at land with Brian."

"He'll probably be out a week," Matthew said. "I don't want to leave Michael and Deborah for that long."

Matthew stripped to his new long johns and crawled into bed. Emily soon joined him in their furry cocoon.

Chapter 63

The doctor checked Michael's wound. The scalp had been shaved and a six-inch opening made in the skin and sutured closed. The crack in the skull was the width of a hair and was Z shaped. On any other part of the body, a broken bone would be more minor. Deborah, Emily, or Jesse nursed Michael twenty-four hours a day even after he moved a muscle now and then.

Katherine left with the outriders after a hurried farewell the morning after Michael's first response. She promised to notify the people of Rough and Ready that Deborah wouldn't be there to teach school until spring or early summer. Deborah definitely wanted the job. She may have to support Michael, their child, and herself for the rest of her life.

Katherine drove her wagon down Main Street following two men on horseback that were leading pack mules. Katherine blew Deborah a kiss; she waved until she was out of sight after a tearful farewell.

Once Deborah could no longer see Katherine she turned back toward the clinic. She saw Brown Eagle entering. The Shoshone was on his way to Fort Vancouver and wanted an update on Michael's condition before he left.

"I'll be there until next spring," he told Deborah holding both her hands. "If you need me, send word. I can be down here in a matter of hours. I may be sent out on short forays looking for lost travelers during the winter, but most of the time I'll just be learning about the army and where forts and out-posts are located."

"Where are you going next spring?" she asked.

"To Saint Louis to join another wagon train," he smiled. "You got any suggestions I can give the ladies?"

"My goodness, yes. Sit down and I'll give you a list as long as your arm. Mainly, tell them to forget everything they know about dressing proper. Tell them to get boy's clothes including boots to wear. And to bring at least three pairs of boy's boots, no button-up dress shoes."

Brown Eagle looked puzzled.

"They should have strong, flat heeled shoes for walking the trail. I thought I was going to ride across country. I didn't prepare for walking two-thirds of the way."

When Deborah finished her list of suggestions, Brown Eagle spoke to Michael as though he was sure every word was understood. He wanted Michael to be assured he wasn't being abandoned. Brown Eagle promised to come back for visits when he got time off his job.

Brian Jamison and his sons started out early that same gray morning. They had a pack mule loaded with sleeping and eating equipment for a week on the road. Robert took a pick, shovel, and gold pan. Brian took emergency medical supplies and sheaves of maps, Josiah took his hunting rifle and a book to read.

Brian held his wife in a loving embrace giving her instructions on the care of their cattle, oxen, and dogs. He was concerned about leaving his wife alone. Her mood swings had him worried. He hoped Emily was right, she was concerned about keeping her family intact awhile longer. At thirty-six years old, she could be starting menopause. His medical studies hadn't prepared him for facing a wife during "the change;" he chose to disregard that possibility.

Robert appeared to have forgotten his distress over missing out on a trip to the gold fields. He was eager to start this manly adventure of exploring Oregon with his father and brother.

Josiah would rather stay in town, he was sure the trip would be boring. He wasn't the least bit happy with the prospect of spending cold nights in a tent and days struggling to find landmarks shown on a map. He knew this was the start of two miserable years of his life. He could hardly wait until he was free to live as he chose.

Matthew shook hands with Brian and said he'd be available if Jesse needed anything. Matthew intended to help Sam with maintenance on the boarding house, get his own set of survey maps to study and help Katie, Deborah, and Emily anyway he could. One more woman under his care would be no trouble.

His first order of business was to reserve a room at McCafferty's. Emily, Matthew, and Jesse went to town soon after Brian and the boys left camp. Jesse went directly to Dr. Forbes to relieve Deborah. Emily and Matthew headed for McCafferty's.

Katie and Sam were putting new wallpaper in the two rooms previously used as a brothel. The mundane ivy print looked much better than the garish red and purple they were covering.

The size of the rooms impressed Emily. Matthew and Emily reserved the room at the front of the house. The view from the window was northeasterly including Mt. Hood, which proudly protruded above the Cascade Range. The eleven-thousand foot volcanic peak looked gray with silver edging as it was back-lit by the morning sun. Matthew stared at the view a few seconds before he realized Sam had asked him a question.

"Matt, you got pasturage for your livestock yet?" Sam repeated.

"No. Nothing arranged. You got an idea?" Matthew responded when the question finally intruded on his private thoughts.

"A friend has a section not far from here. We could ask him to let your animals mingle with his. Probably depend on how much hay he got put aside last summer," Sam said.

"Sounds good. I don't want to sell off the oxen afore I settle into my own place," Matthew said. "I'll need them for dray the first few years."

"What about the dogs? Are they going to be a problem while we live here?" Emily asked.

"Land sakes, no," Katie answered. "Everyone in town has a dog or two. They roam all over the place. Juanita won't allow dogs in the house but they'll be fine staying in the barn."

"Mine better stick close by if they know what's good for 'em," Matthew said sternly.

"I can see you're going to be a strict father," Emily laughed.

"My goodness, Emily! Are you in the family way?" Katie asked.

Emily, slightly embarrassed the subject came up in front of Sam, just nodded.

"Well, congratulations to both of you," Sam said shaking Matthew's hand.

"You're going to have a mighty busy winter," Katie said. "We'll all work together to get baby clothes made for you and Deborah. That'll be a pleasant way to relax after taking care of Michael."

"I'm going to look at land close by so I'll be on hand to help with Michael," Matthew said. "Also, thought I'd see if you want a hand fixing up your place for the winter."

"No land worth having is within a two day drive of here," Sam said sadly. "It was all grabbed up by the Hudson Bay Company employees just as soon as the government notice came out."

"I heard some of the men was already raising hay or running company livestock afore the bill passed," Matthew said.

"Yep. All they had to do was survey and file. No way anybody else had a chance at the land," Sam said. "My friend that has a section of land has had it since 1843. Back then the law was you got that much land free if you built a cabin on it and either lived there yourself or had a tenant. He worked for Hudson's, raised beef for them, already had a cabin built by '44."

Katie motioned for Emily to follow her. They went to Katie and Sam's quarters next to the large parlor downstairs.

"I wanted to give you the new clothes I bought but didn't want to interrupt the men," Katie said. "Both land and clothes are important."

Katie took two boxes out of her armoire. One box contained soft goods, the other a pair of leather shoes.

"Why don't we boil some water and you can take a bath before dressing to go to the clinic. I know Deborah was delighted to do that," Katie dismissed the exuberant thank you Emily gave her.

"I'll just get the towel and soap. You start pumping some water into a kettle," Katie pointed toward the kitchen.

"You have a pump in the house?" Emily asked in amazement.

"No," Katie laughed, "but we do have kettles in the kitchen."

The pump was a few feet from the back door. Emily filled a pail with water and carried it to a kettle sitting on top of the wood burning stove. The fire in the stove had been banked after breakfast and Emily added some kindling and a log. It was soon blazing brightly. Emily added a second pail of water to the enormous kettle before Katie joined her.

"I'll put all the clothes in the bathroom so you can pick which ones you want to wear," she said. "There's a towel and soap on the chair next to the tub."

Emily was soon luxuriating in a private room off the kitchen. She sat in the cast iron tub of water admiring the simple, practical configuration of the room around her. A wash stand held a basin, pitcher, shaving mug of hard soap, and a soap dish. There was a mirror hanging on the wall over the stand, which had candle sconces on either side. A covered wooden pail stood on the floor for waste water.

A series of pegs were lined up on either side of the bathtub. Five of eight pegs had towels on them. Emily assumed there were three tenants in the house including Deborah. She wondered who the fourth and fifth person would be. She knew of only Sam, Katie, and Deborah. Sam and Katie had a private bath off their bedroom. Then she remembered Katie mentioning someone named Juanita. That still left another person, it would be interesting to see who it was.

"Probably Juanita's husband," she thought submerging her head under the warm water.

Chapter 64

*M*atthew made his way to the land office located in the courthouse. The Benjamin Franklin look alike greeted him with bored detachment.

"You look like someone I know," Matthew said. "Did you live in Ohio afore coming west?"

"No," the clerk answered without offering further details. "Here are some maps. I'll explain the land acquisition rules."

The clerk went into his routine speech and spoke nonstop for five minutes.

"Hold on a minute," Matthew finally interrupted. "I'll learn all this stuff but can you tell me what it's really like out here? Where do you go hunting and fishing? Where's the purtiest spot you know? Are the Natives friendly? Where's the Injun's sacred ground?"

The clerk, Rhys Watson by name, relaxed.

"I don't get out hunting and fishing much. My dad and uncle did. Boy, did they have some stories."

Rhys told about trips his father and uncle made across the low-lying coastal range for ocean fishing. The range only rose to about four-thousand feet whereas the Cascades had peaks up to fourteen-thousand feet. There were Native trails and passes in the coastal range for comparatively easy crossings. Once past the hills there were long stretches of sand along the Pacific Ocean. The beaches were broken occasionally by lateral spurs from the mountains. These spurs formed high rocky headlands and spectacular views. Sometimes the Watson brothers, Rhys's father and uncle, came home with saddlebags packed with dried fish and crustaceans taken from the sea.

"What's a 'crustacean'?" Matthew asked.

"Lobster, crabs, abalone—you know animals that live in a shell or have their bones on the outside," Rhys Watson was warming to his story telling.

"I ain't never eaten anything from a shell. You mean snails and such? Are they good eating?" Matthew asked making a distasteful grimace.

"Oh my, yes. My favorite's the abalone," Rhys answered. "You have to pound the heck out of them to get them eatable but they are tasty as all get out when fixed right."

"An you just catch them on a fishhook with a worm?" Matthew asked.

Rhys laughed, "You can't get them that easy. You have to dive under the water and pry them off the rocks."

"That sounds right interesting. Maybe if we are still around when it gets warm you 'n me could go abalone hunting," Matthew said.

No one had offered to do anything social with Rhys for so long he didn't know how to react. Finally, he said, "That's a date! We'll plan on going to the coast in April or May."

After that Matthew could have asked Rhys Watson for the moon and he would've tried to get it. He told Matthew countless secrets about the geology and geography of the valley and foothills. Some areas were too dry, some too rocky. The best farmland had been taken, but there were valleys hidden in the mountains that would make a fine homestead.

"The best place for hunting is way down in the southwest corner of the territory," Rhys Watson rocked back on his chair lost in a memory. "Once Dad, Uncle Jed, my brothers and I went down to the Klamath Forest for a whole summer. It's primitive, not many white men yet. There's gold being discovered along the Scott River and the Klamath, so folks will be flocking in to destroy the place."

"Tell me about your hunting trip with your dad," Matthew suggested.

"There are bear, elk, deer—both mule deer and pronghorns, panthers, wolves, foxes, and even big-horned mountain sheep. We wanted to get a bear or two. The meat's gamey, but my uncle likes it. So does my oldest brother. Dad and I wanted the skins."

"Did you get 'em?" Matthew enjoyed hunting stories.

"Yep. Uncle Jed killed an elk first and we lived off that—along with beans and hardtack—the first month. We had the meat hanging in cheesecloth bags in the trees. That brought in a puma-a panther. Dad shot the cat in the middle of the night. Like to scare the wits out of the rest of us. What a cry that animal has!"

"Anyhow, we lit out looking for bear. Knew we'd find them eating the berries. There are lots of wild berries down there. Sure enough, our second trip out of camp on the Klamath River, we come across a mama teaching her babies how to pick berries. She had twin cubs."

"My uncle was against killing a mother with cubs. He and Dad argued, whispering back and forth, until my uncle jumped up and shouted, 'No!' Course the bears high tailed it out of there lickety-split. That settled that argument. Dad grumbled all evening."

"So next day he and I went one direction and my uncle and brothers went the opposite. Uncle Jed came back to camp with a deer, a nice buck, sometime during the day."

"Dad and I hiked up past the berry bushes into the high country. It took us three hours of climbing. The whole time Dad was following a trail, broken branches here, scratch marks on a tree there, bits of fur on a bush—you know, a bear trail."

"We come to a meadow where two males were having at it. What a fight! Now I was fourteen years old and never saw two animals in a savage fight. I was so scared I nearly peed my pants. They fought for almost thirty minutes before they decided a winner. One male was torn and bleeding and so worn out he slunk off into the bushes."

"The other bear, the winner, stood up on his hind legs and roared. That's when Dad shot him. Shot him in the mouth. He fell over backwards with a crash. Dad reloaded his gun. I kept mine trained on the bear expecting him to rear up and charge us. He didn't. Dad said he was dead before he hit the ground."

"The loser of the fight came back to investigate the commotion. He arrived in the meadow and saw dad bending over his old foe. Well now, he let out a growl and charged. In panic, I cocked, aimed and fired. I hit the bear in the chest and he staggered and fell. When he got up again, he was only a

354

few feet from Dad. Dad aimed his gun and waited until the wounded bear was almost on top of him before he pulled the trigger. He shot the bear in the eye. When it dropped dead, it fell on Dad."

"I dragged the bear off and patched up Dad where a claw raked his shoulder. Dad stayed with the bears while I walked back and got the pack mules and rest of the family. We made it back to Dad nigh on nine o'clock. Wouldn't have found him if he hadn't built a big fire to keep the wolves away."

Matthew was on the edge of his chair. He didn't want the story to be over.

"Go on. How'd you spend the night? What happened on the way back to Fort Vancouver?" he drilled his storyteller.

Another land customer came into the office about then and Rhys Watson took care of business. Matthew fidgeted, tried to look at survey maps, tried to read the land rules, gave up and waited for the clerk to return.

When Rhys walked into the room, he had a scowl on his face. The business interruption made him forget he had been story telling. When he saw Matthew, he immediately brightened.

"Say this is no good. You got business and so do I," Matthew said. "I want to hear the rest of the story. Tomorrow's Sunday. Can I meet you someplace?"

"I'm living in McCafferty's Boarding House over on Pine Street. You want to meet me there?" Rhys asked.

"Perfect. We are moving in there tomorrow." Matthew grinned. He rose from his chair and gathered his papers into a reasonably organized bundle. They shook hands and parted company.

Matthew went straight to McCafferty's. He was elated about finding a fellow hunter. His exuberance didn't last long; he had no one to relate the story to. The only person in the house was Katie. She was far too busy to listen to Matthew.

"I need to finish these two rooms today," she said. "You want a clean room to move into, don't you?"

"Yes, ma'am," Matthew said containing his excitement. "Can I leave these here for safe keeping?"

"Okay, put them in the armoire," she said.

He looked at her blankly.

"Put them in the wardrobe," Katie said. "On your way out, please carry the carpet to the back yard and hang it on the clothes line. I'll beat it later."

He struggled down the stairs and out to the backyard with the heavy, awkward carpet. It was quite a project getting it evenly draped over the line. It reminded him of the time he and Emily had hung heavy, wet blankets on the clothesline when they were youngsters. That was the day he realized he wanted to marry Emily.

He rode his horse to Dr. Forbes where he found Michael propped up in bed. Deborah was spoon feeding him clear beef broth. Emily was on her hands and knees scrubbing the floor.

"Hello, babe," he greeted Emily. "Morning Deborah. How's Michael?"

"He can hear and he can move the fingers on his right hand," Deborah said. "I'm sure he'd like to hear about your activities. I've run out of things to tell him."

Matthew's perpetual smile widened. He gave Emily a hug after she got to her feet. Then he sat down beside Michael's bed and repeated Rhys Watson's story.

Michael didn't respond except for an occasional twitch of his fingers. Deborah assured Matthew he'd heard every word and enjoyed the drama.

"And this man will be living with us this winter?" Emily asked. "Didn't you say he was a boarder at McCafferty's?"

"Yep, that's right. I'm looking forward to hearing more stories. Rhys can sit with Michael and me and tell us everything he knows 'bout Oregon. He's been here all his life," Matthew explained excitedly.

A few minutes later Matthew left Dr. Forbes' home; he had to take care of his livestock. He went to see Sam's friend about boarding the animals on the man's cattle ranch.

"No problem there," the rancher replied spitting a stream of tobacco juice into the soil. "I had a good crop a hay last summer. Got twice as much as I'll need. Figured on selling some when newcomers needed it."

The two men agreed on a fair boarding price including hay and oats for the winter, shook hands and went their separate ways.

The next morning Matthew and Emily loaded their gear for travel, promising Jesse they'd come to Abernethy's pasture often to see her while her men were away.

"I'll be going to help Deborah today and tomorrow while you're settling into McCafferty's," Jesse said. "I might as well ride along with you now. Sam and Katie said they'd drive out here on Friday to make sure everything was all right. Why don't you come Wednesday evening for dinner? We can have a nice visit. Brian will be back early next week and we'll come to town to settle a land claim. Time will fly by so fast, I won't have time to miss them."

Emily felt sure Jesse was expressing false bravado. She knew she'd be a bit scared in a new place all by herself. Surely Jesse had some trepidation.

"Why don't you come stay with us at McCafferty's until Brian returns?" Emily asked.

"No. Don't worry. I'm fine now that I know Brian and the boys are going to settle down here."

Emily and Jesse climbed into the wagon seat. Emily snapped the leather whip over the oxen and they began to move out. Matthew rode horseback herding their cattle. The dogs followed at the stallion's heels. Michael's horse was tethered to the wagon.

Matthew added Michael's mules to his own livestock and took them to the ranch on the outskirts of town. Emily left Jesse off at the clinic and took the Conestoga to McCafferty's.

The rancher greeted Matthew and helped herd the animals into a holding pen. They would be kept there a week or so until they learned this was their new home and family. The rancher had seven of his own stock in the pen. Once the cattle were familiar with each other, they would accept their new herd and not wander off alone.

Matthew was back at McCafferty's by late afternoon. Emily, Katie, and Sam had most of the wagon unloaded. The barrels would be left on the wagon along with the farm implements and cooking utensils.

The room upstairs had several boxes sitting on the floor. It was hard to believe Emily thought she needed so much stuff to live here over the winter.

'I don't want the linens, furs, books and things to get mildewed in the wet weather," she said.

A small fire burned in the fireplace and Emily's rocker was placed in front of it.

"We'll leave the wagon where it is for a couple of days," Sam said. "When you're sure you have all you need off it, we'll push it into the barn with O'Brien's and our own."

"Holler if you need help," Katie added. "Dinner will be at six."

A new phase of their life had begun.

Chapter 65

The dinner bell sounded promptly at six p.m. Matthew and Emily left the unpacking and washed up for dinner at the wash stand in their room.

"My doesn't this look elegant!" Emily exclaimed when she entered the dining room. It was their first meal at a table set with crockery since the party at the Coakley house the last day of May.

Each person had a dinner plate, bread plate, drinking glass, and a cup on top of a saucer. These were set on a white tablecloth with matching napkins.

A middle-aged woman brought in a steaming tureen of split pea soup. Katie followed on her heels with soup bowls and a ladle. Sam was standing at the head of the table slicing a pork roast.

There was a basket of freshly sliced bread, a bowl of whipped butter, and one of strawberry jam already on the table, and the sideboard held two homemade pies.

Rhys Watson and Deborah O'Brien were sitting side by side with their backs to the sideboard. The flickering light from candles placed strategically throughout the room added a glow to everyone's face.

"This is a holiday meal!" Emily said. "Look at all this food! Katie how on earth did you prepare all this after helping unload the wagon?"

"I didn't," Katie said. "Please meet Juanita Garcia, our cook and house-keeper. She and I work together to keep your new home clean and your meals tasty."

Juanita nodded to the newcomers.

"Buenas dias señors y señoras. Bienvenito. I hope you like my cooking. Mrs. McCafferty is teaching me new things. She says man can't live on frijoles and tortillas alone."

"What kind of animal is a tortilla?" Matthew asked taking his place at the table.

Juanita laughed heartily. Her soft brown face wrinkled with delight. "Tortilla is flat bread made from corn or wheat flour and lard. I make some for myself every day. I'll fix you some tomorrow with frijoles for lunch. Frijoles are pinto beans."

"We have a few empty chairs. How many people live here?" Emily asked after Juanita returned to the kitchen.

"Rhys Watson meet Emily and Matthew Kilkenny," Sam said.

Emily and Rhys nodded to each other across the table. "My husband tells me you two have already met," she said. "He's looking forward to getting acquainted."

Rhys blushed slightly embarrassed by acknowledgement of a potential friendship.

"Nice to meet you, ma'am. Matthew and I are planning a fishing trip to the coast next spring. We should know each other pretty well by then."

"Oh, I hadn't heard about that yet," Emily said. "It's been a busy day."

Katie said, "Right now, Rhys is our only regular tenant beside Deborah and you two. Rhys's room is at the far end of the hall upstairs. There are two empty rooms. Deborah has a room downstairs; it'll be easier that way when we bring Michael home. Juanita lives in the servant's quarters off the kitchen and, as you know, Sam and I have a room across from the parlor."

"So you have room for four more people?" Emily asked thoughtfully.

"If they sleep two to a room, we could handle four more," Katie said winking at Sam. "Did you have someone in mind?"

"I hate to think of Jesse out at Abernethy's all by herself while Brian and the boys are looking for land," Emily answered. "Course I don't know if she would want to live here or if they could afford lodging for the winter."

"Let's wait and see how Brian's first trip turns out before we mention anything to Jesse," Sam recommended. "Katie said you would be asking about bringing the Jamisons here."

"Brian probably found the perfect farm by now and is dashing back to get Jesse and his stock," Matthew offered.

"He has to get it cultivated and surveyed," Rhys Watson spoke up. "There's some paper work to validate before it's his. He can't plant a crop until next spring unless he's putting in an orchard."

People ate in silence for awhile. Juanita entered with a pitcher of cold milk and a pot of hot coffee. "I make apple pie so save some room," she said.

After dinner, the men retired to the parlor for cigars and brandy.

"We only offer this treat on Sunday evening," Sam cautioned. "Don't expect it every night."

"Katie and I are going to walk back to Dr. Forbes with Deborah," Emily said leaving the table. "She shouldn't be walking the streets alone after dark."

"If you want to wait until after we have a cigar, Matt and I'll walk with you," Sam said.

"That's okay. I know Matthew wants to hear Rhys's hunting stories," Emily said.

Matthew was grateful. He'd been looking forward to hearing the balance of the bear story.

The men settled into chairs facing the hearth. Sam poured each a glass of brandy. Rhys took a long stick from the fire and lit his cigar; Matthew did the same.

"So, did you tell Sam your hunting story?" Matthew asked.

"No," Rhys said. "We're just getting acquainted. I've only talked to Sam a couple of times. I moved down here from Fort Vancouver last summer. The house had a different manager and tenants then."

"That's okay. You don't have to start over. Just pick up where you left off. If I have any questions, I'll ask," Sam said.

Rhys Watson liked his new living conditions. Before Sam and Katie arrived, he spent his evenings locked in his room after eating silently at a table surrounded by low classed men and women with whom he shared no common interests.

"I was fourteen when I went to the wilds of the Klamath Forests in southwestern Oregon. My father, uncle and two brothers were on a summer long hunting trip with me. The day I was telling Matthew about, was when Dad and I killed two bears. My uncle and brothers were a couple of miles or more away. They had killed a good sized mule deer buck the same day. I found them at the campsite when I returned to get the pack mules. They followed me back to Dad. We arrived about nine o'clock and found Dad fighting off wolves."

"Then what happened?" Matthew said taking a sip of brandy.

"Dad was swinging a blazing branch at the wolves. We shot off our guns and the pack scattered. Dad had a big campfire going and the dead bears were as close to that as he could safely drag them. Our horses didn't want to get too close to the fire or bears. It took a bit of doing to get them tied to trees close enough we could protect them from wolves."

"We put the buck next to the bears. We boys were instructed to build a circle of campfires. Uncle Jed and Dad unpacked skinning tools and packing salt. We'd traded the Karuk Indians a hunting knife for the salt. The men began butchering the deer and had drying racks and kettles for the meat."

"We were up all night cutting, packing, and hanging fresh meat. We kept our guns loaded and fired off a shot if the wolves got close."

"When that was done we built up the fires. Dad and my oldest brother took first watch while the rest of us slept. We took turns on watch. No one slept very well. The horses and mules were skittish and shots were fired now and then because of the wolves."

"By noon the wolves wandered off. Uncle Jed suggested we move camp to an area that was easier to defend. We packed up everything and moved down the mountain to a meadow. Uncle Jed thought we'd have less problems if we got away from the blood of the butchering."

"We found a creek and set up camp. We made fires around a bigger circle. That way the horses and mules were willing to stay inside the circle. We stayed there a week until the meat was cured enough for the long trip home. It took two weeks to get home. All the saddle bags and the pack mules were loaded."

"Uncle Jed kept the deer skin and antlers. Dad made the better bear skin into a coat for himself. It turned out to be too warm for his liking and he traded it to a trapper going to the Rockies. He helped me make the second skin into a rug. I gave it to my ma to put next to her bed. The cold weather gets to her feet and legs now that she's older."

Sam poked the fire in silence. Matthew leaned back in his chair and blew smoke rings into the air. A feeling of comradeship permeated the room.

"Did your dad's shoulder heal up okay?" Matthew asked.

"He had scars but he could use his arm," Rhys said. "We never went bear hunting again. He lost interest, or maybe was a bit scared. We went duck and deer hunting in the autumn and fishing every summer."

"Do you still hunt elk and deer?" Sam asked.

"Not really. Haven't killed anything larger than a Canada goose for five years. Hunting just wasn't the same after dad passed," Rhys confided. "My brothers are married and have families, so they put away a couple of deer each fall."

"I stayed home taking care of Ma after Dad died. I was twenty at that time and working for the territorial government. Didn't have time for hunting or courting. Never married. Don't have a family to feed," Rhys felt compelled to explain why he quit hunting.

"Your mom on her own now? Do you want to put her in one of our empty rooms?" Sam asked.

"She moved in with my older brother. She's getting poorly and needs someone with her during the day. My sister-in-law, Virginia said it wasn't any extra fuss. She's home with the babies all day anyhow."

"Now we know all about you," Sam said. "Next Sunday Matt can tell us about his background and the Sunday after that, I'll tell you the story of my life."

Matthew rose from his chair, "Thanks for the story, Rhys. It was good to hear 'bout hunting, fathers and brothers. I miss my own."

He stretched and declared he needed some fresh air. He left the room and walked idly toward Dr. Forbes'. He expected to meet Emily and Katie on their way home.

He got all the way to the doctor's house and found the women inside. There was a state of excitement. Dr. Forbes had given Michael an eye exam and determined he was seeing light and shadows. He had made another small step forward. The prognosis was that he would regain all his senses and most of his mobility by next spring.

Matthew talked to Michael for a few minutes. He told him a shortened version of the end of the bear story. He suggested they combine a hunt with Michael and Deborah's move south the following summer. They would be going through the Klamath Forest on their way to Rough and Ready in Beaver Valley. He was trying to give Michael a goal at which to aim.

Matthew, Emily and Katie walked back to the boarding house bracing against the cold wind. Sam, Rhys, and Juanita were in their rooms when the trio arrived. Everyone was soon in their respective quarters making plans for the week ahead.

The week went along smoothly. Emily and Matthew unpacked their goods and stored the wagon in the barn. Their livestock mingled with others or the near-by ranch and were content with their latest home.

The Kilkennys checked on Jesse and the Jamison livestock on Wednesday evening and ate dinner at the campsite off of tin plates. They sat at a foot wide board held up by two barrels. Their seats were a bucket, a crate, and an empty barrel. The food was beans and potatoes along with softened buffalo jerky. Jesse was glad of the company and admitted she was a bit scared sleeping in the wagon alone. Matthew promised to check on her on Saturday.

Sam and Katie worked on maintenance of their boarding house, barn, and fences. They wanted the exterior painted and roofs in good condition before the winter rains started in earnest.

On Sunday, the Jamison men returned. Brian had a seven-day growth of beard. He was tired and discouraged. He'd been east of the junction of the Willamette and Clackamas Rivers. After passing the lowlands where the two rivers overflowed, he came to undulating hills covered with fir, maple, and hazel trees. The rivers were moving full and fast over rapids and falls. It was hard to ford any creeks or rivers after the recent rains. Any place the land was capable of being tilled, it had been claimed. Even land too steep for farming was occupied by cattle or sheep. He said he would rest a week then try west of McLoughlin's crossing.

Jesse hugged her depressed husband and said she knew he would find the perfect spot before spring planting time. He had gotten them all safely to Oregon and she was sure he would give them a better life than they had in Philadelphia.

Chapter 66

*I*t rained all week. Some days dreary drizzle dampened everything. Other days it rained hard enough to send sluices of mud racing down Main Street.

Emily and Deborah trudged to and from Dr. Forbes' on a regular schedule. In spite of the wet weather both women were in good spirits. They were happy to be pregnant, Michael was recovering, and their living conditions were excellent.

That wasn't the case for the Jamisons. They were cramped in the covered wagon. Altercations replaced conversations, it was impossible to fix a hot meal and their clothes were continually damp. Jesse and Josiah had chest colds and their coughing kept the others awake all night.

Matthew rode out to the camp on Thursday to hear about Brian's farm hunting plans. He thought he might join him for three or four days since he wasn't needed at Dr. Forbes'. When Matthew arrived, Josiah and Robert were engaged in a wrestling match in the mud.

"Whoa! What's going on?" he asked.

"Josiah hid my book and won't tell me where it is," Robert whined peering out from under his brother's armpit.

"Did not," Josiah said trying to get a grip on his little brother's slippery wrist. "Robert ate the last of the fresh bread. He should have shared it."

The boys rolled over and over, neither willing to concede.

"Hello in the wagon. You in there, Brian?" Matthew called out.

Brian opened the back flap.

"You want to come in? It's a mess in here, not much drier than out there," Brian said ignoring the boys. He held his jacket closed and jumped down from the wagon after Matthew agreed to talk outside.

"We best talk out here, Jesse's feeling a bit surly today," Brian said barely above a whisper.

"Good grief! You people are going to be killing each other off afore spring at this rate," Matthew said shaking his head.

Josiah let out a wail of pain and Matthew turned to see what happened. Robert was sitting on his brother's back pulling his leg up perpendicular to his body.

"You think we ought to stop the fight afore somebody breaks something?" Matthew asked.

"Naw, let them get it out of their systems. Maybe we'll get some peace around here," Brian lamented.

"What's your plans for land hunting? You going out in this weather?" Matthew asked.

"Can't get across the rivers and creeks now. They're rushing like the Columbia. Guess we're stuck sitting in this muck until next spring," Brian looked at the boys to make sure they weren't brandishing weapons yet.

"I searched for a cabin to rent in town yesterday. Nothing's vacant, not even a room in the hotel," Brian's shoulders sagged.

"Sam's got two empty rooms he'll let you have for the winter," Matthew said with excitement. "Jesse will perk right up in a clean house with hot water and hot food."

The boys were suddenly beside Matthew.

"Can we go Dad? Can we? I got to get away from Robert or I'll strangle the little bugger," Josiah said with passion.

"That would be a blessing! Moving to McCafferty's that is, not you killing your brother. Jesse, come out here. We've got good news," Brian called out toward the wagon.

Jesse stuck her head out of the soaking canvas doorway. She was disheveled as though she just woke up. She had, in fact, been hiding under the bed covers hoping to go back to sleep until the rain and the fighting stopped.

"We're going to Sam's house! He's got two rooms. I'll hitch up the team. You get things inside secured for the trip to town."

"Can we take the dogs?" Robert asked.

"Yep, but they got to stay in the barn with Blue 'n Betsy. No dogs allowed in the house. Juanita 'n Katie are particular 'bout a clean house," Matthew responded.

Everything whirled in a state of confusion as the boys raced off to get the oxen and Brian chased riding horses. Brian tripped over a log and slid face first across the muddy meadow. When he caught his frightened horse, he led it back to Matthew who saddled the mount.

The cattle dogs barked and ran about wildly to add to the confusion. It took thirty minutes to catch the necessary animals and prepare them for travel. Jesse drove the wagon. She managed to change into a new city dress and get her hair pushed up under a sunbonnet. She wore a winter coat brought from Philadelphia to ward off the wet mist. Judging from the noise emanating from the wagon, she hadn't taken time to secure belongings.

No one seemed to care, least of all Josiah and Robert. They rode their horses several yards in front of the wagon trying to encourage the oxen to walk faster. Brian and Matthew brought up the rear. The cattle were left behind. Brian could deal with them some day when it was sunny. The dogs trotted beside the men barking occasionally. They had given up their frantic behavior as soon as the wagon started to roll.

Juanita met the family at the back door. She held a broom ready to swat the first person that tried to enter the house.

"It's okay, Juanita. These folks are moving into the empty rooms," Matthew explained.

"Not until they're clean, they're not. They're too dirty to even come into the mudroom. La señora is welcome. Señor y el niños must wash first," she said adamantly.

Juanita motioned for Jesse to disembark from the wagon and enter the house. Jesse walked behind the stout guard and into the mud room. She was unconcerned with her men's problems.

"Which room is mine?" she asked Juanita.

"Upstairs. The doors to the empty rooms are open," Juanita raised the broom threatening Brian when he tried to follow his wife.

"You take bucket of water and clean clothes to barn and wash up. You look like pig. You wash in animal house," Juanita said.

"Now listen here young woman, I'm a paying guest, or will be as soon as you let me in. I should be able to bathe in the house like any other tenant," Brian was offended by the servant's treatment.

"The bucket's right there beside the pump. You wash in barn, then you can come in and take a hot bath in bathroom like decent people," Juanita reiterated pointing to the pump.

"Sam, Sam. Are you in there?" Brian yelled.

"Señor Sam not help you. He doesn't want mud on carpet brought from New York City by big boat," Juanita said.

"What's the matter out here?" Sam came up behind Juanita. "Good heavens man, what happened to you? You better take a bucket of water to the barn and get that mud cleaned off before you come in the house. It would take the women a week to clean up, if you came in here like that. Take a set of clean clothes with you to the barn. Do you need to borrow some of my clothes?"

"I'll not wash up in the barn like an animal!" Brian said. "Can't we wash in the bathroom and clean up our own messes?"

"Yes, you can. But you have to get the mud off first. Maybe you'd prefer to strip your clothes off here on the porch and use a bucket of water on your face, hands and feet. Then you can come in and take a hot bath and get dressed for dinner." Sam was no help at all.

Brian thought of getting into his wagon with his sons and his wounded pride and leaving. He felt the warmth coming from the house; it felt so dry. He smelled the aroma of roast beef coming from the kitchen. The two men stared at each other.

Jesse and Katie walked past the door carrying china cups of tea. Katie said something and Jesse threw her head back and laughed out loud.

Oh, how I love that sound, Brian thought.

"Your fireplace looks so inviting with the rocking chairs and footstools. I'm going to love living here," Jesse said.

"All right. We'll clean up in the barn," Brian conceded. "Can someone start a kettle of water heating for a proper bath? Josiah's already got a cold, he'll come down with pneumonia if he gets chilled."

"No problem with that," Sam said. "Juanita you put a log in the stove, I'll get the water."

"Si señor," Juanita put the broom down and turned toward the kitchen.

"Josiah, get clean clothes for all three of us from the wagon. Robert you bring the water," Brian stalked toward the barn with the dogs at his heels.

Matthew sat on the bench provided in the mudroom and removed his boots. He put on moccasins and went to the kitchen for a cup of hot coffee.

"I think you'll like it here," Katie was saying to Jesse. "We have a selection of books to read on shelves next to the fireplace in the parlor. You're welcome to use the parlor, dining room, or bathroom anytime you want. If you want to fix something in the kitchen, work it out with Juanita. She's in charge of that room. Sometimes she lets me help her make dinner. You're welcome to join us, if you'd like. She might need extra help with this many people to feed."

"Maybe we could continue our women's meetings once or twice a week and include Juanita. We could make baby things for the girls."

"Good idea. I started a quilt for a crib. Planned on making a second one. I know the girls are so busy with Michael, they don't have time to do much sewing. Deborah wants me to teach her to knit," Katie was glad to share her home with lady friends.

Plans were swirling around in Jesse's mind. She had a glow to her cheeks for the first time in weeks.

"I'll get the boys started in school. They need more schooling and they certainly need something to occupy their time. I don't want them running around loose in a frontier town," she said. "Maybe I could get a job in the school or in an office building."

"If you're interested in something like that, you could talk to the young man who lives down the hall from you. His name is Rhys Watson; he works in the land office. He could put in a good word with the Surveyor General."

"Brian might like to work with Dr. Forbes," Katie suggested. "Just until spring, mind you. I know he wants to look for farm land as soon as possible."

"Thank you for giving us hope," Jesse squeezed Katie's hand.

"That's okay, we all need a little help from time to time," Katie set her teacup down. "Shall we look at the rooms and see what you'll need to settle in."

The Jamison boys grumbled the whole time they were cleaning mud off with the cold water. They changed into old but clean clothes to wear until they finished with hot soapy baths in the house.

"Just think of it as preparation for eating a hot meal and sleeping in a real bed," Brian said.

"It'll be good to sit in real chairs and eat off real dishes, won't it?"

"A real bed! Geez, I don't think I could stand all the extra space," Josiah said dreamily.

"Maybe Yvonne will share it with you, I sure won't," Robert said.

Josiah swung his dirty shirt toward Robert but Brian intercepted it.

"Now, cut that out, both of you. I want you to be on your best behavior while we live here. It'll be worse than ever if Sam puts us out on the street after we get used to the comforts of a real home again."

Sam brought a wash tub to the mudroom just as Brian was entering.

"Thought you might like to put your clothes in here to soak overnight. By tomorrow they might be clean enough to wash," he said. "If I didn't know you better, I'd think the three of you were wrestling in the mud."

"We'll be clean by dinnertime," Brian said. "That meat roasting sure smells good. When do you want to talk about rent payment and the rules of the house?"

"Glad to have you in our home, Brian," Sam extended a hand. "We hope you'll enjoy good food, good company, and contentment while here. We can talk about payment tomorrow after we get your wagon unloaded and stored in the barn. I have to go to town on business in the afternoon. Can we get your winter supplies to your rooms in the morning?"

Brian agreed to that and headed for the bathroom behind Sam. "Here's a guest towel and soap. You can use your own equipment after you get unpacked. We just have one empty towel peg right now. I'll put up more soon as I can. Katie and I will share one and Matthew and Emily can share one. That'll give you a couple more spaces for now. Leave your wet towels here when you're finished. Juanita will launder them when we get some sunshine."

"After your bath, maybe you'd like to join me for a cup of coffee in the parlor. I'll tell you a bit about the place," Sam said closing the bathroom door.

Brian submerged himself in the blessed hot water.

Chapter 67

*M*atthew spent time at the land office researching crops and animals that prosper in the Willamette Valley. He found that the Hudson Bay Company employees were raising great quantities of wheat and peas. These were fed to cattle and pigs as well as exported to settlements along the coast of California, Oregon and up into Canada. Some were even shipped to the Sandwich Islands in the Pacific Ocean.

Corn didn't grow well in the valley because of the cool nights in the summer. Apples, pears, plums, peaches and apricots grew well, and berries flourished on the coastal range. There were strawberries, huckleberries, raspberries and blackberries. There were also thimbleberries (a deep pink raspberry that fit like a cap on a finger) and the very sour barberries from spiny shrubs.

The greatest export product was lumber. The huge and plentiful Douglas fir grew twenty to thirty thousand rails to an acre and one man could split three hundred rails a day. The fir trees grew up to sixty feet in circumference and two hundred fifty feet high.

Matthew stopped reading to contemplate becoming a lumberjack. There was no shortage of need or supply. He could keep fit splitting rails while waiting for spring to arrive. Having a job would alleviate the worry of spending land development money before he had land.

He talked to Rhys about lumberjacking and found he could make upwards of fifty dollars a month. That would adequately cover their room and board and lodging of the livestock. Matthew would learn the different kinds of pine, which grew in the Cascades. There were the colorful ones – White, Red and Yellow. There was also Spruce and Ponderosa. Hemlock and Laurel grew in the foothills and was used locally for furniture. Tree felling would require a new education. Whipsawing certainly sounded better than mining. He would be outdoors working in the mountains. Those beautiful mountains he had longed to see his whole life. Matthew went to the lumber mill two miles out of town and talked to the manager.

"We've got plenty of help right now. Do you want to get on the waiting list for a job? We have a few men ahead of you but if there's a gold strike somewhere, a lot of men will leave town overnight," the manager said.

"Can't do no harm," Matthew said giving the man his name and address.

"I'll look for other work. If you need me, send word. I might be glad for the change. There's lots of jobs worse than sawing wood."

The following day Matthew and Brian rounded up Brian's cattle and took them, along with their oxen, to the same pasturage where the Kilkenny and O'Brien stock resided, Walter Kirschner's ranch. After the cows and oxen were safely in a holding pen with some of the rancher's own stock, the men headed back to Oregon City.

"How's the family settling?" Matthew asked.

"Jesse couldn't be happier. She's a whole new woman. Er, really, she's back to being the great old woman I used to know," Brian said contentedly.

"And the boys?" Matthew asked.

"They're putting up a fuss about going back to school. They feel they're men now," Brian related. "I agree with Jesse on this one. They need more schooling, Robert especially."

"Be nice if Josiah could get an apprenticeship—work with a craftsman for a couple of years," the father went on.

"Emily did that. Worked with Dr. Six in Athens for a few years while going to school," Matthew said. "She's lots smarter than me. Don't tell her I said that."

Brian laughed, "I won't. I think you just know different things. Ask her how to mine coal and I bet you come out smarter."

"I suppose. She can read twice as fast as me and figure numbers much faster. She don't say nothing about it, course. She knows I had to quit school to go to work in the mines."

"Maybe you'd like to study with Robert. He'll be starting about where you left off. One of us that was lucky enough to finish high school could help both of you," Brian offered.

"That's an idea. Let me think about it. When's Robert starting school?"

"Next Monday. Both boys start then. There are about fifty kids in the school and two teachers. They could use Deborah's help but she has her hands full."

"Say, maybe Deborah would help me an hour or so a day," Matthew warmed to the idea. "Going to be a busy winter, especially if I get a job. You getting a job?"

"Thinking about working with Doc Forbes until the creeks go down. What kind of work you looking for?"

"Saw a man at the lumber mill today. Heard tell they could use someone on a whipsaw. No luck. They got plenty of workers. I'm just good with my hands. Can't do no thinking jobs."

"How about working for the rancher—what's his name, Walter, isn't it?"

"That's right, Walter Kirschner. Man, you're full a good ideas today. I need some learning about the land. Been scared to tell Em I don't know much about farming."

The two rode the rest of the way home deep in their own thoughts.

Emily was standing at the front gate. She waved frantically at Matthew. He saw her smile so knew she had good news to share. He kicked his horse into a gallop.

"What happened? Did Michael do something special today?" he asked.

"He's fine. There's nothing new with him. We got another letter. It's a good one. Hurry and get washed up so you can read it."

"Who's it from?" Matthew was curious.

"I'm not telling. Come on. I'll put the horse out to pasture. Juanita set up a wash stand in the mudroom for us to use after working outside. Use that," Emily took the horse's reins and led him to the barn.

Matthew hung his coat on a peg and changed from work boots to moccasins while Brian used the wash stand.

Brian had brought a pair of house shoes for each member of his family to the mudroom. They were lined up on the floor along with shoes for the other household members. The Jamisons were getting into the habit of using the mudroom before entering the house. This was a new experience for city dwellers.

"Jesse's hanging up clothes in the side yard, Brian. Come on, honey, you're clean enough," Emily looped her arm through Matthew's and went through the back door.

She hurried him through the hallway and up the stairs. Once they were in their own room, she let go of his arm and went to the writing table sitting in front of the window. Emily brought Matthew the letter. It was addressed to "Mr. and Mrs. Matthew Kilkenny" in a childish scrawl.

"What's this? I thought it would be from Ma. I don't know this writing," he said pulling the single sheet of paper from the envelope. He turned the envelope over again and saw the address "Fort Vancouver, Oregon Territory" was crossed out and "Sam McCafferty's boarding house, Oregon City" was written in. Under the new address were the letters "B.E."

"Read the letter!" Emily said excitably.

"I will. I will. I'm puzzling over where Oregon City, B.E. is," Matthew said.

"'BE' stands for Brown Eagle. He saw the letter in the fort and put our new address on it," she was getting impatient. "Read it."

"I will. Let me sit down in this here rocker and think who it could be from," he teased.

"Matthew! Do you want me to read it to you?" she reached for the sheet of paper.

He twisted out of her way, "Hang on, missy. I'll read it in good time. I can read just fine, thank you. I might be smarter than you think. I might get smarter yet pretty quick," he carefully unfolded the top third of the sheet.

"Let's see. This letter was writ on July 20! That sure got here fast! Are eagle's delivering mail now days? It says, 'Dear Matt 'n Missus Emily.' 'Missus Emily,' that's formal.

'I'm writing like I promised. I writ a letter to my sister yesterday just 'cause I could. Now I'm writing one to youse. Beth says she's going to start teaching me to spell. I'll be the smartest ~~nig~~ (the word was started and then crossed out) Negro in East St. Louie for long,'" Matthew folded the paper up.

"What are you doing?" Emily asked surprised.

"This fella sounds familiar. I want to guess who it could be," Matthew pulled Emily down on his lap.

While doing so, she was able to grab the paper away, "Silly thing. Let me read it. You're never going to get to the good news at this rate."

"Dear Matt and Missus Emily," she read without a trace of Appalachian dialect. "I'm writing like I promised. I wrote a letter to my sister yesterday just because I could. Now I'm writing one to you."

Matthew snatched the paper back again, "I like the way I read better than you. Where was I? Oh, I'll just have to start over."

"Read fast then," Emily begged.

"I don't get a letter every day. I wants to savor it like good brandy—a small sip at a time."

"Okay do it your way," she slid off his lap and sat on the floor hugging his legs.

"Do you want me to read out loud or to myself?" he asked.

She slapped his knee, "Read out loud. Now, please. Not next year."

" 'Dear Matt 'n Missus Emily, I'm writing like I promised.' Let's see who promised to write? There was John, Luke, Ma, Mark...," Matthew said.

"Oh, for heaven's sake! It's from Jerome! Just read it!" she was up on her knees now with her elbows propped on Matthew's knees and her chin cupped on the heels of her palms.

Matthew wondered if ever a more beautiful woman had lived. The excitement of the letter enhanced her natural beauty.

"Okay, cause you asked so nice, I'll read it proper," he gave in.

Matthew read the first third of the sheet without stopping. He carefully unfolded the paper and read on.

"'Beth is right friendly but still sassy. I like that in a woman. She's teaching a whole bunch a kids in the old store used as a school whilst I'm building the new school. We are darn near done. She says maybe she might marry me someday. Soon I hope. I put $10.00 down on some land on Elm Street. We goes there for picnics on Sunday. I'm planning where to sit the house. Me 'n Bill Etheridge is going to start another house soon as we are done with the school. Jim's helping us. Everybody says hello 'n keep safe. Your friend for sure, Jerome Jeffers.'" Matthew held the precious piece of paper to one side and smiled at his wife.

"Have you writ to him?" he asked.

"Of course! I left a letter to each of our mothers, one to the Coakleys, and one to Jerome in Jefferson City, Fort Laramie, and The Dalles," Emily answered.

"Isn't it wonderful? Such a nice man. Now he has peace of mind so he can write letters like any other free man. He has a nice woman and will have his own home in a year or so," Emily reclined on the buffalo robe. She was on her back and used her hands as a pillow.

The fire crackled softy in the hearth beside her. Matthew stood up and closed their door.

"I got one fine woman myself," he said kneeling down beside her.

Chapter 68

The day that Michael was transported to McCafferty's was a Monday. Dr. Forbes wanted as many people as possible *out* of the house. He knew Michael would be exhausted after the exertion; he would need peace and quiet.

Michael could now mumble barely intelligible words, could distinguish the identity of people by sight, and move his arms, hands, and fingers. His hearing appeared to be fine.

Dr. Brian Jamison and Dr. Forbes carried Michael with a shoulder under each armpit. His useless legs dangled between the men. He was laid in Sam's farm wagon on a mattress removed from Deborah's covered wagon.

Brian drove while Deborah and Dr. Forbes sat in the back with Michael. They went slowly to the house on Pine Street and pulled up near the back door.

Juanita made sure there were no obstacles between the vehicle and Michael's bed. She didn't want one of the doctors to stumble. Katie held the door to the mudroom open as far as it would go. Emily held the door to the hallway open.

"Welcome home," the ladies said in unison with bright smiles on their faces.

Michael slurred a sound similar to "thanks."

The bed was made up with sheets fresh from the clothesline. The sun shone in the side window through lace curtains. Michael looked around the immaculate room and nodded.

The men sat him on the edge of the bed and held him upright until Deborah removed his coat. She closed her bedroom door and then they laid him back against the pillows and put his legs on the bed. The three of them worked together to get him into a nightshirt and under the covers. When that was done, Deborah opened the door.

Katie, Emily, and Juanita were waiting outside. They entered the room bearing gifts. Emily laid a slim volume of Henry Wadworth Longfellow's poem Evangeline on Michael's lap. He had mentioned the Acadians struggle for freedom to her a couple of times on the trail. She thought he would enjoy reading a poem by this brilliant new poet on that subject. She had found the book in the general store among farming, animal husbandry, mining as an industry, and other instructional tomes. Juanita held a bowl of steaming bread pudding, and Katie had a cup of tea flavored with brandy.

Michael nodded and gave them a barely perceptible half smile. He lifted the book about six inches off the covers before it slipped from his grip. Emily picked it up and held it level with his face.

"It's a poem about the Acadians. I'll start reading it to you tomorrow."

"Buenos dias Señor O'Brien. I'm Juanita, the woman who will cook you food to make you strong like ox. You'll see."

"Welcome to our home, Michael," Katie said sitting the cup of tea on the table beside the bed. "We're so glad you're here. We'll all help you recover."

His head fell back against the pillows and he closed his eyes.

"Thank you ladies. Michael's put in a full day's work, he needs to sleep for awhile," Brian said.

Everyone except Deborah left the room. She quietly closed the door behind them. She fed Michael a few bites of the bread pudding and gave him half a cup of the tea, one spoonful at a time.

"I'm tired too, darling. Can I rest with you," she tucked herself under his armpit and gently stroked his chest.

Deborah awoke first. The sun no longer came through the window. The room was in shadows. She slipped off the bed and went to the outhouse.

It was late afternoon and Juanita was removing laundry from the clothesline. Deborah emerged from the little building and walked to the side yard.

"Can I help you?" she asked.

"Si señora," Juanita's words sounded musical to Deborah's ears. She'd never heard Spanish spoken before meeting Juanita. "You can start on second line while I finish the bedclothes."

Deborah removed the fluffy, fresh smelling towels, folded them and put them in a clothesbasket.

"The days have been beautiful this week. I hope it last through Thursday," Deborah said.

"Si, fiesta grande. Much company, much work," Juanita sighed.

"I'll help. Michael sleeps a lot during the day. When he dozes off, I know I have a couple of hours to work," Deborah said. "I need to get out of the bedroom now and then."

"Gracias," Juanita said. "Just come to the kitchen whenever you want on Wednesday and Thursday. I'll be there all time both days."

Deborah took a deep breath of the cool air and picked up the basket. She never tired of looking around at this beautiful setting. She made a full turn before following Juanita to the back door.

They carried the baskets to a closet beside the bathroom. Juanita opened it to expose several shelves of linens.

"My, I'll never have that many sheets and towels! It looks like a hotel closet," Deborah said.

"Last boss buy lots of linen. I change beds every day," Juanita shook her head sadly. "He not nice man."

Deborah agreed and then excused herself, "I better check on Michael."

In the evening the house filled with tenants. Jesse paid Michael a courtesy visit before dinner. The uncomfortable boys stood in the doorway, said hello then said they had to do homework.

Jesse explained that she was now working as a clerk's assistant in the Surveyor General's office. It was an important job. She filed maps and papers by the dozens. It was critical she put them in the right place so the clerks could find them when required.

Michael gave her a crooked smile and nodded. He realized how critical it was for Jesse's mental health to feel needed. With Brian back at work as a doctor, the boys in school and very little housework to do, Jesse had few responsibilities. A job was just the thing she needed to keep her balance.

Matthew came into the room smelling of horse sweat. He squeezed Michael's hand and said he'd return after a bath and dinner. He wanted to tell Michael about his new job as a cowboy.

Michael raised an eyebrow and mumbled something that sounded like, "son of a gun."

Matthew laughed, waved, and headed for the pump to get water.

"Señor Kilkenny, I put water on cook stove when I see you ride up. I know you smelly when you come home," Juanita held her nose.

"Gracias," Matthew said. "I'll get my clean clothes and see if I can get the horse 'n cow smell washed off."

Emily was sitting in her rocker with her feet on a tiny footstool. She was knitting.

"What you making babe?" he asked.

"A sweater for Jenny Marie," she said matter of factly.

"Who's Jenny Marie?" he teased.

"Your daughter, of course," she answered.

"Don't put no frills on the sweater cause we don't want folks to think Meriwether is a sissy," he said kissing the top of her head.

"Phew, I'm surprised Juanita let you in the house smelling like that," Emily said.

"She's in love with me, that's why. She even put the bath water on the stove for me," he said taking clean clothes from a drawer.

"Hmmm. I better not catch you flirting with her. I'm usually armed now days," Emily said holding up a knitting needle.

"That sounds like a threat, Mrs. Kilkenny."

"It is. Take it seriously," she narrowed her eyes to look more ferocious.

He kissed her head again on the way past the rocker.

Rhys walked by the open door just as Matthew planted his second kiss. He smiled, content that these nice people were his friends.

Sam announced at dinner that each family could invite one guest for Thanksgiving dinner.

"I'll ask Dr. Forbes," Deborah said immediately.

"I'd like to ask Brown Eagle if I could get word to him in time," Matthew said then looked at Emily for approval. She nodded.

381

Jesse and Brian looked at each other and shrugged their shoulders. "We'll have to think about it. Maybe one of the boy's teachers or the Catholic priest."

"Or Yvonne," Robert snickered.

Josiah kicked him under the table.

Jesse opened her mouth and Brian immediately said, "Jesse tell us about your day at work."

She looked at him caught off guard. Her mind switched gears and she told the diners about the huge flat files for maps.

"We never fold the maps, that causes the ink to rub off at the creases. Each drawer has a different section of the Oregon territory. We have a large map on the wall showing the whole territory. The sections are numbered. The drawers correspond to the map on the wall."

"Sounds complicated," Katie said. "I'm glad Rhys has a smart woman like you to help him."

"Me too," said Rhys. "Life got a whole lot better when your wagon train pulled into town."

"How's your school learning coming Matthew? Hard work isn't it?" Sam asked.

"I'm using muscles that haven't been used in a long time," Matt said pointing to his head. "With Deborah's and Robert's help, I'll get smarter. Got to strengthen the muscle a bit more each day."

"He's taking his spelling words to work so he can memorize them while he's hitting the doggies," Emily said proudly.

Sam and Matthew laughed.

"I think she means cow punching," Matthew said. "We're learning all kinds of new stuff and new words."

Juanita walked into the room with her usual mid-meal servings of cold milk and hot coffee.

"Listen to this," Matthew said to Emily.

"Bwaneus dayus seniora Garcia."

Juanita flashed him a bright smile and chattered away in Spanish for a full minute.

Emily jabbed Matthew's arm with her elbow. When he winced and looked at her, she narrowed her eyes menacingly.

Juanita poured Matthew a fresh glass of milk.

"Grassyass, Juanita," Matthew said and quickly leaned out of Emily's reach.

Katie correctly interpreted the horseplay and said, "You two kids play nice."

"Yes, Mother," Emily said.

She wrinkled her nose at Matthew and he grinned at her.

He leaned over and whispered, "Jealousy makes you turn green, you know."

Chapter 69

*T*hanksgiving morning before daylight, Juanita could be heard in the kitchen chopping, grating and dicing. The O'Brien's bedroom was the closest room to the kitchen and their sleep hours were irregular. It took very little noise to wake up Deborah.

She kissed Michael gently on the cheek and left the bed. Deborah groped in the dark for her clothes then tip-toed from the room. She had just closed the door when a male voice startled her.

"Morning Deborah, happy Thanksgiving," Brown Eagle said.

Deborah nodded embarrassed and bent to pick up her dropped clothes.

"Excuse me, I can't talk to you while I'm in my nightshirt," she whispered and dashed off to the bathroom.

Once she had proper clothes on, she ran to the outhouse with a lantern in hand. She yanked on the handle and found the door locked.

"Oh hurry, hurry whoever's in there. A pregnant woman needs to use it quickly," she said wishing she had used the chamber pot.

Brown Eagle emerged, "Why, Mrs. O'Brien! Fancy meeting you here."

Deborah pushed past him and bounded through the door. She locked it and relieved her aching bladder.

"That'll get worse before it gets better. I mean, that's what I've been told," he called from outside the door. "I'll wait out here to escort you safely back to the house. There might be lions and bears lurking in the bushes."

"Go away Brown Eagle," she pleaded. "I'm fine. I'll greet you in an hour after I've had coffee,"

"I'm leaving. You sure you want me to go? Did you consider the possibility of snakes and spiders in there," he smiled as he saw the lantern move around the interior walls.

"I'm leaving. Okay, I'm gone," he took a few steps in place on the gravel.

"No! Don't go! I'll be out in a minute. Wait for me," she cried out.

She came out of the odorous building with as much dignity as she could muster.

"Thank you for waiting Mr. Eagle," she said taking his proffered arm.

He took the lantern from her and held it out in front as far as he could.

"Watch your step Mrs. O'Brien, we don't want the two of you to fall down."

She was glad it was dark and he couldn't see her flushed face. How did he know she was in the family way?

Oh, yeah, that's right, she thought. I just told him.

Once in the mudroom, she let go of his arm.

"Thank you," she said meekly.

"No trouble, it was on my way anyhow," he handed her the lantern and she went back to the bathroom to wash up and comb her hair.

"Hello," Brown Eagle said to Juanita as he stepped into the kitchen. She stifled a scream.

"Shhhh, I'm a friendly. Don't wake up everyone," he held his index finger perpendicular to his lips.

Juanita slowly backed up to the counter where she knew a butcher knife lay. She gripped the handle behind her back.

"Any chance I could get a cup of coffee," Brown Eagle said sitting down at the worktable.

Juanita hadn't moved, "No, Señor. No coffee made yet."

"Ah, maybe I could make some if that's all right with you," he started to rise from the table. She brought the knife forward and held it high in the air ready to attack if necessary.

He put his hands up and said, "I'm a friend of Matthew, Michael, and Brian. I rode all night to join them for Thanksgiving. I've heard about your great cooking."

Why would a savage bent on rape and mayhem compliment her cooking?

"Where you come from?" she asked narrowing her eyes.

"Last night? I rode from Fort Vancouver. I'm a scout for the army. I came west with Sam's wagon train."

Juanita laid the knife back on the counter.

"There's bucket by pump. You bring water for coffee," she said watching him go. He might be a friend of the men in the house but Juanita still wasn't going to turn her back on him.

Deborah came out of the bathroom clean and groomed for the day.

"Where's Brown Eagle?" she asked.

"No eagle. We have turkey today," Juanita said. "You look pretty Miss Deborah. Be careful, there's an Indian at the pump."

Juanita handed Deborah a paring knife, "Put in pocket where Indian can't see it."

"Juanita! Brown Eagle is our friend. We invited him to spend the day with us."

Brown Eagle returned with the water, "Why Mrs. O'Brien! How nice to see you, what a pleasant surprise. You look lovely today."

"Thank you Mr. Eagle, happy Thanksgiving," she responded with a curtsy. "Have you met our wonderful cook and housekeeper, Miss Juanita Garcia?"

Brown Eagle put the bucket on the table and said, "Miss! I find that hard to believe. A beautiful young woman like you isn't married? You must have to beat the men away with a broom."

"That's a fact. I've seen her do it," Deborah said.

"I just happen to have a bucket of water. Do you suppose we could turn it into coffee?"

The question put an end to the play-acting. The women busied them-selves making coffee, getting cream, sugar, and crockery mugs.

Brown Eagle sat at the table.

"How is life as a scout?" Deborah asked.

"It's a job. No better or worse than any other job," he answered. "I'll be glad when spring comes and I can travel. I'm going to spend a few days with my family on my way to St. Louis."

"Oh, that'll be nice," Deborah said pouring milk slowly from the large pitcher so she would get the cream from the top. She sat the cream container on the table next to the sugar.

"How's Michael?" he asked and saw her shoulders sag.

"He gets a bit better each day. It's such slow progress. We have to fight depression every day," she admitted. "He'll be glad to see you and hear army stories again. Dr. Forbes says Michael understands everything we say. He just can't respond very well yet."

"Can he see?" the Shoshone asked.

"Poorly, but yes. We think he recognizes people."

"You want food Señor Eagle?" Juanita asked.

It took a couple of seconds for Brown Eagle to realize she was talking to him.

"Do you have frijoles and tortillas?" he asked.

She smiled brightly, "I heat them up right away."

Juanita fixed enough for three people and they sat together at the work-table drinking coffee and eating beans. Deborah thought this was a true American celebration—one Native, one Mexican and one woman of European descent comfortably sharing a meal as the sun crept over the horizon.

"You nice man for a savage," Juanita said.

He smiled, "You're a nice lady. I like you better when you don't have a butcher knife in your hand."

Deborah didn't understand but the flush on Juanita's cheeks told her the two shared a secret experience. After breakfast Deborah found Michael awake and gave him some coffee before she bathed and dressed him for the day.

Brown Eagle fetched pumpkins, a bag of walnuts, a bushel of apples, and other food from the fruit cellar on Juanita's orders. It took a half-hour to get all the supplies Juanita needed to start preparing the ritual feast.

Brown Eagle was cracking walnuts at the worktable when Matthew entered the kitchen. He and Brown Eagle greeted each other, poured two mugs of coffee and went to the back yard.

"We best stay out of the kitchen today. Juanita will put us to work," Matthew said.

"I noticed," Brown Eagle chuckled.

They walked to the paddock beside the barn. Matthew fed an apple to his stallion.

"Where's the rest of the livestock?" Brown Eagle asked surprised.

"Happy and getting fat on a ranch east a town. You'll meet the rancher later. He's coming to dinner."

"What's going on with you people?" Brown Eagle asked.

"Lot of changes. Everybody's busy," Matthew said. "Deborah and Emily spend all day with Michael. They are both in the family way and get tired, so they switch time back 'n forth. They are trying to get his muscles to work. Doc thinks he'll be all right eventually."

"So. You're going to be a father! Congratulations. You two will make good parents. And the Jamisons?"

"Jesse and Brian are working and the boys is in school."

"Are they going to settle here in town?"

"They plan on getting land next spring. It's too hard to travel and look for land now."

"Yeah, I had some fast, deep rivers to cross getting here. A normal four-hour trip took me twelve hours. I planned on staying a couple of days but guess I'll start back tomorrow. If it rains very hard it might take me two or three days to get to the fort," Brown Eagle lamented.

"How's life at the fort? They treat you all right?" Matt asked his friend.

"They treat me like an Native one day and like a soldier the next. I keep to myself most of the time. We go on maneuvers once in awhile. The Cayuse don't care to have all the white folks coming west. White people bring disease, alcohol, and trouble. There'll be bloodshed by next year. Hatred, fear, and resentment are building on both sides."

"What's the answer? When gold is found, white men will flock to get it. New immigrants are arriving every day. Too many poor white folks back in the states. They want a better life."

"Just like kids, men need to learn to share. White men have no respect for the Native's land. Natives don't want white men killing all the game and destroying the hunting grounds with farms and cattle. They kill for sport and leave the animals to rot in the prairies. White men think it's wilderness, doesn't belong to anyone, and they have the right to claim it for their own."

"Do you think we are wrong to come here to farm?" Matthew asked seriously.

"I don't know. Natives don't want change, white men do. I don't know who's right—maybe both, maybe neither," Brown Eagle said. "I'm working both sides. I'm a Native because my parents were and I see their side of things. Yet, I'm helping white people come out west and I know they'll take Native land when they get here. But, I'm hoping the white people will bring education—farming methods, guns for hunting, medicine, and an easier, better life to Natives."

"There you are," Sam came up behind them. "How are you, Brown Eagle? It's good to see you."

Sam and Brown Eagle shook hands and slapped each other's shoulders.

"I was looking for a man in uniform. What's this buckskin for?" Sam asked flipping the fringe on Brown Eagle's sleeve.

"It's my day off work," Brown Eagle said. "How are you old man?"

"Don't you 'old man' me. I'll put you in your place," Sam punched Brown Eagle playfully on the arm.

Brown Eagle feigned pain then laughed.

"Isn't this some country?" Sam made a wide sweeping motion with his hand. "Look how green the valley is after the rain. The mountains are gathering snow to water crops all next summer. And we don't have to dig the white stuff to get out of our homes down here in town."

Matthew and Brown Eagle looked at the magnificent scenery.

"It's grand alright. I hope there's enough to go around," Matthew said.

Brown Eagle slapped Matthew on the back, "Don't worry about it. It'll all work itself out sooner or later."

Josiah and Robert raced out the back door and across the yard, "Brown Eagle! Happy Thanksgiving!"

Josiah got there first and thrust his hand into Brown Eagle's extended one, "We were wondering if you'd be interested in a horse race this afternoon."

"My horse is worn out from getting here. He's not fit to race," Brown Eagle apologized.

"We talked to Mr. Kirschner about it last week. He's going to bring in six horses from his ranch. We'll draw lots to see who rides which horse," Josiah explained.

"Where we going to race?" Matthew asked looking at the crowded paddock.

"Down Pine Street to Main, down Main and across River Street to Third, then up Third and back home on Pine," Robert said.

"You boys been planning this awhile," Matthew remarked.

"Yep," Robert said. "And we been practicing. I'm going to win."

Brown Eagle put an arm around Robert's shoulders, "You're on, my boy. But I'll try to win. I won't give you an inch because you're young. Okay? No crying when I win."

"Great! I'll find out what time we're eating dinner. Let's race before dinner. We'll be too fat and lazy after eating all that turkey and pie."

Robert ran to the house.

Josiah shook his head, "Crazy kid really thinks he can beat us men."

"I suppose you think you're a better horseman then your dad 'n me," Matthew chided. "Hah! We'll leave you in the dust."

"I think I'll go in and say hello to Michael," Brown Eagle said walking toward the house.

"Guess we'd better all go in. Emily and Jesse were fixing breakfast when I came out here," Sam said.

"Oh, yeah, that's right. They sent Robert and me out to get you," Josiah remembered.

Chapter 70

"I'm glad we were able to invite Brown Eagle as the Jamison's choice. That way you invited Walter Kirschner as the Kilkenny's choice and he's bringing the race horses," Brian said to Matthew as they finished breakfast. "The boys are as excited about the horse race as they were about swimming the cascades up on Barlow's Pass."

"Walter's a good man. He's by himself out there on the ranch, except for hired help. I was glad to invite him to our shindig," Matthew said. "Course, I'm mighty glad to see Brown Eagle too."

"Dinner's at about four o'clock," Katie announced. "We're only having two meals today."

"What time you want to race?" Matthew asked.

A discussion was held among the racers and cooks and the time of two o'clock was chosen.

"It'll take that long for breakfast to settle," Brown Eagle said.

The women were carrying the remnants of breakfast to the kitchen. Ham, sausage, eggs, fried potatoes smothered in onions and cheese, hot biscuits, canned strawberries with rhubarb and an assortment of homemade jams had been consumed.

"I don't know how you people can work after so much food first thing in the morning," Brown Eagle remarked.

"Our breakfasts are usually porridge and coffee or biscuits and eggs. Meat for breakfast is saved for Sundays and holidays," Matthew explained.

Brown Eagle and Matthew visited with Michael until it became obvious he was tired. They closed the door on the way out knowing he would sleep.

"How did this happen? One minute he was fine, a three minute fight and his life is ruined," Brown Eagle choked on his words. "And it's all my fault! How stupid."

"It's not your fault. You saved us from getting shot! It was an accident. That man could of killed us," Matthew shook Brown Eagle's shoulders. "It ain't your fault."

"I'm going for a walk. I need some fresh air," Brown Eagle said.

"Want company?" Matthew asked.

"Not this time. I'll be back in an hour or so," Brown Eagle headed for the mudroom to put on his boots. He'd been walking around the house in his socks out of respect for the hard working women.

Deborah overheard the conversation. She put a shawl over her shoulders and went out the front door. She saw Brown Eagle headed toward Main Street and quickly walked that way. She came up behind him and slipped her hand into his. He jumped and pulled his hand away.

"Sorry, I didn't hear you," he said and took her hand and squeezed it.

"Didn't mean to startle you. I needed some cool air and exercise after that heavy breakfast," she intertwined their fingers.

They walked several blocks without talking. Neither noticed or cared about the disapproval on people's faces. There were very few people out and about as most of the shops were closed for the holiday. People with families were busy preparing a feast for the holiday.

They came to a stream at the far end of town. The water babbled over basaltic rocks and hurried downstream toward the Willamette River.

She took a deep breath and sighed as she sat heavily on a large rock.

He threw stones in the river.

"Is there anything I can do to make your life a little easier?" he asked.

"Yes," she answered and he waited for a colossal demand.

"Well?" he finally said. "What?"

"Scream with me," she said.

"What?"

"Scream—yell as loud and long as you can. See if you can yell louder and longer than me."

He was puzzled, "That won't change anything."

"No, but I've wanted to do it for weeks and not had the nerve. There is a scream bottled up inside me and I'm going to explode if it doesn't come out."

"Okay, we'll both take a deep breath and then yell until we have no air left."

"Yes," she stood beside him looking at the sky.

They took a few short breaths then one big one and started yelling. A loud long wail of pent up pain and frustration, of anger and hatred, of self-pity and pity for Michael.

Deborah yelled until her vision blurred. She was out of breath and panting for air. Her heart was pounding. She sat down on the rock with a thud and picked up a handful of gravel and threw it forcefully into the stream.

"That was fun. You want to do it again?" Brown Eagle asked somberly.

She laughed. She hadn't laughed out loud since the accident. Now she laughed until she cried.

The tears came slowly at first and she thought they were a product of the laugh. More tears flowed and soon she was sobbing—great violent sobs shook her body.

Brown Eagle pulled her to her feet and embraced her tightly. He felt like crying also. Instead he released a string of foul words shouted loud and clear. He said them in Shoshone, Walla Walla, and French. One word escaped in English and Deborah looked up at him surprised.

"Oh sorry, my mistake," he said.

She smiled and he released her. They stood quietly watching the water.

She broke the silence by saying, "Thank you. I needed that."

"You know something? I actually feel better," he said. "There's been this huge hard lump in my gut ever since Michael was injured and now it's gone."

"What a shame Michael can't scream," she said. "I'm sure he'd like to."

"He's a fighter, Deborah. He'll come back. I just know he will."

She pulled her shawl up close over her bodice and tossed the tail over her shoulder.

"Let's get you home before you catch a cold," he said and took hold of her elbow.

They walked and talked casually on the way home. She told him about the baby and how she hoped it would be a boy. They picked outlandish names for him and laughed. He told her about his sister and her family. He'd never talked about his family to anyone on the train. Now detail after detail flowed out of some private corner of his mind. They were at the front gate before they realized it.

Robert burst from the front door.

"Walter's here. Come see the horses he brought for the race," Robert started around the house toward the paddock.

"Thank you for the walk Mrs. O'Brien. I'll see you inside later," he waved as he followed Robert.

Deborah took off the shawl as she walked down the hallway. She smelled pies baking and decided to put her shawl away and work with Juanita.

She opened the bedroom door quietly so she wouldn't wake up Michael. She gasped, he was sitting on the side of the bed.

"Michael! What are you doing? How did you get up?" she hurried to him ready to catch him if he fell forward.

When she was directly in front of him, he stood up and reached for her. She threw her arms around him. It was enough to throw him off balance and they fell sideways across the bed.

Deborah kissed his face, neck and hair. She laughed and cried for joy.

"Oh, Michael, Michael, Michael," she couldn't find any other words.

He tried to hold her but had expended his strength getting to his feet.

"We'll be all right," he mumbled with the slur of a serious drunk.

"Oh, Michael. Yes. Yes we will."

She got up and closed their door. She wanted to be alone with her beloved. Deborah helped him lie lengthwise in the bed and then she lay down beside him. She dozed off and didn't wake up until nearly three o'clock.

Michael slept also. He was exhausted from the exertion. It had taken him over half an hour to maneuver into the sitting position. He had failed on the first few attempts ending up with one leg dangling over the side and the other lying dead on the bed. He eventually got the second leg to move and got to his elbows. Each movement forward was a giant accomplished. Now he lay awake listening to Deborah breathe deeply in her sleep. He had so much to be thankful for this holiday.

While Michael and Deborah slept, the rest of the household gathered for the big race. Matthew, Brown Eagle, Brian, Josiah, and Robert lined up on Walter Kirschner's horses. The women cheered from the front porch.

Sam started the race. He held a white napkin at arm's length over his head.

"Get ready, get set," he brought his arm down and yelled, "go."

They were off down Pine Street; neck to neck the horses ran.

"Eeeyah," Robert shouted kicking his horse in the ribs.

Josiah tried to make his body one with the horse. He leaned forward against the mane and held the reins beside the horse's neck.

Brian reached Main Street first and made the turn. Because of the holiday, there was no traffic. He glanced over his shoulder and Matthew was second, less than a length behind him. Josiah was third, and Robert and Brown Eagle tied for last place.

Brown Eagle called to Robert, "Their horses will get tired and we'll overtake them on Third Street."

Robert was too intent on the race to answer.

Making the second turn, Matthew reined in his horse ever so slightly and Josiah overtook him.

"Hah!" he yelled as he passed Matthew.

"I'll get you in the homestretch," Matthew called back.

Robert was gaining on Matthew and kicked his horse repeatedly.

"Yah, yah, go boy go," he told the horse.

Matthew rode even with Robert all the way down Third Street. Brian pulled his horse to a stop at the side of the road. The other riders flew past. Robert made it around the corner onto Pine Street a few inches in front of Matthew.

Josiah and Robert were in front headed for home. Matthew and Brown Eagle were right behind them.

"Go girl, go," shouted Matthew. "We can beat 'em. We can do it."

Brown Eagle and Matthew exchanged a quick smile and nod. Dr. Forbes waved a flag indicating the finish line.

Josiah passed him first. Robert was beside his big brother, losing by less than a yard. Matthew was third and Brown Eagle fourth.

There was cheering and stomping of feet from the porch. Rhys whistled between his fingers. Sam let out a war whoop.

"What happened to you, slowpoke?" Matthew teased Brown Eagle.

"Somebody fed my horse rocks for lunch," Brown Eagle laughed. "Just wait until next time."

The boys stood in their stirrups and waved their hats in a big circle over their heads. They accepted the applause and cheering from their admirers. Matthew and Brown Eagle shook hands with the boys and congratulated them.

"I'm going to go see what happened to Brian's horse," Matthew said.

"I'll go along," Brown Eagle took his horse's reins and joined Matthew walking along Pine Street.

Brian came around the corner. His horse was limping.

"Hey, he wasn't fooling around! Something's wrong with his horse!" Brown Eagle said.

Matthew waved to Brian, "You okay?"

Brian nodded. When they got closer, he said, "I think the horse picked up a stone under his shoe."

The men checked the horse's hoofs. Brown Eagle pulled a small knife from a sheath on his sleeve.

"Wow! Remind me not to fight with you. Where else do you have weapons hid?" Brian asked.

Brown Eagle said, "That's a secret."

He took the knife and pried a stone out from the horse's rear left hoof.

"What's the problem?" Sam asked as he, Walter, Dr. Forbes, and Rhys approached the scene.

"Just a stone," Brian said. "Brown Eagle removed it."

"Did you want to race again? We could let the horses rest for a couple hours then try again," Walter suggested.

"No thanks," Brian said. "It was a fair race. Who won?"

"Josiah beat Robert by a neck," Matthew said. "I was third and ole slow-poke was last."

"Hey, I didn't come all this way to be insulted," Brown Eagle feigned hurt feelings.

"I don't think the results would be better if you raced again. We better just salute the better horsemen and leave it at that," Sam said.

The boys were celebrating and accepting praise from Juanita when the men arrived home. The horses were taken to the pasture and the tack put away. Good-humored bantering filled the air as the men rubbed down horses.

Brown Eagle presented the boys with Indian corn and told them to shuck it and he would show them how to cook it in the fireplace. They couldn't imagine being able to eat the dried corn without soaking it overnight. He gave them a pan with a long handle and a lid with a clamp and told them to put a bit of lard in the bottom to melt. When it was liquefied, he put a handful of the dried corn into the pan and told Robert to shake the pan over the flames until the noise stopped. The popping sounds had everyone in the room curious

"It smells good enough to eat," Katie remarked.

"Let me see what's happening," Robert said.

"No, you can't do that until the noise stops," Brown Eagle cautioned.

The funny shaped results were a hit with everyone.

"The Indians sure have some interesting recipes. Is this a Shoshone dish?" Katie asked.

"Oh, I think a lot of tribes have learned it's one way to cook the corn we grow in the summer time. We hang it in the sun to dry in the autumn and then store it away for winter use. Maybe the recipe came from an accident. Maybe someone dropped an ear of dried corn into the fireplace. It would fly all over the room when it got hot," he laughed.

The women worked together preparing food, setting the table, and lining the sideboard and an extra table set in the corner of the room with an array of food. Walter had brought cheeses made from the milk of his dairy cows. They were set out with relishes, fancy bread rolls, jams, and desserts.

The main table was filled with the golden brown turkey, steaming bowls of mashed potatoes, gravy, sweet potatoes, stuffing, and winter vegetables cooked to perfection.

Jesse and Katie had made five pies and Emily made a cake. Juanita fixed a form of Mexican treats with cinnamon and sugar sprinkled on bread sticks.

An easy chair was put at one end of the extended table. When everything was ready, Matthew and Brian went to O'Brien's bedroom to carry Michael to the table. Brian rapped gently on the door. Deborah answered with a radiant smile.

"Is Michael awake? Can we carry him to the table now?" Brian asked.

Deborah opened the door wide and Matthew and Brian saw Michael standing beside the bed. The astounded men let out a whoop that brought a crowd to the doorway.

"Happy Thanksgiving everyone," Michael slurred.

Chapter 71

Christmas was another festive event at the McCafferty household. Rhys Watson took time off work to ride to Fort Vancouver to be with his family. He took a saddlebag of presents to be delivered to Brown Eagle at the garrison. He also had a fruit cake made by Juanita to share with his own family.

The Jamison boys brought an evergreen tree from the forest and it was draped with homemade ornaments. Brian nailed holly and mistletoe over the doorways and bought enough candles in red and green holders to be burned in every window of the building. Emily knitted each member of the household a pair of warm socks. Matthew made a wooden shoetree for the mudroom. Everyone now had a place to hang their shoes upside down so they would dry out before the next wearing. Deborah made fudge and cookies and distributed individual packages to her friends. Sam and Katie presented each person with a fluffy new bath towel.

Jesse organized for the Catholic choral group from her church to sing in front of the house on Christmas Eve. The household sat on the front porch drinking hot chocolate milk and listening to the concert. Afterwards, they invited the chorus into the house to share the savory drink and warm up by the fireplace.

Juanita prepared a feast with the help of Katie, Jesse, Emily, and Deborah. There was enough food to last three days and no one complained about that.

1854 was brought in quietly with the group gathered around the fireplace drinking hot rum drinks and reminiscing with stories of the trip across the continent. Matthew and Emily were the first to agree with Sam. It had been quite a year.

A month later, Dr. Forbes asked Brian to become his partner. He wanted to build a six-room hospital in town. Dr. Forbes no longer had space in his home for all the patients requiring overnight medical attention. After a week of deliberation, Brian accepted the offer. He decided he would rather cure the sick than turn a wilderness into cultivated fields. The Jamisons would be settling in Oregon City much to Jesse's delight.

A site was purchased and plans drawn for the most modern facility available. Emily was as excited as the two doctors to see the hospital take shape. She offered advice based on her work with Dr. Six and was thrilled to see the medical men incorporate her ideas. She suggested a separate room for any treatment that required opening the skin. That room was to be kept immaculately clean. An examining room where people came with colds, measles, cholera, consumption, or any other disease was to be separate from the operating room.

Matthew was concerned Emily would want to live in Oregon City and work at the hospital.

"No, silly," she answered his question. "I'm just glad Lydia Jane will be born in a new modern hospital."

"Who's Lydia Jane? Is that the name Michael 'n Deborah has picked out?"

"Lydia Jane is your daughter. Our daughter," Emily said and gave Matthew a kiss on the cheek.

"I thought Jenny Marie was our daughter. You must be carrying a lot a babies in there because my baby's name is Jefferson Meriwether Kilkenny," he said pulling Emily into an embrace.

She looked at him seriously, "Will you be terribly disappointed if our first child is a girl?"

"I don't care if the first eleven are girls long as you give me one son sooner or later," he nuzzled her ear. "You don't really care if it's a boy do you?"

"No, of course not. I already love the infant. I do want it to be healthy. I'm trying to be careful and not strain myself."

"Course, and I want you to be healthy too. It's kind of scary when I think about it too much. I'd rather not have any kids than..." His voice trailed off. He wished he hadn't told her he was scared.

"I'm a wee bit afraid myself but I trust Dr. Forbes and Brian so whoever delivers the baby will make sure everything's okay."

They held each other in silence for a couple of minutes before Matthew spoke.

"I'm glad you're not wanting to work at the new hospital. I'm sure you'd be a big help to the doctors, but I need you to help set up a homestead."

Matthew saw Rhys waving to him one cold, rainy day in February. He was on his way home from work at Walter's ranch and stopped his horse adjacent to the man on foot.

"Hey Rhys, what are you doing walking around town in this weather?"

"Had some business at the new bank. I stopped by the express on my way home," Rhys said "You had a letter there."

Matthew thanked Rhys for the delivery and put the letter in his pocket. After dinner that evening he and Emily were relaxing in front of the fireplace in their room.

"We got a letter today. You want to read it now?" he asked her.

"Of course! Who's it from?"

"I don't know. I didn't look at it, just stuck it in my pocket."

"Look it's from your mother! It still seems funny that she's Mrs. Caleb Fitzgerald," Emily said taking the letter from Matthew's hand and pointing to the return address.

"I hope it ain't bad news. I'm looking forward to seeing them soon."

Emily opened the envelope with a knife.

"'Dear Matthew and Emily'," she began reading. "'We are all eager to see you in the near future.'"

"Well, that sounds good so far," Matthew interrupted.

Emily nodded, "'We weren't able to get a booking on the ship arriving at San Francisco in June. There was some mix up at the office and they said they didn't receive our request for passage.'"

Emily's heart sank with disappointment. She handed the letter to Matthew, "You read the rest."

He took the letter clearly distraught.

"'We asked when the next ship would sail to San Francisco and the agent said June. Then he told us there was a ship leaving for Fort Vancouver in February! We paid our passage right there 'n then.'

'Now I hope you get this letter while you're still in Oregon City. If not, leave word with Mr. McCafferty where we can find you. We now expect to be arriving in Fort Vancouver the week of May 15. Your loving mother.'"

Matthew and Emily danced around the room in jubilation.

"They are leaving the east coast this month! We get to see them sooner than we thought!" Matthew was so excited.

"It also means you can bring them here from Fort Vancouver which is much closer than San Francisco," Emily added. "And Lydia will be here when the baby arrives!"

"Whoopee! This is great," Mathew exclaimed. "My brothers and step-dad will be here to help establish our farm. Ma will be here to help with little Ian Joshua."

"Say, what's going on in here?" Katie asked as she passed the doorway.

"We just got some great news. Matthew's family is catching a ship to Vancouver this month. They'll be here when the baby arrives."

"Sure solved a lot of problems, heh? Now you don't have to worry about making your way to San Francisco," Katie said.

The news spread quickly through the house. Everyone talked about it at breakfast the next morning.

"They can stay in the rooms we vacate," Brian said. "We're going to build a house on the edge of town as soon as the hospital is finished. The same carpenters will be working for us. That's why we want to wait until the hospital is done."

"We bought some land on a river, well a creek anyway," Robert added. "It's only twenty acres but that'll be enough for our horses. And we can fish and swim in our own front yard."

"I can have a vegetable garden and a flower bed," Jesse glowed with the knowledge that her family was going to stay together and they had stopped traveling.

"We're going to sell the cows and mules in case you hear of a potential buyer," Brian said.

"My family will need pack animals and we planned on getting more beef cows so we'll take the lot, if you want a fair price," Matthew said.

"It'll be fair. We'll work it out," hands were shook between Matthew and Brian, a deal was consummated.

"I bet your oldest brother, Mark, isn't it? Bet he'll be out here within five years," Jesse said.

"That'd be nice," Matthew said. "But I reckon his wife will want to stay near her folks. She's a city girl. Don't know that she'd settle well out here."

"The west doesn't suit most women," Sam said. "Some just follow their men out here and learn to put up with it."

"It takes some getting used to," Katie offered. "Takes strong, independent women like those around this table."

"I've not been strong," Jesse confessed. "But I'm adapting—with your help."

"You're doing a right fine job at the land office," Rhys commented. "We admire the way you're learning new things every day."

Jesse flushed, "Maybe there's a place for women to work right alongside of men. The office, I mean, I know they help with the plowing on farms back in the states. Someday, maybe lots of women will work in offices."

Several people smiled indulgently.

Brian took his wife's hand and patted it gently, "Not likely honey. Just very special women, like you, can do office work."

"Are you going off looking for land early in the spring or waiting for your family to arrive?" Deborah asked Matthew.

"I'll start sorting out places soon as the creeks can be crossed," Matthew answered.

"Are you going to look at Beaver Valley?" she asked.

Matthew didn't respond right away. He took a bite of meat and chewed it deliberately.

"If we find good land in Oregon for the cost of a survey, we'd be plum foolish to go to Californy and pay for land," Matthew finally said.

Deborah stared intently at him. Emily kept her eyes on her plate.

"Let's wait 'n see. Maybe all the good farm land in Oregon is claimed," Matthew tried to smooth the ruffled feathers he knew he'd stirred up.

"Well, Michael will probably be able to travel about the same time as our child," Deborah set her jaw firmly. "We'll be heading for Beaver Valley in July or August. You'd be welcome to travel with us."

"That sounds like a long time away," Emily said, "but time will go fast. We'll have so much to do between now and then."

Juanita burst through the door, "Who's ready for more hot biscuits?"

Chapter 72

*F*ebruary was wet. The weather varied from drizzly showers to icy storms. When it wasn't raining, depressing fog hung heavy in the air. Toward the end of the month, the wind accompanied the rain. No one left the shelter of their homes unless it was absolutely necessary.

"We been having rain for four months," Matthew said to Walter. "The ground can't hold no more. The creeks is busting at the seams and rivers rushing downhill in torrents."

One day the clouds blew away and bright sunshine shone everywhere. Matthew walked across a meadow and examined a tree. He was delighted to see buds forming. He noticed a flock of birds chirping happily.

"Spring has finally come," Matthew inhaled deeply.

"Don't rush it. We'll have another month of tug-of-war between winter and spring," Walter said. "Don't throw away your winter socks just yet."

Grass was sprouting and a light green hue covered the valley for as far as he could see. The sun felt good and Matthew removed his jacket. He left it off for over fifteen minutes, but as soon as he was in the shadow of the evergreens he discovered it was still cold. Reluctantly, he put the heavy garment back on.

Matthew rode off into the foothills looking for cattle. There were mountain lions in the area and he tried to keep the cattle down on the valley floor where pumas were less apt to attack because of the presence of man.

He found fifteen cows and herded them back to the valley. Several cows had full round bellies.

"It is time for birthing everything," he thought. "Emily, Deborah, cows, grass, trees, everything is producing new life."

Matthew was even more optimistic than usual when he arrived home.

"Em, ain't it grand. Spring is here. You want to go on a picnic this weekend?"

The women had been busy celebrating the sunny day also. The house smelled of soap. The clotheslines were full and stacks of folded linens sat on the dining room table.

Emily carried their clean clothes to their room. Matthew stood at the wash stand in his long johns. A pile of dirty clothes lay on the floor next to him.

"Take off your underwear and I'll give you clean ones fresh from the line," Emily said.

"Ain't that just like a woman? Always trying to get a man naked," he teased.

She smiled and put the stack of clothes on the bed. She walked up behind him and embraced him.

"How was your day? Did you enjoy the sunshine?"

"Course I did. The air was scrubbed clean, the trees are budding, grass is sprouting and the cows are in the family way. I could smell the snow in the mountains, but everything down here is ready for spring. How'd you and little George Washington spend the day?"

"We washed every piece of dirty cloth we could find. He didn't seem too happy about doing the work. He was kicking me. You better have a talk with him," Emily said sliding around under Matthew's raised arm.

When she faced him, they kissed gently.

"I won't have no son of mine kicking his ma. What you think we should do about that?"

"Well, it wasn't a very hard kick. Maybe he was just trying to remind me he was in there."

"I don't think you forgot that for a minute," Matthew said rubbing her rounded belly.

Emily said, "Come on, out of those nasty winter long johns. You haven't put on clean work clothes for almost a month. They need to be soaked overnight."

He unbuttoned the dozen or so buttons down the front of his underwear while Emily laid out clean clothes on the bed.

She busied herself putting away the other clothes while he finished washing.

"Looks like everybody's busy washing clothes. Are we getting supper tonight?"

"Juanita put a pot of vegetable-beef soup on to simmer this morning. Katie made cornbread this afternoon. I don't think anyone will go to bed hungry."

He grunted and struggled into stiff clean clothes. Emily changed from her wet work clothes into a dressy-dress she kept on the wardrobe door to wear to the dinner table each evening.

Matthew brushed his shoulder length hair back out of his face.

"Now that spring is here, how about giving me a haircut?"

"Sure. I'll do it Saturday night after your bath. You might trim mine up a bit also. It's getting pretty long. It'll be hot come summer time."

The teasing weather didn't last. Fog shrouded the valley the next morning as Matthew left for Walter's farm. Emily spent the morning hours at the writing table by the window. She wrote letters to her parents and sister as well as relatives in Marietta, Jerome in East St. Louis, Brown Eagle in Vancouver, and Katherine in Rough and Ready.

At ten o'clock Deborah knocked on her door. Her advanced pregnancy made her stomach pronounced under the straight floor length dress. She stood with hands bracing her back at kidney height. She was obviously uncomfortable.

"How are you two doing this morning?" Emily asked.

"We're just fine. Disappointed in the weather," Deborah answered. "I hoped we would have a spell of sunshine. Michael would love to get outdoors."

"How'd he do with exercises this morning?"

"That's what I came to tell you. He fed himself the porridge this morning. He's sloppy of course, but he did get every bite up to his mouth. His arm muscles are greatly improved."

"Say, that's good news. I bet that wore him out. Is he asleep now?"

"No. He was encouraged by his success and wanted to try out his legs. He walked all the way to the parlor and back to bed without assistance," Deborah said smiling.

"He's resting but said he's not sleepy. Would you mind reading to him while I do some shopping with Juanita?"

"Yes, of course. Would you drop some letters off at the express box while you're downtown?"

Later that morning Emily read the newspaper to Michael, "'Mr. Jason Lee of the Methodist Mission has suffered greatly from freshets washing through his establishment again this winter. Most of the mission houses were over-flown by muddy water and much of the fences washed away. Over one thou-sand bushels of wheat have been destroyed.'"

"I hope you and Matthew keep that in mind when you're looking for land," Emily said looking up from the paper. " Good bottom land will flood if the drainage from the hills washes onto it," Emily, along with the rest of the household kept up the pretense that Michael would soon be an industrious member of society.

"'Clackamas County has picked its grand jury. Judge James Nesmith made a statement about the Sheriff and several jurors leaving the states because of the demoralizing effect of alcohol. He commented that they were fine, genteel men having moved to Oregon where no alcohol can be obtained.' Hah! Bet you'd like to tell him a thing or two about people bringing alcohol into the territory."

Emily read one last story about the Cayuse and Walla Walla Indians being upset over the number of immigrants taking up land in their hunting and fish-ing grounds.

"Hope we don't have Indian wars," she said aloud then realized she was talking to a sleeping man.

Walter was right. March weather was unpredictable from one day to the next. When the sky cleared and warm sunshine peered through, everything and everyone rejoiced. More and more birds made their appearance. Trees turned light green as the buds grew and bulbs sprouted flowers. Wild crocus, daffodils, and iris popped up in most unexpected places.

The rain still fell off and on during the month but it wasn't as cold or fre-quent as the previous months. On clear days the Cascades thrilled all within their view. The icy pinnacles glittered as though draped with an abundance of diamonds.

"I want to build our house on the coastal range so that we can look across the valley and see those shiny mountains," Matthew told Emily.

"We'll put a big porch on the front and line it with rockers for everyone," Emily said. "Each afternoon we'll sit out there drinking tea and watching the sunset change the colors of the hills."

During April the sun shone most days. The air was warmer and Michael could walk onto the front porch. He sat watching the activity of the townsfolk wishing he could accomplish something useful. He carried Emily's beanbags in his pocket and worked his hands and fingers making them more and more pliable. He was tempted to try the front steps but thought better of it. He would wait until a man was there to help him the first time or two. Emily and Deborah followed Dr. Forbes instructions massaging and exercising Michael's muscles. As discouraged as he was, he was still making remarkable progress.

Matthew went on forays into the countryside with marked up maps. He took soil samples, checked the lay of the land, water flow, and proximity to other farmers. He wanted to find enough open space where each brother and his stepfather could have adjoining blocks under the land act. Each journey took him further south.

He reported to Michael, "It looks like we'll be neighbors less something happens soon. The land is too rocky, too dry, too wet, or too small everywhere I checked so far."

Michael smiled, "Guess I'll just have to put up with you. I haven't seen Beaver Valley myself, you know. I didn't plan on being a farmer. I'd rather be a rich miner."

"You will. You'll get there. Keep your faith. It might be a year afore you can dig a hole. I got a proposition to discuss," Matthew pulled his chair up next to Michael's bed and spread out maps.

The two men planned and schemed for the next hour. Michael started the session with great enthusiasm. By the end Matthew could see that his friend was haggard.

"That'll give you something to think about. I'll check back with you in a couple days. We'll talk more then," Matthew said folding up the papers. He had offered to do the heavy digging and build a sluice box and cabin. Michael could do the sluicing and panning. Now it was just a matter of finding a motherlode near good farmland. He and Michael would share the expenses and profits from the mine until Michael was ready to take over by himself.

Four women entered the front door of the house as Matthew was about to ascend the interior stairs.

"You look tired as Michael. What you been up to?" he asked Emily.

"We were helping Jesse set up their new home. It'll be ready for them to move into by the end of the week," Emily said sitting on the stairs.

"Why don't you come upstairs and lay down for a spell," he suggested. "I'll bring you some tea."

Deborah passed her friends while rubbing her back with both her hands. "I know I'm going to lie down until supper time. If I'm asleep when the food is ready, don't wake me up."

Jesse and Katie were in slightly better shape than the pregnant women.

"I'll make enough tea for all of us," Jesse offered. "I'll bring it to your rooms when it's ready."

Matthew helped Emily to their room and removed her shoes once she was lying on the bed. She was asleep within five minutes.

Deborah reclined beside Michael and asked him to rub her aching back. It still bothered her and she rolled around trying to find a comfortable position. She fell asleep on her knees with her shoulders on her pillow. She was snoring when Jesse entered with the tea.

Chapter 73

When Matthew awoke the next morning he realized he was in bed alone.

"Em, Em, what's wrong?" he questioned the dark room but got no response.

He lit the kerosene lamp on the bedside table. Emily was not in the room. He decided she must have been restless and gone to the kitchen. He took his time dressing for a fishing trip with Rhys Watson.

When he descended the stairs, he found the house in turmoil. Women came and went between Deborah's bedroom and the kitchen. Matthew walked into the kitchen where he found Katie hanging clean dry towels on an improvised clothesline near the stove and Juanita pouring water into a kettle.

"Morning ladies. Where's Emily?" he asked.

"She's in with Doc Forbes and Deborah," Katie told him.

"Something happen to Michael?"

"Yes, he's about to become a father," Katie answered.

Matthew smiled broadly as he helped himself to a mug of coffee from the stove.

"He's in the parlor, if you want to see him," Juanita said.

Matthew poured a second mug of coffee and carried the two of them to the parlor. Michael was in an easy chair gripping the arms. Sam sat beside him in a rocker smoking a pipe.

"Michael, you want a cup of coffee?" Matthew asked.

"Morning Matt. Michael's a bit nervous this morning. I don't know if he could hold a mug of hot coffee or not," Sam said.

"Oh say, there's nothing to this fathering business. You will be just fine," neither man laughed at Matthew's intended joke.

Matthew sat the coffee on a table beside Michael's chair. He settled into a second rocker facing Michael and sipped hot coffee. A scream came from the back of the house and Michael dug his fingers even deeper into the soft arm of the chair.

"That's a bit unnerving," Matthew said. "You want to go outside Michael?"

Michael barely managed to shake his head and said nothing. Matthew rocked in unison with Sam. He made no further attempt at conversation. Rhys Watson came into the room with two mugs of coffee.

"You want some coffee, Michael?" he asked.

Michael seemed to be listening to something in the distance and couldn't hear people sharing the same room. Rhys saw the mug of cold coffee sitting beside Michael and offered the hot cup to Sam. Sam took it and nodded his thanks.

"Maybe we best postpone our fishing trip for a day," Matthew said to Rhys.

"Right," Rhys said. "This might take a couple of days, you know. First baby and all."

"I don't think Michael could take the pain for two days," Matthew said. "He's wound up tight. I don't think he's took a breath since I came into the room."

The four men sat silently drinking coffee for most of the morning. Jesse came in with tortillas, sliced ham, and cold beans, and handed a plate to each man. Michael didn't respond to her offered meal, so she sat the plate beside the cold coffee. Katie collected the empty plates and mugs and Michael's full ones thirty minutes later.

One by one during the afternoon the men stood and paced the floor. At three-thirty Jesse brought a white bundle into the room.

"Well Michael, would you like to meet your daughter?"

Michael returned from his near catatonic state and smiled. "How's Deborah?"

"She'll be just fine. Emily and Dr. Forbes are still with her. You can go see her in a few minutes," Jesse laid the bundle in Michael's lap.

He looked at the tiny round face completely surrounded by soft white toweling. The other men came to peer into the opening in the cover. No one made a movement toward unwrapping the package.

"Congratulations ole man. That's a fine baby girl," Sam was the first to speak.

The other two men mumbled congratulatory sounds and looked at the little face. Jesse clucked her tongue and told Michael to pick up his daughter.

"I might break her. She's fine where she is," he said beaming with pride.

Jesse sat on the arm of the chair and unfolded the towel so Michael could see the little girl. She was dressed in a diaper and long nightshirt with tiny flowers embroidered on the bodice. The baby's arms waved about, her legs kicked and she puckered up to wail her displeasure at being unwrapped.

"What's wrong with her?" Michael asked alarmed.

"Not a thing," Jesse said. "Babies like to be confined the first few days. They're used to a small space. See, she has ten fingers and ten toes."

Michael put his index finger on the baby's palm. The child grasped the digit. It had the same effect as grasping his heart. Michael felt his chest swell and tighten with overwhelming love. He carefully lifted the baby so he could kiss her forehead. He laid her back in his lap and clumsily re-wrapped her. When that was done the child stopped crying, made a sucking noise and went to sleep. Michael relaxed back into his chair and held his daughter to his chest.

"I'll go see if Deborah is ready for visitors," Jesse said leaving the room.

Michael was completely content holding his tiny daughter to his heart. The other three men felt awkward and wanted to leave. Their duty to a comrade was complete. Sam and Rhys made excuses and left the room.

"You're going to have to make a necklace for her out of your first nugget," Matthew said. "What's her name?"

Michael looked blank and said, "I have no idea. Deborah's mentioned a dozen different names the past few months."

Jesse returned, "I'll carry the baby. Do you want Matthew to help you get to Deborah?"

Michael sat tensely for so long he was stiff. Matthew took hold of his elbows and pulled him out of the chair.

"Put your arm around my shoulders for support. You been through a rough morning," Matthew said helping Michael stagger to the bedroom.

Deborah was sitting up in bed against pillows. She took the baby Jesse handed her and smiled weakly at her husband.

"You all right?" Michael asked.

"Just tired. We're both fine," she kissed the baby.

Matthew helped Michael to the empty side of the bed. Michael sat looking at his wife.

"Why don't we leave you three alone for awhile," Emily said. "I'll be back in a few minutes to put the baby in her crib."

Everyone left the room except the new parents and their infant.

"You look tired yourself, babe," Matthew said. "Why don't you have some food and take a nap."

"Good idea," Dr. Forbes said. "From the size of you, I think we misjudged your time. You may have your own baby any day."

"Oh no, not until my mother-in-law arrives!" Emily exclaimed.

"Babies don't wait for ships to arrive. They have their own timetable," Dr. Forbes nodded to the others and headed for the door. "I better see how Brian's doing at the clinic. If Deborah has any problems, come get me."

The household went about normal business. Jesse dressed and went to work. Emily took a nap. Katie and Juanita did laundry from the baby delivery. Rhys and Matthew organized their gear for an early morning departure to the coast. Sam fed and watered horses.

The following morning Rhys and Matthew were gone before anyone else was awake. They crossed the Willamette River on a ferry and followed a well-worn trail across the valley floor. Farmhouses dotted the landscape and farmers were working in their fields soon after daybreak. Children waved to the passing strangers on horseback and the men returned their greeting. They traveled twenty-seven miles before stopping for the evening.

"We'll be at the coast tomorrow," Rhys said confidently.

"This seems to be a well-used path we're on. Do lots of people from Oregon City go to the coast?"

"This is the Tillamook Indian's trail. They have been coming over the mountains to trade with the Cayuse and Walla Walla for generations."

"That explains the seashell necklace Shinnay wore," Matthew said.

"Who?" Rhys asked.

"One of our guides across the Cascades. She was Walla Walla."

"I thought Brown Eagle was your guide," Rhys said.

"He was across the central plains up to the Dalles. He was supposed to leave us there and return home but decided to join the army."

The next evening Matthew stood in wonderment at the vast Pacific Ocean. The waves hypnotized him with their constant motion. He watched the sunset turn the water to shimmering gold, then red and purple, and finally gray.

Rhys had camp set up in the leeward side of a cove by the time Matthew joined him.

"Say, you done all the work! I'll do it next time we set up," Matthew said.

"We still have a little light. Let's see if we can catch some fish for supper," Rhys said handing Matthew a pole.

He was obviously eager to get started fishing. They carried a lantern to the surf and cast their lines as far into the water as possible. Rhys caught a fish about twenty minutes later.

"This is big enough for two people," Rhys said. "Let's call it a day."

Rhys cleaned the fish while Matthew peeled and chopped two potatoes and an onion.

"That's the ugliest fish I ever did see," Matthew said while they ate. "Sure taste better than it looked."

Rhys offered Matthew a cigar after dinner. They relaxed in the lean-to behind the burning driftwood. The chilled night air didn't dampen their spirits. Matthew was excited about seeing the Pacific Ocean and smelling the salt air for the first time in his life. Rhys reveled in having a friend share a fishing trip with him. They talked of past fishing trips and the big one they almost caught.

In the morning Matthew awoke and slipped out of his bedroll to relieve himself. He walked around the rock barrier between the camp and the ocean. He dashed back to the lean-to and shook Rhys.

"Something's wrong, something is awful wrong!"

Rhys grabbed his gun, "What's wrong?"

"The ocean shrunk! The water's way out there. It ain't up by the shore no more!"

"Tides, Matthew. Ever hear of tides?" Rhys asked.

"No, what's that? What's wrong with the ocean?"

Rhys explained what he knew about tides and assured Matthew it wasn't a disaster. Matthew listened skeptically to a story about the moon pulling the ocean water. Rhys assured him the water would come back later. Matthew took a wait and see attitude.

Chapter 74

Matthew and Rhys spent two days at the ocean before returning home with fish and crab. Matthew took his clay pot cooler with him to keep the fish fresh for the trip home. Juanita was delighted to prepare fish dishes. She made corn tortillas and treated the household to fish tacos, a favorite among Mexicans living along the Pacific Ocean or Sea of Cortez. The boarders were glad for a change from beef and venison. The men planned more fishing trips that included Michael and Sam. For a destination, they had their choice of a variety of rivers and lakes as well as the ocean.

The house was considerably quieter with the Jamisons gone to live in their own home. Jesse stopped by frequently to check on Deborah and the new baby. McCafferty's boarding house was half way between the land office where she worked and her new home. Jesse delighted in passing on maternal advice to Deborah.

Deborah accepted advice from everyone graciously and shared her daughter with the other women who wanted a baby to hold. Michael was a proud father and smiled patiently while the parade of women came and went from his bedroom.

Deborah was confined to bed for ten days after the birth and dependent upon the others to bring her meals and bath water. Emily continued with Michael's therapy though it was increasingly harder for her to get around. Her belly was larger than Deborah's had been at the time the baby was born and she still had a few weeks before her due date. She was worried she might be carrying an enormous baby. She didn't tell anyone about the painful births that she'd witnessed when the child was too large. At times the knowledge gained as an assistant to Dr. Six was unnerving.

Matthew left on May 12, to meet his family's ship at Fort Vancouver. He was eager to see them but concerned about leaving Emily.

"You sure you don't want to come along? I'll drive slow 'n careful," he said.

"No, that would be foolish. I have two doctors right here if I need them. I'll be all right. The trip would be miserable and dangerous," she said packing his bag.

Matthew removed barrels from their Conestoga and hitched the oxen to the yoke. He threw his saddle and bags into the wagon along with the sheep-skin Emily handed him saying it would make a more comfortable seat for Lydia. He secured his horse to the rear of the wagon, gave Emily an intense hug and left the barn yard. Emily waved until he rounded the turn onto Main Street then returned inside.

Katie was returning the emptied chamber pot to the O'Brien's room and called out to Emily.

"Morning Em, did Matthew get off for Vancouver already?"

"Yes, he's on his way. He was like a boy on Christmas morning," Emily smiled.

"I hope the boat's on time. Sometimes they're delayed because of weather," Katie said.

"We know; we talked about it. I promised not to start worrying until June 1. That's a promise I've already broken. I started worrying before Matt was out of the barn," Emily confessed.

"He'll be okay. The Indians don't seem to bother a lone wagon. It's the trains of people arriving they object to," Katie said.

"I still wish he wasn't traveling alone. Here let me take the pot in. I was just going to see if Deborah was ready for her bath," Emily changed the subject.

"Okay," Katie said handing the discreetly covered container to Emily.

Emily knocked on the door and Michael told her to enter. He was par-tially dressed. He had his shirt and trousers on and was struggling to get into his boots. His hands shook with the strain of exertion.

"Morning folks," Emily said tactfully ignoring Michael's dilemma.

They had come to an agreement that she wouldn't help him unless he asked. He wanted to do as much as possible for himself.

"We've decided on a name," Deborah said. "You'll be the first to hear it. Michaela Marie O'Brien. How does it sound?"

"That's beautiful!" Emily replied. "Good morning Miss Michaela. How are you today?"

The baby's bright blue eyes crossed as she tried to find the new voice. They returned to normal and the infant stared at Emily.

"You're so beautiful Miss Michaela," Emily said lifting the girl from her crib. "And oh, so wet. I better get you washed and changed before I help your ma."

Emily kissed the child's forehead and laid her back in the damp crib so she could prepare a bath.

"I'm so glad you're here, Em. I'll return the favor next month," Deborah said.

Emily noted that Michael had gotten one boot in place and was working on the second. She walked past him to the chest and retrieved baby clothes.

"I'm glad for the distraction. Matt left this morning for Vancouver. I'll worry until he and his family are safely in this house. So much could go wrong."

"Now, Em. It's your turn," Michael said. "Think of how they worried while you and Matt were crossing the country."

"You're right, of course. We'll have plenty of stories to trade when they arrive," she said laying out clothes and bedding.

There was a knock on the door and Katie entered with a bucket of hot water.

"Thanks, Katie," said Deborah. "Is there enough water for both Miss Michaela Marie O'Brien and myself?"

"Michaela! Now isn't that nice," Katie responded. "Michaela O'Brien, you have a right proper name missy. And you're named for a right smart father. Morning Michael."

Katie sat the bucket on the floor next to the wash stand and cooed at the baby for a minute before leaving the room.

Michael was finally dressed and tying the thong at the neck of his buck-skin shirt.

"Congratulations, Michael. You did the whole job alone this morning," Deborah smiled lovingly at her husband.

"Was celebrating my daughter's naming," he said. There was still a noticeable slur in his speech but he had improved dramatically during the past two months. Dr. Forbes predicted the slur would be gone within another two months.

Michael could speak, read, feed himself, and get dressed. Now he needed to work on improving each of those skills as well as getting strong enough to do manly work. Dr. Forbes assured him all would return in due time. The frustratingly slow progress made Michael irritable at times.

Emily bathed and clothed the squalling baby and handed her to Deborah. Once the baby was re-wrapped in a little blanket and suckling at her mother's breast, she sighed contentedly.

Emily changed the bedding in the crib and laid out the items needed for Deborah's bath. Michael had gone to the kitchen to eat. The two women spoke easily of the problems and care required after giving birth.

"I read in a book that Indian women give birth in fields and keep on work-ing. Do you suppose that's true?" Deborah asked.

"I don't see how they could. They still have to pass the after birth. And think of how weak you were after it was over. Can you imagine putting the baby in a papoose on your back and going back to picking beans?" Emily said.

"A single bean is about the heaviest thing I could have lifted," they both laughed at Deborah's comment not noticing Michael in the doorway.

"I'll get stronger. Don't make fun of me when my back is turned," he slammed the door as he left.

"Whoops. I better go explain what we were talking about," Emily said.

"No, wait a few minutes. Give him time to cool off. He can't hear when he's angry," Deborah said.

Emily was puzzled but agreed and reached for the sleeping youngster. She held the child upright patting her back gently until a little burp was released. Then Emily kissed Michaela and put her back in the clean crib.

"I put three towels under her sheet. I don't think she'll soak through that many. Would hate for the nice mattress Jesse and Katie made to get smelly."

Emily and Katie cleaned and prepared the vacant Jamison rooms for the Kilkenny men and Mr. and Mrs. Caleb Fitzgerald. Emily planned to put jars of flowers in Lydia's room in a week or so. She figured Matthew and his family would return about the eighteenth or nineteenth of May.

Matthew had no problems along the trail between Oregon City and the Columbia River. He saw many travelers with covered wagons, surreys, and buckboards along the way. His oxen plodded along not paying any attention to other vehicles. Men on horseback passed him at regular intervals and tipped their hats in greeting. Matthew realized that there were a lot of Americans living in the former Indian territory.

By twilight, he was only a mile or so from the river. He pulled off the road into a thicket and found he wasn't alone. Campfires flickered up ahead. He stopped his wagon and listened. He could hear women and children as well as a dog or two. He decided it would be a safe group to join. He smiled cordially at family members and was puzzled by the cool reception. He pulled his wagon into an empty spot in the circle of wagons. Two men approached with rifles across their chests.

"Howdy mister. You traveling alone?" one asked.

"Am at the moment," Matthew said extending a hand. "Name's Matthew Kilkenny."

"This campground's just for families," the original speaker said ignoring Matthew's hand. "'Fraid you'll have to move on."

"Sorry, I don't understand. I'm on my way to get my family what's coming in by boat. Is this a private camp?"

"We gots little children here. We don't want no single men joining us," the second man explained.

"Ah, well. Can you tell me where a man what's alone can get a quiet night's sleep?" Matthew asked. "I been traveling since daybreak."

"Oh let him stay Pa," a pretty teenage girl said openly flirting with Matthew. A second girl climbed onto the seat beside Matthew and smiled coyly.

"You see why we don't want no single men in camp?" the father sighed with distress.

"Your daughters is purdy as pictures but my wife's purdier," Matthew said.

The teenager on the wagon seat stuck out her bottom lip in a pout and descended from the wagon.

"Sorry mister. My daughters are sixteen and seventeen and bound to marry the first gold miner they can get their hands on. I'm trying to be choosy about who gets close to them."

"I see. Do you know of any quiet men's camps nearby? I'm wore out."

"Keep going down the road toward the river 'bout half a mile. We saw a mixed group setting up there. Had families and single riders. Should be okay."

"I'm off then. Good luck with your daughters," Matthew cracked his whip over the oxen's head and they started moving.

Chapter 75

*I*t was mid July 1854 when the caravan got underway. Sam and Katie McCafferty had done their best to talk the easterners into settling in Oregon City to no avail. The Kilkenny brothers, Caleb Fitzgerald, and Michael O'Brien along with their families were ready to strike out for California. The wagons were loaded with as much seed grain and farming equipment as they could haul.

Caleb and Lydia Fitzgerald sat on the seat of a Conestoga. It was their second trip on such a vehicle. They previously rode from the boat dock at Fort Vancouver to Oregon City in the rear of Matthew's wagon.

"I certainly never thought I'd be on such an adventure. Ten years ago, I would have said I'd never get as far as Pittsburgh," Lydia said. Baby Leah, snuggled in her grandmother's arms wore a matching blue dress and sunbonnet lovingly made by Lydia. Lydia wanted to hold her granddaughter rather than lay her in the padded box between Caleb and herself.

Emily drove her wagon ahead of her in-laws. She had her son in a box secured to the wagon seat with a rope. She smiled down at the kicking child.

"Well now, Ian Matthew, are you ready for a long ride?"

The child smiled at the sound of his mother's voice.

Matthew rode his stallion to the wagon's seat.

"You ready for this?" he asked.

"Ian and I are just fine. Would you check on Leah and your mom? I see she's holding the baby. She might want to lay Leah in her crib. Lydia isn't used to the bumpy ride of a wagon, she might want to hold on with two hands."

Matthew nodded and went to his mother's side. Emily didn't turn in her seat to watch them. She was confident her mother-in-law would do what was best for the baby.

Deborah, Michael and their daughter, Michaela, were in the wagon in front of Emily. Deborah held her daughter in a papoose on her back, a gift from Brown Eagle. Michael drove the wagon.

Matthew's brother Luke, who shared a seat with Jack Hans, the new wagon master, drove the lead wagon. Jack had been a wagon train leader on several trips between Fort Vancouver and Sutter's Fort in central California. He now wanted to go to Yreka, formerly called Shasta Butte City and try his luck with gold mining. The area was booming. Large nuggets were being found in local streams. Jack and Sam McCafferty had been acquainted for several years and Sam felt Jack was the ideal man to get the families safely to Beaver Valley.

Mr. Hans had organized the timing of the trip to coincide with the transfer of ten soldiers from the Oregon City army outpost to Fort Jones, located in Beaver Valley. The soldiers, Matthew and his brother, John were on horseback. The military scouts returned from a two-day ride they had made through Willamette Valley and reported to their lieutenant. The lieutenant motioned for the wagons to roll out.

The McCaffertys, Jamisons, and Rhys Watson shouted farewells and best wishes one more time as the wagon's wheels began to creak down Pine Street. Juanita had prepared meals for lunch and dinner. She bustled out the front door of the boarding house just in time to hand a final package to Caleb.

"Vaya con Dios," she said. "Hasta luego. Cookies, hot from the oven for your morning tea."

"Gracias señora; God go with you also," Caleb said. "Thank you for everything."

Lydia waved to the group as their wagon rolled away from the front gate. "I feel twenty years old, exhilarated, and a little bit scared," she said. "How about you old man? Are you frightened at the thought of driving a wagon across a mountain range?"

"I've been waiting for this most of my life. Ian read me his book about Lewis and Clark while we were crossing the ocean to get to America. I caught his fire for the west. I just wish he were here with us. I mean...," Caleb started to explain that he wasn't sorry he was married to Lydia.

"Never mind. I know what you mean. I love you dearly, but I miss Ian every day of my life," Lydia patted her husband's arm.

She checked on Leah Evette who was now awake in her crib.

"Good morning, beautiful. How are you this exciting morning?" the grandmother stroked the infant's back. The baby stretched and stuck two fingers into her mouth. Her only response was a sucking noise.

"Twins," Caleb said. "I still can't get over that tiny young woman giving birth to twins."

"Thank goodness she had an easier time of it than her mother. I remember how scared we were when Emily was born. Julia had a rough time," Lydia recalled.

They were passing through Oregon City and Dr. Forbes waved to them from his front door. He had some trepidation about the troop facing the hardships ahead. Three babies and a semi-invalid man would keep the women occupied on the journey. He felt he had prepared them for the trip to the best of his ability. They were now in God's hands.

Deborah blew the good doctor a kiss and waved as they passed the medical clinic. Michael tipped his hat. There was no way he could express the gratitude he felt for the man who had helped him regain so much control of his body after the freak accident. The hefty payment for services helped build the new hospital and Michael was sure the doctor would use it to cure dozens more people the next few years. Michael occasionally worried about his lack of money in spite of Matthew's promise to see to it that they had a house over their heads before winter. Medical bills and staying at McCafferty's so many months had cost him his army retirement pay, which he had planned to use to establish a homestead for his family. He was optimistic he could make a good living on a mining claim once he got his strength back, but it was the intervening year or so that worried him.

Matthew and John rode up and down the column checking harnesses, dray animals, and wagons. All looked in good shape. The animals were in prime condition after their time on Walter Kirschner's ranch. Caleb bought McCafferty's Conestoga and Luke bought Jamison's wagon. Matthew was familiar with the vagaries of all the vehicles in the train except the army supply wagon.

The soldiers had their individual mounts plus the supply wagon and pack mules. They were hauling artillery and ammunition to Fort Jones. The skirmishes between miners and Native tribes along the Rogue, Klamath, Salmon, Trinity, and Scott Rivers were increasing as the number of miners multiplied.

"You know Mrs. Kilkenny, you are kind of historic," Matthew said to Emily as he rode beside their wagon.

"How's that, Mr. Kilkenny?"

"'It was in 1841 that the first white woman, a Mrs. Walker crossed into Californy over land. Ain't that long ago. Do you feel like an explorer?"

"Not yet, but I might by the time we cross into California. We might be the first white people to cross into California over land with brand new twins. Do you think school children will have to memorize our name?" Emily laughed.

"I'm sure glad gold was found in California," John said joining Matthew and Emily.

"Are you planning on deserting us for the gold fields already?" Matthew asked surprised.

"Nah, but the needs of the miners made a nice road for us to travel on. Rhys was telling me that Hudson Bay Company has been taking wagons south for over two years. The old mule trails are wider and better because of the traffic," John explained.

The first day out of Oregon City the train followed the road along the Willamette River that Matthew and Rhys had used earlier in the spring when they went fishing. The Native trail was now a proper wagon road.

Chapter 76

The small wagon train followed the Willamette River south. They passed farms, ranches, and villages. They were four days into the trip when they came to Fort Umpqua. The lieutenant in charge of the soldiers announced a three-day stop at Fort Umpqua. Not much was left of the fort buildings after a recent fire. Troops were now housed in tents but vast gardens and orchards still existed and were producing crops.

Once they arrived at that destination, the women celebrated the break in the usual manner. Clotheslines were strung between wagons and laundry tubs brought to blazing fires. The men carried buckets of water from the Umpqua River to the fires. By noon the lines were filled with traveling clothes, bedding, and every diaper packed for the trip.

"We'll have a week's supply of baby clothes after today. We'll be settled somewhere before long and have a regular wash day set. I bet you are looking forward to having a place of your own." Lydia said to her daughter-in-law.

"I couldn't have made the trip without your help. Thank goodness you've taken over the responsibility of fixing meals for the adults," Emily said, then laughed. "I have all I can handle giving two babies their meals."

"It won't be long before the babies are sleeping through the night. They're getting nice and fat. I always thought that babies who nursed two years grew up healthier. Modern mothers only seem to want to do it for a year. I think that's why women find themselves in the family way soon after the baby's first birthday," Lydia delighted in having a "daughter" to benefit from her knowledge.

"Matthew and I want a big family but I was hoping to have a home before our children started arriving. These two were in a hurry to get here," Emily hugged Leah Evette. The child immediately squirmed and waved her arms with enthusiasm.

Ian slept in the crib Lydia had brought from Ohio. The name "Baby Coakley" was barely discernible after sixty-six years of use. Ian was on his stomach and had brought his knees up under his body. Emily couldn't resist patting his little behind sticking up in the air.

"I'm going to use the rinse water from the laundry to take a bath," Lydia said. "Do you want to take one first, Em?"

"That's a grand idea. It might be our last chance before Beaver Valley."

John and Luke were greasing the axles on the wagons so Matthew was enlisted to construct a privacy booth for his wife and mother.

"There are soldiers everywhere," Caleb said to Matthew as he helped with the scaffold. "Do you suppose there's Indian trouble in the area."

"I doubt it. The Shasta tribes signed a treaty in '51. They are living on reservations now," Matthew answered.

"Something strange about that treaty. One of the soldiers was telling me about it. Seems like hundreds of Indians disappeared after signing. Some died on their way home. The soldier that told me about it said he thought the gold miners poisoned the Indians at a feast following the signing ceremony," Caleb relayed the gossip.

"What would they do that for? Don't they want peace?" Matthew inquired.

"Sure. But they didn't want to give up good prospecting areas to a reservation. Anyhow, the treaty was never ratified in Washington. No reservation was made," Caleb said sadly.

A look of fear crossed Matthew's face.

"I thought we was getting away from Indian problems by coming south. Brown Eagle said war is stirring along the Columbia."

"Now, I'm not saying we're riding into danger. It's just a good idea to keep your eyes and ears open," Caleb tried to calm the young father's fears. "Besides that, Shasta Butte City is getting' so big, there ain't enough Indians in California to attack it. Supposed to be five or six thousand people there now."

Michael and Deborah returned from a trip to the vegetable vendor. Deborah carried Michaela and Michael was loaded down with produce. They were laughing as they approached.

"What's so funny?" Matthew asked trying to clear his mind of potential danger.

"Deborah thinks we ought to clean everything out of our wagon and fill it with vegetables. We could get a good price for them in Yreka. I told her the stuff would rot before we got there. I don't think we'd get much for rotten tomatoes," Michael chuckled.

"Where's Yreka? I didn't see that on my map. What makes you think you could sell the stuff for more then you paid?"

"Yreka's the new name for Shasta Butte City. A corporal was telling me potatoes are selling there for twenty-five dollars a bushel. Butter is three dollars a pound and eggs are four dollars a dozen," Deborah said.

"How can they get prices like that? Who can afford it?" Matthew asked.

"The miners have to eat. Food is brought in over the mountains from the Willamette, Sutter's Fort, Fort Reading, or Port Orford," she answered. "And guess what else – Beaver Valley doesn't exist anymore."

"What?!" Matthew was overwhelmed with all this astounding news. "What happened to the valley?"

"It just changed its name. Now it's called Scott Valley after a famous miner, John W. Scott. He must have really struck it rich. They've named a mountain, river, valley, and town after him," Deborah said walking off toward the newly erected bathhouse.

"Someday there'll be a town named O'Brien," Michael called after his retreating wife.

"My, them soldiers sure is full a news. Did they say anything about expecting an Indian attack?"

The smile drained from Michael's face.

"Is that what the officers are meeting about? Do you know something?" he asked.

"Just gossip. I thought the Natives was happy on a reservation in the Siskiyous. Caleb says that ain't so. We best find out afore we take our families any farther."

Caleb, Matthew, Luke, John, and Michael marched to the officer's tent where a meeting was in progress. The guard at the door asked them to wait until the meeting was complete before making their inquiries. They waited fifteen minutes standing in the shade of the apple orchard.

"Fruit trees grow well in Oregon," Caleb commented.

That set the men off in a discussion on farming. It was the first time they had actually talked about what type of farming they expected to do. When they saw officers emerging from the tent, they vowed to talk more about farming in the evening.

The men walked toward the lieutenant. Caleb, being the eldest, was designated as their spokesman. He and the officer passed questions and answers back and forth for several minutes. When all concerned felt they understood the Native situation, the meeting ended. The men walked somberly back to camp; each was deep in thought.

"We come a long way," Matthew said. "I hate to turn tail and run away when we're so close."

"He didn't say there was definitely going to be a war. I vote we go on to Beaver, I mean Scott Valley," John said.

Pros and cons were recited. A vote was taken. The men chose to proceed. They would, of course, take every precaution to protect their women and children. It was consoling to know that Fort Umpqua was sending an additional twenty soldiers with them.

The women had finished bathing themselves and the babies. The three children were propped up on pillows in the Coakley crib made by Wesley Coakley, Matthew's grandfather. Michaela, being slightly older was the most active.

"Aren't they precious?" Lydia asked though there was only one possible answer. "What a joy it will be to have youngsters around the house again."

Michael still walked with a hesitating limp. He now went toward his wife who was brushing wet hair.

"Let's go for a walk," he said.

"Okay. Can I finish my hair first?"

"Yeah, sure," Michael didn't move from in front of her and she interpreted his demeanor to mean he had something serious to say. She put the brush aside and tied her tangled hair back with a ribbon. She took his hand and they strolled along the Umpqua River.

"What's going on?" Emily asked Matthew.

The men asked Emily and Lydia to sit on boxes in the shade of the wagon while they explained what they knew.

When they finished, Lydia said, "Why can't people learn to get along? This earth is meant for all of us to share."

"If I plant a crop a corn and tend it all summer, I don't want miners coming along and taking it at harvest time," Matthew said. "That's 'bout what we is doing to the Indians."

"They harvested pine nuts, acorns, animals and so forth from the area for years and years. Now we is plopping down on their land and planting our own food. And destroying theirs. We're chopping down the oak trees, killing and chasing off their livestock."

A round table discussion was held on Natives and farming until tempers flared.

"Hold it," shouted Caleb. "Let's all think about this overnight. We won't get anywhere arguing. Try to think of solutions. We'll talk again tomorrow."

It was Emily who came up with the favored problem solver. The family would buy as much land as they could afford and invite native Ottitiewas to share the work and profits. The Scott Valley Shasta Indians, originally known as Ottitiewa, would be free to do what they liked with their share. They wouldn't be asked to contribute to the original cost of the land because they already considered it theirs. The pioneers felt magnanimous in their decision.

"Sounds good on paper," Matthew teased his wife. "Now if it just works."

Emily spread a blanket on the ground in the shade. She and Matthew each took a baby to the blanket and spent the next hour playing contentedly with their children.

Chapter 77

The uneasy travelers were on constant lookout for signs of Natives. Scouts reported to the senior military officer each morning and noon. Jack Hans, the wagon master, introduced safety measure-keep items in wagons secured in case a fast run was necessary, be aware of your surroundings at all times, don't walk away from the wagons, keep as tight a formation as possible, and so forth. The women were schooled in self-defense using knees, elbows, fingernails, and household items they were apt to have handy when attacked. Lydia was taught to shoot. Deborah and Emily had learned to handle guns on their trip west. Men and women had target practice in the evenings. They practiced circling the five wagons quickly in case of an emergency. Since the space in the center was so small, it was decided cattle would be on their own, they would never all fit inside the circle. The cattle led the train with Matthew and John herding them. Soldiers rode on either side of the procession. The extra soldiers gave everyone more sense of security, but it didn't hurt for them to be prepared for the worst.

On the third day south of Fort Umpqua a scream rent the air. Matthew removed his rifle from the scabbard as did every soldier on the line. The private nearest Matthew slumped and fell to the ground dragging his horse down with him. The arrow protruding from his back barely registered on Matthew's consciousness. Suddenly there was shouting everywhere. Gunfire exploded and more screams emanated from the forest along the rocky road.

Cattle stampeded and oxen followed pulling wagons at break-neck speed over the rough road. Matthew saw Emily race by in a flash. He spurred his horse into action. He chased the bounding wagon trying to yell advice to Emily. No sounds escaped his paralyzed throat.

A second wagon was fast approaching his horse. He glanced at the panic stricken faces of his mother and stepfather. Before he had time to react he saw John dive from his horse onto the back of the lead ox pulling his mother's wagon.

Matthew made the instant decision to trust his brother to get his mother's wagon under control. He heard his infant daughter's frightened cries and prayed she was all right.

He spurred his horse again and again until he was beside the team dragging Emily and little Ian to certain catastrophe. He hesitated only long enough to judge his distance before jumping onto an ox. He was unbalanced and reaching for a handle to hold onto to keep from falling between the oxen. He grabbed the animal's ears and hung on. His legs straddled the yoke but with the bouncing his body was held upright by the strong hands holding the ears. The team reacted by slowing down to a safe speed. When the animals slowed to a trot, he was able to pull himself up onto an animal's back.

Matthew turned to see what was happening with John. He was on the yoke in a stooped position with the reins wrapped around his powerful forearms. The wagon was under control. The brothers maintained their positions for another mile.

They came to Deborah and Michael's wagon and affirmed their family was all right. Luke's wagon could be seen overturned at the next bend in the road, the back wheel was still spinning.

John and Matthew stopped their wagons, dismounted and ran to their brother's side. Luke was sitting on the ground disentangling himself from debris. His leg was twisted at a weird angle and they knew it was broken.

Gunshots along with war cries and horses screaming told them the soldiers were engaged in all out warfare with the Indians. They knew they had to get out of there fast.

A splint was made of broken boards from the wagon and cut leather straps. Luke was quickly carried to his mother's wagon and put on the bed.

John and Matthew ran back to find the wagon master. They found Emily kneeling at his side listening to his chest. She put her face next to his nose in an attempt to feel his breath. There was none. She heard no heart beat and detected no signs of life. The angle his head lay confirmed her suspicions that he had broken his neck when thrown from the wagon. John picked up the man and tossed his body into the back of Matthew's wagon as Matthew helped Emily on board. Matthew climbed into the driver's seat and cracked the whip. The oxen jumped forward and ran around the O'Brien's wagon. Deborah immediately followed the Kilkenny's wagon with Michael and their daughter on the seat beside her. John, driving the Fitzgerald's wagon raced up behind Deborah.

The oxen ran another two miles before Matthew spotted a copse of trees among rocks and vines where he thought they could make a stand. The exhausted dray animals staggered into the trees and bushes as far as they could get. The wagons were still visible from the road.

"It isn't a very good hiding place. The Indians will see our tracks. They will know exactly where we are," Emily said.

"The Indians will know we are waiting for them if they come this way. We can't cover our tracks. We'll have to hide in the rocks," Matthew said. "Maybe there's a cave."

"The babies won't stop crying until we have time to nurse them and calm their fears," Deborah said.

The three wagons were dragged into the thick foliage a few feet further and the passengers disembarked. All except Luke who chose to stay put on the wagon. He couldn't walk and didn't want his brothers to worry about carrying him. John declared he was staying with Luke. There wasn't time for an argument. Lydia was clearly distraught that her sons were in harm's way and Caleb forced her to leave John and Luke and hide away from the wagons.

They found rocks covered with ivy and blackberry bushes. Matthew took off his buckskin shirt and covered the baby in his arms. Caleb and Michael immediately did the same with the other two youngsters held by their mothers.

Caleb went down on his hands and knees and cut a path into the bramble. Lydia followed him into the tunnel pushing aside stickery branches with bleeding hands. Deborah and Emily followed the older couple. Each of them was holding a baby. Matthew carried the last baby into the manmade cave and handed it to his mother. He then backed out and looked for a place where he could defend his family's position. Michael found a hiding place on the opposite side of the tunnel and hoped he could protect his family.

They waited an eternity. The shooting and hellacious noise of the battle gradually diminished. Now was the most dangerous time. The winner of the battle would come looking for them.

The babies had nursed and fallen asleep in the trembling arms of women. Caleb sat inside the tunnel with his two guns loaded and ready. The only way to get to the women and babies was over his dead body. His jaw was clenched so tightly it ached. He felt Lydia's warm back against his own and it gave him enough courage to fight an army.

Matthew and Michael double-checked their weapons. They studied their positions looking for advantage points and hidden dangers. They were ready for battle and prayed desperately they wouldn't have to fire a shot.

John and Luke heard the horses coming. The animals moved slowly. The creak of the supply wagon was distinguished and Luke whispered that it must be the cavalry. The Natives wouldn't have a wagon. The hoof beats got closer and John cocked his rifle. Luke's was ready to fire. John motioned that he was moving to a better spot where he could see who was coming.

The troop rounded the bend. It was the U.S. Cavalry. Some men were missing from their horses and many others were wounded. The supply wagon contained corpses and men too wounded to mount their horses.

John walked toward the column. The lieutenant called a halt and spoke to John. The cavalryman gave orders and uninjured men went to aid the Kilkennys, O'Briens, and Fitzgeralds.

There had been twenty Rogue River Indians who fought fiercely. They were all dead. The lieutenant said it wasn't safe to stay there. The train traveled another seven miles before a defensible campsite was found.

Emily, Deborah, and Lydia assisted the company medic throughout the night. Caleb, John and Matthew helped bury dead soldiers.

Ten uninjured soldiers offered to spend the next day with Matthew and Caleb looking for lost cattle. The lieutenant in charge was against that idea as he didn't want anyone back-tracking into sight of the Rogue tribe gathering their lost warriors. Within an hour, a plan was worked out and the cattle would be retrieved under the stealth of night.

Chapter 78

*K*atherine and her husband, Thomas O'Liddy met the train at Fort Jones the morning after a soldier delivered the message it had arrived. Katherine embraced Deborah, Emily, Matthew, and Michael before the flurry of introductions was made. Thomas and his children were dressed in Sunday finery as was Katherine.

Katherine proudly said, "This is my wonderful husband, Thomas and my children, Clara and Leo."

The girl curtsied and the boy and his father extended their right hands to the nearest males. Hand shaking went on around the group while Katherine and Clara cooed over the babies. Once the general hubbub calmed down, Thomas gave a general description of the valley and told the party it would be fourteen miles to their home in Rough and Ready.

"The roads are good so we'll make it before dark," Leo said.

"I did make us a picnic lunch," Katherine said. "Thought we'd stop and eat about mid-way through the valley, if that's okay with you all."

"We'd better get under way," Thomas said. "I hoped Michael would ride in the surrey with me so we could get acquainted. I know Katherine wants to get caught up on happenings of people she knows. Could she and Deborah ride together?"

"That sounds good to me," Deborah said. "Maybe Clara would like to ride with the women. She could tend Michaela while I drive."

The girl was delighted with her task. She loved babies and hoped Michaela would become like a baby sister. Clara sat on the bed in the Conestoga and entertained Michaela for as long as the baby could stay awake.

The two old friends shared confidences and gossip as they drove through the lush green valley. Deborah told Katherine about Michael's struggle to recover from his injury. She said her every waking moment had been consumed with the care of her husband and new baby.

"But tell me about your life. Are you happy in your new arrangement?" Deborah asked.

"I'm living a fairy tale. Thomas treats me like a queen. He is so kind and thoughtful. Of course, we have our little differences of opinion now and then but nothing major."

"I'm teaching her how to be a mother," Clara said scooting into the seat beside Katherine. Katherine automatically put her arm around the child.

"Is Michaela asleep?" Katherine asked.

Clara nodded and said, "Sometimes Mom forgets she's supposed to be on my side when Leo fights with me. I have to remind her."

"What if Leo's right?" Deborah asked.

"He's never right," Clara said emphatically. "You know how boys are. Mom said you had boys with you on the crossing."

"How are the Jamisons?" Katherine asked. "You said in your letter that they were staying in Oregon City. You didn't say what they were doing. Did Brian go back into medicine or did he become a farmer?"

Deborah brought Katherine up to date on the Jamisons, McCaffertys, and Brown Eagle. Four hours travel had passed by the time the women were caught up.

A picnic lunch was spread out on the rear of the Kilkenny wagon since the back boards could be lowered to a horizontal position. Blankets were spread out on a bed of pine needles under the shade of evergreen trees.

After lunch, Matthew and Caleb rode with Thomas so they could ply him with questions about land and farming. Katherine and Clara rode with Emily.

Luke had been riding with his mother and stepfather since losing his wagon in the Indian fight. He and Caleb took turns driving. He propped his broken leg up on the front boards of the Conestoga and handled the animals without a problem. He was glad to have some responsibility. It would be close to a year before he would walk unassisted and he knew he wouldn't be of much use in establishing a farm. The military medic and Emily had set his leg with gauze, cotton wool, and boards. He had seen a regular medical doctor when the train got to Yreka. The man examined the leg and said he couldn't have done a better job himself. There was nothing more to do but give the bones time to heal. Luke and Lydia had no problem with riding alone in the wagon. Lydia said she wouldn't mind a nap. Luke wanted to absorb the sunshine and scenery.

"What a grand valley!" Matthew said to Thomas. "What's the farming like here?"

"Our garden has been great most years. The only problem we have is with deer not minding their manners. They don't like to share with us. We have to go out at dawn and dusk and shoot off our guns to scare them away. The kids keep them out of the garden during the day. Guess, that'll stop now that we have a school teacher in town."

"What crops do the farmers grow?" Matthew asked.

"Hay mostly. Incidentally, we put in an extra few acres of household vegetables and berries this year because we knew you were coming. We wanted you to have fresh food for the summer and for canning winter supplies," Thomas said.

"Good grief! We didn't expect you to do nothing like that!" Matthew replied.

"You wouldn't want to pay Yreka prices for food. It's crazy up there."

"Thank you very much," Caleb said. "We'll figure out a way to repay you as soon as possible."

"Yeah, thanks. That is some nice welcome to Scott Valley. I'm going to like it here if you is what the people are like," Matthew added.

"Keep in mind, I work at the lumber mill twelve hours a day. The garden is mostly Katherine, Leo, and Clara's project. They are the ones that wanted to make sure you ate good this winter."

"We will be sure to let them know of our gratitude. I have a question about other farmers. They raise hay. Are they mostly beef ranchers then?" Caleb asked.

"Yes. They can graze their cattle in the mountains in the summer and bring them back down to the valley for the winter. By that time they have grown enough hay to supply their own livestock and some extra to sell to the army, the miners, and the city folks in Yreka. Everybody has some kind of hay eating critter," Thomas laughed.

"See those cows over there. They're dairy cows. That area is called Cheeseville cause there is a big family of dairy farmers. They sell milk, butter, cheese, and cottage cheese. 'Course they grow their own hay also. Takes a powerful lot of land and hard work to do all that."

"While I'm pointing out landmarks," Thomas continued. "I'll tell you that mountain over there is known as Sheep Rock, Skookum, in the Shasta language," Thomas pointed to a double mounded mountain that looked like a reclining sheep. It sat majestically above rolling tree covered mounds.

"I like the looks of that place. Do you know if it's for sale?" Matthew asked.

"Don't know that. You'd have to talk to the land management department in Yreka," Thomas answered. "But check on water if you buy on that side of the valley. It is dry over there."

"I got maps from the land management folks when we was in Yreka. I'll look them over and compare available lands with what looks good to us."

"What about fruit? I noticed Mr. Knight and Mr. Short had some nice orchards planted. We stopped at Forest House for two days before starting up the Shasta-Scott Valley Turnpike. They supposedly have about ten thousand fruit trees! Can we plant an orchard here in this valley?" Caleb asked.

"Don't know why not. I've got an apple tree, plum tree, and a walnut tree I planted ten years ago. There again, I just have to teach the deer to share with us," the pleasant driver said laughing.

Leo rode up beside the surrey mounted on Matthew's horse. "Hey Pop. Can John and I race on ahead? We don't like poking along with these slow wagons."

"I don't think you should. That's not your horse," Thomas said. "You ask Matthew."

"What you think, Matt," John was on the other side of the surrey. "We'll be careful. Leo wants to show me around their property afore it gets dark."

"I'm not going against a father's orders," Matthew said. "His dad said 'no'."

"Well, I didn't mean absolutely not. I didn't want him running your horse without your permission," the easy-going father explained.

"Go on, you two boys behave yourself and have fun," Matthew said grinning at his brother.

When they had gone, Thomas said, "Leo built a tree house in a huge oak out behind the garden. He put two bedrolls up there and was hoping one of the men would sleep up there with him. I haven't done it since I get up at four o'clock to go to work."

"I think he found a friend," Caleb said. "John's a good man. You won't have to worry if Leo wants to spend time with him. John missed out on his youth because he had to go to work in the mines early in life. This will be good for him, too. He can be a big brother again."

At eight o'clock the wagon train passed a stage stop called Ohio House.

"Mr. Barnes and Mr. Terry are from Ohio, also," Thomas said. "You'll have to get acquainted with our next door neighbors. Maybe you know some of the same families in Ohio."

"Now ain't that something," Matthew said. "We come all this way and land next to more folks from Ohio."

Chapter 79

"Joshua William Kilkenny, you leave your little sister alone!" Emily shouted from the doorway.

Four-year old Joshua ignored his mother and continued pouring dirt and sand on the head of his squalling sibling.

Julia rubbed her eyes with the backs of her chubby little hands and screamed.

Grandmother Fitzgerald emerged from her cabin and came to the child's rescue.

"What's wrong with you, Joshie? Why don't you play nice?" she asked scooping the filthy two-year-old girl up into her arms.

"Now, now. We'll have that nasty dirt washed off in no time," she tried to console the girl.

"She sat on my mountain," Joshua explained. "Now I have to build it all over again."

"Thanks Grandma," Emily said lifting six-year-old Leah into the wagon. "I'll be home about ten. I'm going to the general store for a few things after I drop Leah and Ian off at school."

As she was pulling away, she turned and said, "Don't forget, Katherine and her family are coming to dinner."

Lydia waved acknowledgement. The baby in her arms was still crying loudly and Lydia's first concern was to get the dirt out of Julia's eyes. She carried Julia to the pump where she found Mungo filling buckets.

"Good morning, Mungo," she said to the elderly Shasta woman. "How're you this morning."

"My bones ache. Winter's coming," the woman complained.

"I'll wash the baby's face then carry your buckets to your cabin," Lydia said trying to be helpful.

She sat Julia on a small stool and tried to pour water onto her face. It was going to be a battle of wills. Mungo picked up the little girl and clasped her to her bosom. She whispered something to Julia and the girl stopped crying.

"That's wonderful! You must tell me your secret," Lydia said.

"When baby is clean, we'll go find a deer," Mungo said picking up a bucket after returning Julia to her stool.

Julia let her grandmother wash her face without further rebellion. When she finished, Lydia carried the second bucket of water to Mungo's log cabin. Lydia loved visiting Mungo and her husband Shastika. Their cabin was always too warm from the continual fire but it smelled delicious. Mungo kept a pot of soup simmering all day so her family could eat at any time.

Today, Mungo's daughter and granddaughter were making baskets on the ground in front of the cabin. Mungo's daughter was expecting another baby soon and seemed uncomfortable sitting cross-legged on the dry grass.

"Nellie, would you like to sit in my rocker? You don't look comfortable down there," Lydia offered.

"Chairs are worse. Then the feathers and beads are too far away," Nellie held up the intricately decorated basket.

"You do beautiful work," Lydia said.

"It's a traditional design," the young woman tossed off her skill as commonplace.

Julia sat down beside the Native child to touch the feathers. The dark skinned girl gave two feathers to Julia and the child smiled brightly. All brotherly misdeeds as well as hunting for deer were forgotten.

Mungo retrieved the second bucket of water from Lydia. "You want tea? I have some made," Mungo said.

"That would be nice. Are you having some?" Lydia asked.

"No. I wash my man. Him not too good this morning. Very hot," Mungo explained.

Alarmed, Lydia asked a few questions about Shastika's health. "I'll talk to Emily when she comes home. She knows a lot about medicine. Maybe she can help."

The women turned toward the sound of approaching horses. John and Matthew rode up to the front of the barn. Lydia saw little Joshua run to his father. Matthew swung the boy into the air and brought him down into a rough hug. Matthew asked the boy a question and Joshua pointed toward his grandmother. John and Matthew waved to Lydia and walked into the barn.

The other men were off in the mountains rounding up cattle from their summer grazing grounds. They would herd the cows down to the valley for the winter months. Scott Mountain and the surrounding range would have snow soon. In preparation for the coming winter the barn was bulging with hay. That wasn't what Matthew and John were looking for.

"Ma, have you seen the book on range cattle Uncle William gave us?" Matthew called out.

Lydia left Julia playing at Nellie's feet to look for the misplaced book. A tack room with a shelf of books was at the front corner of the barn.

"What's the matter? Is a cow sick?" Lydia asked.

"Nah, we need it to settle an argument between Caleb and Tyce Jim's son, Charlie. They been snarling at each other for two hours. John and me is tired of hearing them."

"When do you think you'll have the cattle in the pasture?" Lydia asked. "Katherine and her family are coming to dinner tonight."

"They're in the pass now," John said. "Should be home by four o'clock."

"Good. Shastika is ill with a fever. His sons should be home in case they're needed."

"Where's Em? Can she help him?" Matthew asked.

"She took the twins to school and is going to stop by the store. She'll be home around ten o'clock."

Matthew walked toward Shastika's cabin with his mother. John continued looking for the book.

"I'll check and see if Mungo wants me to do anything afore I go back to the round up."

Matthew stopped long enough to pass the time of day with Nellie and the toddlers before knocking on Shastika's door.

Mungo said she had her husband wrapped in cold wet skins and he should be cooled down soon. She rejected any offer of assistance. Matthew took his leave and joined John at the gate. Joshua was sitting on his father's horse ready to help with the round up. Matthew promised his son he would take him for a ride later. The tact worked and the boy reluctantly dismounted.

Matthew and John rode down the path facing west. They passed homes built by Luke and John for their young families. Luke had married a Shasta lady and they had a son. John married the Methodist minister's daughter, a tall blond woman of Swedish descent. They had two daughters with blond curls bobbing on their heads. The girls now ran toward their front gate to greet their father. John blew them kisses and admonished them to be good girls for their mother. He told them he would be home in time for dinner.

"We're getting to be a big family with lots a beautiful kids," John commented to his brother.

The family complex was surrounded by several hundred acres of fertile land. Matthew's dream as well as his father's had been fulfilled. The Kilkennys were free from coal mines. Three brothers lived off the land and the fourth was a successful businessman in Pittsburgh.

Matthew turned in his saddle to admire the homestead. He, Emily, and their four children lived in the original house. It was two stories of hewn logs with a wide veranda across the front. The porch was lined with rocking chairs and a swing.

A Big Leaf Maple tree had been planted in the front yard. The ground around its base was littered with toys. A sandbox littered with miniature wooden farm buildings and carved animals was located between the tree and the house and a doll buggy sat near the corner of the veranda filled with a variety of homemade dolls.

Caleb and Lydia had a separate four room cabin a short distance to the south of the main house. Their cabin was fenced off with white pickets and the area between the gate and front porch was a flower garden now showing bright yellow marigolds and dormant rose bushes.

On the north side of Matthew's home was a carriage building where farm implements and a variety of carriages were stored. The original Conestogas had been converted to farm wagons years earlier.

A large hay barn sat in the pasture where mules, horses and oxen grazed. The same pasture held a manmade pond where Matthew and his brothers had dammed a seasonal creek. Geese and ducks enjoyed the water as well as their sturdy wooden house beside the pond. The building was separated into two sections. Half of it was filled with nests for laying hens. Chickens, geese and ducks ran free on the farm during the day, but were put in the hen house at night to protect them from foxes and pumas.

Shastika and Mungo's cabin was hidden from view by the Kilkenny house. Their daughter and two sons had separate cabins, which could be seen higher up in the foothills behind the Kilkenny structures. They had a variety of outbuildings and fenced off yards where they kept chickens, sheep, and a few goats.

Duzel Rock, the mountain formerly known as Sheep Rock, stood behind the property. The dry, sparsely treed hills rose in steps toward the double domed sentinel. The lower hill that received moisture from Pelton wheels pumping water from Scott River into manmade channels was covered with grapevines.

On either side of the path leading from the Kilkenny homes there were hay fields now cut to stubble and dormant for the winter. Pumpkins dotted the field closest to the trail. South of Luke's house was the orchard. Matthew knew the next major project would be picking apples and pears. Then the house would be fragrant with the smell of canning the fruit.

All women on the property worked together in the kitchen of the original house canning apples and pears, making applesauce, jams, and jellies. There were always pies and cobblers for a few days after a canning session. About half the crop would be kept as fresh fruit in bins in the fruit cellar dug under the milk house. The large, cold, earthen room stored potatoes, carrots, onions, sweet potatoes, and rows and rows of canned meats, fruits, and vegetables. It was also where the wine from the vineyards would be stored when the vines produced enough grapes.

Turning back toward the west, Matthew took a deep breath of cool autumn air. The soaring mountains in front of him stretched as far as he could see. They surrounded the valley like a cocoon protecting the people from the outside world. The orange and brown oak trees stood in contrast to the evergreens on the higher elevations. Those mountains would soon be marbleized with sparkling white snow.

Emily took the twins to school early enough to spend a few minutes chatting with their teacher, Deborah O'Brien.

"I have thirty-six children in class now. I'll be glad when the new schoolteacher from St. Louis arrives. I hope she gets here before winter. Otherwise I'll have all eight grades for the full year," Deborah lamented. "I do love teaching though and am thankful they held the job open for me six years ago."

"The first couple of years were pretty rough going with Michael unable to make much money mining," Emily said in remembrance. "I'm glad you were able to stick it out."

"Me too. It was scary living in a one room cabin and not knowing whether Michael would ever find enough gold to buy our own place. To change the subject…Michael should be home before long. It'll be snowing in the mountains within a couple of weeks," Deborah said. "I'm always glad when winter comes because I know my man will be safe at home for a few months."

"I bet you have a long list of things for him to do," Emily said. "I can't imagine Matthew being away for seven or eight months. He'd have so much work backed up at home, I'd never get a chance to sit and talk with him."

"The two months Michaela and I visit Michael on the claim in the summer is about all the time I can stand living in the mud and muck. He loves the work and camaraderie of his companions. And he finds enough gold to keep us in food, clothing, and shelter," Deborah shrugged her shoulders. "I can usually find a student's father that will make repairs around the house in town. The winter is our time to get reacquainted as a family."

Michaela skipped up to her mother. Her pigtails bounced with each step.

"Mommy, can Leah and I play on the swing? We won't get dirty," she entreated.

"That's all right but do try to keep your dress clean. I'd like you to wear it one more day," Deborah smiled as the girls raced off hand in hand.

"By the way," she said." "Katherine told me to warn you she was bringing three extra people to dinner."

"Oh? Who's that? Does she have company?" Emily asked.

"Some strangers she met in Yreka. They had just arrived. Came over the Applegate Trail. She said she knew you wouldn't mind."

"I'm sure they're ready for a nice meal eaten off a real table with real crockery. They'll be made welcome," Emily said goodbye and turned to go about her chores.

She did some shopping and picked up supplies from the doctor's office. Emily was the practicing midwife for Scott Valley. She had three patients who would be giving birth within the month.

She was slightly puzzled over Katherine bringing strangers to the homestead but was sure they needed a warm welcome to this country. They were probably trying to escape the unrest back east. Poor President Lincoln sure had some problems to solve. She wondered if people would ever learn to live together in peace.

Emily arrived home to find Lydia baking cookies with the help of Joshua, Julia, and Nellie's daughter, Summer. The kitchen was full of merriment and flour.

"I know you're having company. We'll clean up our mess, won't we children?" The elderly woman's face was smudged with flour and cinnamon, but it was obvious she was enjoying herself.

Emily put parcels in their places while she listened to Lydia describe Shastika's symptoms.

"Sounds like pneumonia. Not good. Not good at all," Emily said.

Emily immediately went to see the ailing man. She did what she could, what Mungo allowed, to help the patient.

When she returned to the main house, the children were eating cookies, apple slices, and drinking milk at a miniature table in the corner of the room. Lydia was scrubbing away the cookie baking remnants.

"You start cleaning upstairs. I'll start here and we'll meet somewhere in the middle," Lydia said.

"Thanks. What on earth would I do without you," Emily hugged her mother-in-law from behind. "I'm so glad you came out west."

The house was clean, dinner organized, and the children dressed in clean clothes by the time Matthew stomped up the front steps. Emily met him at the front door and made him go around the back to the mudroom.

"I have bath water heated and clothes laid out," she said. "You'll have to hurry; our company will be here shortly."

Katherine, her husband, Thomas, and two stepchildren arrived about five o'clock. The Kilkennys were forewarned of their arrival by the sounds of the old hunting dogs barking. Betsy and Ole Blue rarely left the front yard anymore but at least they gave a vocal warning of approaching strangers. The Kilkennys lined up on the porch to greet their visitors. Emily and Matthew were beside themselves with joy when they saw the guests Katherine brought. It was the new schoolteacher from St. Louis, Beth Jeffers, along with her husband, Jerome, and three-year old son, Matthew Michael Jeffers.

40559194R00274

Made in the USA
Middletown, DE
16 February 2017